Praise for *The Girls in the Stilt House*

"Remarkable debut…[a] nearly flawless tale of loss, perseverance and redemption."

—*Publishers Weekly*, Starred Review

"The two young women at the heart of this rich debut come of age under the hardest of circumstances, and Kelly Mustian has given us their world entire. We ache for their sorrows, we cheer for their victories, and we recognize both ourselves and our nation in their troubles and their hopes."

—Jon Clinch, author of *Marley* and *Finn*

"Kelly Mustian's *The Girls in the Stilt House* is a triumph, a heart-breaking and ultimately uplifting debut that's as rich and lush as the Natchez Trace where the story takes place. Mustian's lyrical prose, combined with her deep insight into the resiliency of the human spirit, makes this novel shine. You know a book is good when you wish you'd written it!"

—Karen Dionne, international bestselling author of *The Marsh King's Daughter*

"In a world too cruel to make a place for them, Matilda and Ada become an army of two, fighting a war for their own refuge. This is a gripping novel about friendship, danger, isolation, and the vivid, dripping, moving landscape of a Mississippi swamp. If you loved *Where the Crawdads Sing*, you'll love *The Girls in the Stilt House*."

—Nina de Gramont, author of *The Last September*

"An astonishingly assured debut, *The Girls in the Stilt House* draws you in, holds you spellbound, and will move you to tears. With emotional impact and gut-wrenching power, this unforgettable novel is the best book I've read in a very long time, and I'm sure I won't be the only one who thinks so. A triumph!"

—Elizabeth Letts, #1 *New York Times*
bestselling author of *Finding Dorothy*

"In prose that is stunning and assured, Kelly Mustian forges a powerful story of two young women, thrust together after unspeakable loss and devastation, and their courageous struggle to emerge from their darkest hours."

—Jessica Keener, author of *Strangers in Budapest*

"*The Girls in the Stilt House* is a brilliantly researched, atmospheric page-turner. But best of all, it's populated with characters you really care about. I devoured it in a single weekend, yet the novel's haunting spell remained with me long after."

—Kate Moore, *New York Times* bestselling author of
The Radium Girls and *The Woman They Could Not Silence*

"Readers will be held in this novel's grasp from start to finish…a great new voice in literary fiction."

—Damita Nocton, The Country Bookshop

The Girls
in the
Stilt House

A NOVEL

KELLY MUSTIAN

Published by Sourcebooks Landmark, an imprint of Sourcebooks
P.O. Box 4410, Naperville, Illinois 60567-4410
(630) 961-3900
sourcebooks.com

Library of Congress Cataloging-in-Publication Data

Names: Mustian, Kelly, author.
Title: The girls in the stilt house : a novel / Kelly Mustian.
Description: Naperville, Illinois : Sourcebooks Landmark, [2021]
Identifiers: LCCN 2020047357 (print) | LCCN 2020047358 (ebook) |
    (trade paperback) | (epub)
Subjects: LCSH: Natchez Trace--Fiction. | Mississippi--Fiction.
Classification: LCC PS3613.U8473 G57 2021 (print) | LCC PS3613.U8473
    (ebook) | DDC 813/.6--dc23
LC record available at https://lccn.loc.gov/2020047357
LC ebook record available at https://lccn.loc.gov/2020047358

Printed and bound in the United States of America.
KPC 20 19 18 17 16 15 14 13 12

For all the Adas and Matildas of the world, finding a way

Prologue

The two girls climb down from the wagon and land with gentle thumps on a mat of damp leaves. They move quietly against the dark expanse of forest behind them. Overhead are a hazy half-moon, a few scattered stars. Ada waits as the other girl nudges the mule forward and loops his leather lead around a branch. With a glance back at the wagon, which the girls have steered off a weedy dirt road and close in to the trees, Ada follows her companion, dependent upon the sounds of twigs and old acorns crunching under boots until her eyes adjust to the deeper darkness of the woods. Even then Matilda's face, her arms, her bare legs beneath the hem of her drab dress blend with the night, while Ada considers herself as pale as the moon, conspicuous to anyone passing by. She worries a finger-sized hole in the pocket of her skirt. Surely anyone spotting them would wonder what two girls of their ages—Ada sixteen, Matilda probably some older—and of their sorts were up to out here on this remote stretch of the Natchez Trace near on to midnight. Ada says as much, her voice a hoarse whisper.

"Ain't nobody *passing by* in the thick of these woods this far off the Trace, day or night." Matilda's voice rings through the dark night unhushed, and Ada feels a thrill run up the back of her neck. She is nearly overcome by the newness of the feeling. Anything, it seems to her, might come of this night. And almost anything would be better than what has come before.

Deeper in the woods, a canopy of old-growth trees blots out even the faint moonlight. Matilda lights a small lantern, and an army of moths rises to claim the flame. Ada follows the swinging light, and the girls walk on in silence. After a time Matilda says, "There they are," and stops.

Ada steps up to two lichen-encrusted tombs—brick and limestone—rising just over knee-high from the forest floor. She kneels beside one of them, slides her hand over the cold stone top, and is almost convinced she is not dreaming.

"They're Confederates," Matilda says, and though the girl's voice is still unfamiliar to Ada's ears, there is no mistaking her lack of sympathy. "Somebody laid them out in style, sixty-some years ago. Had the slabs carved up and hauled out here where almost nobody'd ever see them. There's the crack, on that one there." Matilda sets the lantern on the other tomb, and in the small splash of light, Ada can read bits of a worn inscription: *Died October 18, 1862; Colonel; steadfast;* and *Asleep in Jesus.*

Roots of the old trees have worked themselves under the tomb, buckling the brick frame and loosening the stone slab on top, cracking it in two across the sagging middle. Ada runs her hand along the dogleg crevice. She can just shove her little finger through it, which she does, raising the hairs on her neck again.

Matilda tries to lift a corner of the slab. "Give me a hand here," she grunts. Ada fits her fingers under the stone, and the girls pull in tandem. They manage to slide it several inches.

"All right, then," Matilda says. "We found them. Let's go back for the tools."

"And for...for him?"

"Unless you're planning on leaving him buried in hay in the back of the wagon."

The two girls trudge back the way they came. Ada follows Matilda, wordlessly working on the hole in her pocket until she can slide her whole hand through it.

PART ONE
Ada Morgan

1.

Ada smelled the swamp before she reached it. The mingling of sulfur and rot worked with memory to knot her stomach and burn the back of her throat. She was returning with little more than she had taken with her a year before, everything she counted worthy of transporting only half filling the pillowcase slung over her shoulder. It might have been filled with bricks, the way she bent under it, but mostly it was loss that weighed her down. The past few days had swept her clean of hope, and a few trinkets in a pillowcase were all that was left to mark a time when she had not lived isolated in this green-shaded, stagnant setting. When she was a little girl, she had believed she loved this place, the trees offering themselves as steadfast companions, the wildflowers worthy confidants, but passing through now with eyes that had taken in other wonders and a heart that had allowed an outsider to slip in, she knew she had only been resigned to it. As she was again.

She had heard it said that children who lose their mothers early are childlike for the rest of their lives. As it happened, she had *over-heard* those words on the morning of her mother's burial, whispered by the preacher's wife to the preacher, who had cast a doubtful glance at nine-year-old Ada, finding it unlikely—Ada's being childlike—even then. Nevertheless, Ada had held on to the thought, sliding it to the front of her mind often in the weeks that followed until it became undeniably apparent that her mother's death was not, after all, going to usher in an era of ongoing playfulness.

Seven years had passed since then, and if there had been a child-like moment in Ada's life, it had been the one in which she slipped out an open window to run away with the first boy who looked her way. Childlike because she had hardly known him. Because she was only fifteen at the time. Although no one who knew her, or knew her father, would have tried to stop her. She had drifted through the following year in a sweet dream, and when she woke to find she was left with nothing and no one, with nowhere to go but back to her father, the only thing that was surprising to her was that anything as wonderful as Jesse, as their tiny room over the white barbershop on Harlow Street in Baton Rouge, had happened to her at all.

Now she found herself on the last leg of a journey she had prom-ised herself she would never take. She had left Baton Rouge at day-break, traveling first by train, then in the buggy of a charitable stranger, and finally on the back of a produce wagon that raised a cloud of dust in its wake, obscuring all that lay behind her. The vegetable peddler had taken her far beyond the limit of his usual route, well past the last smattering of rickety houses on the fringes of Bristol, Mississippi, to a wild, desolate strip of the Natchez Trace, an old Native trail cut through the backwoods and now only partially passable. He had let her off where the Trace began to swing away from an increasingly marshy terrain, raising an eyebrow before lifting his hat as Ada slipped down from the wagon and murmured a word of thanks. She had watched him maneuver the horses back the way they had come, then disappear behind a new cloud of dust.

Now she pressed on, both hands wrapped firmly around the twisted end of her pillowcase, not thinking about where she was going or where she had been, but only of forward motion. After some time, at a spot where the old road narrowed amid wild overgrowth, she turned off the Trace and onto a grassy trail hemmed in by a dense canebrake on one side and a mixed-wood forest on the other. The sun, not due to set for a few hours more, abandoned her for the far side of the canebrake, and she knew to watch her steps in the false twilight, alert to any stick that might be a rattlesnake, any root a copperhead, as the path curved around the cane and the woods closed in behind her. A mockingbird trilled overhead, lazily acknowledging her presence in his woods, but she did not stop to look at him or to pull up the socks that had slid under her heels and bunched beneath her feet, though she felt the sting of new blisters.

After a while, the trail took a sharp turn. Without warning, but coming as no surprise to Ada, the wall of river cane fell away, and there it was. Familiar as her shoes. As her squarish hands and her long tangle of pale-brown curls. Still, it was alarming.

The swamp. It stretched before her as if she had arrived at the utter end of a dismal world. Shrouded in a thin fog, giant bald cypress trees rose from the still water as apparitions, their gnarled limbs trailing tendrils of Spanish moss, their buttresses bulging above the water's surface, exposed to hordes of insects that chirped and screeched an afternoon dirge. All that was left was to follow the edge of the swamp, and she did. The nearer she came to her destination, the more slowly she walked. In time, she was hardly moving at all. And yet, she arrived. Home.

Small and boxy, the house was raised on a network of cypress stilts facing the swamp. A year had not changed it much. Its bare-wood exterior was still a weathered mushroom gray, its tin roof still rusting through an ancient coat of white paint. The house did not seem of slighter scale, as Ada knew houses often did when people returned to them older. If anything, it was taller than she remembered. More forbidding, somehow. Or perhaps she just felt smaller. It did seem more ramshackle, as if it might fold its stick legs and collapse under a good wind, but she knew that was because Baton Rouge, even Harlow Street, was luminous in her memory. Bright and shiny and as solid as the swamp was soggy.

She stood there for a minute or two, breathing old air from her old life that did not seem to fill her lungs anymore. Jesse was less than twenty-four hours behind her. Her hair still smelled of the mossy cavern under his arm where she had asked, had begged, to keep her head for an extra few minutes before they left the little apartment. She had wasted those moments crying, but he had let her stay nested there until the last second. She doubted he knew how grateful she was to him for that and for every other moment spent with him. But that was done.

There was no sign of her father's wagon. When she rounded the house and checked the pole barn that slumped against the tree line at the edge of the woods, his mule was not there. So he was away, she thought. There would be no gaining permission to reenter her previous life, and Ada was reluctant to barge back in without leave. A thousand insect voices urged her up the front porch steps, pressing her to pull open the screen door and knock. When she did, there was no answer, but even so, she called out before pushing open the front door, then called again after.

The main room was as changed as the swamp was the same. Half living room and half kitchen, it was cluttered with dirty dishes, grimy clothes, newspapers, trash, and empty bottles and mason jars. It was like a way station for roving bandits. A jumble of skinning knives and leather sheaths rested on the roughly hewn pine table, some of the knives standing with their blades lodged in the wood. This was the table her mother had set for supper when Ada was young and that Ada had set for her father in later years. Now a hacksaw lay across the cookstove at one end of the room, and at the other end a greasy sawtooth trap caked with dried blood and matted fur occupied Ada's old bed, a thin straw mattress laid over a narrow rope bed frame. With no female presence to contend with, her father evidently had relocated the tools of his trade from the tin shed out back to the house. All around the room his drying boards, stained with animal oils and pocked with nail holes, leaned against the walls. A wooden barrel, chest high and filled with sawdust, stood behind the front door.

Ada dipped her hand into the barrel and let a mound of sawdust sift through her fingers. Her father used it to clean his pelts, dusting them with it and brushing it through until the fur was soft and shiny. She remembered a time, when she was very small, when she had sprinkled a handful of sawdust into her rag doll's yarn hair, delighting her father to no end. He had squatted down to her level and eyed the doll. "Good girl," he'd said. "Should we scalp her now? Mount her pelt on one of my boards?" He'd held out his hand, and Ada had wordlessly handed the doll to him. Her father had howled with laughter.

"Virgil, please," her mother had said, taking the doll and tucking it back into Ada's lap. Ada wondered what became of that doll, but then she pulled her thoughts back to the present. She had found it was best not to let them stray.

As she stepped around the stove on the kitchen side of the room, Ada choked back a scream. An alligator hide had been nailed to the wall, the creature's mouth frozen in a bisected grin. Spilled from an overturned cup on the floor were what looked to be the beast's teeth, yellow and sharp and curved liked machetes. Ada raised her hands to her face and felt them trembling as she backed away.

She was almost glad her mother was not alive to see this, to have to live with this, which she would have, her mother. Ada remembered that much about her. Her mother had not been the sort to confide in anyone, but it had not escaped Ada's notice, even as a young child, that her mother was well schooled in living with things. With enduring. And until the day Ada met Jesse, she had followed her mother's lead.

She went over to the window. Through a filmy layer of grime that dimmed the room like a shade, the swamp was a blur of green and brown. She had a thought: perhaps even her father was not living like this. The trash, the broken bottles, the foul air—it all squared with abandonment. Maybe he had moved on, somewhere farther north with better trapping. It was possible. Or there might have been an accident while he was setting his traps and snares in the woods or stringing a trotline in that bend of the Pearl River where the current was fierce. Such things had been known to happen. He could have been shot by a hunter taking him for a deer. That last thought was not entirely unpleasant to Ada, and though it shamed her some, she let it linger. Soon she was mentally clearing the house of the tools and the trash, erasing the subtle stink of decomposed carcasses, turning the room back into the clean, spare space it had been when she was a little girl and her mother was young and still somewhat resilient. She stitched imaginary curtains for the windows and twisted rag rugs for the floors. She stuffed dried wildflowers into milk bottles and allowed herself a slight smile.

When she crossed the dim, dogtrot hallway that divided the house into two rooms, intending to make similar improvements to her father's bedroom, all the pretty pictures in her head fell away. She tripped over a tub of greasy tools, and reaching out to catch herself, she caught hold of the cold, smooth barrel of her father's deer rifle mounted on the wall. Her father would have left his leg behind before leaving his rifle, had he moved on. It was much more likely that he was away selling pelts, hauling a load to Jackson or to Vicksburg to be shipped up the river. He would be back. Unless he really was dead. Ada entered the bedroom cautiously. Her father's mattress, lying atop a box bedstead, was bare except for a thin blanket twisted into a rank wad. The window on the back wall was greased black to keep out the sun, but a small circle had been rubbed clear, letting in enough light for Ada to note the array of empty bottles surrounding the bed. Her father had not lost his taste for rotgut. She hadn't supposed he had.

The room was so small a person with some talent could spit tobacco juice on each of the four walls while lying in bed, something her father had been proud to prove to her more than once. She noticed a scrap of her mother's Christmas tablecloth, embroidered with holly leaves and berries, caught in a crack in one of the baseboards, pulled through by mice, she imagined. On the windowsill, within reach of the bed, was another mason jar half-filled with—Ada leaned and sniffed—pee.

She returned to the kitchen and sat down on an old cane chair that groaned even under her slight weight. Living here hadn't seemed so bad, she thought, when she had known nothing else. But now it was nearly unbearable. She shoved aside a dirty plate and rested her forehead on her arms crossed over the sticky tabletop. It wasn't that she and Jesse had had much, but what they'd had was all Ada would have needed for the rest of her life. It had been more than enough. It had been everything. When she left Baton Rouge, she had nothing. And now she had this. This house. In this place. It was less than nothing.

She thought maybe she would try praying, went so far as to fold her hands under her chin there at the table, but she couldn't come up with any words that did not mean "Please let my father be dead" or something just as likely to send her to hell. And what if her father really did not return? What if God chose that moment to answer an unspoken prayer? Who would she look to then? There was no one to tell her what to do, and she had no experience with making plans of her own. She stood up. She opened the front door and let the late sunlight spill across the room. She filled an empty bucket with dirty dishes and dropped in a brittle slice of dirt-lined soap she found wedged in a crack between wallboards in the kitchen. Then she lugged the bucket down the back porch steps and out to the pump behind the house. She would make herself useful.

The woods had crept closer while she had been away, and perhaps the canebrake to the north, as well. In time, she supposed, if left unhindered, they would overtake the entire yard, then the outbuildings and the house, creeping right up to the edge of the swamp.

She dumped the dishes onto the grass and set the bucket under the spigot. With a familiar rhythm, she worked the handle up and down until a trickle of water grew into a stream and she was able to loosen a layer of sludge in the bottom of the bucket. As she bent to replace it under the spigot, she caught a flash of movement in the woods. A quick flicker of light or shadow that could have been anything and was likely nothing, but she thought perhaps she had heard something, too. Something not quite right for those woods at that time of day. She scanned the overgrown edges for anything that might emerge, a raccoon or a fox or a muskrat, perhaps, and told herself that the woods were full of ordinary creatures darting or waddling through the brush, sounding like things they were not. A squirrel dashing through dry leaves could sound like a bear. She knew that. Still, she turned back to her task uneasy.

She would fill the bucket and wash the dishes as best she could. Before the last of the light was gone on this first day home, she would bring in a fresh bucket of water and begin cleaning the house. When it was too dark and she was too tired to work anymore, she would take

Jesse's shirt from her pillowcase and slide it over her arms, button it over her blouse. She would brush the layer of dust off the old oilcloth table cover folded behind the stove and spread it on the floor, find an old pillow. She was a light sleeper. She would wake to his foot on the steps, to his crossing the porch, should he come in the night. She would call out to him. "Daddy," she'd call, and he would know it was her, would put down any weapon he had in his hand. He wouldn't shoot her. What would be the fun in that? And her father, Ada knew, would have his fun with her return.

2.

Ada woke well before daylight, as was her habit. Even in Baton Rouge, where Jesse had slept until noon if nothing kept him from it, then stayed up half the night—musician's hours, he'd maintained—Ada had been up every morning before the milk wagon came around. She ached to hear the clink of the milk bottles again, the rattle of the door in the barbershop below when Mr. Becker arrived to open shop, the distant blast of the steam whistle that signaled a shift change at the mill, anything that would mean her life was still tethered to Jesse. But of course, it was not. She found it difficult to believe it ever had been, waking on the oilcloth mat in her father's kitchen.

She stood, stiff and wobbly as a new colt, and ran her hands down her arms, smoothing the sleeves of Jesse's shirt. She had slept in the shirt without a thought of what her father might have said had he come home and seen her in a man's clothing, but now she hurried to unbutton it as the alligator on the wall stared at her with black glass eyes. She had never known her father to trap a gator, though there were some in the swamp. Most of them farther up, where the water was deeper and the land more marshy.

She balled up the shirt and stuffed it inside her pillowcase, which she slid behind the barrel of sawdust where she could snatch it up quickly if need be. Then she stepped out onto the porch and shook yesterday's dust from her skirt. The starlings were in a frenzy. For as long as Ada could remember, the birds had roosted in the canebrake next to the house. Every evening they flocked in by the hundreds, merging and circling with riotous squawking and squealing until at some point agreeable to them all they began dropping in among the stalks like fat, black raindrops. Each morning, just before the sun broke the horizon, they woke with the same otherworldly racket, eventually lifting off in unison, a shivering black cloud against the pale light of the new day. Ada hated the starlings, hated the canebrake, as well. She had a history with both.

When she was a little girl, still of doll age, her father would occasionally awaken before Ada and her mother and climb onto the roof. Ada would wake to the rip of gunfire as he picked off as many of the glossy birds as he could before they had readied themselves to rise from the canebrake. Under her blanket she would squeeze her legs together for however long it took, suffering a full bladder until he was done with his fun. The real sport, though, came later, sometime after breakfast, when he would send Ada into the canebrake with a gunnysack to collect the dead birds. He kept a tally, or pretended to, as he shot, then sent Ada back again and again until she had collected what he considered a reasonable percentage of the kill. Though she had been quite young, she had learned quickly that the more she pleaded with him to not send her after the birds, the more she tried to explain how the closeness of the cane and the clatter of the stalks, the stink of the roost, the feel of the stiffened carcasses in her hands, terrified her, the more her father enjoyed watching her squeeze her small self in among the green stalks whitewashed with droppings. His daughter bending to his will. He enjoyed it even more when her mother tried to intervene. "Virgil," she would plead, and he would answer, "Either you can do it or she can," and her mother, with her paralyzing fear of snakes, would clamp her hand over her mouth and watch from the porch as Ada disappeared into the canebrake to search out the small corpses and drop them into the gunnysack. Ada never put up a fight. As early as then, there had been no wellspring of rebellion within her. She had been a continual disappointment to her father in that way.

As she grew older, she learned the value of suppressing her response to everything her father doled out. Behind dulled eyes, she watched him become bored with assigning disgusting tasks when she registered no disgust. In the same way, she learned that any gift from her father, rare as his gifts were, was less likely to be taken away later if she showed no excitement over it. These were basic lessons Ada taught herself. By the time she was nine, she had stripped herself of emotion the way another sort of child might have stripped bark off a birch tree. She did not shed a tear when her mother died. In the months, then years, that followed, she did not flinch at being left alone in the stilt house while her father was away trapping or selling his pelts and hides. When she was told at eleven years old that she would no longer be attending school at the old Trace outpost, that she would be of more use at home all day every day, she took that in stride.

But everything was different now. She was different. Now she felt afraid, and she was feeling other things, too—anger and grief and loneliness. They were not full-blown feelings, but they frightened her. She was not sure she could handle herself in the old way. She had loved, and now that she was back, she hated. She felt so assaulted by unaccustomed emotions that she thought it possible she might die of one of them. But there was solace, too, in feeling more human. In feeling at all.

The gaggle of birds grew louder, and Ada headed for the outhouse. The new outhouse, as she still thought of it. She passed the spot where the original structure had stood. Bead ferns were growing thick and lush through years of damp leaf mulch, blending with everything else that was verdant and wild at the outer edges of the backyard. She could not pass the spot without a picture forming in her mind of the way that square of earth had appeared when she was nine, just after the night that had changed everything. The scorched grass, the ashy remains of the outhouse walls heaped around the gaping hole that was absent its board seat. The blackened shards of glass from the kerosene lamp her mother had always taken along on trips to the privy at night because of her terror of snakes. Even now, Ada could have outlined the base of the old slant-roofed structure precisely. She could have reconstructed from memory the pattern the burned shards had made in the dirt, the exact placement of the hole. Her father had had the decency to build the new outhouse several yards away, though he had groused about it at the time, the needless digging of a second hole. Everyone has their moral limits, Ada supposed, her father's being not shitting on the spot where her mother had died.

If her mother had not taken the lamp, had not always slept in that long, flowing nightgown that had belonged to her own mother, had not been too shy to use a slop jar in the night when Ada's father was home, maybe the years following would not have had so many hard edges. Ada wondered. Maybe it would not have made much difference, after all. Maybe Ada's hardships would have been all the worse, sanctioned, as they had sometimes seemed, by her mother's timidity. Her silence. But Ada was pretty sure there would have been some softness.

She lifted the outside latch that kept roving animals out and used the outhouse, then stopped at the pump to splash her face clean. She filled a bucket and struggled with it up the porch steps as the rising sun seeped a spreading pool of bloody orange across the sky and the starlings rose against it like a gathering storm.

Midafternoon, and the two rooms of the house were as clean as they were likely to become with the resources at hand. With meal and lard she found in tins in the kitchen, Ada had made corn bread to have on hand should her father return hungry. It sat cooling under a towel on the stove. Most important had been gathering up all the empty bottles and jars and lining them carefully along one wall of her father's bedroom. He returned empty bottles to his suppliers of bootleg liquor, "Prohibition tea," as he called it. This, she hoped, would be a further sign of her usefulness, an extra incentive to his meeting her homecoming with something other than retribution.

Ada was bone tired. She pushed herself a last few steps to her bed

for a quick nap before she would start in on a pile of her father's socks
that needed darning. She imagined him coming home in the evening,
stepping through the doorway into the transformed living room while
Ada sat in a circle of soft lamplight darning his socks. "So you're back,"
he would say, or some such thing, after taking in her improvements
to the house. She was his daughter, after all. That was what he had
always called her—Daughter—as if that were her name. He had never
struck her. That wasn't his way. Of course, she had never before done
anything on scale with running away with a boy, staying gone all this
long year, living in sin. If she piled up everything else she had ever
done that had riled him, the whole of it would be a pebble next to the
mountain of the past year.

And with that thought came Jesse, front and center in Ada's mind.
She closed her eyes to keep him there as she lay back on her freshly
aired mattress. Then she pulled up her blanket and curled herself
around Jesse's warm, naked backside without a trace of shame.

It was late when she woke, and she opened her eyes on darkness. Or
maybe her eyes were still closed and she was asleep, only dreaming of
waking. Drifting through her mind was a faint impression of having
been awakened by a soft scuttling sound, and she held her breath, waiting for the squeak of the screen door, the thud of her father's boots on
the floorboards. But there were only the ordinary sounds of the swamp
at night. She listened for an animal on the porch or mice running
under her bed, but there was no sound that matched the one lingering
in her head. Even in wakeful daylight it had become difficult for her

to sort out what had really happened in the last year and what she had merely dreamed. Had she really met Jesse? Had he taken her away from the swamp? Loved her, or at least told her he had and believed it at the time? If Jesse was only a dream, he was a dream she welcomed. She closed her eyes again.

Sometime later—a few seconds? a minute? an hour?—she heard, or thought she heard, or dreamed she heard the back door close much more softly than her father ever would have closed it. Too weary to open her eyes again and unwilling to shoo Jesse from her dreams, she sank back into sleep, and sure enough, Jesse was there waiting.

For once, Ada slept through the sunrise and on into the morning. She slept until her stomach woke her with gentle snarls, reminding her that she had not eaten supper the evening before. Nor had she sealed the corn bread against mice, she realized, and it would almost surely be ruined. She untangled herself from the blanket and shuffled into the kitchen. Halfway to the stove, a quiet panic took hold of her like a cold hand on her sleep-warmed shoulder. Something was different. She sensed it before she saw it. And when she focused in on what it was, finally, it was not something frightening like a snake or a swamp rat or a stranger peering through the window. It was a pinecone. Only that. One perfect, tree-shaped pinecone sitting precisely in the center of the big pine table where there had been nothing before.

Her thoughts flew to the sound of a door closing softly in the night. She had not dreamed it, then. Someone had been in the house with her as she slept. She spun a wild circle, taking in every inch of the room. She ran to the bedroom, then down the short hallway and out to the tiny back porch. She raced back through the house and banged open the screen door, flinging herself onto the front porch. There was nothing. No one. Only the swamp with its bald cypresses, the empty dirt trail running alongside it, and the woods that seemed to separate Ada from the rest of the whole world.

She sat down on the top porch step, the open front door behind her. She felt as though she were shutting down, body and mind, but she made herself slog through the possibilities. Not her father, surely. He lacked the finesse of the gesture. He would have made himself known, whether or not he meant to. And he would not have taken care to choose such a pristine pinecone. No one from the colored end of the swamp would have done it. There were only three houses set back there, and as far as Ada knew, no one from the other end had ever come near her father's house. He would not have welcomed them, and they had reasons of their own for staying low, for living on a secret stretch of swamp in stilt houses known only to a handful of people. Her father was always spouting off about the "white-trash whore" living down there with a colored man and "all their half-breed urchins" and how somebody ought to do something about it, but Ada's father shunned attention as much as the colored folks did, and there existed an uneasy peace among the swamp dwellers.

Long ago her father had cut his own wagon trail through the woods to the Trace and insisted on using that rather than the dirt path that stitched the stilt houses together like a brown thread running along the swamp. "Me and mine ain't using *their* road" was what he had always told her, but Ada knew the cutting of the back trail had more to do with hiding the still he and Ansel Jenkins had tried their hands at running before they had their falling-out. That, and keeping secret the places where he hid the animal pelts he stole from other trappers' lines up and down the state. He had walled in an old deer stand in a tree in the woods and trained poison ivy vines to cover it over. He stocked it with the ill-gotten furs, after tanning them, and with his beaver pelts, now that beavers were down to nearly none and the government had outlawed beaver trapping.

Thoughts of Ansel Jenkins gave Ada pause. Farther removed and cut off by the swamp, the Jenkins place was hidden on a spit of land that required hip boots or a rowboat to reach from this side, though his dogs had been known to swim the swamp. Her father had once claimed that Ansel broke out of a chain gang up North and was hiding out, he and his pack of half-wild dogs, on that finger of swampland known for water moccasins that hung from the trees when the water was high. You could hear them dropping from the branches—*plop, plop, plop*—her father had relished telling her.

The possibility that Ansel might have been in the house with her during the night sent a surge of childish need for her father, such as he was, washing over Ada. But then, no. Ansel and her father had too much stacked against each other to play games with pinecones. Each hated the other, yes, but they were bound by a greater hatred of the law and of anyone who might try to stick his nose into either man's business. They held to a sort of outlaw code, keeping each other's secrets with the understanding that neither was going to hold out a hand if the other were drowning. No, that pinecone did not bear the marks of Ansel Jenkins any more than it bore her father's.

Then who?

Back in the kitchen she lifted the pinecone by its tip, only half committing to the act of picking it up, as if it might burn her or bite her or enchant her in some horrible manner. It was beautifully formed. Exquisite, one might say. A gift, if anything, it seemed to her now. And then her heart raced. Jesse? Had he had second thoughts and followed her? It was a ridiculous notion, and she put it away as she would have shelved a beautifully bound book of stories written in a language she could not read. The produce man who had given her a lift and been kinder than was necessary? Maybe more kind than was seemly? But he never could have found this place, even if he'd had the inclination.

She considered the real possibility that whoever had entered the house might still be nearby, in the outhouse, perhaps, or in the barn, the shed, the canebrake. Watching her and waiting—for what? If someone had meant her harm, what better opportunity than during the dark of night with her asleep in an otherwise empty house? No. This was more prank than threat, she decided. She settled in with this idea and numbed her mind to any other explanation because anything else would be too much. It was the way she had handled her fears when she was a little girl left alone in the house. And now, with her grogginess burned away and after having slept for so many hours, it was use the slop jar or make a fast trip to the outhouse. She set the pinecone back down.

Outside, songbirds had taken the place of the departed starlings, lightening the mood of the morning and further calming Ada's thoughts. The swamp took on a dull sparkle under the midmorning sun, looking almost lakelike but for the cypresses, though the smell was all swamp—decay and mold, mildew and moss and animal musk, dung and new growth.

Urgent for the outhouse, Ada snatched up the bucket—one was always in need of drawing water here—and went down the porch steps. She looped around behind the house, keeping her eyes open for anything unusual. At the outhouse, she lifted the latch and propped open the door with the bucket while she did her morning business, still watching.

She made her way tentatively to the pole barn, confirmed that it was empty, then checked the root cellar, little more than a large hole covered with a rotting wooden door so thick with thorny catbrier vines that she was certain no one had entered it. When she opened the lid of the old corn bin built around a frame of stilts beneath the house, a long black snake raised its round head in sleepy surprise. Ada screamed, and the creature scrabbled around the bottom of the crib, looping over on itself until it found the gap between boards that was its exit and slid through it with a sandpaper scrape.

Still somewhat shaky, Ada considered the tin shed. The shed was where her father had skinned carcasses and fleshed pelts and tanned hides before Ada left with Jesse. Where he occasionally had entertained himself by embalming and stuffing animals he deemed unfit for skinning but worth his while, like the tiny two-headed river otter he had sworn he trapped, but which Ada suspected he had crafted himself from two baby otters stolen from their mother. That masterpiece, she supposed, was still on display in the shed, along with other examples of her father's grisly sense of humor.

Ada's fear of that shed, with its black widow spiders and

swamp-size rats, its shelves filled with jars of glass bead eyes, extracted teeth, detached feet, and God-only-knew what else was as full blown as her mother's fear of snakes. In summer, heat trapped by the tin walls lifted old odors from the packed dirt floor so that anyone familiar with such things could pick out the stench of scraped flesh, the delicate tang of old blood, the stink of wet fur. It had seemed a place of horrors to a little girl.

She would not check the shed.

Satisfied that she was alone at the house—the door to the shed was still latched on the outside, as her father had left it—Ada took the bucket to the pump. As she worked the handle, she reasoned with herself again. Whoever had been there had not harmed her. And if someone did pose a danger, if he returned to snuff out the remainder of her life while she slept—well, that wasn't the worst that could happen to her. The worst had happened already. She had lost Jesse.

All the same, she spent the rest of the morning on the porch, where she could imagine herself fleeing down the dirt path to one of the other houses, or through the woods to the Trace, or all the way back to Baton Rouge, though Jesse was not there anymore.

She should not have come back, she thought. Maybe she could have hitched a ride to New Orleans instead and begged for a job in one of those taverns where Jesse had fiddled sometimes, learned to be one of those girls who flitted among the tables taking orders and pouring drinks and listening for her special music to cue her to peel off most of her clothes and climb up on the stage. Learned to smile at men as bad as her father, or worse. But there would have been other kinds, too. Maybe. Some that might have offered her some hope. But then, those girls hadn't looked as if they had any hope, once the band stopped playing and the *Closed* sign went up and all the smiles faded.

Ada sat on the porch, watching and listening, until she was exhausted by the effort to keep herself in each present moment so that her thoughts did not run ahead to evening, then nightfall.

And then, just before noon, she heard the faint laughter of children. Some of the colored kids from down the swamp, she thought. It came again, closer and louder. After a time, the laughter took on a mocking tone, the innocent brashness of young children in cahoots and on an adventure. That was it, then. The mystery solved. Kids and pinecones, a perfect match. Ada let out a heavy sigh, a small moan of relief. She spread her hands on her lap and leaned into the view she had not been able to escape after all, then pushed herself up and went back into the house.

3.

Home six days, and Ada was making her peace with the swamp. There had been no sign of her father. The children, it seemed, had tired of their pranks. She carried on, waiting. Pumping water. Weeding the asparagus that had managed to come up in the patch out back. Getting by. Occasionally she was revisited by the vague sense that there was something hiding in the woods, but of course all manner of creatures lived in those woods, wise to stay hidden so near a trapper's house. It was only her old uneasiness returned, she told herself, and she slipped back into it as if it were an overcoat.

A new thought occurred to her that morning, as she sat on the porch stripping leaves off a bunch of stinging nettles she had gathered, running her gloved hand up the stems from the underside. Perhaps her father was in jail. He had been incarcerated more than once, most often for mouthing off to the wrong person while drunk. Buying bootleg could land a man in jail these days, though it didn't seem to Ada that anyone in Mississippi was paying much attention to Prohibition. Even before the ban, her father had preferred bootleg.

And that brought to mind another possibility. She had heard of more than a few men who had been poisoned by home brew. Ansel Jenkins himself had a close call with one of the few batches he and her father made back when they were still speaking to each other. It was a reasonable conjecture—her father dead from someone's bad liquor. In which case Ada would have the stilt house, such as it was, all to herself. But she would never be able to keep the house standing on her own, keep the woods and the canebrake at bay, the rat population down. The garden would go only so far in feeding a person, even if she tended it well. There would be times when she would have to have money for things from town. So much was required just to stay alive.

The sky that morning was a low slab of dull, white marble mottled with gray clouds that were working themselves up to a long, slow rain, from the looks of them. The surface of the swamp was still, but the beards of Spanish moss trailing from the limbs of the giant trees swayed gently in a slight breeze. Ada's mother had once told her that the cypresses were relatives of the mighty redwoods that grew up into the clouds way off in California. That her own father, the grandfather Ada had never seen, had known all about most every kind of tree there was.

"It's nearabout a miracle for a cypress tree to come into being," her mother had said in her quiet whisper of a voice, which Ada had always had to take care to hear. Her words were timid and delicate, like a candle flame, and just as easily smothered. Ada's father had rarely seemed to hear her at all. "They only make their seeds certain years, and those seeds have to fall onto dirt that's damp, but not too wet. If they land in the water, they die right off. If they land, say, on a rock and dry out, well, they can't grow none. And whatever damp spot they land on has to stay damp—not too wet, not too dry—for *years* before that seed'll sprout." Ada remembered the look on her mother's face when she gazed out over the swamp from that same porch and declared, "Ever tree out there is a miracle," like that was proof of something she wanted to keep believing.

Ada paused with her hand fisted around a nettle stem and picked out a cypress in the distance, followed its trunk up and up, a hundred feet and more, then back down to its bulbous base. It was an old tree ringed by a dozen cypress knees, woody cone-shaped growths that jutted a foot or so out of the water near the trunk, standing guard with their pointed ends up like short, thick spears. Ada wondered if the trees would be able to reach such glorious heights without the knees. And the knees—would they have their own chance to grow tall if their big tree died? Would they die themselves without it? Or would they stand alone, stunted and useless, only just clearing the brackish water through the long centuries of a cypress lifetime.

That afternoon Ada was on her knees in front of the woodstove, cleaning out a mountain of old ash coagulated with sap, her face smeared with soot. She was scraping the bottom of the firebox with a square of scrap tin, her ears ringing with the sound, when goose bumps started up her spine. She froze, her arms inside the stove up to her elbows. Without looking, she knew there was no child holding out a pinecone behind her. No ghost of Jesse that her longing had summoned was there to comfort her. It was *him*, come home. And her in just the sort of compromised position he would have hoped for, had he known to expect her. She had felt no thumping of footfalls through the floor-boards under her knees; there had been no warning sounds. Just a feeling like a cold draft wafting across her soul. A voice in her head offered that it might be only an animal—she *had* left the fool door open—or nothing more than a cloud blocking the sun from the doorway. But she knew. Slowly, she slid her arms out of the stove, then spent some seconds brushing them off without turning around. She wiped her hair out of her face with a sooty arm.

"Daddy," she said. It wasn't a question.

"Well, look what the hell the damned cat done dragged in."

Ada stood up. She turned around. Eyes lowered, she focused on the front of his shirt. He was wearing one of his "good" shirts, which was how he referred to one not yet bloodstained or ripped. This suggested that he had been away selling pelts, which further pointed to his likely having had drinking money on the way home. A moment later she wished she had looked him full on from the start instead of creeping a nervous gaze up his shirtfront, past his collar, up his thick, ruddy neck, and over his bearded chin so that it arrived at its inevitable destination through half-raised eyes.

There was a Christmas morning look on his face, and Ada stood there like the present she was.

4.

He was a little boy once. Ada stood looking at the man who had trampled her soul her whole life, trampled her mother's, too, and she pictured him as a ten-year-old, a five-year-old, an infant cooing and trying out smiles. Maybe it wasn't his fault, the way he turned out. Probably he hadn't been done right himself and didn't know anything but what he gave out.

She watched him taking in all she had done to the house. A slanted beam of sunlight streamed through the clean window glass, and he squinted as if it hurt his eyes. He rolled a glance around the room, passing over the cleared-off table, the stove devoid of its coat of grease, the clear pathways from front door to kitchen, kitchen to hallway, hallway to back door, finding nothing worth pausing over until he saw her bed in the corner, the mattress bare except for a blanket folded over the foot of it, her old pillow laying claim at the head, the greasy trap gone. Without a word, he crossed the room and looked through the doorway of his bedroom, noting his own aired-out mattress, the clean sheet and blanket, the bottles lined up tidily along the baseboards. He crossed his arms and turned back toward Ada. The veins in his neck bulged with what Ada knew was effort to restrain himself. She dug a fingernail into the soft part of her hand at the base of her thumb and let the pain drive the dread from her face.

When he finally spoke, he said, "There's supplies in the wagon." He looked Ada in the eye and worked his jaw forward, blinked a few times with slow, steady control. "A ham hock and some bacon. Eggs. Some oil and feed and such. And there's some jars that'll need bringing in real careful." He reached up for his rifle and tucked it familiarly under his arm, then started down the hall toward the back door. "I got traps need checking," he said, walking away from Ada. At the back door he stopped. "I'll be wanting supper when I get back." Ada nodded silently to his broad back. "Make sure there's biscuits," he said, as if Ada had been in the outhouse for ten minutes rather than in the next state for more than a year. Then he shoved open the screen door and let it slam behind him.

Ada knew her father well enough to know he was biding his time, the same as when he was stalking a deer or hand fishing for catfish. He would not lose the prize by striking too soon or going about things in the wrong way, the prize, in this case, Ada, his daughter come home shamed and needy and looking to him. He needed time in the woods to work out how he was going to humble her up, to balance what Ada could do for him against what he could do to her, and set some parameters.

Ada let out the breath she had been holding and dropped into a kitchen chair to regain herself. Some might think her father wanted people to be afraid of him, she supposed, but she knew that what he wanted was to feel like a big man. It was that need that fueled the worst in him. Her father had so mixed up respect and fear that he could not discern one from the other, and it fed some desperate thing in him when people or animals felt helpless in his presence.

Ada remembered a time when her father let a trapped fox loose after the poor thing had gnawed its foot half off, the one time Ada had wished her father would go ahead and kill an animal. Leaving it wriggling in the trap, he had rushed home to find Ada and hustle her back through the woods to give her a lesson in how it was up to him, that fox's fate. She had watched it chew through its own flesh, had heard bone crack between its teeth before her father stepped over to spring the trap, freeing it so his daughter would think him grand. "He deserved it, you see," he told her as the fox limped away, dragging the dangling foot behind him. "He rose to the challenge."

He would challenge her, too, she knew, and she would do her best, and in that way she would get through the days until one or the other of them passed out of this world. It did not matter much to her which one. She could not see anything ahead of her beyond that.

She unloaded the food from the wagon and arranged it in the kitchen cupboard. Two crates of mason jars filled with clear corn liquor were too heavy for her to lift, so she brought them in three jars at a time, hurrying to get the last of them inside before she would have to begin supper.

Her final trip to the wagon was for a bundle of dirty clothes tied up in one of her father's shirts, the sleeves and shirttail knotted together. She dragged the bundle across the wagon bed, and with it came a small rag, sun-dried and stiffened into a coarse ball. Though it was crusted with old grease, Ada could see the pattern underneath, yellow daisies on a sky-blue background, and a sob rose in her throat. Before Jesse, she would have been able to swallow it back down, but now it loosed itself in a high, thin whine. The rag was a scrap torn from one of her mother's dresses. Ada had slept with that particular dress tucked under her blanket every night from the day of her mother's burial until the day Ada ran away with Jesse. In her excitement, she had not thought to take it with her. In every memory Ada had of her, her mother was wearing that dress. Probably she had not worn it to muck the barn or lye the outhouse or keep the poison ivy vines cut back, jobs that had fallen to Ada's thin and delicate mother, but some trick of Ada's memory dressed her in those yellow daisies for her every appearance. Ada stuffed the rag into her pocket and rushed inside to fry up bacon and cut out biscuits before her father returned from the woods.

There was an empty liquor bottle in his hand when he opened the door, a small bottle that did not seem to have done much damage, and he set it on the table already laid for supper. Then he sat down without washing his hands, though Ada saw that they were in terrible need of washing. She drew the bread cloth off the biscuits, uncovered the bacon and the boiled eggs she had kept warm on the stove, and set the food on the table. Her father leaned back in his chair, his belly like a pillow in his lap. He was taut and well muscled everywhere else, but his belly told a tale of heavy drink.

With a damp dish towel tied around her waist, Ada leaned over to set a cup of fresh coffee next to her father's plate. As she did, he reached out and, with one finger, slowly tipped over the empty liquor bottle. The two of them watched it roll across the table, fall over the edge, and shatter onto the floor. Ada straightened. Her father slid his eyes her way. So this was how it was going to be, she thought. A thousand quiet punishments, day in and day out.

Silently, Ada went for the broom while her father laid into his supper. With trembling hands she began picking up the broken glass. When she cut her finger, she turned away to hide the blood, wrapping the wound in the towel around her waist and sweeping up the remaining glass one-handed. Her father said nothing. Ada tore a page from the same catalog she had been using to stock the outhouse before she left with Jesse—her father used leaves and dry corncobs—and swept the glass splinters onto it, then twisted it tight and put it in the trash bucket before sitting down and taking a now-cold egg from the bowl on the table. Her father seemed satisfied. He shoved the plate of biscuits toward her with a grubby hand.

"Most times, them things're crawling with red bugs," he said, lifting an elbow toward the pinecone that still sat on the table like a centerpiece. He stuffed half a biscuit into his mouth. "You ourtn't put such on the table with the food."

Recalling the layers of long-hardened meals she had scraped off that table in the last few days, Ada laughed in a place so deep inside herself that it did not show on her face. She stayed in her chair long enough to finish chewing a bite of bacon, then picked up the pinecone and took it out to the porch. She found that she was reluctant to let go of it, as if tossing it over the railing toward the swamp was breaking a tie with someone out there other than her father. A child, she reminded herself. A colored child who could not offer her a bit of help.

Later, Ada washed the dishes and put them away while her father started on a second bottle. He filled a pipe with tobacco and tamped it with his thumb. Then, breaking a long, cold silence, he said, "Weren't an easy time, I reckon. All them months you been gone."

It had been the most glorious time of Ada's life, but she answered, "No, sir."

"I turned the whole Trace upside down looking for you. Knocked on doors. Made a fool of myself asking where my own damned daughter might could be."

"I'm sorry," Ada said.

He eyed her midsection, staring at the bloodstained towel around her waist. It felt as if he had touched her, his look was so intense, and Ada wanted to fold her arms over the towel, but she held them stiff by her sides. He put down the pipe unlit and took up his bottle, swigging and staring at the stains until Ada could not stand it.

"It was the broken glass," she offered as explanation, lifting her finger to show him the cut.

He looked at her hard, at her face, not her finger, then back at the towel. For a moment, he seemed at a loss. "It was wrong, what you done. What you've been doing. Off wherever you've been."

And though the word was like a desecration of all that was holding her together, Ada whispered, "Yes."

"You asking pardon?"

"I'm sorry I put you to such worry."

He took up the pipe again, held it in one hand, and waited, letting her know that what she had said was not enough.

"I'm sorry I shamed you." Ada would have chewed off her own leg to escape the look of derision her father fixed on her.

"Sorry for living like trash? Like a harlot, so's I heard. Sorry for going off whoring, when I brought you up better'n that? Is that what you're saying?" He was getting louder, less controlled, and Ada twisted her hands to keep them from shaking.

"I'm asking forgiveness. For all I done."

Ada's father used his shirttail like a pot holder to work the hot chimney off the kerosene lamp, and Ada looked away from the white swell of his bare belly. He held the pipe between his teeth and leaned into the flame, sucking on the stem.

"Daughters ain't like sons," he said around the pipe as he replaced the chimney. "Girls is always looking to be took care of. And I ain't never shirked on taking care of you. You ain't never gone hungry here."

"No, sir."

He sat back in his chair. "Comes a time, though, when a daughter starts giving some back. When the father's on the needing end of things. You run off when I was in need. My wife gone. Nobody what to clean and cook and mend and such."

"Yes, sir. I'm sorry."

He blew smoke out of his mouth in quick puffs, spreading his lips wide with each one and showing a black gap in front where one of his dull yellow teeth had rotted out. Then he grinned.

"You ain't forgot how to skin a muskrat, have you? Like I showed you that one time?"

Oh, dear god.

"'Cause there might be some call for that. That and some other jobs I figure there ain't no reason you couldn't learn. To carry your load, big as you are now." He dragged on the pipe, his eyes drifting back to the bloodstained towel her fingers had not been able to unknot. "Course, you'd be willing to do whatever you could, I expect. After all you done."

Ada knew to keep her face blank, a cold mask of granite slightly softened with shame.

"Might make half a trapper out of you yet."

She pictured him learning to walk, unsteady on fat baby feet. Tottering and landing on a padded bottom, clapping his pudgy baby hands. Had he been born to different parents, he might be somebody else entirely, she thought. Somebody who might have put an arm around her when it was warranted and been a soft place for her to land, times like this.

Ada excused herself, tore a few pages from the catalog, and went out the back door at the end of the hall. Halfway between the back steps and the outhouse, the eggs from supper came up. She dropped to her knees and let them go, clutching her stomach, her long hair swinging in her face. When she had swiped her mouth with one of the catalog pages and dragged a slimy lock of hair off her cheek, she stood and looked back at the house. Her father was sitting on the top step, watching. Not grinning, as she would have expected. Just watching. She moved on toward the outhouse, leaving a slick yellow puddle in the dirt behind her.

A little later, Ada sat darning her father's socks in the chair by the window while he sat on the porch with his bottle. The starlings arrived in bunches, swooping in over the swamp on their way to the canebrake.

Just before nightfall, when the sky was still a charcoal gray, her father stepped back into the house, surprisingly steady on his feet. He looked at Ada there in her chair, her hands lit with lamplight, and made a show of stretching his arms over his head, putting forth a huge yawn.

"Fixing to turn in early," he said. "Been a long day. Likely you're worn, too. I can see you been busy around here."

Ada was taken aback by his taking notice. By his mention of her effort. She was unaware of the tears in her eyes until she felt one spill down her cheek.

"I am some tired," she answered, letting a measure of gratitude sound in the words.

"Well," he said. Then he went over to her bed and lifted the mattress from its rope frame. Calm and quiet, he rolled it up with her blanket and pillow inside and set it on the floor at the front door. He reached behind the sawdust barrel and swung her pillowcase from its hiding place, then balanced it on top of the bedroll.

Ada sat with her mouth open, gratitude dissolving into confusion.

Her father put on a look of mock disbelief. "You weren't thinking you'd just waltz back in here and set yourself up in my house, were you?" He could not hold back a rough snicker. "You can see I done moved my tools in here. I need room for my work. Especially now you're asking me to add you back in to everything else I'm keeping up."

Ada could not speak. She could not even close her mouth, so she just raised her hand and covered it.

"You thought you'd drag my stuff out of your way and take up what space you wanted for yourself?" He was getting worked up now, though Ada could see him straining to rein himself in. To make it last. To squeeze every bit of satisfaction he could out of the situation instead of blowing it all in one big explosion. She recognized the look on his face as the same one he had leveled at her mother years and years before. Ada had an eerie sense of slipping into her mother's skin and feeling what her mother had felt for so long, of looking at her father through her mother's eyes. And now she knew exactly how her mother had felt. She had felt trapped. She'd had no other family. No friends. No other options. And Ada's father had known that. Just as he knew those same things about Ada, now that she had come home.

"I done cleared out the shed," he said, and Ada felt everything within herself go limp. She thought she might slide right out of her chair and onto the floor, but somehow her body kept itself upright.

"There's plenty of room for you to sleep out there." Ada's father was all grin now. "I just spread half a bale of fresh straw for you. You're more'n welcome to it. Daughter."

He slid his suspenders off his shoulders and began unbuttoning his shirt.

"Lord, I am tuckered," he said, yawning again. "I'll be looking for breakfast at sunup. Door won't be latched." Scratching his chin under his wiry red and gray beard, he ambled into the bedroom and shut the door behind him.

5.

Virgil Morgan had no change of heart. He did not show up at the door of the shed to spring Ada from his trap in a grand show of benevolence, as he had done with the fox those long years ago. The tin walls held in the day's heat, but Ada shivered from fright on the mattress she had laid out on her father's abandoned worktable. She had wound her blanket so tightly around her body and over her head that when she woke in the night in need of air, she could not move her hand to her face. She flailed around on the worktable until her head broke free, then sucked in a mouthful of air that went in like damp dust. She remembered where she was and quickly rewrapped herself against everything unseen in the dark, dank shed.

Outside, the swamp played its night music—the hum of crickets, the deep bellow of the bullfrogs, the occasional croak of a heron, the familiar cracking and creaking and watery plopping that had signaled sleep to Ada for so long, but now kept her from it. She reminded herself to move through the night one moment at a time, but her thoughts jumped ahead to the multitude of nights like this one that stretched before her. Some, surely, would be worse. But she pushed aside those cold thoughts for warm thoughts of Jesse.

She would never have met Jesse if Peggy Creedle's father hadn't come down from Baltimore and bought a large parcel of farmland on the other side of the Trace a few years back. Or if Mr. Creedle had not paid the iceman extra to drive his wagon way out the Trace to a far-flung last stop between the two girls' vastly different worlds. Or even if there had been any other girl of an acceptable age at the ice stop that spring day, almost exactly one year ago, when Peggy accompanied the farmhand who fetched her father's ice.

Ada was fifteen that spring, Peggy seventeen. Ada had emerged from the woods pushing her father's rusty wheelbarrow lined with newspaper. Every Saturday, Ada pushed the wheelbarrow through the woods to meet the ice wagon, then hightailed it home, the block of ice sweating and sliding as she bumped over roots and rocks and sticks. Sometimes, before she could get it home and shove it into the icebox, the ice took on streaks of brownish orange from the rust and dried animal blood that scabbed the sides of the wheelbarrow. Ada was surprised to find a girl she had never seen before waiting at the ice stop. She lost a quarter of her ice block that day politely listening to Peggy's complaints about living "a million miles from anywhere" and how awful it was to have a two-story farmhouse with just a pump in the kitchen sink (*a pump inside the house!* Ada thought) instead of civilized plumbing and to have to pour a pail of water into the toilet (*an indoor toilet!*) to flush it. Ada was careful not to weigh in for or against the girl's living conditions, in case Peggy was making fun of her.

"It's positively primitive," Peggy declared about life on the opposite, swampless side of the Trace. "Don't you think?"

Ada felt cornered. She pointed to the block of ice shrinking in the wheelbarrow and mumbled an apology, then escaped into the woods and back to her own two-room swamp house, wondering what it would feel like to flush an indoor toilet or draw water right from the kitchen sink.

After that, Peggy showed up at the ice stop along with the farmhand, Eugene, every week. She barraged Ada with unwanted invitations—to her house, to ride with her into Bristol for ice cream, to meet her in her father's cotton barn where she had hidden a bottle of peach brandy. Peggy persisted until Ada ran out of excuses, which is how Ada eventually found herself sitting next to her new friend atop a bale of hay in Peggy's father's wagon, refusing swigs from Peggy's bottle of brandy while Eugene pretended not to notice.

Eugene drove the team to the outskirts of Bristol where a traveling carnival had been set up in a farmer's pasture. Ada's father was two counties away peddling illegal beaver pelts and was not expected home for two more days. That was the night Ada met Jesse. After that night, she never saw Peggy again. By the time the ice wagon came around the following Saturday, Ada had already slipped away with Jesse, leaving without ever having seen Peggy's father's farmhouse or his peach orchards or his cornfields.

But she would be forever grateful to Peggy for that night. She had begun it sitting woodenly in the wagon, wishing she were back home enjoying her father's absence, and worrying that there would be consequences to this trip. When Eugene stopped at the carnival grounds, Ada climbed down reluctantly.

"Come *on!*" Peggy shouted, dragging Ada behind her as she made a beeline for a row of sideshow boxcars painted in garish colors, the barkers out front besting each other with claims about the bearded lady and the bird boy, an elephant girl, a mermaid skeleton. The girls were too young to be admitted into the hoochie-coochie cars at the end of the line, but Peggy was undeterred by the crossed arms and stern stare of a burly, bald man guarding the entrance to a boxcar painted like a scene from *The Arabian Nights*. She devised a plan for sneaking inside, a doomed plan, to Ada's mind, because it hinged on Ada's nonexistent ability to flirt. But the barker simply snatched their ticket money and waved them in without a second glance.

Inside the shadowy boxcar, Ada pressed herself against the back wall. A ragtag band of musicians started up a slinky minor-key tune, and Peggy rocked and swayed, keeping time with the music and mimicking the action on a low stage up front featuring a half-dozen dancing girls in swirling veils. Other than the dancers, Ada and Peggy were the only females in the boxcar. It was packed with men hooting and catcalling and shoving each other for spots closer to the stage. Ada stood stock-still as Peggy carried on, her head thrown back and her arms swinging over her head, making a spectacle of herself. Ada stared at her feet to avoid the girls and their shocking undulations, but she did allow herself a quick glance at the musicians—a fiddler, a conga drummer, and an old man playing a harmonica. In the split second she looked up, the fiddler made eye contact. Instantly, Ada went back to the safety of her Sunday shoes, or what would have been her Sunday shoes had she come from a churchgoing family, which she had not. But still, Ada recognized a den of iniquity when she saw one.

Peggy spun herself around, swinging her skirt, and Ada slid away from her along the back wall. She sent a shy glance back to the fiddler, thinking he had been looking at Peggy all along, but there he was, staring straight at Ada as if Peggy had not, by then, gained a small audience of her own. His face resting on the fiddle was serene despite the surrounding chaos, and Ada, feeling a bit unbalanced by all the sin swirling about, grounded herself in his gaze. As if in warning, he raised his eyebrows the instant before he trilled two high notes that prompted a wild flinging of veils followed by a roar from the crowd. Ada felt her face go hot.

"I told you this would be great. Let go and *live*," Peggy gushed, tossing her hair and rolling her shoulders as the fiddle double-stopped and the harmonica dragged out a low, slurred scale and the two men nearest them began directing their catcalls to Peggy.

Ada's stomach lurched. It all seemed so dangerous—the wild music, the smell of alcohol, the pull she felt toward the stranger playing the fiddle, and Peggy, who was standing much too close to the man next to her and laughing at something he was saying. Leaning against the wall of the boxcar of the Sultan's Sinsational Harem, Ada thought she might faint. She raised her hands to her hot face and looked up, and the fiddler caught her eye again. He nodded encouragement, and Ada, unaccustomed to small kindnesses, felt the first tears she had cried in years spill down her face. In response, the fiddler jerked the instrument from under his chin and planted it on his head, sliding his bow neatly across the strings as the dancers swung into their climax.

Ada laughed. A few patrons booed at the distraction, causing one of the dancers to stumble and another to stop flat-footed in midspin before they both collected themselves and caught up with the other girls, shimmying frantically and jingling the coins strung around their bare midriffs. The fiddler, his fiddle back under his chin, shrugged and winked, and Ada, overcome with it all, bolted for the exit, shoving her way through the crowd with her thin, sharp elbows as the dancers lost the last of their veils.

An hour later, the fiddler found Ada standing in line for the circle swing that Peggy and one of her admirers from the boxcar were insisting they all ride. Ada had not made up her mind. It was a frightening contraption, a high metal tower strung with long cables that whirled small, dangling, boat-shaped carts in a wild circle through the air.

"Hi, there," the fiddler said as an empty gondola swung into place in front of Ada. "You mind?" he asked Peggy, sidestepping her and her new friend and ushering Ada into the gondola. He fastened the rope grip and sent a two-finger salute to the attendant whose job was to secure the riders. Peggy giggled and waved.

"Jesse Parker," the fiddler said. He whipped off his hat, revealing a thick crop of burnished brown hair, then held out a hand to Ada. She grazed his fingertips, then pulled her hand back quickly. It was the first time she had touched a boy. Not a boy, she thought, a man. She noted his broad shoulders and the laugh lines at the corners of his eyes. He smiled at her, and she looked down at a molten lemon drop between the toes of her shoes. She asked herself what she was doing here with this boy—this man—she did not know. A man who traveled around the country with women who danced half-naked and who had sought her out for reasons she could not fathom. She had no answer for that, but she did know that if life stayed true to form, and so far hers had, this would not end well.

"That boxcar was awfully hot," Jesse said. "There's hardly any air in there. I've known some of the girls to pass flat out right on the stage, and them not wearing anywhere near the amount of clothes you are." Ada half smiled. She was probably the only girl at the carnival wearing a sweater. She pulled it tight around her and held it closed with crossed arms. When the ride jerked into motion, beginning a slow rotation, she clutched Jesse's wrist—the second time she had touched a man when the touching had not been absolutely necessary. He pressed his hand over hers, and she did not move a finger. One step above a brazen hussy is where she supposed she was, but when Jesse leaned over and kissed her cheek, she did not object, and then the ride was picking up speed, the gondola swinging up and out.

Back on the ground, they held hands and wandered among the animal pens and the shooting and tossing games—"rigged, all of them," Jesse told her—until Jesse had to head back to the boxcar for the last Sinsational show. Shortly before the carnival shut down for the night, he found her again, and they sat together under a blanket of stars as the music died down and the animals were fed and boxcar doors slid closed with a wooden thud and the metallic clank of the locks. Ada kept Peggy and her friend, and Eugene and a friend of his own, in sight, the couples assembled separately on a strip of grass behind the sideshow cars, hidden from the dwindling groups of carnival-goers.

"I'm quitting the show after Bristol," Jesse told her. "We pull out Tuesday morning for Opelousas, and I'm jumping off at Baton Rouge. Got a job lined up there with an old carny who jumped off last spring. Construction," he said. "But he plays banjo with a band, and he says there's lots of places we can play." By then, Jesse's head was in Ada's lap. He told her he was nineteen and that his father owned a brick factory. More than likely, he would end up working for his old man one day. "But not yet," he said. "Still got things I want to do before then. Like lying here looking up at this pretty face." He traced the curve of Ada's chin with his finger.

Ada found it difficult to believe that she might seem pretty to anyone. But then, only a few hours ago, sweeping the porch back home, she would not have been able to imagine, not in any dream, that she would be here with a man lying across her lap telling her about his hopes and plans.

"What about you?" he asked. "What's the story of Ada's life? Or is there a story yet?" He touched her lips with the tip of his finger, and Ada's story poured out. She did not try to stop it.

Jesse listened to the hard-cut account of Ada's existence with her father, without her mother or any other family, without laughter or joy or even a spark of fun. She told him about the swamp and the fire in the outhouse that took her mother, about the slaughtered animals and the stink of the shed, the isolation, her father's peculiar cruelties. She told him more than she had ever told anyone in her life.

When Ada finished, Jesse sat up and looked intently into her eyes. "Come with me," he said, pressing that magic finger to her lips again when she tried to apologize for having gone on so. "Why not?"

Ada did not dare take him seriously. She made a chuckling sound in the back of her throat to show that at least she knew that much.

"I mean it. Just pack some clothes and I'll meet you in three days. There's a room comes with that job in Baton Rouge. Over a barber shop. Nobody as pretty as you should have to live on a swamp with a man like that."

"I...I can't. I'm fifteen."

"My mother was married when she was fourteen."

Ada's breath caught at the word *married*. She made sure she didn't show it, but her heart was fairly humming with it.

"Where does she live, your mother?"

Jesse laughed. "Texas," he said. "Red Dog, Texas. Can you believe that?"

Ada smiled. Jesse was someone who could be believed. She could feel it.

"It's your life," he said. "You get to live it how you want. Just reach out and take it. I'll help you."

Ada saw a star fall in the sky and made a quick wish that any part of this night might be real. She thought maybe the star was a sign.

"It's your chance," Jesse whispered in her ear, gently catching her earlobe with his lips, and as fast as that falling star, Ada's heart dropped into Jesse Parker's hand.

Three days later, the same day Ada's father returned from his trip, Ada slipped out the front window of the stilt house in the wee hours and took the path through the woods to the Trace. Jesse was waiting for her in a yellow gig with the words *Dog Lady and Hercules* painted inside a red heart on the back, pulled by a white horse with a plaited tail. It was as close to a fairy tale as Ada had ever been. Jesse smiled big as the world and tossed her pillowcase into the gig. Ada sat with her leg pressed against his all the way to the carnival grounds, by then a deserted pasture strewn with hay and carnival trash and punched-ticket confetti. The carnival had folded itself back into its boxcars, which were lined up on the tracks and ready to be linked up at dawn.

Jesse unhitched the horse and started toward the area where the animals were stalled. He turned and motioned to Ada to join him, and she followed him across the pasture. She would have followed him anywhere.

God damn it to hell! The shout came from outside the shed and startled Ada awake a second time that night. She heard the clanging of the metal bucket as it was kicked across the porch over at the house, followed by more drunken swearing that grew louder and more profane as Ada's father closed the distance between the house and the shed. Slowly, she freed herself from the cocoon of her blanket and sat up. The shed had only the one door. The only latch was on the outside, but Ada had lodged two bricks against the bottom of the door to keep animals from pushing it open. Four wide, short rectangles had been punched out of the tin walls for light and air, but they were too high to reach and had been sealed with burlap.

Ada sat hunched on the worktable in the dark, her arms wrapped tightly around her knees. As she had known she would, she heard the rattle of the latch, then the *scritch* of the tin door as it moved over the dirt floor, taking the bricks with it. Then he was in the doorway, a black hulk against the moonlight reflected in the swamp. He disappeared into a dark corner and scratched around for something, then the shed lit up like a lamp, revealing him, one suspender hooked onto his pants,

his work shirt unbuttoned and hanging like curtains on either side
of the sagging white mound of his belly. He held a lit lantern in his
hand and swayed on his feet until he managed to lower himself onto
a bench, where he sat and swayed. Usually Ada found her father more
dangerous when he was not drunk, but now there was a look on his
face that she did not recognize.

"I come out here—" He lost his balance, almost fell off the bench,
and to Ada's relief, he set the lantern on a milk stool. "I come here
needing to know…" He thrust out an arm and pointed a shaky finger
at Ada's lap and said, "To know what in the hell you plan on doing
about *that*."

Thinking he meant to torture her over ruining the dish towel still
knotted around her waist, Ada mumbled something about cold water
loosening blood and about taking care of it first thing in the morning.

Her father laughed a horrible laugh, a strangled howl of a sound.

"Don't take me for no fool, girl," he warned, standing up. He braced
himself against the wall.

Thrown by her father's anger over a stained rag, Ada let down
her guard and pleaded for a chance to show him how the stains would
come right out with cold water and how that towel would be as good
as new, but she trailed off in midsentence, confused as his expression
cycled from anger to disbelief to contempt, like a moon-face clock
moving through its phases.

"Too goddamned dumb to know," he said, shaking his head. "Too
mortal dumb." He seemed unprepared for this turn of things and
annoyed at having to adjust for it in his condition. He swiped a fruit jar
from a shelf, twisted off the lid, and swilled a mouthful of liquor before

he spoke again. Ada watched a mosquito feeding off her forearm, but did not move.

"Just like your mother," her father said, and the words lit a tiny light deep inside her. "Trash from trash," he said, and her light went out. "Your *mother…*" He spat the word and Ada winced. "She was cheap. Easiest I ever had." He laughed, his shoulder bumping against the thin wall. "Lifted her skirt soon as I met her. But she thought she was too good for me. A man can't live with that. And you, over there." He waved a wild arm at Ada. "You think you're too good, too, don't you?"

He sat down hard on the bench again. "Two damned peas in a…" He raised his jar and slugged. "It's in your blood, both of you." With bleary eyes he looked up at Ada sitting on the table, clutching the blanket to her chest. "Trash blood." He bared his yellow teeth in a drunken smirk and hurled the jar over Ada's head.

She did not flinch, either from years of practice or because she didn't much care if the jar hit her. It bounced off one of the tin walls with the eerie gong of a musical saw, and the sound seemed to confuse her father. He lurched off the bench, wobbled, and held out his arms to balance himself.

"Sorry for being a goddamn whore?" he slurred, then answered "Yes, sir" in a high squeak and howled again. Then he rushed the work-table and slammed into it, managing only to rock it and gash his left arm. "Damn it all to hell." He stumbled backward, holding his arm in his hand. Ada was on her feet now, the worktable between herself and her father.

"Come looking to me after you been whoring," he shouted across the table. "Come looking to me with some man's seed done sowed. And

I take you in like the fool I am." His voice thundered between the thin walls. "I took you in, Sylvie. I married you."

Ada's eyes went wide. *Sylvie*. Her mother's name.

Virgil lunged over the table, grabbing for Ada's arm, but she ducked back. "Fifteen years old and already ruined, but I took you in. When your own family wouldn't keep you. Raised your filthy seed. Provided for him till the day he died. And for you, Sylvie." Another lunge, and he fell over the worktable. He stayed there, bent over, face down.

Run. An unknown voice in Ada's head shouted the word, but her own voice answered *Where?* and she held her place.

"You never loved me. All I done, and you never goddamned loved me." He broke into drunken sobs, slumped over the worktable.

Ada stood as still as a rail. Her mother. Fifteen years old, younger than Ada was now, pregnant with Benjie and nowhere to go except, somehow, to this drunken monster. Her mother had told her about Benjie, her first baby. Three years old when he died just days before Ada was born. Benjie, who would have been family to her, had he lived. Her father raised his head, sniveling and wiping away snot with his arm. He pulled himself upright and staggered the length of the table.

"You ourt to have been more thankful. I knew you was planning to run off," he said, his eyes unfocused. Ada did not know if he was talking to her or to her mother, but she moved down the table away from him. "I found them clothes, yours and the girl's, packed in a sack. Hid in the stove. The girl, she got up in the night—you in the outhouse. Pulled that damned doll out of the stove, and I saw that sack. Saw you was going whoring again." Virgil was inching back up the table toward Ada. "Weren't nothing else I could do," he said. There was an emptiness in his face that turned Ada cold. She kept her eyes on him, her mind on the door behind him, waiting now for a chance. "It made me crazy, Sylvie. And you in that outhouse...all that straw on the ground. I didn't start out to kick over that lantern, latch that door shut. But I wanted you to know I knew all you was planning. That I weren't nobody's fool. I had to do it."

Ada thanked God her stomach was empty. She dry retched without taking her eyes off the man who had murdered her mother.

He watched her closely, raised a hand to his face, and rubbed his stubbly cheek. Still staring, he took a step back, then shook his head as if trying to clear his mind and fit Ada into her proper place in it.

"You think I don't know, don't you?" His mouth turned up in a stupid smile. "I saw you sick out back of the house. You run off from here and come back with that..." He glared at Ada's stomach with disgust. "That hump-lump you think you can hide with a rag." Ada clutched the table as his meaning hit her. "I was glad you was back. After everything, I was glad when I seen you squatting in front of that stove. And then I looked more careful later on. Saw you was going to spit out a brat—a trash brat—and look to me to raise it." He shot out a hand and snatched an iron rod from the shelf, jabbed it across the table, just missing Ada's head. Ada screamed with all she had, hoping to wake Ansel Jenkins and all his dogs and God himself.

"You ourtn't of shamed me," her father said so quietly that it was terrifying. He backed toward the open doorway, swinging the rod. "I ain't raising no more trash babies." Before Ada could piece together a plan, her father raised his foot and kicked over the milk stool. Ada reached out a helpless hand as the lantern landed in the half bale of straw. It went up with a loud, hot *whoosh*, sparks flying like lightning bugs in the dark.

"Daddy!" Ada screamed over the crackling and popping of the young flames taking hold. But her father was backing out the doorway, grinning in the firelight, his hand already reaching for the outside latch.

And then, with the door still open to the swamp, he pitched forward, arms outstretched, and landed with a dull thump on the dirt floor.

Behind him, a shadow stood just outside the doorway, a dark silhouette against the moonlight, out of reach of the light from the fire. A woman, Ada saw, about as tall as her mother. As the flames caught the blanket lying on the ground near the table, Ada wondered if her mother had come to usher her out of this world and into the next, an angel come to fetch her. But there was a hammer in the angel's hand, lit now by the spreading fire, and Ada felt herself slipping out of her body and onto the ground, as if her father were dragging her with him to hell.

6.

Something had a death grip on her arm. Her eyes fluttered open. Her vision was hazy, as if she were sun blind. She could hear only a ringing in her ears. Ada had expected more of the hereafter, and she feared she was drifting somewhere between where she had been and where she was going, lost and forgotten by whatever entity had been charged with transporting her. And then she was being dragged across the ground. She tried to get her feet under her, to stand, but her legs were limp. Then she was sliding again, and she remembered—the shed, her father, the fire. Her face still warm from the flames, she found herself outside under a starry sky. After a few seconds, she could make out a person. Not her father, thank God above. In the moonlight, she recognized the figure she had seen behind him when he fell. A few seconds more, and she realized the figure was shouting at her.

"Get up and help me!"

Ada could only turn her head. This woman, this girl, her angel, flew back into the blazing shed. To save her father, Ada supposed, and she heard herself mumble a protest. Her mind was clearing, her legs and her senses coming back to her, and she sat up on the ground, bracing herself with her elbows locked behind her. The angel was pounding out the fire with a canvas tarp, flinging it with a fury, as if it were light as a sheet, as if everything that ever was depended upon her putting out that fire. As she worked, she cursed the flames and cursed Ada's father, and Ada was glad for that. She saw the lumpy form of her father on the ground inside the shed. He was not moving. He was not being moved. Ada was glad, glad, glad. She saw now that the angel was indeed just a girl. A colored girl. Likely a bit older than herself, but not by much. The fire was burning low to the ground now. The flames did not seem to have caught much wood, just the straw and the blanket and one leg of the worktable; but the girl beat them out with a wildness the smoldering remains did not seem to justify, until the shed went black.

Ada raised her hand to her head, and her fingers came away wet and sticky. Then the girl was beside her, standing over her, breathing hard and smelling of smoke and sweat.

"You'll live, I imagine." The voice was ragged, but strong.

"I'm all right, I guess."

"You ain't sorry he's dead, are you?"

"He's dead?"

"As can be."

"Thank the Lord."

"Huh. You might could start off thanking the one dragged you out of there."

Ada turned and looked at the other girl in the moonlight. She was a little taller than Ada, her features bold, as far as Ada could make out in the night. Her hair was a dark cloud around her face. She bore a look that would not be crossed.

"He set the fire," Ada said. "He was fixing to lock me in."

"Cold-blooded, crazy bastard."

"It's what he done to my mother," Ada said, "when I was a little girl. I learnt that in there."

"Well, he's the devil himself."

Standing between Ada and the moonlit swamp, the girl slapped straw and ash off the britches she was wearing. Men's britches, Ada noted, held up with a cloth cord, but she had a shape no one was likely to mistake for a boy's.

"I'm sorry about your mother and all," the girl said. "But it ain't nothing to me."

"It's nearabout everything to me," Ada said softly.

"I was in the woods. Heard you scream. Heard some of what all he said. Your daddy, I guess."

Ada glanced toward the shed, the door still open, her father still there somewhere in the darkness inside. Dead. Unless she woke to find herself back in the shed, under the blanket, or on the oilcloth mat by the stove in the kitchen, or in Jesse's bed in Baton Rouge, any of which seemed as likely as her being here with this girl she had never seen before.

"Lucky I had this with me," the girl said, twirling a ball-peen hammer she had picked up off the ground. Ada thought she heard a whisper of threat in the words, but she could not be certain. It was odd, to be sure, that anyone would be in the woods behind her father's stilt house at night, but she did not care about that. There was so much else to think about. Her life was in pieces, and she needed to pull her thoughts together so she could start sorting them out. *Her father was dead. He had killed her mother, trapped her inside a burning outhouse. Her mother had planned an escape for the two of them.* And there was the other thing her father had said.

"He claimed I'm going to have a baby."

"I heard."

"He had me all mixed up with my mother in his mind, but..." Ada trailed her hand over the bloodstained towel still around her waist, over the tight little bulge that she had thought was nothing more than her stomach knotting up like it always did when she was anxious. "Do you think it could be true?" Ada asked this question of the shadowy girl as if she might still prove to be a heavenly being.

"I think I saved your sorry ass and you ain't said spit about that, is what I think."

$$\sim$$

The girl's name was Matilda, and Ada was careful to thank her for killing her father. She'd had only a few moments at the pump to wash the blood from her forehead—she'd hit her head on the worktable during the fire—before Matilda led her back to the shed and started asking questions.

"How long before somebody comes looking for him?"

"Who do you mean?" Ada peered into the night, twisting her hands.

"I mean who is the first person going to notice him missing? Who does he meet up with regular?"

"Nobody, I don't think," Ada said.

Matilda was all business. She found another lantern in the shed and lit it. Then she turned out Virgil's pockets and came up with a pouch half-full of money, a knife, a pack of tobacco, and a fishing lure, all of which she stuffed into her own pockets. "You telling me ain't a soul in the world going to miss this man?"

"He mostly kept to himself."

"Family?"

"None to mention." Ada was unsettled by the way the other girl rolled her father over by yanking on one arm and flopping him onto his back. His head fell to the side, and his eyes stared at them accusingly.

"None to mention or there ain't any family? We got a serious situation here, girl. We got to think this through and get it right."

Ada did not want to admit that she had never met a single one of her father's kin and that there had been only the one quick visit by her mother's sister, back when Ada was still sucking her thumb. That after her mother died, she had longed for any of those missing, unknown relatives to appear, and when they had not, she had opened the Sears catalog and cut out a paper doll family for herself—a father, a mother, a big brother, grandparents.

"There's nobody on *his* side," she said with a jerk of her chin toward Virgil's slack face. "And he didn't see eye to eye with my mama's family. They don't come around. Never have." Ada did not say that she didn't even know any of their names, not even that one aunt she remembered mainly because of the purple feather in her hat. She was afraid Matilda might walk off out of sheer disgust and leave her there alone to deal with her father. "It was just us three. And then my mama died."

"Friends?"

"None to men— I mean, no. No friends. Not up to the time I left home a year back."

Matilda kicked up a clod of dirt with the toe of her boot, a man's dusty black boot. "Anybody he works with?"

Ada bit her lip, then shook her head. "Hunts and traps by himself. Fleshes and tans here. Sells pelts different places. Vicksburg. Jackson. I don't know where all. He falls out with people," she said. Her forehead was beginning to throb. "So he's always got his eye out for somebody new to sell to."

"What about women?"

"Women?"

"Can you answer a question straight on? Women. Girlfriends. You know what I mean."

"I'm sorry. I'm just nervous," Ada said. *Nervous because there is a dead body lying there and I don't know you from Adam and I might could be going to have a baby and I don't have any kin.* She tried to convey these thoughts with a forthright look, but the look she got back from Matilda stopped her short.

"So has he got a woman someplace, or not? Somebody who might come looking for him? Or be asking around in town?"

"Never been any women I knew of excepting my mother."

"A man like that ain't likely to draw many women, safe to say."

"No," Ada agreed. "Oh, wait," she said, holding up one finger, eager to offer something. "Whoever he's buying his liquor from. That's who'll miss him, for sure."

Matilda cracked her first smile. "Bootleggers don't chase down customers. Ain't no need." She said this with some authority, but Ada did not ask any questions. Matilda seemed to be easing up a little, and Ada relaxed enough to feel the ache in her shoulders from their having been tensed so long.

"No neighbors likely to check in on him," Matilda muttered, looking off in the direction of the dirt trail that led to the other end of the swamp.

"No," Ada said, embarrassed again.

"Anybody who comes around to see you?"

Lying was out of the question, so Ada didn't try. "I was born right here in this house, and hasn't anybody ever come to see me."

Matilda seemed to consider that for a moment. Then she glanced at the sky. Clouds had blotted out some of the stars and dimmed the moon that was creeping toward midnight. "Still early enough," she said. "We can get it done before daylight, but we got to move quick." She grabbed hold of one of Virgil's big, heavy boots and tugged.

"Get what done?"

"Good lord, girl, what do you think? We done committed us a murder. Get that other leg and pull."

Ada was nearly numb with shock, but she rolled that word *we* around in her head and filed away a tiny exception to it.

They dragged the body to the wagon and propped up some boards as a ramp. Inch by inch they pulled him feet first into the wagon, his shirt bunching under his armpits as he slid along the boards, one uncompliant wrist catching the side rail to no avail. Ada found a mud-filled slit in the sole of the boot in her hand and locked her gaze there until they had him laid out in the wagon bed. They dismantled the ramp and shoved the boards into the wagon along with some things Matilda hurriedly gathered from the shed—rope, Virgil's deer sled, a horse blanket. Then they broke open a bale of hay and covered over everything.

Light-headed and queasy, Ada rushed to the pump and splashed her face with water, washed her hands raw. When she came back, her father's boots were sitting side by side on the ground, the red leather laces he had tanned and dyed himself unloosed. Matilda's britches were smeared with blood from the gouge in Virgil's head, and she shucked them off there in the yard. Ada saw that she had been wearing a dress underneath, the hem tucked into the britches, and she wondered at that as Matilda slipped Virgil's knife into her dress pocket, then folded the britches and stashed them in the shed. Then she freed Ada, finally, from the dish towel around her waist.

"Let's get the mule." Matilda headed for the pole barn, and Ada fell in behind her.

7.

Matilda held the reins. She knew where they were going, what they were about to do, and she had not found it necessary to seek Ada's opinion on either matter. Neither was she compelled to converse as the two of them—the three of them—rode down the back trail, Matilda holding a lantern high over the rough terrain, the mule moving through the night at her bidding. At the end of the trail, they snuffed out the lantern, the thinly veiled half-moon giving light enough. They turned onto the Trace, headed away from town and toward the old Choctaw boundary where hardly anyone ever had cause to go. They had not traveled far when a big blond dog raced out of the woods and into the dirt road, barking into the silent night, snarling and snapping at the wagon's creaking wheels.

"Hellfire."

Matilda breaking her silence seemed a call for some sort of action, so Ada felt along the floorboard and found a shriveled apple core Virgil had left there. She flung it over the dog's head into the woods, hoping he would go after it, but he only yipped at it as it flew by. Then, to Ada's horror, he leapt into the back of the wagon. She hissed at him and waved her arms, but the dog simply turned a couple of tight circles and curled up contentedly on the bed of hay. Ada scrounged for something else to throw at him, but Matilda said, "Leave him be," so she sat back down. They rode on.

The Trace narrowed, sunken here between dirt banks that rose on either side, reminding Ada of the parted waves of the Red Sea as the children of Israel passed through them, a story her mother had told her. Recalling it now and remembering her mother and the way she had died made this journey seem less unholy.

Her father was dead, and Ada had never felt more alive. She was very nearly buzzing with life—with fear and hope and horror and something that might be anticipation. A cloud uncloaked the moon, drifting past it in the dark sky, and Ada stole a glance at the strange girl next to her on the driver's seat. This girl she had not known was a part of the world a few hours before and with whom she now shared something dangerous, a secret that bound them, though neither had earned the other's trust. She hoped there was justice in what they were doing, in what they had done already. That there were exceptions to *Thou shalt not kill,* or at least mercy enough to cover this night.

They pulled in close to the woods under shelter of overhanging trees and tethered the mule to a branch. First, they left Virgil where he was and hiked into the woods by lantern light, looking for a spot where Matilda knew that two old, long-forgotten Confederate tombs, knee-high brick enclosures topped with limestone slabs, rose from the undergrowth, one so conveniently cracked and buckled that it almost invited a second occupant. Once they found them, the one slab loosened and broken in two just as Matilda remembered it, they went back for Virgil, hoping the dog, who had been unwilling to budge from the wagon, had not already dug him out of the hay.

With the lantern turned so low it was barely a flicker, though the Trace here was uninhabited and utterly desolate at night, the girls climbed into the wagon and rolled Virgil onto the deer sled. Matilda looped a length of rope under the sled and around Virgil's chest, anchoring it under his arms. Then she pressed her boot firmly on the knot as she double tied it. Stomped on it, really, Ada thought, reminiscent of the way Matilda had beaten out the last low flames in the shed with what seemed like a personal vengeance. They strung another piece of rope under the sled, and Matilda tied it off at Virgil's gut. When her boot came down hard on his stomach, his head shifted slightly so that the lantern lit his face. His tongue protruded between his lips as if he would speak his mind about his fate yet, and Ada's old fear flared. She sprang off the back of the wagon to watch from below as Matilda tied the last rope around Virgil's knees, securing him firmly to the sled.

Matilda tossed the blanket over the body, tucking it under the ropes to keep it in place. She shoved a crowbar under Virgil's back, then the two girls began laying out the board ramp again. Virgil had mounted wheels to the bottom of the sled, and it rolled smoothly down the ramp when Matilda gave it a push. In the dim lantern light, Ada saw her reach quickly under the driver's seat, take something out, and hide it in a fold of her skirt. Then, on the ground, she turned away and slid whatever it was underneath the blanket.

The turning and the hiding made Ada uneasy. Two images came to mind—Matilda's ball-peen hammer and the broken tomb, room enough in the latter for a third occupant. But when she and Matilda each slid an arm through the sled's leather harness, there was nothing to do but press ahead into the woods toward a place from which Ada feared she might not find her way back, should Matilda not lead her out. And yet this danger, this alliance with a stranger who had appeared out of thin air, had an intoxicating effect on Ada as she strained against the harness and they pulled the sled behind them, the dog bringing up the rear of their odd funeral procession. She attuned her gait to Matilda's, their steps marking time to a new and unfamiliar song.

With the broken slab already loose atop the brick frame of the tomb, the two of them were able to slip the flat end of the crowbar under one of the halves. Matilda pressed her full weight against the other end of the bar, while Ada shoved the cold, hard slab. A count of three, a press, a shove. The unnerving graveyard sound of stone scraping over brick in the still of the night. Slowly, they managed to slide the stone over the side of the tomb and rest one edge on the ground. Then the other half—count, press, shove. As Ada leaned over the widening opening, the malodorous scent of old death polluted her every breath, and she understood why Matilda had moved the lantern aside before they began, had set it on the ground near the sled. She could see nothing but impenetrable darkness inside the tomb.

"We got to move quick," Matilda said, her breaths hard and fast. She took Virgil's knife from her pocket and passed it to Ada. Matilda stripped the blanket off the sled and declared Virgil too heavy for them to make short work of lifting him over the side of the tomb, even if she were willing to take barehanded hold of him, which she made it clear she was not. So they left Virgil tied to the sled, and together they upended it near the foot of the tomb. Both girls strained to hold it up until Matilda could slip beneath it. She bent her knees slightly and planted her hands on her thighs, her back bearing the weight of the sled, Virgil nearly vertical. Ada stood in front of her father with his folded pocketknife gripped in her fist, desperate to keep her eyes from traveling up to his lifeless face. Her trembling fingers felt for the groove in the long blade, and she pried open the knife.

"I can't hold this blame thing up forever." Matilda groaned, stooping under the weight.

So close to Virgil's body, Ada was assaulted by the combined odors of old liquor and excrement. She fought nausea as she slid the knife blade, keen, as a trapper's always is, underneath the rope tied tautly around his chest. As Ada sawed at the rope, Matilda shifted position, straightening just as the rope snapped, and Virgil's weight yanked the sled off her back. Ada reeled sideways as body and sled fell forward, her father's head dropping onto her shoulder, his cold lips grazing her neck before she ducked away. They heard his skull crack as it banged against brick, starting the yellow dog howling. It was all Ada could do to root herself where she stood instead of running blindly into the woods, away from the flicker of the lamp and the mad howl of the dog and those cold lips that had taken a final revenge.

With the heel of her boot, Matilda shoved the sled and centered it over the opening. She took the knife from Ada's hand, sliced the remaining ropes, and Virgil collapsed into the darkness of the tomb. The dog jumped in behind him, scratching and snuffling until Matilda cuffed his backside and he leapt out, dashing off through the woods. Using the crowbar and the last of their strength, they managed to work the halves of the slab back onto the tomb and slowly shove them together. Before the final push to close the crack, with Ada kneeling over the tomb, Matilda reached under the blanket next to the lantern for what she had hidden earlier—not the ball-peen hammer that had killed Virgil, but a corncob, picked clean and dried. She dropped it through the opening with evident satisfaction.

Ada stood up, faced her. "What's that for?"

"For me," Matilda said.

Ada stared at her.

Matilda stared back. Then she said, "I wonder where that blame dog is."

When they returned to the wagon, the mule was waiting quietly under the tree, acclimated, it seemed, to being hitched up in the dead of night. And there was the dog, lying again in the hay in the back of the wagon, contentedly chewing on a bone the Confederate soldier no longer had need of.

⌒͜⌒

When the starlings flew into the dawn, the mule was back in the barn. The dog, having been shooed off the wagon on the Trace, was back wherever he belonged. The girls were outside the stilt house, exhausted but still running on nerves. The hay they had used to cover

Virgil's body had been swept out of the wagon and scattered in the woods, the rust-red horse blanket hung again over the stall door, and the harrowing night was behind them.

The rising sun brought with it the first day of a new life for Ada. That was her thought as the sky lightened, tinting the edges of the clouds pink, then orange, then yellow. She took her first full-on look at Matilda in daylight. Her hair was short and parted on one side. Her dress was pinned together in front and looked to have been made from the striped ticking of an old mattress cover. As Ada studied her, Matilda turned, caught her watching, and Ada thought the look on the girl's face conveyed a suspicion that Ada knew about all the wrongs that had ever been done to her and had a part in them. It frightened her a little. But she was more frightened about what she would do when Matilda went back to where she had come from and Ada was truly alone in the world, with things so different now, and with all these new, unfathomable feelings.

Matilda laid a firm hand on Ada's shoulder and easily spun her a half turn. "I figure you're about…" She squinted at Ada's side view. "About four months on."

With those words, Ada's condition became real to her, as if Matilda had spoken it into being.

"Turns out," Matilda said, "I'm needing a place to stay. And I figure anybody four months on and blind to it is somebody going to be needing some help."

Ada nearly swooned with gratitude. She was going to have a baby. There had been no time to wonder about that in the course of the night they had just passed. And now she was too dazed and depleted to think clearly about anything.

"We need sleep," Matilda said, turning toward the house.

"He won't let me…" Ada began, then realized the absurdity of what she had been about to say, that her father would not allow her to sleep in the house. She put her hands over her mouth and laughed until she could hardly catch her breath, until she lost control and the laughing felt like screaming, then she laughed until she was all screamed out. She looked at Matilda, and Matilda shook her head.

"You don't think I could hurt it, laughing like that?" Ada moved her hands to the hard little lump just under her belly button and caught her breath, worried now.

"I think you're plumb crazy, is what I think," Matilda said. Then she strode up the porch steps like someone already more than half owner of them.

8.

"Was it you left that pinecone?"

In the few days since she and Matilda had set up housekeeping together, Ada had forgotten about the mysterious pinecone. But now it came to mind.

"Maybe."

Ada kept her eyes on the dough she was rolling out, but showed a shy smile.

"Door wasn't latched. Guess it scared you."

"I wasn't scared. Just at first, I was."

"You'd best toughen up; a baby's a whole lot scarier than a pinecone."

A *baby*. It seemed to Ada a word with no dictionary definition, just a blank space she would fill in with whatever truth replaced the baby-doll image she now held. There was so much she did not know about taking care of herself, having grown up without the guiding hand of a mother all these years, and soon there would be someone else to look after and keep safe. And yet, even as the horror of burying

Virgil still hung in the air of the stilt house, Ada felt a new lightness of heart now that she had someone other than her father to work at life with.

"We'll put in a garden this week. It's some late, but I know where I can get some plants so we don't have to start everything from seed. Over at my other place. My last place." Matilda paused and Ada thought maybe she was leaving space for a question about where she came from or who her people were or why she'd had a hammer with her on the night of the fire. Until now, Matilda had made it plain that she was not open to inquiries. She had simply stepped into Ada's world without a word about whatever world she had stepped out of.

But Ada did not care where Matilda had come from. She cared only that she stay. "Down the swamp?" she asked, mostly for conversation. "With the others?"

"The other what?" Matilda asked, and Ada's face clouded over with worry.

"Oh, lord," Matilda said. "How'd such a mouse come from that devil of a man?"

Ada relaxed. "My mother was the mouse." She almost spoke up about what it had been like living with her father, for herself and her mother both. But she was being careful not to drive Matilda away, and she thought it best not to overload her with shameful details.

"And no, I do not live on the swamp. Not till now. I come from over the other side of the Trace."

"Oh, do you know the Creedles?" Ada asked. "Peggy Creedle? She lives over there somewhere. I knew her just a little."

Ada thought she saw Matilda's face flinch, just a slight slackening of her generally steely expression, but Matilda shook her head vaguely and did not seem interested enough to ask who Peggy might be.

"Let's forget about everybody you used to know a little," Matilda said. "We need to lay low now. Somebody you used to know could get us sent to the penitentiary, or worse. It's just you and me right now. That's the way it's got to be."

"I know," Ada said.

"And don't be talking to nobody on this swamp, either. I mean nobody. People talk, and we don't need anybody talking about us. We just need some time to go by. Then, if anybody asks, Virgil went off with a load of pelts and never came back." They picked a date to use for the day he left and memorized it. "And he hired me to look after you while he was gone," Matilda instructed Ada. "Said he might be gone a long while, but wouldn't say where. And when he didn't come back, I stayed with you out of the goodness of my heart, a baby coming and all."

Ada nodded at everything.

"But don't go mixing up what's real and what's made up. I do *not* work for you. We straight on that?" Ada nodded more, and Matilda seemed satisfied.

Ada was in awe of Matilda. She felt as if a switch had been turned on inside herself the moment Matilda showed up. With Matilda, life had new possibilities. Life itself seemed a possibility. She tossed a sprinkling of flour over the dough, and something, perhaps her better judgment, threw up a memory from her childhood: a leggy gray bird she had watched crossing the swamp on a gator's back. But if a gator was of a companionable mind, what safer place in the world than on its back?

"There is one person I'm thinking about, though," Matilda went on. "One person we need, that I can trust. Her name's Gertie Tuttle. 'Miss Tuttle' to you," she said, looking over her shoulder at Ada cutting out dumplings. "She's a midwife."

"Oh." Ada had been hoping that Matilda would lay out a plan for the coming of the baby.

"I'll have to make a trip over there one night, see if she can get over to take a look at you. We don't need anything going wrong with what you've got going on."

Ada had not considered that problems might come with her pregnancy.

"I'm grateful," she said.

"Well, don't get too grateful. I ain't taking responsibility. Not for you nor any baby. This is a scratch-each-other's-back situation." Matilda strode over to stand face-to-face with the alligator on the kitchen wall. "You ain't attached to this thing, are you?" she asked, and when Ada said "Good heavens, no," Matilda picked up a skinning knife and began prying the nails out of the wall. "I don't like it looking at me." When she had the whole hide down, she rolled it up and carried it out the back door. Afterward she said, "We'll have to pay Gertie something when she comes. And down the road, we'll be needing more money." She looked around the room, taking inventory of what she might be able to sell. Virgil's fresh supply of corn liquor was first on her list. "And we might could sell some of his tools and traps later on. After a time. I don't guess he's got any extra money hid up somewhere?"

"Usually he'd just keep it on him, I think. When he had any," Ada said, but she mentioned Virgil's stash of tanned beaver pelts, and Matilda said she knew someone who might be interested.

The next afternoon, they reloaded the liquor into the wagon, rode into the woods, and raided Virgil's deer stand, taking care to avoid the bear trap Virgil had planted at the base of the tree lest anyone try to steal his stolen pelts. Back at the house, Matilda waited until night settled over the swamp, then rode down the back trail with Virgil's things in his wagon, leaving Ada to wonder where she was going and if she would return.

Matilda did return. Before the night was out, she came back in a wagon that was not Virgil's, pulled by a mule who was not Jax. "Traded them," she said, unhitching the older mule from the smaller wagon. "Can't keep his old wagon here and say he rode off in it both, if it comes to that. Same with the mule. Not that I think it'll come to that." She stroked the mule between his eyes with her fist. "Had to trade down some, but it couldn't be helped."

Ada was happy to go along, happy that Matilda had returned. She did not ask about the pelts or the liquor or any money that had passed hands in the night. She didn't ask why Matilda had not consulted her about the wagon or the mule. A baby was coming, and she would not be alone on this swamp in her father's hideout of a house when it happened. She had long believed, though she realized it only at that moment, that all one needed to get along in life was a true connection to one person. And Ada was setting her hopes on Matilda's being that person.

9.

The midwife's hands were wrinkled with age and work-worn. The veins were thick and ropy. But those hands roamed Ada's body with a firm sureness that gave her comfort and courage, and when Gertie proclaimed everything "right and good," Ada sighed with relief.

"Now, you come for me if anything seems off," Gertie told Matilda, and Matilda said she would. "I been called to catching babies, Mattie," Gertie said sternly. "Called by the Lord. Anything seems off, you make sure you come for me right quick."

"I said I would." Matilda picked up a strawberry from the basket Gertie had brought. She rolled it between her palms.

"See as you do. And you'll know to collect me for the catching when the pains come regular. When there's a nip in them. A nip, Mattie. Don't wait for a bite. Don't wait too long. You hearing me?"

"Regular and a nip. Ain't that hard." Matilda dropped the strawberry back into the basket.

Ada could see there was a history between Gertie and Matilda, wondered if maybe they were kin, but she did not feel that she was on strong enough ground with either of them to pry. Gertie's holy calling notwithstanding, Ada wasn't sure the midwife would tend her if not for Matilda, and she was not entirely certain about Matilda's going for help when her time came if not for Gertie. So she kept quiet and let the two of them work out the details of her child's birth.

"Should be up around the middle of September, it looks like," Gertie said.

"I'm some scared," Ada ventured.

"You should be. Having a baby ain't no walk in the woods. You just mind the time for fetching me, and it'll be all right, God willing. And you eat you some of that fruit."

Gertie turned to Matilda while Ada pulled up her underpants. "Pastor'll ride me over now and again."

"Just you and him, now. I don't want anybody else knowing I'm here."

"I know about what all you don't want. Ain't many that even knows about these houses back up in this swamp."

"Somebody might see you riding over and wonder."

"Ain't the first time I been over here. Job Farley, just down there a piece, he comes for me some. Irene's working on number six. Don't hardly need me no more, but Job's the worryingest fool for a woman ever was. He brings me regular. I can stop in them days, too."

"It's taking chances," Matilda said.

From across the room, Ada tuned in to their conversation and the nervous undertone in Matilda's voice. After all Matilda's warnings about not saying anything to anyone, had she told Gertie about Virgil?

Gertie's gravelly voice softened. "I'm taking care, Mattie. Ain't nobody but me and the pastor knows nothing, and he's done held a service."

A service. Ada pondered what that might mean. She busied herself with smoothing imaginary wrinkles from her skirt, listening.

"You don't got to worry about Job or Irene or nobody else down that way. They don't look to the right nor the left about other folks' business. Job, he could school anybody on taking chances." Gertie buttoned her crazy-quilt medical bag and hooked it over her arm, sighed and shook her head. "Ain't never been a man loved a woman no more'n that one. Carries him a vial in a secret pocket everywhere he goes, in case there's trouble."

"A vial?"

Gertie and Matilda looked at Ada as if they had forgotten she was there. Neither answered her, though Gertie seemed to weigh the prospect. It didn't matter, though. By then, Ada had remembered Virgil's rants about the "white trash whore and her half-breed urchins" down the swamp and how somebody should do something about "that nigger man." When she considered what form that "something" would likely take, she understood the purpose of the vial in Job Farley's secret pocket.

"I won't be crossing over the Trace anymore until her time comes, unless there's trouble. Not even at night. Too many eyes over that way," Matilda said, walking out to the porch with Gertie.

Ada watched them from the window as they went down the steps talking low about things they knew and she did not. She puzzled over all she had heard. In truth, she did not believe that anyone was going to wonder about her father's absence, let alone tie it to Matilda. He had been coming and going for years without anyone taking an interest. And she doubted that anyone way out here would pay any mind to a colored girl crossing the Trace. Surely there was something more than the disappearance of Ada's father in what those two were talking about out there, heads close together, Gertie's arm around Matilda's waist. *Turns out I'm needing a place to stay.* That was what Matilda had said that first night, and now Ada wondered why. But the promise of a midwife when the baby came and a friend in the meantime, maybe even for the long run, kept her from spending any more time on that.

At breakfast the next morning, Ada put a few strawberries from the basket onto Matilda's plate. "Have some of these, Mattie."

Matilda looked up and raised an eyebrow. Ada had learned to gauge her standing with Matilda, day by day, by whatever played across the other girl's face, and Matilda was not having Ada's use of a nickname.

"I heard Gertie…"

"You ain't Gertie. And it's 'Miss Tuttle.'"

Matilda shoved back her chair and went outside without touching the berries.

Ada picked up one of them, bit into it, and tried to figure things out. Sometimes it seemed as if Matilda was punishing her for something. Something other than everything white people had done to colored people. It was unsettling. She ate another strawberry. *Unfair is what it is,* she told herself, still stung by Matilda's harshness. After all, wasn't Matilda living in Ada's house? Hadn't she taken charge from

the beginning, and Ada been nothing but grateful? Treated her like
family? Her thoughts took a rare bold turn, leading her down a sloping path that eventually ended with *Even though she's colored.* Those
words flattened her with shame as she tasted her father's poison on
her own tongue. She felt a trace of fear as well. Sometimes it seemed
that Matilda could see right into Ada's soul and read her thoughts,
even through her blankest expression. It was frightening. And exciting.
Ada swept her mind free of all her dangerous thoughts and cleared
Matilda's plate from the table.

The following morning, Ada emerged from the outhouse in time to
see Matilda walk off into the woods on the back trail with Virgil's
boots under her arm. The boots Matilda had pulled off his feet before
they loaded him into the wagon. Sometime later Ada was at the pump
filling a bucket when Matilda returned, a burlap sack slung over her
shoulder. The sack was bulging, and moving.

"Two laying hens and a clutch of chicks," Matilda said, swinging
the sack onto the ground in front of the shed door.

"For the boots?"

"Something like that."

So she was meeting someone in the woods. Ada stood holding
the bucket awkwardly, waiting to be told who the someone was.
The chickens made their displeasure known as Matilda dumped
out the sack in the doorway and shooed them inside the shed,
latching the door behind them.

"You going to take that inside, or not?" Matilda asked, flicking her thumb at the bucket, closing the subject.

That afternoon, Matilda wound a roll of Virgil's chicken wire around a frame of cane stalks to section off a small chicken yard. She spent the rest of the day nailing up a coop made of Virgil's old drying boards topped with sheets of tin. All together, a good return for her father's work boots, Ada thought, listening to the cheerful peeps of the chicks.

The next thing to go, a few days later, was Virgil's trotline, coiled into a cumbersome mass of cord, fishing line, hooks, floats, and weights. From inside the house, Ada watched Matilda roll it out of the shed in the wheelbarrow and disappear down the trail. Several times more in the two weeks that followed, Matilda walked into the woods with or without some item of Virgil's and returned shortly thereafter with something they needed—seedlings for the garden, three cotton shifts Matilda made do with though they were considerably too large, a stack of thick rags that would be useful for monthlies.

One day a rooster appeared. By then Ada had pinned down the meeting time to every third morning around eight thirty. Matilda never presented an explanation, and Ada did not ask for one. She just watered the seedlings and took in the side seams in the shifts, happy for whatever turned up. The chickens were the best things of all, because Matilda would sit on the porch of an evening and talk about how many eggs they would have for trading, or to sell, when the chicks started laying, and Ada would take that as a commitment, adding up the months that Matilda was sure to be there.

After those two weeks, the trips into the woods stopped. The last delivery was two tablets of lined paper and a box of pencils. Matilda took those out to the shed, which she had claimed as her own private space with no objection from Ada. Matilda had installed a latch on the inside of the door, and she began spending hours at a time closed up in there, making no noise for Ada to hear when, on occasion, Ada crept around to one side of the shed and listened under one of the cutout windows. One day she was doing just that when her foot thudded against something soft that had not been there the day before when she had stood in that exact spot listening for any sound from within. She looked down and clamped both hands over her mouth. Staring up at her with four shiny black eyes was Virgil's two-headed baby otter.

10.

Matilda talked in her sleep. She slept in the hallway on a pallet of overstuffed quilts that Gertie had brought, Virgil's bedroom having taken on the air of a netherworld behind the door that Ada had closed the night they buried him and had not opened since. When it happened, the sleep talk came early in the night, not long after Matilda's breath slowed into a deep, raspy rhythm. Sometimes it flowed as a gentle stream of soothing words that Ada could not make out, meant, it seemed, to comfort someone in her dreams. Other times it was more lament than talk, haunting and sad and exactly matching the way Ada felt when she thought of Jesse or her mother. Sometimes it sounded like crying. Ada was not sure it sometimes wasn't. She never spoke of it, but she took to staying awake as long as she could each night, her ear against the wall between them, hoping to capture some of the elusive words.

One night she was awakened by the sound of Matilda thrashing on her quilts. Ada sat up quickly and pressed an ear to the wall in time to hear the smothered, impotent, mouse-squeak shout of one trapped in a nightmare, followed by slurred words that sounded, in turns, bitter, desperate, and resolute. A vow, it seemed to Ada. An unintelligible pledge. Matilda woke herself with her tossing and quietly opened the back door. A moment later Ada could make her out walking along the edge of the swamp under the full moon, pitching rocks into the still, black water.

Something, surely, was tormenting her. Something altogether unlike the guilt that often clawed at Ada over their having disposed of her father in the way they had. There was a sadness about this girl, something deep and raw. Ada knew sadness well enough to recognize it for what it was, no matter how much it sometimes looked like indifference or annoyance or hostility. Perhaps in this one area, she understood more than Matilda did.

"Did you sleep all right?" she asked gently over breakfast that morning. She would show she cared. She would hold that out, and Matilda could do with it what she would.

"What's that supposed to mean?" Matilda set down her spoon and glared at Ada as if she had asked if the sun would rise the next morning. But behind the glare, Ada believed she saw something—a silent plea that Ada not call her out, not acknowledge that she knew about her troubled nights. And then it was gone, Matilda's harsh countenance back, demanding an answer.

Ada stirred her grits nervously. "I just meant, you know, did you sleep good. Something to say, is all." She scooped up a spoonful of grits, raised it halfway to her mouth, then returned it to the bowl, stirred some more. She hated the way Matilda could fluster her so easily. Even after that glimpse behind her mask.

"I don't sleep good and bad," Matilda said. "I just sleep. Every night."

After breakfast, Matilda saw to the mule and the chickens, as usual. But instead of starting in on turning over a new section of the garden during the cool first hours of morning, as she had done for days, she came back inside the house.

Ada's guard went up as Matilda roamed aimlessly about the room, picking up a cup here, a work glove there, picking up, setting down, moving on. Finally, Matilda spoke. "You know, we got that whole room in there going to waste," she said, speaking of Virgil's bedroom. She sat down on Ada's low-slung bed, ran her hand over the drab green blanket.

"I don't mind you taking it," Ada said quickly. "The bedroom."

"I was thinking you ought to," Matilda said, rocking Ada's bed as if it were a porch swing.

Because I asked after her sleep. Shined a light on a weakness. Ada took a breath and held her ground. "I don't like going in there."

"Maybe I don't like sleeping in the hall. And he was *your* father."

It sounded like an accusation.

Later that day, Matilda brought in a hammer and nails and reattached a board that had pulled loose from one side of Virgil's bedstead, a low wooden box made of rough lumber, so that the bed stood firm and level. Ada stood outside the bedroom doorway and politely admired Matilda's work, but that night she settled herself into her old bed while Matilda sat on the porch, cooling down after the warm day. She was still out there when Ada fell asleep.

Sometime in the night, Ada woke with remnants of a dream in her head. It had a bad feel to it, but she lay there with her eyes closed and tried to piece it back together. In the dream, she was sleeping in Virgil's bedroom behind the closed door, lying on his mattress atop the newly repaired box frame. The tobacco-stained walls leaned in over her head. She was wearing her mother's daisy-strewn dress, blue and yellow, the only color in an otherwise sepia-tone scene that had the ghostly aspect of a tintype photograph. Bone-colored moonlight leaked in from the window and spilled onto the floor. She caught sight of a corner of her mother's Christmas tablecloth sticking out from between the mattress beneath her and the bedstead. She got up and slid the flimsy mattress aside to draw out the cloth, which to her delight was of a whole piece, as fresh as the day her mother had hemmed it. It smelled of Sylvie's homemade soap, scented with gardenias. She held it to her chest, reclaiming something of her mother, comforted by the fragrance and the tiny holly berries her mother had embroidered with her small, delicate hands. But when she reached for the mattress to slide it back in place over the bedstead, she realized it was not a bedstead at all, but a tomb, brick and limestone. She knew to turn and leave, warned herself to step away quickly, but this dream was the sort that compels one to walk up a foreboding flight of stairs or to open a wisely barred door. She leaned over the bedstead tomb, peered into the dark cavity, and there he was. Her father. Restless. His eyes closed as if in fitful sleep. He was still wearing the clothes they had buried him in, his feet absent the boots Matilda had removed. Ada stood over him, paralyzed, until he opened his eyes and grinned.

"I can't do it." Ada was sitting at the table in her nightgown when Matilda woke that morning. "No matter what, I can't sleep in that room. I'll sleep in the hall. I don't mind. Or I'll sleep here by the stove. But I can't never sleep in there."

Matilda dipped herself a cup of water from the bucket on the table and slowly drank it all. She set down the cup. "I changed my mind," she said. "I like the hall. It's private."

"Then take my bed. I'll take the quilts. It's only fair. I don't mind a bit."

"Gertie made those quilts," Matilda said.

That night, Matilda undressed for bed earlier than usual. She took the lamp and fished through a box she had found in the shed, filled with old books and magazines that had belonged to Ada's mother and were mostly gone to mold and silverfish. She carried a book and the lamp to her pallet. Ada heard her turning pages for a long time, the lamp sending flickers of yellow light dancing on a small patch of ceiling in the main room near the opening to the hall. Matilda was still turning pages, the lamp still lit, when Ada blew out the candle on the kitchen table and went to bed. Ada did not keep herself awake listening for words through the wall. She was the first to fall asleep. After that, nothing more was said about sleeping arrangements, and Virgil's door remained closed.

A few days on, almost as if in apology, Matilda taught Ada to drive the wagon.

"You mean that snake never even taught you to handle a wagon? To ride yourself out of here if you needed to?"

"He liked being the one who knew how to do everything, after my mama was gone," Ada told her.

Matilda walked her through harnessing the mule and hitching him to the wagon until Ada could do it without any help. On Virgil's trail, Ada learned to maneuver the wagon, to signal the mule to turn, to stop him and get him going again, to set the brake. Things she had seen Virgil do, but had never attempted herself.

"You did good," Matilda said back at the barn as she slid the harness over the mule's nose and handed it to Ada to hang on the wall.

Ada liked knowing she could handle the mule and the wagon. She felt less trapped, less at the mercy of her circumstances. She was gaining ground, she thought, and she was grateful to Matilda for that, though she knew better than to tell her so. Matilda kept an emotional distance, and Ada respected that.

As time went on, Ada learned to work her days around Matilda like the harmony in a simple two-part melody. If Matilda was of a mind to cook or do chores in the house, Ada worked the garden or brushed down the mule or lit a fire under the wash pot. If Matilda was out in the shed, or in the garden, or tending her chickens, Ada took up whatever needed doing inside. On occasion she was rewarded, as with the driving lesson, with a kindness that worked itself into a brief period of camaraderie between the two of them. But for every kindness, there was a coldness. As if the one required the other.

Even so, Ada pushed aside any misgivings that arose about Matilda and made way for a new concern—the faint butterfly fluttering inside her that Gertie had said was the baby moving.

11.

Summer arrived and showed itself in color and increase, deepening the green of the woods, yellowing the leaves on the cane stalks so that they fell under the harsh sun as if it were autumn, and yielding a bountiful harvest from the garden. Ada canned everything that could be put up in Virgil's empty mason jars. Matilda fished the river and shot rabbits and squirrels with Virgil's rifle and, to spare their supply of bullets, caught them in string traps and deadfalls she made with sticks and rocks and wood scraps. Neither of the girls had a heart for Virgil's cruel traps with their foothold jaws and rusted teeth.

Ada's pregnancy ripened so that by midsummer she often had to reach up a hand to Matilda for help getting out of bed. Their birthdays—Ada's seventeenth, Matilda's eighteenth—passed a week apart with little more than a mention. Gertie had come around several times to examine Ada as what had been only a modest swell beneath her skirt grew into a sizable mound that the midwife, one early August day, predicted would be a girl.

"How do you know?" Ada asked her.

"Carrying high. That and other things."

"A girl," Ada said. She was glad. A boy might look like Jesse and be a reminder that he had not loved her, or loved her enough. Or he might look like Ada's father, and Ada might not be able to love *him* enough. A girl was good.

"Should be on to four weeks, maybe on up to five," Gertie said. "No more'n that."

The time for fetching Gertie arrived sooner than she had predicted, and during a heavy rain. Ada was cutting out biscuits with a glass jar, and Matilda was writing out numbers on a new deck of homemade playing cards.

"Matilda!" Ada took a step backward and looked down past her hard, round belly, floured with handprints, to a puddle on the floor. "Something's bad wrong." Sliding down the side of the stove, she lowered herself to the floor and squeezed her privates, afraid her baby might run right out of her.

After a quick glance, Matilda finished the ten of hearts and laid it on top of the deck before she got up from her chair and made her way over to Ada.

"Is it dead?" Ada whispered.

"Ain't nothing but your water broke." Matilda looked down at Ada on the floor and shook her head.

"So it's all right?" Ada struggled to get to her feet, feeling for the stove behind her and climbing back up it.

Matilda walked to the front door and lifted her rain scarf from its hook. She began tying it around her head.

"Where're you going? Don't leave me."

"Either I can go for Gertie or you can have that baby on the floor while I feed the mule. Both ways, I need my scarf. It's raining."

"But I need you with me."

"Well, none of this was my idea. Gertie and me are fixing to get soaked, and this wasn't neither one of our doing."

"So it's time, then? But it's early. She said four, five weeks, and it hasn't been but three."

"Coming on to time, for sure, when the water breaks. Look, this ain't nothing half the women in the world ain't already done. Don't go acting like you're the only pregnant woman ever was."

"All right," Ada said. She moved herself over to the table and sat down. "So you'll bring Gertie."

Matilda gave her a sharp look.

"Miss Tuttle. You'll bring her?" Ada asked as if she wasn't sure of the answer.

"Or feed the mule," Matilda said, opening the door. "I ain't decided."

The baby was still. Maybe too still, Ada thought, sliding her hands over her belly while she waited for the next pain to come. She should have given more thought to the backache that had hounded her for the past two days. But it was manageable, this pain. More like bad digestion than what she had imagined labor pains would be. It would worsen, she knew. Matilda had been gone more than an hour. Maybe two. Maybe longer. Surely Gertie would show up in time. But Ada remembered the look on Matilda's face just before she left the house. It had been a look meant to throw Ada off-balance, to leave some doubt as to how much of a hurry she would be in with the fetching of Gertie. Or whether she would go at all. A look that warned against Ada's taking her for granted. Ada had seen it before. She did not believe Matilda would leave her on her own with the baby coming, though Matilda always seemed on the edge of deserting her, like a bee who lights on a flower but is just as likely to fly off as to drink.

Her stomach clenched around a dull ache that suddenly turned sharp, and Ada fixed her thoughts on Jesse, planting him in her mind before things got bad and she wouldn't remember to call him up. Would Jesse ever see his child? Ada wondered about that. She had wanted to try to contact him once she fully understood that she was carrying this baby. It had seemed right to let him know. But Matilda had forbidden it.

"We have committed murder, Ada. Who's to say anybody'd believe we did it to save you?"

Ada had taken note of the word *we* again as she gave in. But at least Jesse would have no chance to turn away from her once more. That first time had been pain enough.

The next cramp had a considerable bite. Ada groaned softly and lumbered over to her bed. She sat down, propped up in the corner with her pillow behind her back and her legs splayed out in front of her.

What would Jesse think of her, the way she looked now? He had always told her she was pretty, and she had always been embarrassed to hear it. It was Jesse's kindness talking, she knew. Jesse was kind. Even though he left her.

Something had changed between the two of them that last month in Baton Rouge. Jesse had changed. Could he have known she was pregnant? Virgil had seen it. Had Jesse? He had been away from their little room most of that last month, working on a big construction project in Metairie and living in a barracks. When he did come home to her, he was drained of his usual energy. He had lost his eagerness for her body and seemed to be fretting over something. Then came that awful day when he announced that the Metairie job was finished and told her he had decided to return to Red Dog, Texas, back to his real home. He was sick of construction work, he said, and it was clear that fiddling was never going to pan out for him, not in any way he could count on. He was going back to working at his father's brick factory. He sat down on their bed and took one of Ada's hands so gently that it terrified her. There was a girl back in Red Dog, he told her. A girl he had been thinking about lately.

"You are so beautiful, Ada. You're a sweet girl. And I have never in my life wanted to take care of somebody as bad as I've wanted to take care of you." He ran his hand softly over the back of her head, following her hair down her back to her waist, and Ada could have lost herself in that one tenderness if she had not already been withdrawing back inside herself, retreating to the place where she had kept herself hidden before Jesse. "But being here together all these months, this whole year, I'm seeing things with us different. It's almost like you're my kid, if you can understand what I mean. The responsibility of it. I'm not ready for that. I don't know as I ever will be." He buried his head in his hands, his long musician's fingers laced through his thick hair. Finally, he looked up. "There's someplace you can go, isn't there? Someplace besides back to *him*. I couldn't let you go back there." He dropped his head again.

Ada watched him hunched over, shaking his head as if he had done a bad thing, and she said, "Yes," very quietly.

Jesse looked at her, and the hope in his eyes rent Ada's heart in two.

"Really? There's somebody?"

"My mother has a sister," Ada said. She did not say that she no longer remembered this woman's name and did not know where she lived, or even if she was still alive, and that this woman would not want to take care of her any more than Jesse did, anyway.

"I'll put you on the train next week," Jesse said. "We'll get you there."

Ada nodded.

"I'm sorry, baby."

"It's okay," Ada told him.

"I wanted to be a hero for you. To save you, you know? But you deserve somebody who really loves you. Like a husband ought to. And you'll find that someday."

Somebody who really loves you. Ada had never once dared to believe it when Jesse told her he loved her. She had never considered a day of their year together as something real and solid, but had known it to be a wonderful misunderstanding that would someday be cleared up. And that someday had come.

She let Jesse take her to the train station and buy her a ticket for Jackson, where, she told him, her mother's sister lived. He wanted to believe her so much that the weight of that want nearly knocked Ada over. In Jackson, she spent most of the money Jesse had pressed into her hand when he said goodbye to buy a ticket to Bristol. And from there, she had found her way back to the swamp.

No, she did not believe Jesse had ever suspected she was going to have his baby. Jesse was a good man.

The birth pangs were intense now, the space for catching her breath between them closing up. One hit with such force that she cried out into the empty room. She focused on the front door, praying for it to swing open on Gertie and Matilda. The next one ripped through her like a knife, lifting her off the bed. She stumbled through it, heaving herself over to the table and into one of the chairs. When she could breathe again, she drew in a succession of quick, ragged breaths and clamped her fingers around the chair bottom, bracing for the next wave of pain. And when it came, she had resigned herself to it. She closed her eyes and gave herself over without a sound.

12.

"Well, you got you a girl." Gertie held up the wet, squirming baby by its heels and gave its backside a slap. A thin tinkling wail came from its red bow of a mouth.

"Don't think it'll stay like that—that sweet little angel sound. This one here'll be waking up the dead a few days on." Gertie wiped down the baby with a boiled rag and wrapped it in a blanket she had brought.

Gertie and Matilda had only just made it in time. Matilda had gone for the midwife on foot through the woods, avoiding the road, and someone—the pastor, Ada supposed—had given them a ride back. The two of them had come through the door to find Ada with her underpants off and squatting over the mattress she had laid out on the floor, sweat rolling down her face. Once they had gotten her onto her back, pillows doubled under her shoulders and head, knees spread wide, Ada had borne the entire ordeal with nothing more than hurt-dog whimpers to let Gertie know when to tell her to push. Three good pushes was all it had taken.

Gertie gave the baby first to Matilda to tend while Ada pushed once more to expel the afterbirth, which, after a careful examination, Gertie wrapped in layers of brown paper.

"You know what to do with this," Gertie said soberly, taking up the baby again and passing the paper packet to a reluctant Matilda. "Go on, now. Take it out back and bury it somewhere secret. Somewhere nobody won't come acrost it. Next to a young tree, like I showed you before. And cover it over real good with leaves. Ground'll be soft after that rain."

Matilda did not hide from Ada her feelings about having to take on this job, and Ada managed a weary "Thank you. Thank you, both."

Beyond holding out her arms to receive the baby from Gertie, Ada had no idea what she was supposed to do. The old woman gently worked Ada's blouse up around her neck. She loosed the blanket from the baby and laid her on Ada's chest, leaving her to find her way. "They most times do," she said. She praised Ada for the good job she had done and told her she had been blessed with an easy birthing. "You was farther along than I thought; you just didn't look it." Ada watched the baby root around until she found a small, milk-hardened breast and pressed her little face into it.

Gertie cleared away the rags scattered on the floor. She dunked the scissors she had used to cut the cord into a kettle of water slow boiling on the stove, then dried them off and dropped them into her bag.

Matilda returned empty-handed. Gertie raised her eyebrows, and Matilda nodded.

"Good," Gertie said. "Now we got to make out the receipt." She pulled a small ledger and a pencil from her bag and sat down at the table. The tip of her tongue slid over her top lip as she carefully formed letters on the page. "You got a name?" she called out to Ada.

"Ada Lovella Morgan," Ada answered.

"I was meaning for the baby," Gertie said. "But we can start with you. The mother. How you spelling that—Lovella?"

Ada spelled out her name haltingly, long out of practice with spelling, and Gertie wrote the letters slowly.

"Now, what about for the baby?"

Gertie had been as adamant about not speaking the baby's name before the birth as she had been about burying the placenta.

"Well…" Ada could feel her body regaining some strength, but her voice was still weak. "My mother's name was Sylvie. Maybe that?" She looked up as if she were asking permission.

"You want me to put that down? It'll be official then. I'm certified by the county."

"I like 'Annis,'" Matilda said firmly.

"Mattie," Gertie said low. There was reprimand in her voice.

"I just like the name, is all."

"You watch yourself, girl. You making your own bed," Gertie muttered.

Ada was only half listening. She lay still while the baby worked on her nipple, hoping she was doing everything she was supposed to do.

"And," Matilda went on, raising her voice, "I think it's time Ada started thinking on new things." She looked everywhere except at Gertie. "'Annis,' now. That's a new kind of name. Don't you think so, Ada?"

"Janice?" Ada asked absently, tracing a tiny blue vein at the baby's temple.

"*Annis*. No *J*."

Gertie growled a low "unh, unh, unh" in the back of her throat.

"It's a name people won't forget," Matilda said, fixing a meaningful look on Gertie.

Gertie shook her head.

"Ain't nothing to me, though, if you don't like it," Matilda told Ada.

"I like it," Ada said quickly. She tried it out. "Annis Morgan. I like it real good."

"Don't matter none to me what you call it," Matilda said. "It's your baby. Not mine."

"Write that down, please, Miss Tuttle. If you would. Annis."

"You sure on that?" Gertie paused with the pencil in the air.

"I'm sure," Ada said.

Gertie wrote, and Matilda looked pleased with herself. Ada noticed and was happy for it.

"You put this somewhere careful," Gertie said, tearing the sheet of paper from the ledger and laying it on the table. "I got it in my book, too. It's official."

"You the one fixing to have to live with that name," Gertie told Matilda later at the door. She wrapped her scarf around her head, ready to head back out into the misty air to meet a wagon that had pulled up at the end of the trail in the woods.

"Guess if I could live without it all this time, I can live with it," Matilda said.

Ada was almost asleep with the baby in the crook of her arm, and while the words puzzled her, she was not certain she would remember them when she woke.

13.

It was after midnight. The baby, three days old, was asleep in a bushel basket beside Ada's bed. A little earlier, Ada had awakened at the first sound of Annis's stirring and nursed her until she fell asleep at her breast, then laid her back in the basket. Now Ada sat up in bed again, alert to a new sound. Her gown was still open, her nipple still moist and swollen as she pressed her ear against the wall. She had not stayed awake to listen for Matilda's sleep talk in a long time, but here it was, the familiar cadence, the slurred dialogue. She held her breath, willing Matilda to say something that would help Ada to understand whatever had made her the way she was. There was some silence. Then a deep breath. More silence. Then a low moan. After that, three distinct words broke through: *Annis. Mama. Springhouse.*

At the end of each day, when Matilda lay down on her pallet in the hall, one thin wall separating her from Virgil Morgan's daughter, and now his granddaughter as well, she welcomed the velvet refuge of night. In the first vulnerable moments, alone with her thoughts, she sometimes called on her mother's practice of dwelling only on what was good in the world. In this way, she kept evil at bay. But sometimes sleep betrayed her and she woke in the predawn darkness, sleep having let in some horrible thing to lie beside her. As had happened this night. Now she lay awake as her mind turned over, like so many cold stones in a barren field, the unspeakable events that had led her to this place: what she had seen, what she had done, what she had lost.

She hadn't meant to kill him.

PART TWO
Matilda Patterson

14.

Virgil Morgan was the devil.

Matilda had known him for what he was with the first word she heard him speak. *Boy.* Directed at her father. It was nothing new, that word used in that way, but coming from the likes of Virgil, it carried more than its usual sting. It had come, that first encounter, on the heels of Curtis Creedle's having told Virgil to "get on home" when he came around looking to buy liquor on a Wednesday afternoon when Curtis, as Virgil well knew, only sold to locals on Sundays. Sunday morning, nine to noon, when those most likely to object were tucked away at church. It was safe enough, selling hooch to pagans on the Trace while Prohibition was only just taking hold, but Curtis did not need Virgil's business. And he did need Matilda's father. On the Creedle farm, Dalton Patterson, a sharecropper, was more important than Virgil Morgan. Matilda knew that, and Virgil knew it. So Virgil took him down a peg every chance he got.

Virgil lived on the opposite side of the Trace. Way up in the swamp, so Matilda had been told. With the rest of his sort, she supposed. Reptiles and rats and slugs. Those useless little gnats that never let up. Chiggers that get under your skin and leave their marks if you pick the wrong flowers or take the wrong shortcut through a field on the way to somewhere you'd like to go. Pesky, inconsequential little things that would be easily squashed if all of nature did not conspire to provide them such cover, give them such an advantage.

She caught sight of Virgil's wagon one day when she arrived for school at Miss Bodie's house, an old cabin leaning on the shoulder of the Trace. His mule came around a bend in the road, followed by his rattletrap wagon, Virgil swaying on the driver's seat, already three sheets to the wind and the sun just up.

Headed toward town, thank God and everything good, Matilda thought. She watched the wagon until it disappeared around another turn, then she went inside mad.

Matilda attended school when she wasn't in the fields, mainly to make her mother happy. But she looked beyond the teacher's lessons for most things, seeing science in the stars and the heat lightning and the long-legged skimmers skating across the pond, art in the agates she collected in the gully, and history in the bones and arrowheads and bottles she dug up in the sandy creeks. As for religion, she looked at the moon and knew there was a god. She saw Virgil Morgan's wagon coming down the road and knew there was a hell, because Virgil was going there, no question.

After school that day, she followed the creek bed home, picking a path around anything that might punch a hole in the cardboard soles she had cut out and slid into her shoes that morning. The hem of her dress swung uneven at her knees, and she swatted at a loose thread that nagged the back of her leg. As she neared the outskirts of Curtis Creedle's farm, his *plantation*, as he liked to call it, the woods thinned on either side of the creek and a breeze that smelled like rain stirred the new leaves on the trees. A wild-eyed yellow dog she didn't know bounded from a clutch of scraggly pines and ran a frenzied circle around her, then veered off across a fallow cornfield as if he had sized her up and matched her with the run-down shack across the creek from the Creedle house. And when Matilda arrived there, the dog was waiting, hanging back at a sagging corner of the sun-bleached shack, tail thumping expectantly, as if he were something more than a passing stray. She stomped her foot and he scuttled back, then slunk forward again, low to the ground, eyeing her hopefully. Matilda turned away. She was not getting attached to anything new on the farm. As it was, she was already working on detaching herself from everything holding her there.

Her mother was hanging dry clothes on a line strung across the front porch, humming a hymn around a clothespin tucked between her lips. She was airing out the clothes, a "wind washing," she called it, stretching the life of things too ragged to survive the boiling pot.

"Hey, baby," Teensy said, the clothespin flapping. Matilda answered over her shoulder as she slipped inside the shack, the screen door slapping shut behind her.

It seemed to Matilda that every blame thing in her life was ragged, the shack being the prime example. Flies flew in and out no matter how much newspaper or straw mud Teensy stuffed between the warped clapboards, as did wasps, harvesting the dry wood for their paper nests lodged in the porch rafters. Furniture in the main room consisted of a square table with three straight-back chairs, one for each Patterson; a three-legged stool Teensy sat on when there were visitors; a shuck mattress on a base of apple crates pushed up against the back wall, where her parents slept; a small woodstove; and a hammered-tin pie safe wrapped in a pick sack filled with sawdust and straw, making do as an icebox when there was ice.

A tar-paper wall sectioned off a narrow space just long and wide enough for a wobbly, four-drawer chest with one drawer missing and Matilda's pallet of quilts. It was a sorry sanctuary, but it gave Matilda a private place to think at night. She slept on quilts because she could not abide the sound a shuck mattress made beneath her when she turned over, so much like the dry rustle overhead when a snake was holed up in the attic, which was the case as often as not. Two ginger cats—even they were battle-scarred and scraggly—were on perpetual guard against mice.

Her mother always referred to the shack as "our house," though to Matilda's mind it wasn't theirs and it fell way short of a house. Her father was of like mind. Matilda had never heard him speak of it as anything but *the place*. "Go back to *the place* and fetch me a dry sweat rag," he might say, mopping his forehead with a damp scrap of cloth when Matilda checked on him in one of the cornfields or the peach orchard.

Like most of the sharecroppers Matilda knew, her father wanted a place of his own, a piece of land that *was* his, with something he could rightly call a house sitting on it. But unlike most of the others, her father had a plan for bringing that about. It required making a deal with a devil—there were plenty of those besides Virgil Morgan—but he had done it because it looked to be a way out. Not just for himself, but for Matilda and for the baby her mother was carrying. The prospect of owning land was what drove him, day and night. It was the reason the shack was stuffed chock-full of illegal home brew—jars of corn liquor in the attic and the meal bin and the corn crib, bottles of peach brandy in the crawlway under the floor. It was the reason there was a false bottom in the bed of his wagon.

Not one of those bottles or jars belonged to Matilda's father. Not any more than the shack did, or the fields he worked, or the team he used for plowing. It made Matilda crazy. Her father wanted his own place so bad he couldn't think in a straight line, and not many straight lines in Mississippi ended at a colored sharecropper owning his own farm. Matilda knew that.

Still, her father had gotten himself tangled up in a deal to hide Curtis Creedle's liquor and to transport it in the rigged-up wagon. Twice each month he filled the hidden compartment with crates of liquor that he drove to the train station in Canton, handing them over to someone else beholden to the Creedles, who, in turn, loaded them into a freight car and sent them on to Vicksburg. From there, a steamboat captain floated them up the river to St. Louis, then shipped them on to Chicago. Dalton did this in exchange for Curtis's promise to write off, at the end of one year, the debt Dalton owed him. The typical crippling sharecropper's debt for seed and rent and poor crop yield that kept men like her father from ever getting out of the hole with landowners.

Back when Dalton was still mulling over his decision, or what passed for a decision between croppers and landowners, Matilda had said what she and her mother were both thinking—that Old Man Creedle, with all his outbuildings and his 140 acres, only hid liquor in the shack so he could point to Dalton as the bootlegger should anyone catch on to his enterprise. Her father was no fool. He knew what was what with regard to Curtis Creedle. But he so wanted a chance in life that he was willing to take the risk.

"One year's all I need," he'd said. "Then we're out of here, free and clear."

Her mother, in contrast, had learned to take joy in a warm slice of strawberry pie or a cooling breeze visiting the porch on a hot day. Teensy held that life was short and she was not about to miss any good thing right in front of her, looking ahead for something that might never be.

Matilda tried to find her own way between the two of them, a way around all those low expectations, but there wasn't a path to anywhere that she could see from where she was. The problem—one of the problems, as she saw it—was that a person, at least a person in her own circumstances, couldn't have a respectable dream in a place like this.

Foraging in the pie safe for something to eat before she'd have to plant a few rows of strawberries ahead of the coming rain, Matilda found a day-old biscuit and an almost empty tin of cane syrup. A fly had died a sweet death stuck to the side of the tin, and Matilda flicked it off with her fingernail. She stabbed the biscuit with her thumb and dribbled the dregs of syrup into the hollow, but before she could take a bite, she heard voices from the porch.

"Mattie! Miss Creedle's here."

Good lord. A long day just got longer. Peggy Creedle looking for some-body to get in trouble with. Matilda had never known a girl as old as Peggy was—seventeen—with so much time to spare and so little sense about using it.

She took her time strolling out to the porch. She wouldn't have gone at all if she hadn't known her mother would start offering up apologies to "Miss Creedle" for her daughter's dawdling, and Peggy would say "It's okay, Teensy, she'll be coming," and there was just so much wrong with a scene like that.

"Hey, Peggy."

Teensy had asked Matilda more than once to address Peggy as "Miss Creedle," but Matilda called her "Peggy" when there weren't any other Creedles around and avoided calling her anything when there were.

"Miss Creedle brought you a letter," Teensy said, and then Matilda was interested.

"Eugene picked it up at the post office this morning," Peggy said, flapping the envelope like a paper fan. Eugene was an extra hand hired to help with spring planting and to run errands. "He carried it back to the house for you," she said, meaning the Creedle house, as even Peggy knew that shack was no kind of house, the same as the other two cropper shacks on the place, way over on the peach orchard side.

"Who's it from?" Teensy asked, looking at Peggy politely, and Matilda reached in front of her mother and slid the letter from between Peggy's fingers before Peggy could pretend she hadn't already read it. She had done a sloppy job of resealing the envelope. Matilda took a few slow seconds to examine the seal, making a silent issue of it. She swept a quick glance across the face of the envelope at the postmark—Cleveland, Ohio—and the handwriting—Rainy's. She would have pointed out the postmark to her mother instead of stating her own business in front of Peggy, but Teensy couldn't read.

"It's from Rainy," Matilda said. Then she looked over at Peggy and added pointedly, "From Miss Day."

Peggy's face pinked up, and Teensy said in her prim, white-folks-are-listening voice, "Well, that's nice," and Peggy—*God be praised*—said her goodbyes and headed back to the Creedle house, auburn curls bouncing, tail end swishing—trouble looking to happen.

"Mattie, keep a civil tongue," Teensy said the minute Peggy was out of earshot. It was more plea than rebuke, delivered with so much worry around the edges that Matilda would have offered something to ease her mother's mind if she had not been so eager to see what Rainy had written. So she just went inside by the front door and out by the back door and took a path that climbed a hill and ended at the rim of a gully that fell off into the creek. A rocky outcrop near the top, hidden by a buttonbush growing out of the bank, was her place for being alone, and she sat there and opened the letter.

Five months had slogged by since her best friend, Lorraine Day—Rainy—and her family left the Trace for Ohio. Plenty of people were leaving. There were jobs in the North, people were saying. Up North, railroads and factories and meatpackers and stockyards were looking for Negroes to hire. So people said. Rainy's mother had an uncle in Cleveland who ran a Negro newspaper—*now there was a dream worth having*—and he had written to them about an anti-lynching law some people were trying to get passed in Washington. He was hopeful, he had written, though many in the country opposed it.

Matilda had asked herself then how anyone—*anyone*—could be against an anti-lynching law. But there were people, she knew, who would resist any law handed down by the federal government. People who did good things, who went to church and gave to the poor and helped their neighbors and loved their children, and at the same time would stand against making it a federal crime to hang people from trees, or beat them to death, or burn them, or douse them with acid. Year in and year out such things were happening, while her mother's mind was stayed on cool breezes and wildflowers and berry pies and her father longed for a piece of this godforsaken, blood-soaked land to put down roots in. None of it made any sense to Matilda.

Even before Rainy left, Matilda had decided that as soon as she could manage it, she would board a train headed north and take her chances. She had thought it through. First, she would get herself to Jackson and find work. Most every white woman in Jackson had a maid, and most were always on the lookout for a cheaper one. Or one less likely to catch a husband's eye. So Matilda had heard. She could do maid work for a while, if it came to that. Maid work was far and away better than chopping cotton, which is how she had spent every late spring and early summer since she had been big enough to hold a hoe. Or she could bus tables. She was only sixteen, but she'd be seventeen by the time her mother's baby was born.

Matilda was counting on the new baby to soften the blow of her departure. She had a friend in Jackson she could stay with in the room she rented. She would have to put up with the latest bad boyfriend— Leeta always had a boyfriend, always a sorry one—but she could handle that. She would give herself a year there to save up. She figured she could stand anything for one year. And she would be careful not to let herself get sidetracked by things like love and marriage and children, because if you did that, you could almost always forget about ever getting out. She had not told anyone about her plan. Not even Rainy.

And then Rainy had left first. Without warning. When no one was paying attention. The preferred manner of departure when leaving Mississippi for the North, taking the South's secrets.

Matilda tore open the letter. It was short, just a few lines. Rainy was working as a laundress, earning more for a day's work than she and Matilda had earned in a week chopping cotton. They were living, the six Days, in the top half of a house—four rooms to themselves. There was enough space for Matilda, and work, too. "Get your skinny butt up here quick as you can."

This was a real plan. Something concrete to take the place of all the daydreams about leaving that Matilda had only half believed in. Doing laundry had not figured in her dreams, but it was a beginning. She could send home some of her pay, she told herself. Help her father buy his own team, his own seed. He might not ever have a chance to own his own farm, but he could move up from sharecropping for Curtis Creedle to tenant farming for somebody else. Get out from under Old Man Creedle's thumb, out of his nasty business. That was something. A start.

Matilda slid the letter into her pocket and Cleveland, Ohio, into her heart.

15.

"Not that one, that other'n."

"This'n here?"

When Matilda reached Gertie Tuttle's place, just beyond the gully, Virgil was in his wagon on the road out front messing with Gertie's granddaughter, Stella Mae.

Stella Mae was ten years old, the sweetest thing on the Trace, and not right in the head.

"No, the brown one. Over there," Virgil said.

The dirt road was full of rocks, all some shade of brown and buried in the dirt like paving stones. Stella Mae was earnestly digging up rock after rock and holding each one up toward Virgil, him sitting there in his wagon with an idiotic grin on his face, shaking his head and pointing from one side of the road to the other while Stella Mae crisscrossed in front of the mule. She looked up when Matilda entered the picture.

"There's a sharp rock out here gonna hurt Jax's foot. I got to move it," she said.

Matilda looked at Stella Mae, then up at Virgil.

"Exactly which rock you looking for her to move?" Matilda met Virgil's bloodshot gaze with a cold, hard stare. She had a particular soft spot for Stella Mae. Virgil looked away first, then chuckled and flicked the reins.

"Watch out, Jax!" Stella Mae shouted to the mule as it moved on down the road. Matilda took hold of her hand and walked her up the large, flat river rocks lined up as steps leading to Gertie's porch. Nailed to the house, just to the left of the front door, was the familiar tin shingle painted white and hand-lettered in black: *Gertie Tuttle, Birthing and General Nursing.*

"Is Jax a donkey?" Stella Mae asked as they entered Gertie's shack, an old one-room cabin left over from slave days that was slowly crumbling around her, despite the labors of Dalton and others to keep it standing. She declined all offers from those who tried to convince her to live with them, including Teensy. If asked, Gertie would say she lived there because she liked the feel of the spirits in the cabin, but Matilda knew she lived there because no one else had claimed it and she wanted something of her own. The same reasons she was raising Stella Mae, who wasn't really her granddaughter.

"Ain't but one jackass out there, and he's driving the wagon," Matilda said, emptying the basket of cucumbers Teensy had sent from their garden. Stella Mae made a show of laughing at that, falling onto the floor and kicking her feet in the air.

"Awright, Stella Mae, that's enough. Go out and play," Gertie said, and Stella Mae trotted outside.

When Stella Mae was gone, Gertie turned a look on Matilda.

"Don't you go teaching her disrespect. She got enough problems without you adding more."

"He had her out there digging up rocks, moving them out of the road—never the right damned rock."

"I saw it. Didn't do her no harm. And watch your mouth."

"There's different kinds of harm."

"You let me worry about Stella Mae. And I got my plans for that one," Gertie said, nodding in the direction of the road.

Meaning Virgil, Matilda knew. Meaning some hex Gertie'd come up with—sprinkling salt on the road or filling his wagon tracks with ground-up dirt dauber nests or some such thing that wouldn't make a whit of difference to Stella Mae or Virgil Morgan or any other soul on the Trace.

"He been passing by a right lot, of late, that man," Gertie noted, asking without asking.

"Poppa says he's working off a debt he owes Old Man Creedle."

Gertie nodded. Neither mentioned the buying or selling or manufacture of liquor, neither acknowledging the dangerous subject that was understood between them.

"He came around a few times loaded up with furs," Matilda said, watching the way Gertie was folding a pile of rags into diapers, then joining in, their arms moving in the same rhythm. "Paying with pelts, I guess. But now Old Man Creedle's got him working in the back field doing I don't know what. I'm happy enough I don't have to see him back there."

"How's school?" Gertie asked, moving to a safer subject.

"Same," Matilda said. "Just one day left." School always let out early for spring planting before the cotton chopping season started.

"And your mama?"

"Good, far's I can tell."

"You bring her this." Gertie handed Matilda three oranges tied up in a red rag. "She's in the month for eating oranges."

"Where'd you get oranges?" Matilda scraped a fingernail across the bumpy skin of an orange and raised it to her face, breathed in the sharp, sweet fragrance.

"Never mind. I have ways," Gertie said, the implication being that she had conjured them or prayed them into her hands. Matilda did not argue. She didn't believe in Gertie's conjuring, but knowing that Gertie was hexing people like Virgil Morgan made her smile. Nobody else seemed to be doing anything about him or anybody like him. Not in Mississippi, anyway. But in Cleveland, Ohio, there were Negro newspapers and people weren't afraid to read them. Matilda kissed Gertie's wrinkled cheek and tickled Stella Mae breathless on the porch, then headed off down the road with her basket and the bundle of oranges, thinking about the North.

She was already on the train in her mind. She could picture Rainy waiting at the station, waving as the train slowed, then stopped. The two of them laughing and jumping and carrying on. She was so caught up in it all that she didn't hear the wagon until she was back on Creedle property, until she looked up and saw it ahead of her on the farm road. Virgil.

Hellfire. Old Man Creedle must've sent him back out as soon as he showed up. She squeezed through a gate into the cow pasture on her right and started picking up dry twigs as if collecting kindling, laying the sticks in her basket, not looking up, waiting for the evil to pass. When the rattle died away before it should have, she knew he had stopped behind her. Head down, she reached to one side for a twig, watching him out of the corner of her eye. He just sat there on the wagon seat. She supposed he was going to ask her to do something like move a rock or swat a fly off the mule's ass or some other useless thing any white man could tell any colored girl to do and expect it to be done or have her answer for it. But Virgil did not call out to her. Instead, she heard the groan of the axle as he climbed down from the wagon and the thump of his boots as they hit the ground. She cut another sideways look his way and saw him cross to her side of the road and fumble with his suspenders.

Pick up a stick, move a step away, pick up another one. Matilda looked again just as Virgil dropped his trousers and sent a sparkling arc of piss into the field between them. Whipping around, her back to him, she stood rigid. She heard his smug laughter, the snap of his suspenders as he replaced them, and finally the splintery creak of the wagon as he heaved himself up. She wanted to hurl every stick in the pasture at the back of his greasy head. But she just stood there, straight-backed and still, her face burning with shame and fury, listening to the sigh of the leather traces as the mule strained against them and moved off.

Starting for home again in the dust the wagon had thrown up, she thought of all the things that might happen to Virgil Morgan if there was anything fair in this world. The diseases he might contract, the plagues and pestilence and adversity that heaven might rain down on him if heaven and hell and the worlds between made any sense at all.

16.

"I'm thinking on hiring myself out to Caleb Gill."

Matilda sat on the three-legged stool in the middle of the room, putting some distance between herself and her parents finishing up supper at the table. It was well into May by then, and all three were used up after a day's work on the farm, then chopping weeds by twilight in the small patch of cotton that Dalton grew on his own each year, the only exception to his one-third/two-thirds sharecropper split with Curtis Creedle. It added to their workload, but allowed a little money for winter provisions—shoes and woolens for the three of them, kerosene for when the days grew shorter, winter feed to fatten the chickens.

"'Tain't the best time," Dalton said, sopping up a puddle of cold flour gravy from his plate with his last bit of bread. "What with the cotton needing chopping and the garden still going in and your mama slowing down some."

"I'm keeping up," Teensy said, standing up and swiping the dirty dishes from the table as proof.

"I got to start in on the second planting in the front field at sunup, so that's leaving our cotton to you. And Gill's already got people lined up to work his place by now. Not much chance he'd take you on this late, anyhow." Dalton leaned back in his chair and crossed his arms over his broad chest. Matilda had often wondered if her baby brother, born three years back, would have favored their father—tall and muscular, a quick smile, handsome as the day is long—if he had lived more than one day.

"I can chop both places," she said. "I'll get ours done first. And Gill'll take me on. He knows I'm fast."

"*Mr.* Gill," Teensy said, heading out to the porch with a bucket.

"Mama, wait. There's something I want to tell you, while you're both here."

Teensy's eyes narrowed slightly, but Matilda took a deep breath, steeled herself, and went on.

"Well, here it is plain. I got that letter from Rainy a while back."

"From way up in Ohio…" Teensy said, as if that in itself was worth sitting back down and spending some time on. "Ain't been no word from Marlene. Expect she's been too busy up there."

"Well, Rainy had some news. About her and her mama both." Matilda told them about Rainy's bringing in more money in a few weeks than Matilda could make all season hiring herself out to Caleb Gill and anybody else who would give her field work. Then she told them her plan to get herself to Cleveland as quickly as she could manage and to send everything she could spare back home to Dalton. "To buy your land, Poppa," she said, though what she really meant was to at least get him off the Creedle farm and on to tenant farming somewhere else before he ended up in prison for driving Curtis's liquor.

"And how you figuring on getting train fare clear up to Cleveland,

Ohio?" Dalton looked to be taking his empty cup more seriously than Matilda's proposition.

"Chopping. I can work the Porter place after the Gills'. And come July, Mrs. Porter'll hire me to do her canning. Other white women up that way, too."

"It's four miles walking to Gill's place and more to Porter's, lessen you're wanting me to leave off my work to haul you up there."

"I'll walk it. Or catch a ride. Ain't no problem."

"In them shoes?"

Matilda tucked her feet, clad in the ruins of her only pair of shoes, underneath the stool.

"I'll get by."

"Rainy planning on feeding you up there? Putting clothes on your back? It's cold up North. Snow and all. Them shoes ain't gonna cut it. Them clothes, neither."

"I got my coat. It still fits." The elbows were worn to threads, and she couldn't button it across her chest, but she'd manage. "It's as good as what Rainy had when she went. And they're paying, for a day, what we'd get in a week here, chopping."

"Maybe for a grown man. Not no little girl. I ain't believing that."

Rainy's pay, worked out over a year, was more than Dalton would see in twice that time. Matilda answered carefully.

"It's what Rainy makes. A man probably makes double that. Maybe more. They'd probably jump at hiring you, if you went up there."

"Hmph. I ain't working in no sweatshop factory for no amount of money from nobody." Dalton shoved his cup across the table. "That's what Rainy's doing? Factory work?"

"Laundering."

"Well, that figures. Move all the way up there and end up taking in laundry, same as down here," Dalton said, but Matilda could see he was running figures of his own.

"You could have your land in half the time," she said, playing her final card. "Have some money put back for it after your year's up." Then she fell silent.

"It's down to ten months, now," Dalton said, but he was chewing on his mustache, thinking things over. "You want this real bad, Little Bit?"

It was the last thing Matilda had expected her father to say, and the pet name he hadn't used in years caught her off guard. She felt her eyes water up, and then the dam broke. She sat on the stool and cried, red-eyed and snotty, until she was so embarrassed that she stumbled back behind the tar-paper wall to compose herself.

She knew it would be hard for them if she left. Especially as they had no real family on the Trace other than Gertie, who was family by choice, not birth. Dalton's kinfolks were scattered across the state, and Teensy had grown up an orphan. Her parents had both died in a massacre in the Carroll County courthouse after two colored men brought charges against a white man. There were still bullet holes in the courthouse walls when Dalton and Teensy got married and Teensy left Carrollton for good. Teensy never spoke of how her parents died, but Matilda knew enough about what had happened to understand her mother's meekness, even with girls Peggy's age.

When Matilda reemerged, Dalton and Teensy were still at the table, talking low, Dalton's hand over Teensy's, Teensy's chin almost touching her chest.

Matilda sat down and rested her head on Teensy's shoulder. She looked over at her father and said, "To answer your question—real bad. I want it real bad. For all of us. It's a chance for…" Cleveland, Ohio, was a chance for so much that Matilda could not fit it all into a few words, and her father stopped her from trying.

"We think you ought to go," he said. "It's a chance for a whole life."

He understood. A whole life instead of a sunset here and a cool breeze there and a dream of landowning that wasn't likely to ever come true. He believed it was possible, a whole life up North instead of a little scrap of one down here. Matilda was so grateful that she promised herself, and her father, that she would live on as little as possible, on potatoes and onions, if need be, and send every spare penny back home to him and Teensy, who was crying softly, tears dropping onto the little baby bump in her lap.

"When?" Teensy asked.

"Not till after the baby comes. Till you're on your feet and don't need me as much."

"Was on my feet by suppertime, the day you come," Teensy said, wiping her eyes fiercely with the back of her hands as if she were done with crying forever, and Matilda knew her mother was giving her blessing.

17.

"Looks like this one's gonna take." Gertie ran sure hands over Teensy's belly, kneeling beside the shuck-and-crate bed. Matilda reached out a hand to help her up when she had finished, but the old midwife swatted it away. "Time comes I need help getting on my own two feet, I'll let you know," she said, making her own slow way up.

"It's early, still," Teensy said, asking to be told that didn't matter.

"It ain't just time that tells," Gertie said. "What I'm seeing is everything the way it ought to be."

"I was worried maybe I wasn't putting on enough weight." Teensy reached up to Matilda, who pulled her up with two hands. "Like that one time."

In the years since Matilda was born, Teensy had suffered three ill-fated pregnancies: one lost to miscarriage at four months; another, a girl she'd had to labor hard, awash in grief, to deliver dead at seven months; and a son lost the day after he was born, blue, but the spitting image of

Dalton. Three large, round stones from the gully, painted with white crosses and the words *Beloved Baby*, marked the tiny graves, three rock humps like something monstrous rising from the earth in a makeshift cemetery in the clearing behind Gertie's house. "Comes with the trade," Gertie had said when Matilda told her it was disturbing, all those gravestones right up in her yard marking the unborn and the barely born of mothers Gertie had tended. Gertie had claimed they were angels looking out for her from the other side, and Matilda had not said what she thought, that they weren't doing much of a job, judging by Gertie's living conditions. But she knew better than to feel sorry for Gertie or to speak ill of the dead, even those who had never been born.

"She's big as she needs to be," Gertie said.

"She?" A smile broke over Teensy's face.

Gertie answered with a curt nod. "Things pointing that way."

Teensy beamed. Matilda shook her head.

"Ain't up to you believing a thing to make it true, Mattie." Gertie wound up her tape measure with sharp, quick circles and packed it away in her bag. "You got three months, most," she said to Teensy. "Any swelling—feet, hands, face?"

"Not that I notice."

"Good. Now, take hold of this. Squeeze hard as you can." Gertie held out a carrot, soft with age, and Teensy closed her fist around it. "Umm-hmm," Gertie said, eyeing her hold, then she shot out a hand and jerked down on the carrot. Teensy held tight. "No swelling and a strong grip. From everything I'm seeing, you going all the way this time."

If Teensy was beaming before, she was an absolute sunrise now.

"Oh, come on. You never have any fun. The fields are soaked. Nobody's working. Live a little!" Peggy Creedle sat on the porch swing at the shack, one foot tucked beneath her and the other keeping the swing in motion with the toe of a T-strap pump that was so ridiculous on a farm, especially after an all-night rainstorm, that Matilda felt less embarrassed about her own rainy day footwear—her father's old town shoes, newspaper stuffed inside the toes and a length of twine tied around the one with the sole that flapped.

"We won't be long. I promise. I just need a few things from town, and we have to pick up the mail. If you don't come, I'll be stuck with Leon the whole time, and he never talks about anything anymore but that college he goes to. He wouldn't even have come down here for the summer if Daddy hadn't made him."

Leon was Peggy's older brother, making his first appearance at the farm. From what Matilda had seen of him in the two weeks he'd been there, he seemed as decent and level-headed as Peggy was rash and full of herself. Talk was, he did not get on well with his father.

Theirs was an odd arrangement, the Creedles'. Matilda knew that Mrs. Creedle had refused to live on the farm when Curtis bought it three years before. He had moved into the farmhouse alone, hiring new hands and issuing orders, allowing Dalton, who had sharecropped for the previous owner, to stay on. Peggy and her mother had remained in Baltimore, and Curtis visited them there on holidays and during slow seasons at the farm. Peggy had shown up only a month ago, arriving all down in the mouth about leaving Baltimore and claiming that she had been exiled to the Trace for being what her mother called "a handful" and what her father called "a spirited girl."

Matilda found Peggy tiresome and kept her distance, though she sometimes agreed to walks around the farm or up the road past Gertie's or along the creek to pick dewberries. On those occasions, Matilda didn't mind listening to Peggy go on about how she was going to be an actress and travel the world, maybe marry a Frenchman and live on a cliff overlooking the sea. It was a pretend world that Matilda was not against visiting from time to time. On one such walk she had learned that Leon had one more year to go at the university in Pennsylvania where he was studying, as Peggy told it, "rocks and bones and all that." He had been to Palestine, she said, digging things up, and to England to the British Museum.

"Say you'll come," Peggy said now. "We'll get ice cream," she added in a singsong voice, as if speaking to a child.

"The road'll be awful muddy," Matilda said, wondering if she could put up with Peggy's prattle all the way to town and back. She didn't care about the ice cream, though she wouldn't turn it down, but there was a letter she wanted to mail without anyone else reading it first. "And it might rain some more."

"We're taking the buggy. We'll put the top up if it rains. Please. I'm so bored in that house with Daddy and Leon that I could *die*." Peggy put on a pretty little pout and turned it toward Matilda.

"Good lord, stick your lip back in. I'll go."

"You will?" Peggy bounced out of the swing. "We'll come by in an hour. You can help me pick out material. I'm having some dresses made. We'll have the best time." Peggy trotted off down the muddy road, and Matilda lamented the ruining of a pair of shoes, ridiculous as they were.

Although she believed Peggy meant well, most of the time, there was something about the girl that wore on Matilda. The way she seemed to feel entitled to barge in on whatever Matilda and Teensy were doing at any given time, for one thing. *As if we'd all light up like a Christmas tree at being worth her time.* It didn't help that Teensy made such a fuss over her, either. "I don't know as I've ever seen a dress pretty as that one there," Teensy might say to Peggy, Matilda standing next to her in a feed-sack skirt and a flour-sack blouse. All in all, though, Peggy wasn't so bad, really. She just couldn't abide a minute of being by herself, and she was pushy. And nothing made her happier than breaking a rule and getting away with it, unless it was dragging somebody else in on it. Eugene had almost been turned off the farm because Peggy had talked him into driving her to Bristol one night for a traveling carnival she had led him to believe she had permission to attend. Since then, Peggy had been mostly farm-bound, other than mandatory trips to church every Sunday.

Still, it wouldn't be the worst thing, riding into town in a double buggy instead of the way Matilda usually went, crammed into the back of a wagon with as many people as would fit picked up along the way. And she needed a break. Besides her chores and her field work for Caleb Gill, she'd been hiring herself out to white farm wives for canning and pickling. The coffee tin she kept her Cleveland money in was almost half full. But truth be told, fields too muddy for working were a welcome sight on this day.

She took a paper sack from the kitchen and cut a square scrap from it with a sharp knife, being quiet so as not to wake Teensy, who was, according to Gertie, "in the month for sleeping." Behind her wall, she pulled out a pencil stub, took a minute to whittle it sharp, then thought about how to word the letter. Peggy was not the only person prone to opening other people's mail. Matilda knew that and took pains to keep her business to herself. She licked the pencil lead and wrote a few lines about the weather and the garden and the yellow dog who wouldn't go away. Then she wrote:

Baby due in Sept. Waiting on that. Keep your fingers crossed about that laundry job. I plan on taking it, come Oct.

She felt under her pallet for the envelope Rainy's letter had arrived in and carefully erased her own name and address, replacing it with Rainy's. Then she lit a candle and dribbled wax to reseal the envelope and slid it into her pocket.

She knew the buggy was pulling up when she heard the dog carrying on outside like it was the last day for barking. When the blame thing had refused to leave after that first day, she had been forced to feed him scraps ever since. To keep him from dying on the front porch, she'd told her mother, and having to cart him off. But she had secretly named him "Go Away," so she could call him without admitting to wanting him around.

"Have fun with your friends," Teensy said, all full of sleepy optimism when Matilda shook her shoulder and told her where she was going. "We're getting ice cream," Matilda said, because she knew that would make her happy, and Teensy smiled as if she had been hoping for just that, her daughter having ice cream with friends. Matilda looked on all her mother's hopefulness and love and wondered for a quick second if a new life in Cleveland would be anywhere near a fair exchange.

❧

Halfway to town, Leon pulled to the side of the road and stopped the horses as a Ford sputtered toward them, spitting up mud and digging itself in as much as it was moving forward. Matilda sat on a short, springy seat wedged into the back of the buggy like an afterthought, glad the top was raised so that in her small, cramped space she could see out without being seen. The way she liked it. Peggy sat up front wearing a feathered hat and another pair of silly shoes, waving wildly to the three young men in the Ford.

"*Why* don't we have a car at the farm?" Peggy turned around and looked at Matilda as if she had the answer, which she did.

"Don't make sense on these roads. There's your proof, there," she said as the Ford dipped into a mudhole and only just extracted itself.

Leon flicked the reins, and the horses had sense enough to move around the mudhole.

Matilda studied the back of Leon's head. He seemed to be a rare Creedle, humble and considerate and respectful. On Saturday he'd brought Teensy a block of ice from the ice wagon, and he stopped by the shack to ask if anyone needed anything whenever he rode into town. He carried a book around with him most everywhere he went, and Matilda had seen him disappear into the springhouse or the peach orchard or the deep bed of the hay wagon with a book, sometimes two, under his arm.

"You sure you don't want to come up here with us?" Peggy called to Matilda. "I can make room, see?" She slid up against Leon, creating a few vacant inches of seat.

"I'm okay here."

"But we could talk better if you'd come up." Peggy kept on until Leon said "Let her be," and by some miracle, Peggy did. "Fine," she said. After a blessedly quiet minute, she twisted around on the seat and began firing off questions—*When was Teensy's baby due? Had they picked out names? Didn't Matilda wish she lived in town, even though Bristol barely qualified as a town compared to Baltimore?*—shouting to prove her point about the distance between them.

When Peggy ran out of questions, Matilda asked Leon what he had dug up in Palestine.

"My best find was a first-century oil lamp, still in one piece. I was just a student tagging along, though, so I mostly hauled off loads of rocks and sifted pails of dirt. But the team found the foundation of a structure going back to the Roman occupation."

"You're going to bore her to death," Peggy said.

"No, it's interesting. I just dig up stuff in the creek," Matilda said.

"What kind of stuff?" Leon asked.

"Oh, just old bottles. Arrowheads. A button that looks real old. And I found a big tooth, about a hand's width long. Hardened into rock, but you can see where the roots were. I thought maybe it came from a dinosaur," Matilda said, feeling uncommonly shy.

"If you don't mind, could I take a look at it sometime?" Leon asked. "I've seen some fossil teeth. Maybe I could find out what it is for you."

"That'd be good," Matilda said.

Then Peggy cut them off with a list of things she needed from town—a hat, writing paper, a handbag—and with a detailed description of a dress design she had in mind. She was hoping to return to Baltimore at the end of the summer, and she seemed set on spending as much of her father's money as possible in the meantime.

When they got to town, Leon set out for the hardware store. Peggy went into the drugstore and came out with two cups of ice cream from the soda counter, which she and Matilda ate on a bench outside the Masonic Temple. After what seemed an interminable time in the dressmaker's shop as Peggy wavered between crepe de chine and organdy, then organdy and linen, then linen and crepe de chine, Matilda slipped her hand inside the pocket that held her letter to Rainy. "Let's go check the mail," she said, glancing up the road at the small, square post office.

"Leon'll get it."

"No, I want to go myself," Matilda insisted, and Peggy wilted a little, the issue of Rainy's unsealed letter rising again between them.

"Sure," Peggy said, linking her arm through Matilda's and sauntering off for the post office, nodding fiercely at people along the way as if daring any one of them to wonder for a second about the propriety of her choice of friends. Peggy breaking rules again, Matilda thought.

In the post office, Peggy stopped to chat with a girl she had met before, and Matilda slipped away to the counter. She stood back while all the others came and went—the white others—claiming their mail and mailing their letters, and when everyone else had cleared out, she placed her envelope on the counter and laid out her two cents for postage. The clerk tossed the letter into a bin of outgoing mail, and it was on its way to Cleveland.

Leaving the post office, Matilda and Peggy made their way through the usual congregation of men clustered around the entrance, talking or arguing, smoking or spitting tobacco, laughing or cursing, or both. Leon had not returned from the hardware store. As the girls walked in that direction, a large red-faced man with a coppery mustache barreled past them on the wooden sidewalk. He stopped in front of a young couple who had just emerged from the colored entrance to what was both the train station and the telegraph office. Standing in the middle of the sidewalk, the couple was engrossed in a telegram they were reading, smiles on their faces, unaware that people were detouring around them until they looked up and saw the man standing there. They quickly stepped out of his path.

"Move on off," the man barked, meaning, as Matilda well knew, that he expected them to step off the sidewalk onto the dirt road while he passed them by. Matilda had seen this before, though generally, in Bristol, moving to the street side of the sidewalk placated all but the most insufferable of townsfolk. And today, after so much rain, the edges of the dirt road were ankle-deep mud.

The young husband assessed the muddy road, then assessed the red-faced man, then took off his hat and said, "Mister, my wife here's been sick. And these're the only shoes she's got. And that road there ain't nothing but mud soup." He offered the man a pleasant and somewhat nervous smile, pulled a cheery, yellow-and-green-plaid handkerchief from his pocket, and blotted his forehead.

"Move off. I ain't going to say it again, excepting to the sheriff."

There were snickers from the men in front of the post office. Matilda looked back and saw that five or six of them had moved forward and were watching with particular interest. She held her place on the sidewalk, and Peggy gripped her arm.

His hat still in his hand, the young man put an arm around his wife and moved to the far side of the sidewalk. "I don't mind none," his wife said, about to step into the mud, but he held her back.

"Like I said, mister, she's been sick. You understand," he said, standing there balanced on the outer edge of the sidewalk, the heels of his shoes hanging over the road.

Matilda was paralyzed with anger, and Peggy, for once, was speechless. The big man hesitated. He looked back at the men behind him, some of them smirking, all of them waiting to see what he was going to do next, and what he did was draw back one massive arm and land his elbow against the young man's jaw, sending him sprawling into the mud, blood dripping down his chin, his jaw knocked off-kilter.

"Let's go," Peggy whispered, but Matilda held her ground. Somehow, the young wife had remained on the sidewalk as her husband tumbled past. There were hoots from the post office as she stepped into the mud to help him up.

Before she knew she was going to do it, Matilda stepped into the road as well and reached out her hand. With the man on his feet, she dug in the mud to retrieve a pocket watch he'd lost in the fall, tarnished silver inscribed with the letters B. J. and attached to a chain with a fob shaped like a sailing ship. She handed it to the woman. The young man, his crooked jaw cupped in his hand, left his hat in the mud and led his wife to the firm strip of packed dirt in the center of the road, away from everyone gaping at them.

Matilda stepped back onto the sidewalk. Her father's old shoes were so heavy with mud they seemed made of cement, and she could feel mud oozing between her toes inside them. A jowly shopkeeper standing in the doorway of her shop made eye contact, then swept a reproachful gaze down to the muddied sidewalk, as if that were the tragedy of the situation. There were sympathetic glances from a pair of towheaded little girls whose shocked faces mirrored Matilda's despair, her powerlessness, and she began stomping the mud off her shoes in defiance. She stomped until her feet hurt, until she thought she might break through the wooden sidewalk. Then she glared at the crowd of men, who sent back looks more amused than angry, and Peggy, to her eternal credit, turned a glare of her own on them all and threaded her arm through Matilda's.

Just then, a man stepped out of the post office. A tall, slender man a few years older than Leon, with a thin blond mustache and a cavalier air.

"Frank!" Peggy squealed. She clattered up the sidewalk in her patent leather pumps and threw her arms around the man's neck. Then Frank, gazing over Peggy's shoulder, raked Matilda head to toe with a look that left her raw.

18.

Frank Bowers. Peggy's cousin. Mrs. Creedle's nephew. He sat up front next to Leon while Peggy squeezed in beside Matilda in the back of the buggy. Peggy kept up a stream of conversation directed at Frank, who answered her questions with a distracted tolerance that drove her to try harder. Leon and Matilda said nothing, and Matilda imagined a solidarity in their silence. With Peggy's voice clanging in her ear, Matilda gleaned that Frank had recently graduated from law school and that he had arrived on the Trace at Peggy's mother's suggestion. He would spend the summer harvest season working for Curtis before trying to get in with a law firm in Baltimore.

"Unless I decide to set up my own practice somewhere else," he said. "Which would mean scraping up the start-up cash, hence my offering myself as a farmhand for the summer. No pipeline to the family money for me, you know," he said, tacking on a shallow laugh. "Either way, after a year or so, I'll run for office."

"What office?" Peggy asked.

"Whatever's easiest to win," he answered. "And of more immediate concern, I promised Aunt Rose I'd make sure you don't get yourself into any more trouble. She's paying me extra for that."

"Ha! As if Mother would send one black sheep to look after the other."

"You're right, there. She probably has Leon down here to report on both of us. Why *are* you here, Leon? Finally had to put in an appearance to keep the college money flowing? Or are you taking an interest in farmwork these days?"

"Oh, leave him alone," Peggy said. "Look at this place. Why would anyone want to come here? I sure didn't. Daddy needed him to sign some paperwork. Some legal something or other—I don't know. And *he* won't say." Peggy rolled her eyes at Leon. "There's no point in asking."

As if to prove her right, Leon gave the reins a needless snap and offered nothing.

"Safeguarding the inheritance from the ne'er-do-wells, no doubt," Frank said. "Though I expect Aunt Rose forked over a chunk of it to buy Uncle Curtis a farm. Peaches and corn, is it? Me, I'd have leaned more toward downtown property investment in Jackson. But then, I'm only a lawyer with extra coursework in real estate finance. Good move on Granddaddy's part, leaving everything to your mom."

Leon cleared his throat.

"But your mother got her share, too, right?" Peggy leaned over the packages stacked in her lap and folded her arms over them defensively.

"My mother. Now there's a ne'er-do-well to put the two of us to shame. You two got the good sister, in Aunt Rose."

"I've heard Mother say you're smarter than the rest of us put together," Peggy said. "She's always loved you especially."

"Ah, pity is close kin to love," Frank said.

Peggy fell silent then. Leon shifted uncomfortably on the seat. Frank watched him in a deliberate and obvious manner, and Matilda watched Frank, hoping the summer would pass quickly.

⁓

Peggy adored Frank. Matilda watched her follow him around the farm, hanging on to everything he said as if he were the prodigal son come home, but seeing the looks Frank passed Leon's way, Matilda saw him in more of a Cain and Abel light. So now, whenever Matilda left the shack, she had in mind avoiding both Virgil Morgan and Frank Bowers. She had only three months left at the farm, and she did not plan on inviting any kind of trouble over for dinner before she boarded that train for Ohio.

She was working so many jobs, on the farm and off, that in the evenings she had time only to rinse out the most necessary items from the laundry pile, too busy to set aside a whole day, as was usual, for building a fire under the big iron pot outside and cycling through a first rinse, a soapy boil and scrub, a second rinse, then the hanging to dry. Teensy, too far along with her pregnancy to manage a laundry day alone, did a lot of wind washing between harvesting, canning, and drying the yields of their own garden. Those were grueling days, but Matilda's coffee tin was filling up fast, even as she passed on a portion of what she brought in to her father.

Just before nightfall one evening, she was standing near the garden rinsing out Teensy's church blouse when she saw something moving underneath the shack. A raccoon, most likely, she thought. They liked burrowing under the porch, and if you didn't get them out as soon as they showed up, it was near impossible to get rid of them. She stepped closer, and before she realized what she was looking at in the twilight, Frank Bowers backed out of the crawlway like a bug from a hole, clutching four bottles of peach brandy to his chest. He stood and bent to brush off his creased pants, and Matilda stopped in midstep, just as she would have if he had been a snarling dog or a rattlesnake within striking distance. He turned around, and their eyes met. If looks could kill, Matilda knew, she would have been lost to the world right then. Frank's lips curled into an empty smile, and he raised the bottles over his head in an arrogant greeting.

"You know what's good for you, you'll keep your mouth shut about this." His voice fell over her like an icy rain, and she stood frozen, a garden statue at the end of a row of field peas, until he turned and strolled off down the wagon path. Teensy's wet blouse raining on her bare feet brought Matilda back to herself, and she wrung it mercilessly between her hands, then went inside.

"'Tain't nothing to do about it," Dalton said when Matilda told him what she had seen, out of earshot of Teensy, already in bed. "It'd be my word against his. Best to wait it out till he goes back where he come from, end of the summer."

Matilda thought of Curtis's meticulous record keeping, his accounting of every bottle and jar stored in the shack and in the crawlway and under the false bottom of the wagon. She suspected her father was thinking of that, as well, wishing he had never agreed to drive Curtis's liquor to pay off his debt, wishing he had not stayed on when the farm changed hands, wishing he could leave the farm without fear of arrest, or prison, or forced labor. Wishing for a different kind of world.

In the hottest part of a hot day, Matilda and Teensy were sitting on the porch shelling peas when Dalton came in from the fields to refill his water jug and cool off in the shade of the porch. Teensy met him in the bare dirt yard, took the jug, and went off to fill it. Before Dalton could sit down, Virgil Morgan came around the side of the shack. "Boy," he said, pointing at Dalton and looking down his outstretched arm as if he were sighting a deer. "There's a big old jack possum done died in the stream, caught up in them rocks. Get on over and fish him out 'fore he spoils the water." He stood waiting, the usual vapid grin pasted on his face. Waiting, Matilda knew, to watch her father take out his shovel and head over to the stream because he'd been told to. Dalton stood on the porch looking down at Virgil all puffed up like a rooster and too full of himself to know that Curtis Creedle was, at that moment, walking up behind him.

"Morgan."

Virgil's grin drooped.

"He don't have time for that. You take care of it. I got you here to work off a debt, not give orders."

Virgil slapped a look on Dalton that was meant to be threatening, but since it was followed by a quick "yessir" to Old Man Creedle, it fell away like a handful of dry dirt. He slouched off toward the spring-house. Curtis put one foot on the bottom porch step and said, "Mind?"

Dalton waved him up, and Matilda knew something was coming. Old Man Creedle asking for leave to stand on the porch was a preamble to bad news, no question. Dalton sent her a glance, her cue to make herself scarce, but she picked up a pea pod instead, slit it with her thumbnail, and shoved the peas out so that they pinged into the tin pot in her lap. She was careful not to catch her father's eye.

"Mattie," he said, and there was nothing to do but set the pot on the chair and head inside. She closed the door behind her, but stayed close, listening through the drafty wall while Teensy was still out with the water jug.

"Sorry about Morgan," she heard Curtis say. "Used to be a good customer, now he's just a pain in the ass. Man like that—best to keep him full of liquor and obliged instead of dry and running his mouth. Long as he stays in the dark about the out-of-state business. Nobody looks twice at a little neighborly brewing, but there's not enough money in the county to pay off everybody who'd be holding out a hand if word got around about me shipping up North. And Leon—you know I can't have him knowing about any of it. Or Peggy."

Matilda had already figured out why Old Man Creedle insisted that Leon take Peggy to Bristol for church every Sunday, rain or shine. Peggy blamed it on her mother, but Matilda knew it was to get the two of them far away from the farm during Sunday morning business hours. Curtis saw to it that all the local buying and selling, as well as the manufacture and bottling, took place off the farm.

Her father had no role in any of that, thank God; even he didn't know where Curtis hid his stills. But Curtis had a place set up in the woods somewhere, beyond the Creedle property line, where customers picked up their orders, and they used a short stretch of the farm road, up near the fork, to get there. So Curtis sent Peggy and Leon off every Sunday.

"They're only here for the summer, those two," Curtis was saying to Dalton. "And I mean to have Morgan off the place by then, too."

There was a moment of silence, and Matilda pulled out a clump of wadding from a chink in the wall and squinted through the crack.

"There's something I want to talk to you about, though."

"All right."

"Frank, now. He's a smart guy. Had a hard upbringing, but he's set to be a lawyer, now. Needs money—"

"Here's your jug." Teensy came into view, her shoulders framed by the slit in the wall as Matilda peered through it. "Hello, Mr. Creedle. Powerful hot day."

"That it is."

Matilda heard Teensy climbing the porch steps, and as the door opened, Matilda scooted behind the tar-paper wall and rustled about, as if there wasn't anything worth listening to going on outside.

"He said Frank'll be driving half the loads, here on out," Dalton told Matilda that night after Teensy went to bed. Since the day Matilda announced her plan to go to Cleveland, her father had been letting her in on things he would not have before, looking at her a little differently, she thought. "I'll be glad for it," he said, but they were both unsettled, thinking about Curtis's record keeping and Frank's pilfering.

"Frees me up some for working the crops. Lord knows Virgil Morgan ain't no kind of help out there. Leastways, it'll cut by half the chances of me getting caught with a load."

"Frank getting caught in your wagon is the same blame thing. Can't you tell Old Man Creedle you're done with it? We ain't slaves."

"Too far in." They glanced at each other. "Most likely he just took them few bottles that one time, and that's the end of it."

"Maybe," Matilda said. And maybe he was lining up customers of his own behind Curtis's back. "Leon still doesn't know about the running?"

Dalton shook his head. "Rule number one with Old Man Creedle. He don't want his boy knowing nothing about none of it. Thinks he'd make a fuss."

"But he trusts Frank?"

"Trusts him or don't care as much what Frank thinks about him. Don't ask me what a Creedle's thinking. Don't ask me about none of this. You know more'n you're supposed to, anyhow. Creedle would call my debt tomorrow if he knew what all you know. And you and me got to look out for her," he said, glancing over at Teensy blowing little puffs of air between her lips, her arms wrapped around her middle, cradling the baby that Gertie kept promising was going to make it.

19.

"Here it is," Matilda said, joining Leon in the front yard where he was waiting for her. She handed over her best find from the creek. Dusky gray. About four inches long and an inch and a half thick, with bony ridges down the front and root grooves at one end.

"It's the nicest one I've seen," Leon said, tracing a ridge with his fingertip.

"You know what it is?"

"It's a fossil tooth, all right. Like you thought." He turned it over in his palm. "From a giant ground sloth. I've seen a photograph of the skeleton of one of these guys. Twelve, maybe thirteen feet tall. Imagine, this tooth belonged to an animal that lived during an ice age."

"Maybe you should have it," Matilda said.

"No, you keep this. It's very special." He handed the tooth back to her. "Can you show me where you found it?"

"I dug it up at the creek. In the sand."

"I'd like to see just where, if you don't mind showing me. I might dig around a little myself, while I'm here."

They walked up the road around the front fields and the pasture and climbed the hill toward the rim of the gully mostly in silence. As they scuttled sideways down the steep bank to the sandy creek, Matilda felt self-conscious and, because she couldn't help it, concerned about Leon's good shoes. "On about here," she said, standing on a strip of white sand that cut a few yards into the creek.

"And you say you've found other things down here?"

"Mostly bottles and stuff. And arrowheads. Got a slew of them."

Leon sat down on a damp log and scratched in the sand with a stick. "I have a book with sketches of arrowheads from this part of the country. From a course I took last year. I brought it with me because I hoped I might come across some myself. Say, I could lend it to you and maybe you could find out what you've got."

"That'd be good," Matilda said. She was a little nervous, hidden away down in the gully with Leon Creedle. "You must've seen a lot better than arrowheads over in—where was it you went digging?" *Palestine*. She remembered, but asked anyway, hoping he would tell her more about the places he'd been.

"Palestine. It was amazing. But the things I saw in England— those were the best. Things they looted from the old Egyptian tombs. That's where I'd go—Egypt—if I could go anywhere."

"Egypt, huh."

"Yep."

"I'd be happy being anywhere but here," Matilda said, then she worried that Leon might take that wrong. "I mean, just to see...anywhere." She felt flustered. She didn't like the feeling.

"There are women archaeologists working now," Leon said. "Famous for what they've done. Hetty Goldman, for one. And Harriet

Hawes. She rode around Crete on a mule looking for things just like your tooth here. Made amazing discoveries. She lectures at a college in Boston, now. I heard her once."

He was being kind, Matilda knew, but it ruffled her a bit, too. It was all fine and good that those women were so amazing, but there wasn't a snowball's chance that any colored girls from Mississippi were riding any mules in Crete, wherever the hell that was. She wasn't sure what he was getting at.

"It starts with digging in the creek," he said. "And who knows where it goes from there."

Matilda smiled a little at that, which made her mad. Leon Creedle was not taking into account that the world they lived in, his world, wasn't offering up its best dreams to everybody. He hadn't come out and said that it was reasonable to believe that a colored sharecropper's daughter might someday see the places Matilda dreamed about seeing—he'd only said that there were white women who were archeologists in faraway lands— but maybe that was what he'd meant. Maybe he was talking down to her. But maybe he believed it was true. She almost thought he did.

A few minutes later they were both down on their knees digging in the sand with their bare hands and laughing when they heard something rustling in the brush above and behind them. Matilda whipped her head around, thinking instantly of Frank. But it was Peggy, clutching the limber trunk of a sapling growing horizontally out of the bank a quarter of the way down the gully. She was watching them with wide eyes and a look on her face like she was just about to bite into the most delicious sweet treat that ever was. "Well, you two look like you're having big fun," she called to them. "Help me down."

Leon washed his hands in the creek, then climbed up to her. Matilda waited as they descended, Peggy stepping cautiously down the slope, holding on to Leon's arm. At the bottom, she paused briefly to catch her breath, then looked at each of them in turn and asked, "What were you doing down here?"

"Just digging around," Leon said, his face flushed. "Looking for those arrowheads you told me people find around here. She was showing me where she's found things before. I asked her to."

"I see," Peggy said, and Matilda understood that what Peggy saw was a lot more than what really was.

"I'll be getting on back, now," Matilda said, self-conscious again. "I got supper to start and laundry to tend to," she said, meaning to send Leon a message about the difference between her life on his daddy's farm and the lives of those famous women he'd told her about, and for that matter, the life of his sister, who might could get herself to Crete someday, and to Egypt and England and to the moon and back if she had a mind to. "And peaches to pick at first light." Halfway up the bank, she wanted to turn back and thank him for telling her about her fossil tooth, but Peggy was down there smiling and poking Leon all playful-like and Leon was shaking his head at whatever Peggy was having so much fun saying to him, so she just kept climbing.

Peggy stopped by that evening, all smiles and innuendos.

"He just wanted to see that old tooth I dug up," Matilda told her on the porch.

"I know," Peggy said, sounding like she knew that and a lot more and thought it was all too delightful for words. "I won't say a word to anybody." She drew a big X across her chest with her finger.

"Ain't nothing to say," Matilda said, "except that you are one crazy girl."

Curtis Creedle came around during the noon meal one day, asking for Dalton. Hat in hand, he waited while Dalton got up from the table and went out, closing the door behind him. Matilda could hear the two of them on the porch, heard Curtis clear his throat, then say, "What with Frank driving half the loads now, I can't see my way clear to calling us even after that one year we talked about."

Matilda could picture Curtis turning his hat in his hands, a sorrowful look arranged on his face. She could picture her father working to keep from showing how crushed in spirit he was. Then the voices trailed off as the men walked out into the yard together.

"Two years" was all Dalton said when he came back inside and knew with a glance what Matilda had heard. "Minusing the four months I already put in." He sat at the table clenching and unclenching his fist.

"You could lay him out, easy." Matilda said what her father wouldn't. She said it for him. She saw a corner of his mouth turn up some, and she smiled at him.

"That'd be the weak thing," he said.

"What's the strong thing?"

"The strong thing," Dalton said, "is picking up and getting on a train for Ohio with nothing but a raggedy old coat and them cardboard shoes of yourn."

They passed a look between them that spoke of love and pride and hope and regret. Then Dalton got up and stuffed a clean sweat rag in his pocket and took his hat off its hook. Teensy came in with a mess of string beans from the garden and made her labored way over to the table. Dalton passed close to Matilda and said, "Don't tell her nothing till she's done having that baby," and Matilda nodded.

So it hadn't ever been a lust for land driving her father. She saw that now. It had always been about her mother. He wanted to put Teensy in her own house on their own land and to make their own way, spare as it might be, working the land, that thing he knew best. He wanted to put what distance he could between her mother and everything he could not change.

They had been there a good while, Teensy in the porch swing, her bare feet dangling, Matilda sitting with her back against the porch railing, legs stretched out on the planks that had still been warm from the day's heat when she sat down. They had said little as dusk came and went and evening settled over them. The purple martins and dragonflies and mosquitoes had long since finished their twilight feeding frenzy, swooping and darting, risking predator for prey in the dying daylight. The lightning bugs had finished their show and moved on to some secret place. Night had fallen in earnest, clean and clear, and a gentle wind had blown away the last trace of mugginess. When Teensy spoke, it was in a hushed voice that seemed appropriate under the stars assembling in their constellations overhead.

"Don't tell Gertie, but I done got the name picked out."

"You gonna say it before she's born?" Matilda had been calling the baby "she" as if she believed in Gertie's signs. It was a pre-parting gift to her mother.

Teensy turned her face toward the night sky. "Don't have to. You hear that?"

Matilda heard crickets chirping in the field and leaves rustling in the big tree that spread out over the porch. A dog barking from a long way off. "Hear what?"

"The wind passing through the sycamore tree. Listen to it—'annis-annis-annis.'"

Matilda listened, and there it was, sounding for all the world like exactly that.

"The wind named this one here," Teensy said, caressing her swollen belly.

"Annis? That's her name?"

"Shh. Gertie says it ain't safe to say till after the birth."

"You believe in that, Mama?"

"I believe in Gertie." Teensy cut a look across the porch that Matilda felt more than saw. "And in respecting your elders." Then she went back to rocking the swing and watching the night sky, and Matilda got up and sat beside her, her pretty little mama. She hoped the baby really would be a girl, a girl the wind named, and that she would be the best of company for Teensy after Matilda was gone.

20.

"Here, girl." Virgil called Stella Mae like he would a bird dog. "I got something for you."

Stella Mae dropped Matilda's hand and trotted right over, all smiles and goodness. They were on the trail that wound between cornfields and pastures to the orchards where Matilda and Stella Mae were going to spend the morning picking peaches.

"What is it?" Stella Mae clasped her hands behind her and rocked her shoulders, skirt swinging, waiting to be done a kindness. Matilda walked up behind her as Virgil slid his hand into the deep pocket of his pants.

"It's a little toy I made. Made it a long time ago for my little girl, but she's gone off now."

"Where to?" Stella Mae's face crinkled with concern.

"She run off a while back," Virgil said, playing with a sorrowful expression that had the intended effect on Stella Mae, who now wore a matching look on her own sweet face.

"She's a very bad girl," Virgil said, shaking his head.

"Well, we got to get on." Matilda put an arm around Stella Mae's shoulder and nudged her aside.

"Wait, now, I done found it. In my other pocket all the time." Virgil kept his eyes on Matilda as he withdrew his hand, letting her know his gift was mostly meant for her, Dalton Patterson's daughter. Payback for his having had to fish the dead possum out of the stream. "My girl used to carry this around ever'where she went. I'm happy to pass it on to another little 'un."

He held out his fist. Stella Mae opened her hand and into it dropped a stuffed swamp rat with a leathery hide and glass bead eyes, a long bald tail that Virgil held by the tip to make the rat dance on Stella Mae's palm. Matilda gasped, and Stella Mae laughed, clutching the tanned rat and pressing it under her chin as if it were a doll.

"Drop that thing." Matilda pried open Stella Mae's hand and slapped the rat to the ground just as Frank Bowers rode up in Curtis's buggy.

Matilda gripped Stella Mae's wrist, holding the offended hand in the air until she could get her back to the stream and wash it off.

"What? She don't like my present?" Virgil squatted down in front of Stella Mae and whined, "I brung it just for you." Then he looked up at Frank in the buggy. "She don't like it," he said.

"I *do* like it." Stella Mae stomped her foot and turned a fierce look on Matilda. "I *love* it."

"It's a dead rat, Stella Mae. That's what it is. A blame dead rat. It's filthy." She looked directly at Virgil with those last words. She curled a protective arm around Stella Mae and led her around the back of the buggy in the direction of the stream. Frank, who had watched their little encounter without comment, snapped the reins and moved on without acknowledging Matilda or Stella Mae. Or Virgil, standing on the path with the stuffed rat at his feet.

That night, Matilda sat on the porch with the yellow dog beside her, thinking about how she had acquired two grown-men enemies without having done a single thing to either of them. Worse, she had shown them both a weakness—Stella Mae. She did not know enough about Frank Bowers to judge the danger there, but a weakness was exactly what a man like Virgil Morgan, a snake like Virgil Morgan, was on the lookout for. She would have to step carefully. If Curtis Creedle was true to his word in this case, at least, both men would be off the farm before fall. And come October, unless hell itself stopped her, Matilda would be in Cleveland. And now she was determined that when she got there she would put together a plan to get her parents and the new baby up there, too. And Gertie and Stella Mae, if Gertie could be persuaded.

"Maybe I'll even get you up there, somehow." She rubbed the dog's head, and he looked up at her with soulful eyes.

The middle Porter boy met Matilda on the Trace, just beyond Miss Bodie's house. The Porters had company, he told her, so the canning Mrs. Porter had hired her to do would be postponed a day. Matilda was more than happy to turn back, even though she would have to take the same route again for the afternoon canning for Mrs. Riley. A couple of hours of free time was worth walking a few extra miles. The swap pile behind the church had yielded a rare find, a book of short stories, and she thought she might steal a few minutes to read a story or two before setting out again.

It was still early, but already the air was stifling. Matilda's shoes were hooked over her fingers to save them wear—she had only brought them to wear in the Porters' kitchen—and she had in mind, too, a quick detour to the spot where the creek emptied out of the shadowy gully and narrowed to a sunny stream, past the big shady rocks that copperheads favored on days like this. She was halfway down the hill on the farm road, a fenced field on her left, the old well house up ahead a ways on her right, when something struck her as odd. The well-house door was open. Gertie might have seen that as a warning from a soul gone on before, Teensy just as reason enough to turn around and go back the way she'd come, to take another route home, one that offered no unnerving surprises. And though Matilda heard their whispers, Gertie's and Teensy's, she strode forward, an open door, to her, only that.

The old, slat-wall structure housed a well gone dry many years ago and in disuse for so long that Matilda had never seen the door open. It had been built by a former landowner, and Old Man Creedle had padlocked it to keep curious children and wandering livestock away from the hole. Had the door been open when she passed it earlier going the other way? She couldn't be sure. Leon might have taken a book into the well house, she thought, looking for a cool place to read. But even with the door open, it would be too dark in there for that. Dark enough for

Peggy to get into the sort of trouble Matilda suspected she'd gotten into in Baltimore. Peggy had taken up lately with the son of a farmer farther up the Trace, a friend of Eugene's, and Old Man Creedle *was* off the farm for a few days. They might be in there staying out of sight. Of course, Peggy would have had to locate the key to the padlock first. Matilda slipped her shoes on. Whatever the reason for the open door, she wanted to be at her best advantage when she passed by it.

As she got closer, she could see the back end of a wagon—her father's wagon—partially hidden behind the well house and a persimmon tree next to it. Odd, as Dalton had left the shack just before Matilda left that morning, and on foot, planning on a full day's work in the peach orchard. Still, the presence of his wagon made whatever was going on there more a curiosity than a concern. Until Frank Bowers appeared in the doorway, pushing a wheelbarrow stacked with wooden crates full of bottles. Crates marked with the yellow flash that identified Old Man Creedle's premium brandy.

Matilda thought of squeezing through the fence on her left and taking cover in the cornfield before Frank saw her, but the wire was strung too tightly for that. Getting stuck in the fence or caught trying to hide in the field would be worse than meeting Frank head on. Her instinct was to show no fear, and she walked on, hoping to slip past without being seen, hoping he would disappear back inside the well house.

But Frank did not go back inside. Instead, he began sliding the crates into the compartment under the false floor of her father's wagon. In broad daylight. This would never have been allowed by Old Man Creedle, had he not been off the farm. And it was strange that there would be crates in that old well house at all. Strange that Frank would be loading the wagon himself, and on a Monday. Dalton, and now sometimes Frank, ran Curtis's liquor to the Canton depot every other Thursday, and Dalton had made a delivery the Thursday just past. It wasn't time for another one.

Ain't nothing to me. Matilda wore that thought like a uniform as she strode on, eyes on the last fence post where the road curved around the cornfield just short of the well house. If she could make that turn without being noticed, she could slip into the cornfield through the gate. Frank had his back to her, clumsily hoisting the crates into the wagon while Matilda made as much speed as she could without running. This did not look to her to be evidence of Frank's selling a paltry few bottles of liquor to locals on the sly. It looked like Frank hiding a load of Curtis's best stock in the well house and waiting for Curtis to leave the farm for four days so he could drive it behind Curtis's back. Dalton had said that Frank was keeping count of the brandy bottles and liquor jars now. Was he shorting the numbers and shipping stock off himself? Ciphering off some of the family money he'd talked about in the buggy that first day?

Nothing to me. Not one blessed thing to me. Matilda was almost home free, almost at the corner post. Frank turned just then and swiped his face with his sleeve. He peered into the sun, shaded his eyes with his hand, and spotted her. Matilda looked straight ahead and picked up her pace, turning, finally, around the end of the cornfield and away from the well house. Now that she had been seen, she strode on past the gate. She could see the board straddling the stream that marked the line between cropper and landowner, the shack in sight beyond it, when she heard a quick pounding of footsteps behind her. *Frank.* Following her.

"Want a ride?"

Matilda felt a blow to the back of her knees. The wheelbarrow. He'd butted her with it so that she nearly fell into it, but she managed to keep her footing. His was not a question to be answered, and though her heart was banging in her chest, she kept walking.

"Hold up," he said, and Matilda slowed, but did not stop. He sidled up beside her, so close that she could feel his breath when he spoke into her ear.

"I know you are not a stupid girl. Not nearly stupid enough to go mouthing off about things that don't concern you. Because that…that would be very stupid." The wheel of his wheelbarrow squeaked with each revolution as he walked slowly beside her, and Matilda knew she would never forget that sound, not even in Cleveland.

"First off," he went on, "there's your daddy to consider. If you decided to be stupid, I'd have to tell Uncle Curtis that I caught him—your daddy—with liquor he'd been hiding in the well house. Crates of Uncle Curtis's liquor he was loading up to haul off and sell while Uncle Curtis was away. Or maybe I'd just say I'd seen him passing bottles around to some of his friends and that maybe we ought to take a new bottle count over at your place."

Matilda was trembling with anger. She quickened her step, but Frank stayed with her, the hair on his arm tickling her elbow.

"And then there's your boyfriend."

Matilda stopped and turned a look on Frank that made him take a step back.

"My boyfriend?"

Frank's face went hard. "You and the golden boy, the big world-traveling son, hidden off down by the creek, rolling around in the sand. Wouldn't Uncle Curtis like to hear all about that."

Peggy. Peggy who could not keep quiet about anything that happened to anybody anywhere. Peggy making something dangerous out of nothing.

"I just showed him where I found an old tooth," she said, struggling to keep her voice even. "Him being interested in—"

"Oh, I heard how *interested* he was," Frank said. He sat down on the end of the wheelbarrow next to a woody shrub growing through the fence and snapped off a twig, twirled it lazily between his fingers. "I'd be interested, too, if you wanted to meet me down there and show me something." He reached out with the twig and lifted the hem of her skirt with it. "Real interested."

Instantly, Matilda snatched the switch away from him. She heard the windy shriek it made as she whipped it through the air and brought it down on the back of his soft, pale hand, slicing the skin and nicking a vein. They both stared as beads of blood rolled down his hand, off the tip of his middle finger, and into the dirt.

"Well, now," Frank said, calm as death, still sitting on the wheelbarrow. "I'd say we've got us a whole mess of secrets to keep now." He held up his hand and let blood drip down his wrist. He looked at it thoughtfully. "This," he said, "could be from me stringing barbed wire and not being careful. Or it could be from a drunk sharecropper cutting me with a broken bottle when I caught him stealing my uncle's liquor. You get to decide."

Matilda thought she could hear blood splashing in the dirt. She felt dizzy, felt her anger turn to fear, her hard edges melting, leaving her soft and vulnerable. She turned her head to keep Frank from seeing any of it.

"I'm keeping up with the bottle count for Uncle Curtis now. You just forget you saw me today, forget there was ever anything in that well house, and my numbers are all going to add up just fine," Frank said. "I don't say a word to anybody unless you do. You remember that."

Matilda broke into a run. She did not slow down, was not sure she even breathed, until she was in the yard, up the porch steps, inside the shack. Panting, she stood to one side of the window and watched Frank standing where she had left him. She kept her eyes on him as he stood there for what seemed like half her life, the sound of the squeaky wheel still in her head. Finally, he raised his hand and waved at the window, grinning like the cat that ate the rat. Knowing she was watching. Then he bent over the empty wheelbarrow and rolled it back down the road toward the well house.

It would kill her mother. Telling her parents would crack the fragile world Teensy had made for herself of things she could see that were beautiful and good. She might well lose her "last-chance baby," too. If that happened, Teensy would never be the same. And telling Dalton would put him at risk. Was he safer knowing, or not knowing? After an hour alone behind her wall, her thoughts twisting like snakes in a sack, Matilda slipped out through the back door and took the long, rough path through the pine thicket behind the garden and into the woods beyond, taking no chance of being seen by Frank on the farm road as she set out for her afternoon job.

In Mrs. Riley's kitchen, anytime Matilda could not push Frank Bowers from her mind, she grazed a finger across the boiling water in the canning pot on the stove. She cleared her mind of him over and over until there was nothing but the clink of the jars in the water bath, the sweltering heat from the stove, the pop of the lids as they cooled on the table. When she left for the day with new coins for her coffee tin in her pocket, there were burn blisters on four of her fingers.

Over supper that evening, she casually asked Dalton where his wagon had been that day. "I didn't see it when I came in," she said. *Maybe he knows. Maybe he's already put together what Frank's up to.*

"Bowers took it. Had to haul some lumber in from the sawmill this morning, and Eugene had the field wagon off somewhere. Frank still ain't brought it back around. Guess that city boy's getting his hands dirty," he told her. His easy smile at the idea of Frank loading lumber laid aside any notion that he shared her secret, or that there was any justifiable reason for Frank to be driving a load of liquor that day.

As soon as the dishes were washed and some clothes rinsed out, Matilda escaped to her room. She did not yet trust herself to think things through, so she poured out the contents of her coffee tin and counted her savings, beginning anew each time her mind wandered, until she gave that up and stowed the tin behind the false back Dalton had fitted into the bottom drawer of her chest of drawers.

When she knew her parents were asleep, she let the dog in. Lying on her pallet with Go Away curled up beside her, she worked on deciding whether or not to tell her father what she had seen at the well house. If she did and Old Man Creedle questioned him about missing bottles, he might try to feign ignorance and seem guilty. Despite his deal-making with Curtis, her father was an honest man, unaccustomed to lying. And nothing good could come of his accusing Frank outright. Even if Curtis believed him, he would never side with a cropper over family. She did not for a moment consider telling her father about the liberties Frank had taken with her, or his insinuations. There was no accounting for what Dalton might do if she did. Or what might be done to him.

She thought about Rainy's uncle and his newspaper, remembered thinking that there would be some people down here who would walk a wide circle around such a newspaper if it were set out free for the taking. She had thought herself so much bolder than the older folks, when she had only been younger and more foolish and untried.

Not long before the sun rose on another day, Matilda made her decision. She would not say anything to her father about Frank. Not yet. It was a calculated decision in what she was coming to see as a game she could not hope to win, did not care to play, but for all of their sakes, must not lose.

21.

The sky was dressed for sunrise in streaks of pink and gold when Matilda opened the front door the next morning. Nature carrying on, consecrating a new day for those who set their step by such offerings, like her mother. Matilda had hardly slept the night before. She stepped onto the porch, then had to remind herself of why she had opened the door—because she had to work for Mrs. Porter this morning and for Mrs. Riley in the early afternoon. She crossed the porch and stopped again at the head of the steps, looked toward the brightening horizon, and there was Frank. On the far side of the road that led to the Creedle house, his arms crossed over a fence post. He was talking with her father across the fence. Dalton saw her, waved a cheery greeting, then Frank did the same, a broad smile on his face, his arm making a wide arc in the air. *See? As long as you stay quiet, your father's just fine.* That was the message Frank was sending. Matilda knew that by smiling back, waving at them both, she could seal the deal, but she dipped her head, went quickly down the steps, and struck out for the Porters'.

By the time she reached the Trace, she wished she had raised her hand to Frank. What difference would it have made? She would be leaving soon, and even before she left for Cleveland, Frank would be leaving the farm. Was her pride worth so much? She asked herself the question and answered it easily. No. Not her pride. But dignity is what raising her hand to Frank would have cost her. And Frank Bowers would not rob her of that.

The day's work seemed endless. Afterward, Matilda hurried home. Again, she would have liked to wade the stream, cool her bare feet after the long walk, but she rushed across the board bridge, settling for the satiny coolness of a patch of clover on the other side. Go Away slinked out from under the porch and ran to meet her. When she opened the screen door, she saw that Gertie was there, her hands spread over Teensy's middle, Teensy in a chair at the table.

"Kicking like a mule," the midwife said. "Want to feel her?"

She took Matilda's hand and laid it just under Teensy's navel. Right on cue the baby delivered a gentle kick that set off smiles on all three faces.

"Everything right as rain," Gertie declared later, after a thorough examination on the shuck mattress. "And now I need to get on back. Gus'll be bringing Annie over this evening. Might be carrying twins, that one."

"Lord bless her," Teensy said.

"You seen Stella Mae out there when you come up?" Gertie asked, and Matilda shook her head.

"Go hunt her and tell her it's time. Check out back. Like as not she's eating up your tomatoes. Child has no shame when it comes to tomatoes."

When she didn't find Stella Mae in the garden, Matilda circled around to the front yard, calling her name, then checked the spring-house. Stella Mae loved the cool stone floor, the stream running through it. She wasn't there. Then Matilda cut across Dalton's cotton field and up the hill to the clearing where Stella Mae liked to chase butterflies, still calling with no answer. She met the farm road and followed it back down, passing by the well house, the door closed, the padlock in place.

Just beyond the well house, she peered around a row of fat, round cedars and spotted Stella Mae in the empty bull pasture, sitting in the grass between Frank Bowers and Virgil Morgan, their backs against a water trough inside the open gate just ahead. Matilda froze. She had a good view of them, though they hadn't yet seen her. She tried to hold herself back for Stella Mae's sake, to take a breath and think about what to do instead of picking up the two-by-four lying in the tall grass between her and the gate and cracking somebody's skull, which was her first thought. She stepped behind one of the cedar trees and moved aside a prickly branch so she could keep her eye on Stella Mae while she got herself under control.

Frank bumped the toe of his boot against Stella Mae's bare heel, and Virgil sat there looking all full of himself, as if he'd found some momentary footing with a member of the mighty Creedle family at last. He reached behind Stella Mae and slapped Frank on the back in a way that Matilda knew would not have happened if Virgil had not been sloshed. Frank ignored him. He sat with his long arms draped over his knees, his eyes glued to the farm road ahead, as if waiting for something. Then it dawned on her. He was waiting for her. He'd heard her calling and was waiting for her to find Stella Mae.

Matilda looked through the cedar branches at the scene he had set, a new warning playing out for her benefit. If her father's well-being wasn't incentive enough, he'd add Stella Mae to the mix. Stella Mae stared straight ahead, her eyes so empty that Matilda could almost believe her soul had flown right out of her. Virgil asked her if she wouldn't like to have her load lightened some, like he had. He took hold of her small hands and wrapped her fingers around his mason jar, then he cackled and nudged Frank with his elbow behind her back. Frank seemed annoyed, but his gaze remained locked on the dirt road.

Stella Mae looked back and forth between the two men as if she didn't know whether to cut and run or cry, and Matilda stepped back a few paces, then called, "Stella Mae! Where are you, girl? Gertie wants you." Then she stomped into view of the three of them. Stella Mae started to wriggle up, but Frank pressed his shoulder into hers on one side and Virgil followed suit on the other and she was pinned where she sat, like a sweet little butterfly in a schoolboy's cigar box for show-and-tell. Frank looked Matilda in the eye and laid his big hand on Stella Mae's bony knee, a challenge. Matilda met it by reaching for the hidden two-by-four, but before she could pick it up, she heard someone behind her.

"You got the tie vines pulled off the fence in the northwest field, Mr. Morgan? My father was asking about that. Said he wanted to make sure it was done before the day was out."

Leon. He went up to the gate and into the pasture. Virgil sank in on himself like a tire with a leak, and Frank stood up and walked over to face his cousin. Frank stood a head taller. "Uncle Curtis said that?" he asked, another challenge, but Matilda could see that a son carried more weight than a nephew, and Leon did not offer an answer. He held out his hand to Stella Mae and she grabbed onto it like it was a lifeline. Frank laughed and headed off in the direction of the house, and Virgil just sat there in the grass looking around as if he were trying to remember where the northwest field was, or what a tie vine was, or what he was doing sitting in the bull pasture.

Stella Mae flew to Matilda and wrapped her arms around her, burying her face in Matilda's dress and sobbing.

"Shh. It's okay," Matilda said, stroking her back. She looked at Leon and could not bring herself to thank him for what he had done, because gratefulness just then seemed like a concession to all that was wrong with the world and because she was so angry she could not speak. She just met his eyes, then turned around and walked Stella Mae back to the shack.

When Matilda stepped onto the porch the following morning, Frank was leaning against the same fence post where he had been talking with Dalton the day before, alone this time. He and Matilda looked at each other for a moment, then Frank smiled and waved, two wide arcs back and forth over his head. Matilda glanced behind her to make sure Teensy was not watching from inside. Then she lifted her hand, signaling defeat.

A day passed, two days, three, and Frank made no more appearances. Matilda had not expected him to. He knew—had known from the moment he butted her with his wheelbarrow—that she would keep his secret. If not for her coffee tin of Cleveland money, full now, she would not have been able to bear his knowing that. Then Dalton came in Saturday evening and announced that Virgil had been turned off the farm.

"Excepting regular Sunday morning business hours, and then he ain't allowed past the fork."

"Old Man Creedle turned him off?" Matilda thought maybe there was some hope for Curtis Creedle after all.

"Bowers did it. They was both fed up with him. Funny thing, though. Bowers come around the orchard today. Told me to tell you Morgan's been turned off and won't be bothering nobody no more."

Frank Bowers keeping up his end of the bargain she had made with that wave of her hand. Stella Mae would be left alone, Virgil's absence a bonus.

"Now, what I want to know is why would he say that?" Dalton's tone did not allow for a careless answer.

"I told Peggy about Virgil sending Stella Mae all over the blame road digging up rocks his mule might step on. You remember that. I guess she told Frank."

Teensy came in from one of her increasingly frequent trips to the outhouse, both hands pressed against her back, steering her baby belly across the room. Dalton looked hard at Matilda, then dropped the subject as if it had the power to rob Teensy of yet another baby, and Matilda knew she had been right to shield both of them from what had happened at the well house on Monday. Things would go back to normal—back to the ordinary, everyday walking on eggshells and looking over one's shoulder, the usual staying alert to anything that might arise out of nothing, the going about one's business with the familiar sense of foreboding that had been the background music to Matilda's whole life. Except that now Matilda understood that Frank Bowers was far and away more dangerous than Virgil Morgan.

22.

That Sunday morning, a large crowd of worshippers filled the barn-turned-church behind Pastor Brown's house. The plank and cinderblock pews were tightly packed, the youngest children sent to sit in the swept-dirt center aisle. Older boys who had not shown their faces at services in months, maybe years, huddled just inside the wide doorway, present but not committing to anything holy. Most all of the croppers that Matilda knew from the nearest farms were there, along with the Braswells and the Owenses, who worked parcels of the Creedle property. She recognized some of the mamas Gertie had tended who belonged to another church, there with their families. More than a few people who had long since moved farther up the Trace or to Bristol were sitting again in their old spots on this day. Something had happened, or was about to happen. Gertie was there with Stella Mae, as always. There were whispers and the sounds of shushing, but no one was laughing or sporting the usual pious Sunday countenance or clapping anybody on the back and asking about crops or cotton prices.

"What's going on?" Matilda looked at her father sitting next to her, and he just shook his head. He knew something.

"Best to hear it from the preacher," Teensy said. "Whatever it is, God'll give him the words."

A hush fell over the room as Pastor Brown started up the dirt aisle, stepping over and around children, his black homespun robe billowing ecclesiastically. He made his way to the front and took his place behind the scrap-wood pulpit, then raised his arms in his usual manner, though the congregation had already stilled.

"Most times," he began, "it does me good, seeing folks filling up the house of the Lord. Even on a hard day—most especially on a hard day—this here's a blessed sight, all these faces of God's children turned up to Him, every ear open, every eye on the path been set before us, every heart reaching for the comfort nothing but Him can give."

Pastor Brown was the worst farmer on the Trace, but he had a gift for speaking and a heart for the Lord. He came around to stand in front of the pulpit, and the timbre of his voice brought the faithful to their feet as he proclaimed, "But we would not have you ignorant, brethren, concerning them that fall asleep; that ye sorrow not, even as the rest, who have no hope." Then his arms fell to his sides. "First Thessalonians 4:13," he said softly, as if defeated by chapter and verse.

The funeral verse, Matilda thought. *Somebody's dead.*

Behind the pulpit again, the pastor began swaying to a melody only he could hear, humming low, but when he rolled out the first word like a moan, those congregated could hear it, too, the melancholy music of a soul in need, and they joined in the song, filling the barn with a cry for comfort for whatever burden the Lord God would be helping them bear on this day.

> *There is a balm in Gilead*
> *To make the wounded whole...*

There were more songs and a sermon on the barren fig tree, and then Pastor Brown pointed into the crowd. "Sister Esther and Sister Rayelle," he said. "I'd be beholden if you'd take the young ones outside where they might can find some popcorn balls to spoil their dinners with while I have some words with the grown-ups."

The children whooped and cleared out of the barn, leaving about half as many people inside. Stella Mae did not catch on to his words right away and stayed in her seat, but when Gertie leaned down and whispered in her ear, a broad grin broke over her sweet face and she raced down the empty aisle. Then Doreen Braswell closed the door, despite the heat, and Pastor Brown got down to why so many people were in the barn that day. He was the bearer of news that many, Matilda could see, already knew. She sat between Dalton and Teensy, one row behind Gertie. The paper fans in the women's hands stilled, and every gaze was on Pastor Brown as he swiped his face with a cloth that matched his robe.

"We know," he started off, "about a law been set down in this state, set down in nineteen and twenty. A law saying anybody making arguments about all men being equal is guilty of a crime." There were tuts and mutters from the congregation, and Pastor Brown quieted the crowd. He raised his voice and declared, "So there will be no arguing here today. No calling right 'right' and wrong 'wrong.'" He blotted his face and sang out a crescendo of condemnation: "No crying forth that a man is a man and that all are precious in the sight of our Lord Jesus Christ." He raised his hands to heaven and shouted, "No reminding them that set such laws that 'There is not Greek and Jew, circumcision and uncircumcision, bondman and freeman; but Christ is all, and in all.' No!" And the words shook the walls of the barn and the ground beneath them and the trees in the earth outside. Then he bent over the pulpit, crumpling inside his robe, and softly repeated, "No."

The barn resounded with shouts from those congregated, and Pastor Brown raised himself up and said, "What we *will* do here today is throw ourselves at the foot of the cross and cry for mercy for our sister, Cassie Jones. Some here might not know Sister Cassie, but you know her grandmother, our sister Myrtle—in the front row right there, every Lord's Day." He pointed to the bench in front of him. "And this morning Sister Cassie from over at Bristol is sitting here with her, without her husband." He motioned for them to stand. Myrtle, a slight woman about Gertie's age, rose first. Then the younger woman, a cloth pressed to her cheek, stood up next to Myrtle. Her face was shiny with tears.

Watching this woman rise and turn made Matilda catch her breath. Cassie was the young wife Matilda and Peggy had seen outside the telegraph office in Bristol. The woman whose husband had not let her step off the sidewalk into the mud on that rainy day. The wife, surely, of the man for whom Pastor Brown had instructed them to sorrow not, as those who have no hope.

And then Pastor Brown eulogized Buddy Jones, husband to

Cassie, father to two little girls. A brickmason in Bristol, he told those assembled, until the Monday just past, when he had come to the Trace for a last look at a piece of land he was set to buy.

"Our brother Buddy was blessed in everything he set his hand to, and he had a mind to try farming. Not cropping, farming his own piece of land, bought with what he worked for and laid aside, year by year."

As the pastor told it, Buddy Jones had come to the Trace on Monday to walk the property lines one last time before a deed was to be drawn up on Tuesday. He and Cassie had long been planning to settle on the Trace. They had friends in the sharecropping community, and they wanted to be close to Cassie's grandmother, to help look after her now that her husband was gone. And they had wanted to get away from Bristol, where more people meant more skirmishes. Where Buddy himself had recently been assaulted, right on the main street.

Buddy had stopped at Myrtle's house on Monday before heading back to Bristol, telling her he would return in a week to mark the foundation for a house. But he never made it back to Bristol, not that night and not anytime in the three days that passed before his body was found caught in a deadfall in a crook of the Pearl River, a gash in the side of his head, Buddy already "passed to glory" a mile from where his wagon had been found. A deputy had been around to some of the farms over the past two days, asking questions, but no witnesses had turned up, no answers had been offered to the deputy or to Cassie.

Matilda could not take her eyes off Cassie, the young woman's shoulders shaking under her grandmother's spindly arm.

"Sister Cassie here will be staying on with Sister Myrtle for a time, her and her two little ones. 'Pure and undefiled are them that visit the fatherless and widows in their affliction,'" the pastor offered, and Cassie gave herself over to sobs and to the host of women who left their seats and lavished her with Christian love.

The service let out early. The congregation walked outside in a common daze and gathered their children, whose mouths drew up tight with worry when they saw their parents' faces.

Dalton and Teensy and Matilda were mostly silent on the ride home, each grappling with what they had experienced at church, each taking on a share of Cassie Jones's grief. Just past Gertie's cabin, where the road forked alongside a stand of corn left unfenced in a vain attempt to lure raccoons and squirrels and deer away from the crops still maturing in the fields, they met Virgil Morgan's wagon. Not too proud to come back for his Sunday corn liquor, Matilda thought, even after being banished from the farm. Dalton halted the mule when Virgil slowed to a stop beside him. The ground there was littered with chewed-clean corncobs.

"Hop on down, boy, and gather me up some of them cobs for the outhouse."

Matilda saw her father's jaw clench. He didn't move. Then Teensy blurted out as cheerfully as she could manage, "I'll get you some," and struggled to hoist herself up.

"Like hell," Matilda mumbled. She jumped down from the wagon and yelled, "I'll get the blame cobs." She marched through the tall john-songrass at the edge of the field, cursing chiggers, and snatched up an armload of dry corncobs. Then she launched them, one after another, into the back of Virgil's wagon, landing them with pops like rifle fire.

"Need to get control of that one there, boy," Virgil shouted to Dalton before slapping the reins and moving on.

When Matilda climbed back into the wagon, Teensy was shaking and Dalton's muscles were so taut they looked about to burst, but no one said a word as the wagon clattered down the road toward the shack. There was too much grief among them.

23.

Teensy declared the remainder of the day a Sabbath rest. She set out a cold meal of fruit and garden vegetables. Buddy Jones, his wife, and their two little girls were among them at the table as surely as if they could be seen. Afterward, Dalton took his fishing pole and strode off toward the pond, but neglected to take any bait.

"Meeting up with some of the men about that business the pastor told of," Teensy said. "Doesn't want me to know. Thinks I might break in two worrying, so I don't let on."

"You do look tired."

"I ain't made of china glass, Mattie," Teensy said, but a few minutes later she was sitting on the bed. "I figure the baby could use a nap." She stretched out and turned toward the wall.

Matilda took her swap-pile book out to the porch swing, hoping Peggy would not come around on this, of all days. She tried to read, but couldn't get Buddy Jones out of her mind. The way he and Cassie had looked so happy outside the telegraph office, heads bent over their telegram. How that yellow-and-green handkerchief had seemed so gay and fanciful peeking out of his pocket and so lurid and garish when Buddy, lying in the muddy road, wiped his bloody jaw with it. The hardened hatred on the face of the man who attacked him. She wondered if that man might have had something to do with what everyone knew was a murder and what Pastor Brown had said the deputy was calling "the accident."

While Teensy slept, Matilda slipped back into the shack and quietly slid two paper sacks from behind the pie-safe icebox. In her room, she opened the seams and spread the sacks over the floorboards. She sharpened her knife on the brick she kept for that purpose and cut the sacks into sheets of paper, punched a hole in a corner of each, and tied them together with a bit of string to make a passable notebook. Then she headed for the gully.

Sitting on the rock ledge embedded high in the sloped bank, Matilda let the wildness of the gully embrace her. The buttonbush was close on one side, and a stand of tall trees rose behind her, shading her and offering cover. For a while, she watched a trio of vultures reeling overhead in a patch of blue sky between sunlit clouds. Here, near the top of the bank, she could watch the creek flow downhill in the ravine below, then on through wilder brush where it narrowed to a silver thread of stream. If she dug an opening in the buttonbush, she could see in the distance the back of the shack, the squared-off garden, the neatly stacked woodpile, the outhouse, the clothesline. Home, despite it all. She leaned back against the dirt bank and opened the notebook, took out her pencil.

There was something nagging at her. A bothersome detail hiding itself like a word that won't come when you need it, though the shape of it, the feel of it, is there in your head. It had something to do with Buddy Jones. She thought of Cassie sobbing in church and the way Pastor Brown had carefully packed his outrage into his Sunday sermon. "A brickmason in Bristol" is how the pastor had described Mr. Jones. Until the Monday just past, when he had come for a last look at the land before laying out his money for it. *The Monday just past.* The day Buddy Jones disappeared. *Monday.* The day she had seen Frank at the well house loading the wagon with brandy. As that fact presented itself, everything else seemed to stop—the water flowing in the creek, the crows vying for the highest branches in a tree on the opposite bank, the breeze through the gully, her heartbeat, her breath—and she almost expected the rock to tumble down the bank under the weight of it.

But what connection could there be between Frank and Buddy Jones? Neither was from the Trace. They had no history with each other. No past scores to settle. Frank was evil itself, but Matilda could not imagine him bothering with anything or anyone who did not affect him directly. He did not have Virgil Morgan's fragile pride. He was motivated only by his own concerns. She had seen that. She bent over the notebook and listed everything she knew about Buddy Jones and what had happened to him. *Brickmason. Bristol. Two little girls. Land purchase—where? Wagon found—where? Monday. Frank at well house. Red-faced man from town?*

For some time, there on the rock as on a biblical judgment seat, with a jury of trees assembled behind her, she considered the evidence. She wondered if Mr. Jones had filed a complaint about what happened that day in town. Unlikely, she thought. He'd been so close to buying his land and leaving Bristol for the seclusion of the Trace. Other than herself and Peggy and the two little towheaded girls in town, the witnesses on the sidewalk that day had seemed a hostile lot. She read back over her notes and thought again of the man who had shoved Buddy off the sidewalk. Circumstances pointed more to him than to any connection with Frank. Didn't they? Or did she only need to believe that? To believe that Frank would leave the Trace soon and she would board her train for Cleveland as planned and her father would work out the remainder of his time, then be free of the farm.

Three unwelcome boys invaded the woods where Matilda was taking a break from the heat of Mrs. Porter's stove. It was Monday. Just a week since she had seen Frank at the well house and only a day since she had learned about Buddy Jones, yet it seemed as if she had been carrying those loads much longer. She knew the three boys. Harold and Luke—the Porters' sons, eleven and twelve. Ollie Riley, also twelve. They looked as if they were up to something. She did not care what it was. They hadn't noticed her sitting on a stump some distance behind where they stood bunched together over something in Ollie's hands.

"Promise you won't never tell," Ollie said.

"Just hurry up, we got to get back." Harold, Matilda thought.

The boys were covered in hay, fresh from the Porters' fields where a group of men were loading wagons and building haystacks. Ollie opened a folded cloth and dealt out hand-rolled cigarettes like a round of cards, three apiece.

Should've waited for that promise, Matilda thought. Webb Riley, Ollie's daddy, was not one for sparing the rod and spoiling the child. Matilda had spent enough time over Mrs. Riley's stove that summer to know that.

Luke produced matches, and all three boys lit up.

"This ain't homegrown; it's store-bought." Ollie blew a stream of smoke out the side of his mouth with veteran precision. "Almost lost ever one of these babies last week," he said. "I was hiding 'em in a knothole in a tree I know, off the road down past the school. Where I go to smoke, most times."

The outpost school. A little Baptist church where the handful of white kids, farmers' kids, most of them, from that part of the Trace had lessons on school days. Those who went to school at all.

"Had 'em in my hand when I heard a wagon coming down the road, so I holed up behind the tree and waited..." Ollie took a long, slow drag, taking his time with the storytelling while the other boys puffed quickly, eager to be off without being found out. Matilda was not any more interested in Ollie's story than the Porter boys seemed to be. She slid her feet out of her thin shoes and into a clump of cool moss at the base of the stump. Her mind drifted around vague thoughts of Cleveland.

"And then just when that wagon gets right even with me on the road, I hear one of the wheels crack. And then here comes another wagon, going the other way, toward town. A colored man's in that one, says he's got some tools and he can help the white man fix the wheel. I ain't never seen neither one of them before."

Matilda's mind cleared instantly. She sat motionless, listening so hard she barely breathed. Luke pinched his skinny cigarette between his thumb and forefinger, smoking it down to a nub.

"So the colored man gets his tools out and they start working on the wheel, and the white man asks him if he lives around there, just passing time and all, and the colored man says no, not yet, but that his wife has family there and he's thinking to farm a little piece of land close by to them. They chew the fat till the wheel's good to go, then the white man says thanks for the help and good luck with the farming. Asks him where the land is, and the colored man says it's that tangled-up strip of woods just this side of Bayou Ford wouldn't nobody in his right mind try to clear. And then the white man stood right there in the road and said he'd pay him fifty dollars if he *didn't* farm that land."

The other boys looked at each other and shook their heads. "That place ain't even good for hunting," one of them said. "It's eat up with poison sumac trees. You can't even burn them things without getting sick. And that's where Kenneth Joe's daddy got bit by that rattlesnake and died. Ain't nobody'd go up in there on purpose."

Ollie went on. "Then the colored man said, 'preciate the offer,' but he didn't go for the deal, just climbed back up in his wagon, and the white man got mad. Said his family was already using them woods for something else. I could tell he wasn't gonna let it go, and that's when I dropped ever one of these smokes." Ollie let the smoldering nib of his cigarette fall to the ground, and Harold, the only one in shoes, ground it out. "Soon as I picked 'em all back up, I hit it back through the woods to where I was supposed to be."

Buddy Jones. Had it been him fixing that wheel? It must have been. Ollie had said it happened last week. Was it Monday? The day before

Mr. Jones was supposed to buy his land? The last day anybody saw him alive? The day she'd seen Frank loading the wagon at the well house?

"We better get back before somebody comes hunting us," Harold said, and then Matilda was alone again.

It didn't have to have been Frank—the man on the road that day. The man she had made an unspoken pact with to safeguard her parents, to keep Stella Mae safe, keep herself safe. There were other white farmers on the Trace who would not look kindly on a colored man owning land. *Land nobody in their right mind would try to clear.* That was what Ollie had said. And then that one thing took shape for Matilda. Land that was no good for farming or hunting and thick with poison sumac. Land everybody knew to stay away from, but that the white man's family was using nevertheless. A perfect place for a bootlegger to hide his stills. And if what Ollie had witnessed *had* happened on Monday, Curtis Creedle had been out of the county then. The day before and two days after, too. It couldn't have been him. Eugene had gone somewhere in the farm wagon that Monday. But it made no sense that Eugene would say his family was using that land. He had only his mother and a little sister, and he wouldn't have had fifty dollars to wave around. But then, it might have been anyone. Any of the farmers, any of their hands. It might not have happened on Monday at all. It didn't have to be Frank.

One thing Matilda was sure of was that she was the only person in the world who knew both what Ollie had witnessed and that Frank had driven off with a wagon loaded with liquor the day Buddy Jones disappeared. She wanted to keep the two events separate in her mind, because together they were explosive. She had no proof of anything.

Even with proof, her word would not count for much. And Frank knew the law. Matilda did not doubt his ability to keep himself out of jail and to put her father there for running liquor. She felt as though the fates of everyone she loved most were in her hands—her pregnant mother, her hopeful father, sweet, innocent Stella Mae.

She wished she were already in Cleveland. Maybe she could pack up Mississippi and take it on the train, unpack it in Cleveland and hang it on the line for everyone to see. Maybe someone would care. Would do something.

24.

Matilda switched kitchens—Mrs. Porter's for Mrs. Riley's—hardly noticing the walk between farms. Her hands, washing and peeling and chopping, filling jars and sealing them, seemed to work on their own as she grappled with her thoughts. Did she owe it to Cassie Jones to speak up? And what might she set in motion if she did? Should she confide in the pastor? In Gertie? Should she tell her father everything?

Her hands continued their independent work until Mrs. Riley told her she looked peaked and sent her off early. She walked without thinking of where she was going, without noting that she turned off the Trace at Miss Bodie's house, took the left-hand fork past Gertie's, walked down the hill, and crossed the straddling board. She looked up, and she was home. Gertie's walking stick was on the porch. She heard her father's voice inside while the sun was still bright over the fields in the afternoon, and that was wrong. She pulled open the screen door. Her mother was in bed, Dalton stroking her hair and telling her everything was all right.

"I can't lose this baby."

"You ain't gonna lose this baby," Gertie said. "This ain't nothing but too much work and you letting yourself get too dry. I see it plenty when the last weeks is this hot." Gertie turned to Dalton. "She'll be fine. You just keep her drinking and resting. A little water every hour till bedtime, then wake her up a time or two in the night to drink. Something salty to chew on now and again. And from here on out, till the baby comes, keep her out of the sun. She don't have to stay in bed, but don't let her work up a sweat or get dried out. This'll pass."

"I could take a little milk," Teensy said weakly.

Gertie nodded at Dalton, and Dalton looked up, found Matilda in the room.

"You feeling all right?" he asked when he saw her, his voice so strained there was only one answer Matilda could give him that he would be able to take on.

"I'm good. I'll get the milk."

She went out the door, down the steps, across the road to the springhouse. She opened the door of the little stone structure, and for an instant she mistrusted her eyes, suspected her overburdened mind of projecting its fears onto the physical world. Because there was Frank, sitting on a stack of empty crates upturned on the cool, stone floor of the springhouse. He was sitting beside the stream, turning a small object over in his hand. Matilda seemed to have startled him out of whatever had been playing in his mind, and she thought he looked almost glad to see her, as if there was something he hadn't yet said to her, some new indignity he had been saving up. But then he saw her staring—and she could not stop staring—at the object in his hand. Something she had held in her own hand in a muddy road in front of a telegraph office. A tarnished silver pocket watch on a chain with a fob shaped like a sailing ship.

Frank looked down at his hands, then back at Matilda, and his face turned stony. He stuffed the watch into his pocket. Matilda's body was urging her forward, toward the milk jug in the stream; her mind was warning her to appear as if she had not recognized the watch. She did not know if Frank had seen her pick it up that day in town. He had stepped out of the post office after Buddy and Cassie walked away. After all of Matilda's own stomping on the sidewalk. She looked at the jug in the stream. Two steps forward and she could reach it, take it out in an ordinary fashion, any nervousness she showed to be expected after what had happened between them at the well house. But she could not prevent her gaze from drifting back to the pocket that held the watch. Frank stood up, drew her eyes to his, and the truth shot between them like an electric charge. Matilda backed out of the doorway, and Frank did not move to stop her.

Teensy was asleep when Matilda reached the shack. No one asked about the milk. Dalton and Gertie held a whispered argument about him wanting to hitch the wagon and drive her back to her cabin, and, as usual, Gertie headed home under her own power.

"Gertie says it ain't as cut and dry as she made out," Dalton told Matilda on the porch. "Too much work and too much worry, and she could lose another'n."

Her mother would not survive the loss of this baby. Matilda knew she would lose herself with it, one way or another.

"She worked too hard over supper," Dalton said. "Go on and eat. I'll fix me a plate later on. I want to sit with her some and wake her up when it's time to drink. You look tired. Get you some rest." He dragged a chair from the table to Teensy's bedside. Before sitting down, he pulled a cloth from his back pocket and mopped his brow with it. A handkerchief. A yellow-and-green-plaid handkerchief.

"Where did you get that?" Matilda was not sure she had spoken the question aloud until her father answered.

"Found it in the wagon yesterday," he said, looking at it as if for the first time. "Caught behind the latch."

Which meant under the false floor of the wagon bed. In the compartment that would have been empty after Frank delivered the load of brandy to the depot, or wherever he had taken it. Room enough inside to hide a body on the way to the river.

Teensy stirred, and Dalton sat down, took her hand.

It was all too much. Matilda felt that she was losing her hold on herself. She whispered that her head was aching and she might lie down a while, then hurried to get to her pallet while her legs still held her up.

Matilda woke sometime after dark. Dalton was in bed beside Teensy, both of them asleep, the front and back doors open to the hope of a breeze. She stepped softly across the room and cracked the screen door for the dog, who silently slipped inside and padded to the pallet behind the wall. Then she hid her knife in one of Dalton's old shoes and set it next to her pillow. She lay awake for a long time, until she could pick out cracks in the wall that needed chinking as the last hour of true night began to gray. Go Away got up then and slinked silently back around the wall. Matilda heard the screen door close softly behind him. She turned onto her side and waited for the first sound of her father's waking. She would catch him before he brought in the morning water. She would tell him everything. She would let him decide what needed to be done. Let him decide how to protect her, instead of the other way around, as he would want it. She would not let him walk out the door without understanding the danger Frank Bowers posed to them all. The evil he was capable of. What would come, would come. They would face it together.

Usually Teensy stirred first, putting together a breakfast Dalton could eat on his way to the fields, but with the birth so near, Dalton had begun leaving earlier, moving quietly so as not to disturb her sleep. Matilda wasn't sure he would leave at all this morning, after Teensy's having been so weak. Matilda felt weak herself. Drained of all resources. She rested her eyes for a moment, and when she opened them again, full-on sun was shining through the chinks. She heard pots rattling in the kitchen, her mother singing a hymn. She shot up as if Frank might be standing outside the door waiting to murder them all, and banged into the chest of drawers as she rounded the wall.

"Where's Poppa?"

"Out in the fields. Been gone more'n an hour, sleepyhead." Teensy was smiling, her hand atop her baby belly, everything as right as Gertie had told her it would be. She glanced at Matilda and her brow puckered. "What's the matter?" She set down the cup of water she had been faithfully sipping and started toward Matilda just as the door swung open and Dalton walked in, a wide smile on his face.

"Can't stay but a minute," he said. "But I got some news." He picked up Teensy's cup and handed it to her, motioning for her to drink. "Creedle threw Frank off the place this morning."

"How come?" Teensy was already filling a sack with biscuits and butter for Dalton.

"Didn't nobody see fit to tell me," Dalton said, but Matilda knew by the way he rubbed the side of his nose as he spoke that he was not telling all he knew.

She followed him out to the porch and didn't have to ask. Dalton looked at her and sighed, as if they had passed beyond his trying to shield her from the dangerous aspects of his work.

"Creedle caught him red-handed, stealing his best liquor. Been running his own loads. Somebody at the depot got wise to it and sent word. Owens heard them arguing over in the orchard this morning. Creedle told Frank to pack up, he was putting him on the first train to Baltimore. Told him not to show his face around here again. To keep clear of his wife, too, or he'd make trouble for him. I think she's soft on him."

"So he's gone for good?"

"Looks like it. Saw them ride out myself, in Creedle's buggy."

Frank was gone. It was almost too much for Matilda to believe. Her mother would have her longed-for baby. Matilda would make it to Cleveland. And her father would get himself free of this place without whatever danger the laying of her burden on his shoulders would have brought to him. It wasn't justice, but it was grace, nonetheless.

That night Matilda got on her knees beside her pallet and said her first prayer in months. It started and ended with *Thank you, God.*

25.

The other side of the news that Frank was gone was that Dalton would be making all the runs to Canton again. Buddy Jones's death was on everyone's mind, and Dalton could not hide his apprehension the next time he climbed into the wagon with a load of concealed liquor.

In the days following, Dalton took on the countenance of a man trapped and ill-fated, his enthusiasm about owning land dulled by the extra year Curtis had added to their deal. Matilda threw out the prospect of running off to Cleveland in the night, all three of them, just as the Days had, but her mother was too near her time and her father was too unsure of a place he did not know and jobs he had not tried before. And running out on a sharecropper debt was more dangerous than driving a load of liquor, either of which could strip him of what little freedom he had. Aside from that, as Dalton pointed out, a coffee tin full of coins would not take three people very far or keep them there very long.

Then one day Dalton had word from a friend two counties over. He and another man were putting every penny they had into a parcel of land big enough for both of their families and Dalton's, too.

"Over in Eller's Bottom," Dalton told Teensy and Matilda. "Land's low, and rocky, but once we get it cleared, ain't no reason we can't farm it. Course, it floods some on one end, but that's all right. Good for the soil. Rayford, he's setting aside a spot for us to put up a house," he told Teensy. "And he's willing to settle for whatever I can send, whatever time I can send it."

Teensy looked like she had taken her first full breath in weeks.

"It'd mean I'd have to put in our cotton money," he said. "To hold our stake in the place till my time's up here. And I been studying that time. With Frank gone and me doing all the driving again, I'm gonna talk to Creedle about going back to our old deal. One year, minusing the months already passed. Or splitting the difference, leastways."

"Won't hurt none to try," Teensy said, hope threading its way through the words.

"That's my thinking," Dalton said. "I'll hold off a while, let things settle down some first. Then we'll talk."

While her parents made plans that Matilda could not bring herself to believe in, she got back to her own plans. *Get to Cleveland. Work double time. Scout out a job for Poppa. Talk some sense into him about getting out of Mississippi.* She would wait two weeks after the baby came, make sure Teensy could manage, and then she'd go. She could hold herself together that long. Even though she had not been able to shake off the image of Frank turning over Buddy Jones's watch in his hand, his eyes boring straight through her. Sometimes she broke out in a cold sweat from holding in what she knew about him. It ate at her like a poison.

"You been talking in your sleep of late," Teensy told her one day.

"Just gibberish," she said, and Matilda laughed. One more lie, that laugh. Or maybe one more kindness. She didn't trust herself to know the difference anymore.

～

Three weeks into August, Peggy came by to say goodbye. She and Leon would be off the next morning for Baltimore.

"Bye, Teensy," Peggy said, and Matilda noticed her mother's misty eyes as she hugged Peggy goodbye. Her mother, she thought, was perhaps the most tenderhearted person there ever was.

"You take care of yourself," Teensy said. "And come back and see us."

"I'm not sure when that would be," Peggy said. "Mother wants me back with her…" She seemed to be grappling with explaining her family situation, and Teensy rushed in to spare her.

"Course she does. I expect she's had a terrible time missing you this summer."

"And Leon." Peggy turned to Matilda. "After Baltimore, he's going back to Pennsylvania. Back to college. And then he has a job waiting for him up there when he graduates. Teaching."

Teensy took note of Peggy's apologetic tone and watched her daughter, concern setting in around her eyes.

"I'm so glad. He'll be a real good teacher, I know," Matilda said, showing no trace of regret, and Teensy's worry lines faded.

Matilda was picking cotton at Caleb Gill's farm when Peggy and Leon stopped by the shack the next morning on their way to the train

depot in town. When Matilda came in that evening, Teensy pointed
to a box sitting on the hearth, Matilda's name written across the top.

"Peggy left it."

"What is it?"

"Open it up and let's see."

Matilda opened the box. She pulled out a dress and held it up so
Teensy could see. It was made from the fabric she had liked best when
she and Peggy were shopping in town, a mossy green with a slight
gold sheen that Matilda would have felt silly wearing if Peggy had not
thought to have it tailored with simple lines and a modest cut. Matilda
thought back to the letter from Rainy that Peggy had surely read,
and she wondered if this was Peggy's way of urging her to make the
trip to Ohio. Maybe it was just Peggy being Peggy, playing dress-up
with a poor sharecropper's daughter, but that dress, Matilda thought,
had Cleveland written all over it. Under the dress, Peggy had packed
a tin of shortbread cookies and a silver-handled mirror. And under
that, a pair of sensible shoes, black leather with block heels, in exactly
Matilda's size.

"That Miss Creedle's something, ain't she?" Teensy said, holding
the dress under Matilda's chin and shaking her head in wonder.

"She is that," Matilda said. She reached into the bottom of the
box and took out a paper sack with Teensy's name on it. Inside were
a dozen diapers, a tiny white nightgown, a flannel blanket, and a silk
baby bonnet. Teensy went off to pack them away in the cradle Dalton
had made years ago for one of the babies who hadn't been born after
all, along with the other things she had knitted and sewn already.

There was one last item in the box. Matilda lifted it out. A book, bound in burgundy cloth. The book Leon had told her about: *Flints, Arrowheads, and Spearheads of the Indians of the Lower Mississippi Valley.* Inside were dozens of sketches, many that looked familiar to Matilda. As she flipped through the pages, appreciating the fine artwork and Leon's thoughtfulness, a folded sheet of newspaper fluttered to the floor. She stooped to pick it up. It was a clipping, just a few weeks old, from a newspaper from somewhere bigger than Bristol. A real city newspaper, that was clear. Maybe even from Pennsylvania. The headline read "Queen Bessie—The World's Greatest Woman Flier," and under that was a grainy picture of a young woman wearing an aviator's cap with goggles pulled up over her forehead. A colored woman. Matilda scanned the article. *Bessie Coleman…daughter of sharecroppers…walked an hour to school every day…enrolled in a colored university she had to leave when her money ran out.* And yet she made it all the way to Paris—Peggy's Paris—and became the first colored woman with a pilot's license. The article was about an air show soon to be held in New York, where Bessie was expected to amaze spectators with her stunt flying.

So Leon, Matilda supposed, *had* been encouraging her when he told her about women traveling the world and making discoveries. And he had left her this clipping. There was a lump in her throat she wouldn't let herself pay attention to, but she did allow the thought that Peggy was lucky to have a brother like Leon and crazy to have wasted the little time she'd had with him on the farm trailing Frank.

26.

Dalton was in Canton that day. Matilda spent the morning hours picking up pecans in the orchard beyond the Creedle house. Like picking money up off the ground, she thought, working for a rare fifty-fifty split with Old Man Creedle. She got home around noon. Teensy was sitting in the porch swing knitting for the baby. Abiding by Gertie's instructions, she had cut back on work and was resting more.

"There's fatback biscuits on the stove," Teensy said. "Brung by Doreen."

Doreen Braswell was the youngest of the three sharecropper wives on the farm. The Braswells and the Owenses worked forty acres each on the other end of Curtis's 140 acres. They knew more than they had been told about why Curtis grew so much corn, so many peaches, and they kept a discrete but cordial distance on the farm, saving socializing for church and singings and taffy pulls and quiltings and other events held elsewhere.

"Was right nice of her. There's fried pies, too. Sweet potato." Teensy cast off the last row of stitches in a tiny sock and held it up. "This'll be about right come winter," she said, then started in on its mate, casting on a new row with her thumb and one of the polished-wood needles Dalton had made for her last Christmas.

Matilda took a biscuit from the stovetop and fished a fried pie out of a greasy paper sack. She took her plate and a cup of water back out to the porch.

"Sorry I couldn't help pick up pecans," Teensy said. She put down the knitting and closed her eyes.

"Tired?" Matilda asked, and Teensy held up a finger but didn't open her eyes.

Matilda finished off her biscuit, watching Teensy until she picked up the needles again. They clacked away for a few minutes until, once more, Teensy laid them aside and closed her eyes.

"Mama?"

"Shh." Teensy seemed to have gone off someplace and didn't want to be brought back by words. Matilda waited. When Teensy opened her eyes, she smiled. "I been keeping a count on the pains for a time now," she said.

"Pains?" Matilda moved her plate out of her lap.

"It ain't bad. Hardly right to call it pain. But coming regular," she added, laughing softly, like pain was something funny. Then she groaned and went away again.

"Mama."

Teensy held up her whole hand, firmly, and Matilda waited until she was back with her.

"I think it's time to go for Gertie," Teensy said, the words coming in a rush.

Dalton had taken the wagon, and Eugene wasn't on the farm that day. Matilda had no idea if Old Man Creedle was up at the house. She could get to Gertie's quick enough running, but it would take some time for Gertie to walk back. "I could go over to the Creedle's…"

"No, I got a good while yet. There's plenty of time. Just run on up to Gertie's."

"I'll run back quick and let Gertie come behind. Won't be gone long."

Matilda ran as much of the way as she could, going around the front field, past the cow pasture, and up the farm road past the gully and the fork that led to Gertie's, praying for all she was worth that when she got there the old chair on the porch would not be upturned, Gertie's signal that she wasn't home. And that Gertie could walk back to the shack double speed.

～❧～

Gertie came through the doorway with a birthing quilt over her arm, already issuing orders.

"Lay this out over the bed, Mattie. And where's my bag?"

Matilda had run ahead with the medical bag and a bundle of rags. "On the table," she answered from in front of the stove.

"Got water on to boil?"

"Yes'm."

"How fast they coming?" Gertie asked Teensy.

"Quick and hard" was all Teensy could manage.

Gertie laid a watch on the hearth and minded the time while Matilda soaked a towel in hot water.

"We'll be needing two washbasins down the line—one for her and one for the baby. Just warm water in them. You got two full buckets from the spring?"

"Right here."

Once Teensy was undressed and on the quilt, Gertie swabbed her with petroleum jelly and massaged and stretched the birth canal, pressing down and outward with her thumbs, while Teensy sang shaky snatches of hymns between labor pains. Even her moans went up like prayers.

"Need a hot towel," Gertie shouted. Matilda handed one over, and Gertie pressed it between Teensy's legs.

"Feels wonderful. Thank you, Gertie."

"Ain't gonna let you tear," Gertie said. "Don't push yet. Not till I tell you."

"Everything's all right this time?"

"Everything's just right." Gertie took the towel away and went back to massaging. Matilda filled the basins with warm water and laid out a baby-size blanket.

After another towel and another massage, Gertie told Teensy, "We gonna push next time, all right?"

"She's almost here," Teensy said with what breath she could muster. "Or he. It don't matter which."

All was well as the baby crowned. Gertie had Matilda raise Teensy upright, to a squat. To hinder tearing, she said, and Matilda sat behind

Teensy to prop her up, her arms around her mother's shoulders. Teensy pushed or did not push, as she was told.

All was well, too, as the baby's head emerged, as one more push freed the rest of the perfect little body, and as Gertie caught Annis and held her in her hands.

Nothing seemed amiss as Gertie tied off the cord in two places with strips of boiled rags and made an expert cut between them. Or as she laid the baby on the blanket and had Teensy push once again to deliver the afterbirth. Or even later, as Gertie gently cleaned the baby with warm water and Matilda dropped the scissors into the boiling pot and Teensy lay in bed smiling as if the world had finally lined up with her best hopes for it.

Before Matilda realized what was happening.

Before Gertie, her voice ragged and thick with grief, said, "Sweet Jesus, no. I seen it twice't before. Ain't nothing for it."

And though Gertie's expert hands continued their work—checking for a pulse, massaging the stomach, crossing the legs and holding them high—she was already gone.

Lying on the blood-soaked quilt, Teensy was gone.

27.

Gertie knelt beside the bed kneading one of Teensy's lifeless breasts for its colostrum. "It's better'n gold for this baby," Gertie said, her tears falling into Teensy's still face as she helped the baby latch on, let her drink the golden, honey-thick liquid. "Teensy'd want her to have it. It'll start her off strong. She's got to have it," the old woman said, frantically milking Teensy's other breast and pushing it into Annis's tiny mouth as if doing this one thing was the reason she had been put on the earth.

Matilda stood back, out of the way, watching as blood—every last bit of her mama's lifeblood, it seemed to her—seeped through the birthing quilt and onto the shuck mattress. She stayed as long as she could bear what was happening, what had already happened. And when she could bear it no longer, she flew out of the house, left Gertie and the baby and the earthly shell of her mama and fled to the rock in the gully, crying so hard she could not catch her breath. Crying because she would never again have a single moment with her beautiful mother, then because her mother had never had a chance to be whatever she would have been if the world had offered her a choice.

She cried because Teensy had never had a decent house or anything to spare or some fine thing for herself, and because there were three painted rocks behind Gertie's cabin with Teensy's failed babies buried under them. And now that one had made it—Annis, named by the wind—Teensy would never hold her in her arms, not one time.

Matilda cried about everything her mother would never do and all that she had been made to do, all that she had never had and all that had been loaded upon her narrow shoulders, every mean word and hard look and unkindness that her mother had borne without ever once returning evil for evil.

She cried because she was never going to make it to Cleveland, or to Egypt or England or Palestine or Paris, and because she was low enough to think of herself when Gertie was back at the shack doing all she could alone.

Then she got up off the rock, went back home, and took her baby sister from Gertie's arms, took her out onto the porch and rocked her in the swing until she fell asleep. As she rocked, she prayed that God would show her how to keep this baby safe in this perilous world. Annis opened her eyes for just a moment and peered up at Matilda. She seemed to look straight into her big sister's eyes as if she were making a connection that could never be broken, and Matilda knew then where Teensy had gotten her strength, why she had overlooked so much and insisted on living in a bubble of happiness encased in the awfulness around them. She could almost hear her mother whisper a long-ago promise to make the best and brightest possible world for Matilda. And there in the swing, though she knew she did not have her mother's strength, Matilda made the same promise to Annis.

Dalton dragged himself to the fields each morning and back in the evenings. He ate the supper Matilda cooked, held his tiny daughter in his strong arms, asked Matilda what she needed him to do, his eyes showing no heart for any of it. Working, eating, sleeping, answering when spoken to, one foot in front of the other.

Gertie got them through the next few months. She found a wet nurse for Annis among her other mothers, a woman fresh off the loss of her own baby girl. And largely because of the warm wash of joy that Annis bathed them in day after day, they all began to pull themselves up out of the grief and despair in which Teensy's death had stranded them. Things were not good, but they were bearable. Then they were more than bearable, because Annis was such a delight. And there was purpose, because she needed them.

28.

Winter brought an easing up of farmwork. Except for a few winter crops, the fields were resting. Chores were mostly preparation for spring—stacking new wood, walking the fences, ditching, broadcasting the fields. Most of Matilda's hours were occupied with the baby. In time, Gertie devised a formula Annis could tolerate—a mixture of goat milk and water and cod liver oil—and Matilda weaned her off the bereft wet nurse who had taken to looking at baby Annis with such hungry eyes that Matilda had become uncomfortable with her. Winter was a slow season for moving Curtis's liquor, too. Dalton's trips to Canton were fewer, and there was relief in that, as well.

In all this time, Matilda had seen no more of Virgil Morgan, and there had been no word of Frank Bowers. No letters had come from Peggy, nor from Rainy after Matilda had written to her about losing Teensy and Rainy had sent a shocked reply. It was as if all creation was slowing down to let Matilda and Dalton regain their bearings, learn what was to be normal now, and begin healing so they could look to raising Annis. Things were so peaceful on the farm that Matilda thought maybe she could learn to live on birdsong and rustling leaves and the patter of rain on the roof, as Teensy had.

Eventually, Dalton threw himself wholeheartedly into his plan to move the family onto the land at Eller's Bottom. He had held his place there with his cotton money and had sent along what little else he had been able to manage since then. Matilda could see that at least some portion of his old hope had been renewed.

The secrets Matilda carried were buried now under fresher tribulations, and she sometimes went several days without Frank Bowers entering her mind, although Cassie Jones seemed to have taken up permanent residence there.

Now that she and Dalton had resumed going to church on Sundays, Matilda avoided sitting where she could see Cassie, who was living now with her grandmother on the Trace. Holding back the things she knew about Frank felt like thievery. When the other women fussed over the two little girls and lavished Cassie with invitations, Matilda stood apart. So she was surprised one Sunday when Cassie, passing by, laid a bird-light hand on her arm and smiled at her as though there was a bond between them. It felt like forgiveness, that touch, and Matilda thought she must have somehow given something away, worn the truth on her face, but then she remembered Buddy lying in the mud and knew the familiarity of that touch was in remembrance of her having lent her hand to Buddy that day.

Near the end of February of the new year, Dalton came in one evening wearing his old smile. Matilda was feeding Annis her first carrots, pulverized and watered down, and Annis, five months old now, was deciding whether or not she liked them—scrunching her face as if they hurt her feelings, then giving them a second chance with a baby-bird open mouth.

"Talked to Creedle," Dalton said, shucking off the ragged jacket he hadn't spent any of the cotton money to replace. "Going back to the old deal. I'll be clear come May." He took up the forked stick leaning against the fireplace and stoked the small flame in the grate with a flourish, then jigged over to Annis and tickled her belly until she laughed her little tinkle of a laugh.

May. In less than three months, they might really leave this place. It hardly seemed possible. "Here, you feed her for a minute." Matilda handed Annis over to her father. "Be right back."

Matilda passed behind the tar-paper wall and opened the nook in the bottom drawer of the chest where she kept the book Leon had given her, her homemade notebook, and her coffee tin of Cleveland money. She had not taken out the tin in months. She hadn't let herself think about it. She worked off the lid and the metallic ping it made threatened to bring back the old excitement, but she tamped it down into a place she did not visit anymore. She suspected that come May, Old Man Creedle would come up with some new sum her father still owed, a reason to keep him working the farm, and she was ready for it.

"Here," she said, depositing the coffee tin on the table in front of her father. "For your land. Our land," she said, brushing a finger over

Annis's sticky orange cheek. "In case of any extra expenses when your time's up."

Dalton looked at the tin, full to the top with money. He did not move to touch it. "It don't mean you ain't never getting north," he said. "I know that's what you was living for."

"I'm living for something else now." Matilda took back the spoon and sailed it into Annis's mouth like a steamboat.

"Day'll come I'll pay it back. And if I have my way, I'll put you on a train going north myself."

"If I have my way," Matilda said, "we'll all three of us be on that train."

Two dreams going in opposite directions, and Annis sitting at the crossroads.

"Be interesting to see what comes, won't it, Little Bit?"

And just like Teensy's cool breezes and strawberry pies, the return of Dalton's interest in the future was all Matilda needed to be content, for that day at least.

The next day brought more cheer.

"Creedle's going off the farm for three weeks," Dalton reported. "Going up to Baltimore to visit the wife before the spring planting. Leaving me in charge."

"In charge of what all?" Matilda had in mind the secret stills and the Sunday morning sales, things with which Dalton, up to now, had never been involved.

Dalton knew her mind. "He already put up the red flag." A red flag signified no liquor sales until further notice. Matilda had never seen it, but she knew that Curtis hung it somewhere down the other fork at the top of the road when he was closed for business and that customers knew his rule about no one coming down the hill to the farm, ever, with or without the red flag up.

"Can't be sure," Dalton said, "but it's sounding to me like Creedle's about got his fill of farming, and all that other business, too. I think them men on the other end been giving him some headaches."

"What men?"

"Them he sells to in Chicago. Might be he's thinking on pulling out of here."

If that was true, maybe they really could leave the farm in May. "When's he leaving for Baltimore?"

"Tomorrow morning."

"We'll have us a party in the afternoon, then."

Dalton smiled at that, and Annis woke up from her afternoon nap making sweet baby sounds.

29.

Influenza.

It sounded like a death sentence the way Gertie said it, so woven through with dread, and for seven days straight, they thought it might be.

Matilda and Gertie, on the porch with Stella Mae and the baby one afternoon, had seen Dalton stumble crossing the stream as he came in from the fields. Gertie stood up from the porch swing and squinted over her spectacles. When Dalton fell to his knees in the yard, she waved a finger between Annis and Stella Mae and said, "Get them two out to the backyard and don't come inside lessen I tell you." The fear in Gertie's voice kept Matilda from arguing. She scooped up Annis and grabbed Stella Mae's hand and led them through the house to the backyard.

Minutes later Gertie appeared on the back steps and uttered the dreaded word, her voice trembling in memory of the epidemic just four years past.

"I thought that was over with," Matilda said.

"They's always the chance of getting it. Might not be as bad as what come through here before. They's different kinds. This time tomorrow I'll know more. He ain't blue. That's a good sign." Gertie was breathless but fierce with her instructions. "You take them two up to my place. I got diapers there, and bottles. Food enough. You got goat milk in the springhouse, and Stella Mae'll show you where I keep the cod liver oil. Cordie Wade down the road, she'll watch them two when you come down to check on him, and you can draw water for us when you come. But don't come no closer than the steps. Not till I say so."

For three nights Gertie slept on Matilda's pallet and nursed a fevered and delirious Dalton. She treated him with cold-water rag baths and herbal concoctions she had Matilda bring down from the cabin. On the fourth day, Matilda left Stella Mae and the baby with Cordie and marched into the shack unannounced, refusing to leave. She relieved Gertie of emptying Dalton's slop jar, tried to keep a dry sheet under him, and boiled sweat rags and underclothes. She dribbled as much broth and water down his throat as he could stand.

Late that night Gertie announced, "Thank-you-Jesus, the fever's done broke. He can have him a blanket now. Just one." She eased herself into one of the kitchen chairs, finally showing how worn she was.

With Curtis away in Baltimore and his house shut up and locked, neighbors felt free to come around, the women with food for Matilda and Gertie, the men to put their shoulders to Dalton's work, carrying his load and their own. Cordie looked after Stella Mae and Annis. Pastor Brown paid a visit. On the seventh day, Gertie said, "I'll be going on home tonight, coming back in the morning. He needs rest."

"I won't let him get up," Matilda vowed.

"He couldn't fight you on that if he tried. Way too weak. It's a job for him just lifting up his head. You scrub down everything. It's been enough time that it ain't likely to be catching anymore. And me and you look to be in the clear. But you keep a watch on yourself. You start to feel any little bit funny, you tell me."

Gertie looked ready to fall over. "You're tired," Matilda said. "I'll let Poppa sleep and drive you home."

"Ain't no need. I know the way."

"Talking sense today?" Gertie was back with the sun, as promised.

Matilda was feeding Dalton applesauce.

"She don't float my spoon like a boat, Gert," Dalton joked, his voice frail as a winter leaf. "Like for Annis."

"If you call that sense," Matilda said.

"Cordie's gonna go on and bring Annis down in a little while," Gertie said. "Got somewhere she needs to go, and I told her it looks safe enough now."

Dalton coughed weakly, then again with a hoarse bark that caught in his chest. He moaned, coughed again.

"Hurts some, that coughing?" Gertie asked, and Dalton nodded. "Put on some water, Mattie. I'll brew up something to slow the cough, and I brought something else to make him sleep."

Dalton swallowed a few sips of Gertie's tea, and his coughing calmed. Then she poured something from a fruit jar into a cup and lifted his head, held the cup to his lips. "A tonic for sleeping," she told him.

"You killing me the rest of the way, woman," Dalton said when he tasted it, but he drained the cup, as Gertie directed.

"Rum cherry bark and a little something extra. Best they is for sleeping. And that's what's gonna get you where you need to be. Lots of sleep." Gertie laid out a row of small pouches on the table and instructed Matilda in how to steep them for Dalton's cough, then she set out two quart jars of the tonic. "Every day this week, when you put Annis down for a nap—morning and afternoon, now—you give him a cup of this here and them two'll drop off together. The little baby and the big one," she said, pulling Dalton's blanket up under his chin. "You liked to scared us to death," she told him. "Too ornery to die, though. I knowed that the whole time."

Dalton took hold of her hand and looked her in the eye, grateful.

"Well, I got mamas to tend to. And Stella Mae's likely done forgot all about me, staying over to Cordie's so long. Mattie, fetch my walking stick."

"Let me drive you back."

Dalton raised a hand against that. Matilda knew why, and she figured Gertie did, too. No one was allowed to drive his wagon when it was loaded with liquor.

"Walking's good for keeping alive," Gertie said. "Which I plan on doing. Any need, you fetch me." She went out the screen door swinging her hickory stick, and when Matilda turned back around, Dalton was already asleep.

She heard voices outside, Gertie talking to someone on the porch. Matilda was surprised to see Eugene out there, as he wasn't supposed to be on the farm that week.

"Met a car on the Trace a little while ago," Eugene told Matilda when she stepped outside. "Man from town. He was bringing a telegram out here for your father."

"A telegram?" Who on earth would be sending her father a telegram, and who would pay to have it brought so far out on the Trace?

The answer was on the paper Eugene held out to her. The telegram was from Mrs. Creedle. Curtis was dead—a streetcar derailment in Baltimore. She had hired someone to oversee the farm until it could be sold, and she was counting on Dalton to take care of things until the new man's arrival in about ten days.

The sorrow in Matilda's heart for Peggy and Leon was quickly overcome with worries: her father bedridden and weak, the wagon and the shack itself loaded with liquor bottles, and only ten days before a new man arrived. What would this mean for them? If she could have managed it, she would have packed up her father and Annis and Gertie and Stella Mae and headed somewhere, anywhere, as fast as they could ride.

"Old Man Creedle promised to cancel Poppa's debt come May," Matilda told Gertie after Eugene left.

"Did he get that wrote down?"

"I don't know," Matilda said, but she figured he had not. "I'll ask him when he wakes up."

"No. Not till we get him rested up a little more and on his feet. Worry'll set a person back quicker'n anything. He's got to know, but he needs more time. Two days, if we can keep him sleeping like he's been doing. Then we'll ease off the tonic and get him up and moving around some. We'll tell him then."

Cordie arrived with Annis, sound asleep, and handed her over in a rush. She had tucked her into the bottom half of an old cardboard suitcase. "You keep it," she told Matilda. "It makes a good bed."

Matilda and Gertie thanked her for all she had done. As soon as Cordie was gone, Annis woke, babbling and smiling. It was like the sun coming up after a week of rain.

"And what is you about today, baby girl?" Gertie leaned over the suitcase where Annis was waving her arms and legs like a bug on its back. Annis answered with the furious waving of a small fist, which Gertie caught and closed up in her wrinkled hand. "Don't you back-talk me none, missy. Got a mouth on you like your sister." She kissed the captive fist and set it free.

The ground was crusted with a light, late frost when Matilda went out with a bucket at dawn the next morning. Teensy would have had something to say about the way it sparkled under the first rays of the sun and how she could feel winter on her feet and smell spring in the air at the same time. Matilda missed her mother so much that if Dalton and Annis weren't due to wake any minute needing her, she would have left the bucket and walked all the way to Gertie's to lay her hand on Teensy's stone in the baby cemetery.

One of the Braswells' little girls met her in the yard with a jar of fresh milk for Annis and a message for Dalton that the girl's father and Mr. Owens were carrying Dalton's workload just fine, that he shouldn't worry. It would fall to Dalton to tell them the news about Curtis's accident once he was on his feet, once he'd learned the news himself.

Matilda was able to light a fire in the stove before Annis's first sleepy cries. Dalton woke himself coughing. Matilda gave Annis a sugar-teat to suckle in the cradle while she put on a pot of water to brew up a cup of Gertie's cough remedy. She was still holding the dipper over the pot when Go Away started barking as though the thing he hated most was out in the yard. Matilda heard cursing, then a banging on the door that sounded like it might bring the whole shack down.

"Mattie. You and Annis get out of sight." Dalton fought to sit up, but lost the battle as the door flew open. Then Virgil Morgan was standing there looking around as if he were shocked to have found the inside of the shack on the other side of the door.

"You," he said, pointing a shaky finger at Dalton.

Matilda snatched up Annis's sugar-teat from where it had fallen and shoved it back between her lips before she could cry for it. The tremor in Virgil's hands told her why he was there.

"Get up and get me my order."

"What order's that, Mr. Morgan?" Dalton rolled to one side to better see Virgil.

"You know good and goddamned well what order. My standing order. Ever week."

"Mr. Creedle ain't on the place right now. Didn't speak of any orders. Wish I could help you, but…" Dalton's voice was waning. Matilda was afraid he might pass out trying to get out of bed. Then he was coughing again. The room was cold. She hadn't yet lit the log in the fireplace, and Dalton was easily chilled, even with the fever gone. Annis was wide-eyed, sucking the sugar-teat.

"I know there's liquor down here, boy. Or leastways you know where some is. I'm a regular customer, and it's my time. Ain't nobody up at the house. I been there. And I'm telling you to get me a bottle."

"I'm a cropper here, Mr. Morgan. You know that. You got business with Mr. Creedle outside of farming, I can't help you there. He'll be back…" He looked at Mattie, not sure how much time had passed. "Two weeks on?"

Matilda nodded.

"Two weeks," Dalton said.

"Get your black ass up and sell me my liquor, or you'll wish you had."

"Now, Mr. Morgan, it's Mr. Creedle you want. Let's just settle down and wait on him to get back." Dalton's coughing started again. When it let up, he spit into the rag in his hand and rolled onto his back.

"You telling me to settle down, boy?" Virgil kicked over a chair and let off a string of words as nasty as any Matilda had ever heard. Annis wailed. Matilda skirted Virgil and picked the baby up out of the cradle, set her on her hip and bounced her so fast that she was startled quiet.

Virgil sent a wild gaze around the room. When it lit on the stoking stick by the fireplace, he made for it, grabbed hold of it, and raised it over his head.

"I got children here. I don't want nobody getting hurt." Dalton's voice was only a whisper now, but he slid one leg over the side of the bed, doing his best to push himself up. He motioned for Matilda to take Annis outside, but she laid the baby back down and stepped between her father and Virgil.

"My father can't get up," she said. "He's sick with a fever. It's influenza."

Virgil's breath caught with a sloppy gurgle. He reached out into empty air, unbalanced.

"He might not pull through, and it's bad catching. You know about the influenza. Ain't nobody supposed to be in here but us. You'll likely come down with it a few days on." She could see her words were having an effect on Virgil. Influenza had taken out whole families on the Trace and in town, those few years before.

Matilda moved a few steps closer to him, and he moved as many steps back, toward the open door. "But there's some men working the field, and I can bring them right over here with one loud holler, if you need them." She sent that out like a threat, and she could see he took it that way. She almost laughed. Virgil stood there looking like the loudmouthed coward he was, and there wasn't anything a loudmouthed white coward in Mississippi was more scared of than a bunch of colored men in a field with nobody else around.

Matilda moved around him to the door. "We'll be sure to tell Mr. Creedle you came down here asking about liquor while he was gone. That you were up at his house looking for him," Matilda said, holding the screen door open.

Virgil aimed a last vile look her way, then hurled the stick across the room. It hit the wall behind Dalton's head, and Virgil half ran half fell down the porch steps and out to his wagon, looking like a scared rabbit and cursing like the devil.

30.

The next morning, Matilda was more concerned about clearing the shack of liquor than she was about Virgil Morgan. The word *influenza* was as good as an iron bar across the front door against him. The old coward obviously did not know about Old Man Creedle's accident, and that alone was enough to keep him from coming down the forbidden farm road again. Once she had the go-ahead from Gertie to tell her father about Curtis, Matilda would figure out how to handle the crates. Most likely, they would have to enlist the help of Mr. Braswell and Mr. Owens. Dalton was much too ill to do it himself, even with Matilda's help. And it was better not to involve Eugene. But where would they put the stuff? And what would happen when the deliveries stopped arriving at the depot? Questions for her father. But not today.

When Dalton woke, Matilda propped him up and gave him a cup of soup that Opal Owens had brought. After a few sips, he rolled over, put his feet on the floor, and reached for his work pants.

"Poppa, you got to stay in bed. Gertie says it'll set you back, getting up too soon." Matilda put her hand on Dalton's arm to try to stop him from doing whatever he had in mind. "Another day resting and sleeping, Gertie said. You ain't in any shape—"

"I think I know better'n you what shape I'm in," Dalton snapped, pulling on his pants. "I ain't asking permission to go to the outhouse."

Matilda stood in the doorway as Dalton went out onto the back porch and stopped, taking in the three wooden steps between the porch and the ground. Matilda moved out of sight as her father turned around and began his halting trip back to the bed, sliding along the wall for support. To spare him, she occupied herself with Annis, unpinning a dry diaper and pinning it back on as Dalton sank onto the bed. Without a word, she reached for the slop jar, set it next to him, and took Annis out the front door.

After a scant lunch in bed, Dalton tried again. He stumbled to the front door, then, light-headed, grabbed onto Matilda halfway back to the bed, almost taking them both down. By the time Matilda put Annis down for her afternoon nap, Dalton was so done in that he did not argue over the dreaded cherry-bark tonic. He welcomed the blessed sleep it would give.

"You'll wake up stronger for it," Matilda said as her father closed his eyes, both he and Annis already drifting off.

Matilda wandered out to the porch and called up the image of her mama in the swing, the sound of a hymn sung in time with the wooden clack of her knitting needles. Matilda's loneliness on the empty porch was crippling. Even Go Away was off on some adventure. The limbs of the sycamore tree showed nubs of spring leaves soon to come, the last spring, she thought, that she and her family would pass on the farm. The months ahead were a newly plowed field sown with unknown seeds.

The future was too worrisome, the past too sad, the porch too empty of her mama, so she checked on Annis sleeping soundly in her cradle near Dalton's bed, Dalton already so deep in sleep that Matilda had to look hard to see the gentle rise and fall of his shirt as he breathed. Annis was the best-sleeping baby there ever was. It would be a good three hours before she stirred if no one woke her, and Dalton, fatigued by the sickness and his stubbornness, would sleep at least that long under the influence of Gertie's tonic. They had run out of the pouches for Dalton's cough, and there was time for a quick trip up to the cabin for more and to update Gertie on Dalton's progress, maybe save the old woman a walk down to check on him.

Matilda had not left the shack, except to fetch water or milk from the springhouse, in all the time she had been nursing her father. Doreen and Opal, as well as Gertie, had urged her to get some fresh air and exercise, and she had always refused to leave, even for a short walk. But this looked to be a good time for it. Mrs. Creedle's hired man wasn't due for a few days more, and even if he showed up early, Matilda would see any buggy or car that came down the road. She could be back in just over an hour, in plenty of time to have supper ready when her father woke. She thought about going for one of the Braswell or Owens girls to come sit at the shack while she was gone, but it would take her as long to get to their side of the farm as it would to get to Gertie's.

She quickly filled a basket with corncobs from one of the kindling barrels behind the shack. Gertie always welcomed a fresh supply. Dry cobs were the best kindling. They burned faster and hotter than twigs and got a stove going in no time. And there was something else

Matilda wanted to do. One more thing she needed to clear out of the shack before anyone came snooping around. She took an extra minute to slip behind her wall and snatch up her notebook.

In the months since her mother died, Matilda had filled the notebook with all the dangerous things she had otherwise held to herself: what she had seen at the well house and all of Frank's threats; what Ollie Riley had told the Porter boys over smokes in the woods; her walking in on Frank at the springhouse, Buddy Jones's watch in his hand; her father finding Buddy's handkerchief in the hidden compartment of the wagon. She had kept her sanity by keeping this record and, more than that, by telling herself that she would use it when the time was right. She would find a way. But now, she had to get it out of the shack.

The walk was as curative as one of Gertie's healing tonics. The chill of the previous days was gone, the early March sun declaring winter over. In one of the fields, a redbird courted a would-be mate. Matilda stopped to watch him swoop down to where his intended sat fluffing her feathers at the base of a tree and place a delicacy in her beak, like a kiss. So far, Matilda had missed out on kissing. She was seventeen now, and she would not deny being curious about kissing, and other things. Not that there were many suitable candidates on the few scattered farms on the Trace. She had planned on swearing off boys until she got to Cleveland, but she didn't think about Cleveland anymore. There was no need to. It might as well not exist.

At Gertie's cabin, the chair on the porch was upturned. She was away, probably tending one of her mothers. Just as well, Matilda thought. There would be time for her other errand. She emptied the basket of cobs into the kindling box on the porch and went around to the little lean-to where Gertie kept some tools. She borrowed a rusty spade and set out for the gully. Once there, she allowed herself a few moments in her favorite spot, the sky wide and blue above her, the rock cool and solid, the creek murmuring far below—all things she could count on. She sat there just long enough to pretend that she and her mother were there together as the sun crept lower in the sky and the shadows of the tall trees fell down the ravine. *And who's to say we aren't?*

Behind the buttonbush in the bank, Matilda hollowed out a snake hole with the spade. She rolled up her notebook and slid it into the hole, then sealed the opening with a plug of moss and dead leaves. Reluctant to leave just yet, she peered through the twiggy shrub, bare but for its first fisted buds, spring green with a rosy blush. There in the distance was the back of the shack, the garden that would not yield another harvest before they left the farm, if all went well. The back door that led to the room where her father and Teensy's longed-for baby slept inside. Matilda had been away for less than an hour, and suddenly she was longing to be back with them more than she had longed for the peacefulness of the gully. She stood up to start back, and as she did, she caught a glimpse of something moving in the yard. A faraway figure, a man, coming into view between the garden and the shack. Not her father. Shorter, and stouter. Not Mr. Braswell or Mr. Owens. Not Eugene. Her gaze traveled the path the man had taken, ending at a wagon parked on a rough, rarely used trail through the woods between the Trace and the farm. She knew the wagon, the mule. Her eyes flew back to the man. Virgil.

She was more angry than worried, certain that Virgil would not enter the shack, too afraid of Dalton's illness. She had known he would not be bold enough to go back down the farm road a second time against Old Man Creedle's orders. He had taken the old trail so he wouldn't be seen; that was clear. Intuition urged her to climb back up to the road and run home as fast as she could, but now she saw Virgil at the back wall of the shack, messing with the barrels there. Searching for liquor? If so, he would find the barrels filled with only corncobs and bundled cornstalks that Dalton stockpiled to stretch their firewood. She could not tear herself away as Virgil bent over something he held in front of him. Then in one quick instant, with a steep slope and a creek in one direction and two pastures and a cornfield in another between Matilda and her loved ones, flames rose from the kindling barrels and Virgil was moving off toward his wagon.

Matilda sprang off the rock, threw herself onto the sloping bank above her. She reached for a sapling to steady herself, and her hand closed around nothing. She was aware of losing her footing, of tumbling down the creek bank and rolling through brush and branches, of banging her knees and slitting her thigh on the way down, and then she was no longer aware of anything.

She came to at the bottom of the gully, not knowing how long she had been there. Creek water was rushing over an ankle swollen twice its normal size. Her skirt was drenched. She struggled to stand, squeezed her eyes shut against the pain as she tried her ankle. Then she heard a car passing on the road above and was glad for it, even if it brought the new man come early while the shack was still full of liquor. A car would arrive there long before she could. Someone would be there to help. To pull her sleeping sister and father out of the shack should fire take hold of the old wooden walls, which it almost surely would. Or had.

With no hope of climbing up the bank to the road, Matilda let her tears run freely as she hobbled along the creek through thicker brush and wild brambles, cursing Virgil Morgan and every Morgan that ever was and ever would be. She found a thick stick that wasn't much help, but she clung to it and splashed into the knee-deep water, the coldness soothing to her ankle. She waded into the current and followed the creek until it broke free of the brush and narrowed to the grassy stream that ran through a thicket of young pines. When she finally neared the edge of the thicket where she knew she would be able to see the shack, the shack was not there.

There was only fire. Orange flames raging from a mass of old lumber collapsed on the ground. Crackling and popping. Sparks flying. A wall of thick black smoke. The occasional sound of a mason jar or a brandy bottle exploding. The blackened brick chimney standing apart. Everything else gone. The porch. Teensy's swing. The tar-paper wall and Matilda's pallet. The crate and shuck bed. The cradle. She could not think beyond those objects.

Tut Owens was there, his shirt singed. He was bent over, his hands on his knees, Charles Braswell's hand on his shoulder.

She could make no sense of what she saw, could not form thoughts or remember how to propel herself forward.

Then Charles was shouting. "Go back! Get them out of here!"

He was yelling at his wife and their two girls running through the pasture toward the shack. "Nothing left but ashes," he shouted. "They're lost. All three of them. Didn't nobody get out."

Matilda could not move. She couldn't scream. Couldn't race the distance to the shack and fling herself into the fire so that she would not be left behind alone, the thing she wanted to do above all else once the meaning of Mr. Braswell's words settled into her head, her heart.

They're lost. All three of them. The words were a death knell ringing in her head. Her father was gone as surely as her mother was, as surely as there was no trace of sweet baby Annis's soul left in the smoldering remains of that miserable shack. Shock and grief. That was all there was.

And then she saw the car. The car she had heard from the gully. Saw the man standing beside it, away from the others, wearing creased pants and a white shirt and lighting a cigarette. Frank Bowers.

Up through the shock and grief that numbed her so that she seemed to have melded with the ground beneath her and the trees around her, a needle of fear pierced her consciousness. Frank's head was down as he cupped a hand around the match flame, but she could still feel his steely eyes on her in the springhouse the day before Curtis sent him away, those eyes that had drawn from her the truth that she knew what he had done.

No one knows you're alive. Frank thinks you were in the shack. The message came to her as if from a friend she had not met but knew to trust. It raised her to her feet, her hands gripping the stick for support. Instead of moving forward toward the fire and into the hands of Frank Bowers, she limped back into the woods and made her slow, painful way back to the gully. Then, grasping roots and branches and clawing at dirt, she pulled herself up the bank inch by inch until she reached the rock. She rested there. There she was bathed in a glorious sunset, the sky a sea of gilded orange waves, and she believed her mother had sent it, urging her forward, insisting that there would be beautiful things yet.

As darkness spilled into the gully, then overflowed it, swallowing the trees and the road and everything beyond, Matilda felt her way up the last few yards of the bank, and under the stars her mother had loved, her heart directed her to Gertie's front door.

31.

She dreamed there was a snake in the attic, then woke to the sound of Gertie's shuck mattress rustling beneath her. Gertie was wrapped in a blanket in her wooden rocker, keeping watch at the front window.

It all came back to her. Except she did not remember agreeing to take Gertie's bed.

"It's daylight," she mumbled, and Gertie turned.

"Sun's been up for hours. It's the tonic," Gertie told her.

Matilda did not remember drinking any tonic. She remembered clawing her way up the creek bank. And before that, wading in the creek. Mr. Owens bent over. Orange flames and black smoke. Frank's shirt so white it seemed to glow. *They're lost. All three of them.* She remembered.

Her ankle throbbed with pain, and the slit in her thigh burned. Both were wrapped tightly in rags, as were her knees, the rags there soaked with blood.

"They's something I need you to hear, soon as you can listen good. I gave you some other things last night, aside from the sleeping tonic. You hearing me clear?"

"Yes'm."

Gertie stood and dragged her rocker to the bed, then sat back down.

"Gertie." Everything Matilda could not form words to speak sounded in that one guttural moan, and Gertie heard it all. She held out her arms, and Matilda sat up and fell into them.

"The fire."

"I know. You told me last night."

"Did I tell you everything?" Matilda spoke into Gertie's lap and felt Gertie's answer rumble inside her.

"Everything."

"I should've been there. It was my fault. Did I tell you that?"

"A hundred times. And a hundred times you was wrong."

"It's too much. This is too hard."

"Seems that way. To me, too." Gertie stroked the back of Matilda's head. "But it always happens you get what you need, a little at a time. You get through an hour, then a day, then a week. Then you look back and it's been a year, and then more years, and good things found a way in, too. And in time, you see that them you lost are holding you up and moving you on. Helping you see the good. You ain't done with good things to come."

PART THREE
Ada and Matilda

32.

MATILDA

AUGUST 29, 1923

She hadn't meant to kill him.

Matilda lay awake on her bed of quilts in the hallway of Virgil Morgan's house and was unable to stop the flood of memories swirling in her head: her mother's death and her baby sister's birth; the fire that took her poppa and the baby and every last thing left to her; the sliding shut of the limestone slab over Virgil's body; Ada spread-eagle on her mattress here in this house and Gertie catching her baby. Matilda's naming that baby "Annis" and calling her that until, after only three days now, it hurt too much.

She had come unglued at Gertie's after the fire. That was the only way she could reconcile her being here in this place. Even now, after more than four months on the swamp with Ada, more than five since the fire, she was still trying to make sense of the choices she had made. More than anything, it had been the sameness—of the road in front of Gertie's cabin, of the trees along the gully, the baby cemetery, Gertie's healing hands—that had become intolerable. Ordinary life going on around her as if she were a boulder in a fast-moving stream, as if the tearing away of two innocent souls had left no mark on the earth. As if she deserved the singing of birds, the pattering of rain, the new sweetness in the air—nature insisting that spring had arrived.

She should have been at the shack when Virgil came round.

Those weeks at Gertie's were still foggy in her memory. She had been only vaguely aware of the danger in which she had put Gertie and Stella Mae, hiding in the cabin while those around them assumed she was dead, gone to the fire that had been blamed on the woodstove. Of Frank Bowers, she had told Gertie only that she knew something about him that was worth killing over, and Gertie had hidden her, had furthered the myth of her death in the fire. Matilda had not trusted herself in those dark days to judge what was safe to speak, to determine right from wrong or even what was real from what she might have imagined. Each morning Gertie reminded Stella Mae to keep the secret about Matilda's being there, about her being alive at all. It had been difficult to ask that of a child who understood so little, but Stella Mae promised with her whole heart to never tell a soul, and Matilda knew she never would, no matter what. That had frightened her as much as anything.

Other than Gertie and Stella Mae, the only person who'd known she was alive was Pastor Brown. Gertie had insisted on that one confidence. She was too old, she said, too close to heaven, to lie to the pastor. She told him that Matilda had reason enough for hiding out, and he took Gertie at her word and did not press for details. He requested of Frank that he be allowed to claim the remains of the Pattersons after the fire. He removed them himself, what little was left. Then he held a memorial service for all of them—Dalton, baby Annis, and Matilda.

At Gertie's, Matilda closed her mind to everything other than the void inside her. But Virgil Morgan would not let her rest. He kept her awake, setting fire to the corncob barrels behind the shack again and again, night after night, as she drifted in the dreamy state between sleep and wakefulness, between then and now. During daylight hours, he crouched in a corner of her mind with his match, waiting for the sun to go down, mocking her inability to stop him once it did. She stopped sleeping except in short snatches while the sun was up. During those times, Gertie kept vigil at the window or on the porch, ready to send her out the back door and into the woods if anyone approached the cabin.

As soon as her sprained ankle could hold her weight, even as it still pained her, Matilda began going out at night after Gertie and Stella Mae were asleep. Into the woods. Or to the gully. To the church to sit alone in the darkness, ready to refuse forgiveness if it were offered. Every night she punished herself for having taken that walk on the day of the fire, for each second she had sat on the rock in the gully enjoying being alone while Vigil made his way to the shack. She became reckless, climbing barefoot in the night-black gully with no regard for its dangerous inhabitants or the ease with which she might fall, as she had before.

Finally, one moonless night, she walked down the farm road, a ghost returning home. She went all the way to the Creedle house and slipped into the carriage house where the car in which Frank had arrived was parked. Word had come to Gertie that he had moved into

the house, planned to stay for a while. Matilda opened the car door
and slid onto the seat, daring Frank to find her there. Not caring if he
did. She thought of leaving something in the car to unsettle him, or
writing "B. J." in the dust on the hood. But Buddy Jones was not why
she had come.

She left the carriage house and walked along the road again in
darkness, crossed the stream on the board bridge, and walked on until
she knew to stop, where the porch had been. The charred rubble still
smelled of fire. Her feet knew the number of steps required to reach
the spot she wanted, and once there, she sat down. She filled her hands
with the ashes of what had been her father's bed. Then she lay down.
There on her father's funeral pyre, she smelled the smoke of the raging
fire. She felt the heat of the flames and opened her arms to them. She
put herself there, where she should have been, on the night of the fire.
She begged her father to call her to him, to not leave her here alone.
But she felt nothing of him in this miserable place. With a trembling
voice, she sang one of Teensy's hymns to Annis, who was no longer
constrained by time or place and might be comforted by it still. After
a while, she fell asleep there, and when she woke, there was a pain
in her side. Something hard pressing against her ribs. The ball-peen
hammer her father had kept under his bed. She put it in the pocket of
the cast-off britches Gertie had found for her in the swap pile and left
the Creedle farm for the last time.

After that, every nightly journey took her to the same destination,
the swamp on the other side of the Trace. She haunted the woods
behind the stilt house, having coaxed its location from Gertie, who
knew that dirt path way up in the swamp and thought Matilda had

in mind avoiding any encounter with Virgil. When she found the house, it was empty, the wagon and the mule absent. Several times over several nights, she went inside the house, shining lantern light on the disgusting evidence of the life Virgil led there. She supposed he had disappeared after setting the fire to distance himself from the act, but there were signs that he would be back. She returned every night, waiting.

A girl appeared at the house first. Ada. Matilda watched her for a few days, messed with her some with that pinecone. And when Virgil showed up, she watched him, too. Saw him come in and go out that day, saw Ada puke on the way to the outhouse, watched her tote her bedroll out to the shed. Matilda stayed in the woods that night, curled up with her hammer on a horse blanket she took from the pole barn, unable to leave, unable to advance, unable to sleep. Thinking only of bringing down biblical vengeance on Virgil Morgan, a vengeance she would never have found it within herself to carry out—she knew that now—had it not been set before her that night as the only good and right thing to do, as if divinely decreed that Virgil be hit with that hammer.

She had heard the cursing and the shouting, had seen Virgil cross the yard and open the door to the shed. She had crept up close to the back wall and leaned her head against the cool tin, listening to his ravings. When that devil lit the shed on fire and Ada screamed to high heaven, the hammer had come down on Virgil's skull before she realized she was standing behind him and had lifted it high over her head.

She had done it to save his daughter's life, a fact that brought her both redemption and defeat.

The instant he fell, all the boundaries that had seemed so blurred snapped into focus: she was a colored girl who knew two white men's secrets—Frank's and Virgil's—and she had just killed one of them. But the fire was catching hold and the girl was passed out in the shed and instead of allowing the sins of the father to be visited on the child, instead of racing back through the woods and across the Trace to Gertie's cabin, she had pulled Ada out of that shed and fought those flames as if they were the very flames that had taken her father and her baby sister, as if by beating them out she could change everything.

Afterward, the stilt house hidden away on the swamp had seemed like an answer from on high for all of them—herself, Gertie and Stella Mae, even Ada. Here, she could hide until Frank sold the farm and went away. Here, she would be close to Gertie. And she could not lose Gertie now. Here, secluded from the rest of the world, she could try to put herself back together.

Convincing Gertie had been difficult. Gertie had known since the night Matilda crawled to her door on her hands and knees that Virgil had set fire to the shack. Keeping up the pretense of Matilda's death had also meant telling no one what Matilda had witnessed from the gully that night, a bitter enough pill to swallow. But the idea of Matilda setting up house with Virgil's daughter, of trusting Ada to keep quiet about what had happened to her father, was unthinkable. In the end, Matilda suspected that only Gertie's calling and Ada's coming baby had given the old midwife any peace about the situation. They had agreed that it would be a temporary arrangement, just until Matilda could regain herself sufficiently to make a plan for getting away from the Trace and starting over somewhere safer, and that in the meantime,

Ada should be told nothing of Matilda's history with Virgil or her life on the Creedle farm.

Now she had passed months in this house, and she was still sleeping in this hallway, still bound to the Trace as if there was something she could do from only here that would grant her some relief from the rage and guilt and grief that consumed her and some kind of escape from the past that presented itself day after day as proof of how little control she had over anything. She had thought there might be some satisfaction in taking possession of Virgil's house and his land, his worldly goods, but there had been none. Just as no relief had come of bestowing upon his granddaughter the name of the baby whose life he had taken, so that Teensy's gift of a name lived on despite him, a rebuke every time anyone spoke it.

And yet, she remained here. Even with Frank Bowers still at the farm, still driving Dalton's wagon up and down the road in front of Gertie's cabin, as Gertie had told her. And still shipping liquor north, Matilda surmised. Maybe she had stayed *because* Frank was there. Because she held some grand notion that she might yet find a way to bring some measure of justice for Buddy Jones without raining down harm on the innocent. It all seemed so foolish now. There was no noble purpose for her here. Nothing grounding her to this place anymore. She belonged to the Trace in the way a child belongs to a callous parent. The Trace belonged to her because she had collected its dirt on the bottoms of her feet her whole life. Its birdsongs were the ones she knew, and the stars that had looked down on her and her mother when they sat on the porch of the shack were aligned in just that way only there.

But to really belong somewhere. Matilda had never known that. Gertie always maintained that she did not belong to this world at all, that her citizenship was in heaven. "In this world, but not of it," she declared of herself. "Like the Good Book says." But was it too much to ask of life that one be provided with a place that seemed to fit, where things were understandable and tolerable and maybe even more than that? Her mother had fashioned her own world of beauty and goodness, and her father had dreamed of carving out a satisfying place for himself here with his hands and his sweat. But without her family, Matilda wanted only to walk out of this world and into another one. Not at the end of her life, Gertie's hope, but in time to set a meaningful course for herself. If she did not do something soon, she would go crazy, if she hadn't already. She had to start thinking again about getting out.

She would write to Rainy. She would not ask if the Days could still take her in after all this time. For now, she just needed to remember that there was someplace other than this swamp, this Trace. Not Paris or Egypt or Palestine, but someplace where somebody she knew was living a different kind of life. She would write to Rainy, and maybe something would come of it.

A wail came from the other side of the wall, and Matilda fought the old instinct to scoop up a hungry baby, as she had done so often with her own Annis. But she lay still and listened to Ada soothe her newborn daughter.

33.

ADA

Nursing did not come easily for Ada. A few weeks after she gave birth, there were scabs on her nipples and traces of pink in her milk.

"Won't hurt her none. Just keep on feeding her," Gertie said when she came to check on them. "Don't let her fall asleep on the tit. That's the trouble. And some babies, you got to take a hand in the latching on. Like this here." She took Ada's breast in her hand and shoved it into Annis's open mouth, rolling her little lips back. By then, Ada was in such pain that she cried out when Annis latched on. "It'll get better," Gertie said, and as with most everything else, Gertie was right.

Because the baby's appetite was skimpy, Ada had to drain her breasts herself after each feeding, squeezing them between her hands to empty them and keep up her milk supply. When she wasn't working at breastfeeding, she was boiling the diapers Gertie brought. Boiling diapers and nursing Annis and squeezing her breasts dry. It was an endless, exhausting cycle.

Matilda took on extra chores, but as weeks passed, Ada noticed that Matilda avoided contact with the baby. She never laughed at Annis's silly faces or offered a finger for her to grab on to when Ada marveled at the strength of her grip. But Matilda knew things. She knew that babies cried after eating because they needed to be burped and that a second diaper folded into the crotch of another would last Annis through the night. That touching the dulled point of a safety pin to her scalp would oil it so that it slid more easily through a diaper. She knew to make a sugar-teat from a bit of rag tied with twine to quiet Annis between feedings.

"It's almost like you'd had a baby yourself, with all you know about," Ada said one late September afternoon as she stirred a thin stew made from a rabbit Matilda had caught. Annis was napping in her bushel basket on the table, her skinny arms slung over her head, her little potbelly rising and falling contentedly with each breath. Ada had expected to be first in this one area, assuming a mothering instinct to be a natural consequence of childbirth, but in motherhood, too, she found herself looking to Matilda for guidance.

"I never was a trapper's daughter, and I skinned the rabbit in that pot." Matilda was sharpening one of Virgil's knives at the table. She spat on the whetstone and scraped the knife over it, up, then down, flipping the blade with each stroke and keeping up a steady, musical rasp.

"What's that got to do with babies?"

"Maybe it's got more to do with why you don't know how to skin a rabbit."

"I never was showed how."

"I never was either."

Ada was surprised. Matilda had skinned countless rabbits and squirrels in the past months. "How'd you learn to do it?"

"By doing it. Because it had to be done. Maybe you ought to take a turn doing some of the things you think I just know about."

Ada thought back to the day Virgil had brought home a muskrat and handed her a knife, made her slice around its back feet, around its neck and tail, then hold on tight as he peeled the skin away in one piece, like stripping off long underwear.

"You been doing all the hard stuff," she said. "I'm sorry."

"Sorry don't put a rabbit in the pot," Matilda said, but there was no bitterness in her words, and Ada was grateful for that.

Matilda tested the edge of the blade against her thumb, then left for the shed. She was spending more and more time there, and Ada worried that maybe a new baby was turning out to be more than Matilda had bargained for. Because Matilda knew so much that Ada did not, Ada sometimes forgot that Matilda was only a year older.

She put the lid on the pot, checked to make sure that Annis was sleeping soundly, then took an empty basket out to the clothesline. As she worked her way down a row of dried-stiff diapers, unpinning them and dropping them into the basket, she heard sounds coming from the shed. Curious, she left a diaper hanging by one pin and moved toward the sounds. She had not tried to eavesdrop since the day Matilda left the two-headed otter in her listening place, but now she crept close to the back wall again, taking care to make no sound and leave no footprints. She leaned in without touching the tin and listened. Scraping. Scratching. The clink of tools. The pounding of a hammer. Sounds so reminiscent of Virgil with his traps and fleshers and mounting boards that for a moment Ada lost her place in time. She saw her father's image bent over his worktable as if she could see through the thin sheet of tin. The familiar tremble revisited her hands, and she felt the creeping paralysis of her old leaden resignation. Her father still had a hold on her. He would have liked knowing that. Maybe he did know it. Maybe he was watching her from wherever he was. Making those sounds in the shed. Maybe they were sounds only she could hear.

She stumbled back to the clothesline and tried to talk sense to herself, as she had done so often as a child. Her father was not in the shed. He was not in the bedroom sleeping off his liquor, as she sometimes caught herself imagining. He was not in the woods hunting or away selling pelts. He was gone, dead, rotting in that Confederate tomb, and the sounds from the shed were new ones. She shook him off as best she could, rubbing the coarse fabric of a diaper between her fingers to bring herself back to what was real and true. She had a child to take care of now, and she would not raise her to be afraid.

She left the basket in the grass and strode back to the house, went inside, and crossed the hall to the bedroom with purpose. The hinges squeaked as she swung open the long-closed door, another old disquieting sound that raised a dusty sense of dread. She sent herself into the room to confront her father at last, opened the window to banish any wisp of him that remained. Standing at the foot of the bed, she spoke her mother's name aloud, a ward against her own fears, reminding herself that Sylvie, too, had once inhabited this room. She left the door open and went to the kitchen for a pail of water and a brush. Then she returned to the bedroom and began scrubbing the tobacco juice stains from the walls as if erasing her father from her memory.

That evening the air was thick and humid, low clouds hoarding what might have been a welcome, cleansing rain. Ada and Matilda sat on the porch listening to the sounds of the swamp, Annis at Ada's breast.

"The chicks are big as the hens, now," Ada said, looking to start a line of talk that might somehow end up at what it was that Matilda was doing every day in the shed.

"I'm thinking on breaking down the woodbin, using the boards to nail up a better coop," Matilda said.

"That old woodbin's falling down anyways. We haven't used it in years."

"'We?' You ain't forgot he's dead, have you?"

"I mean *he* stopped using it years back," Ada corrected herself. "But sometimes I do forget. Sometimes I think I see him coming around the barn. One time, I could've swore I heard him snoring in his room when I woke up in the night."

Matilda propped her bare feet on the porch railing and tipped her spindly chair onto its two back legs.

"And sometimes I think I hear him in the shed, working with his tools." There. She'd laid that out. Opened up a place for Matilda to laugh at her and her ghosts and tell her she was crazy. Tell her what she was working on out in the shed with those tools, the door latched.

"There's people that say spirits come back around to where they spent their last minutes," Matilda said. "Especially when they've been killed off sudden. I don't believe it, but there's people that do."

Ada's mother had sworn she saw the ghost of her dead grandmother floating over the swamp late one evening. "Mawmaw, clear as day," she'd told Ada. "It was like she was trying to get to me."

Ada looked out over the swamp and wished she could find her mother there among the bald cypresses and the tupelo trees. She wished, too, that Matilda would talk to her in the way she imagined that friends talked to each other, openly and warmly, taking comfort in one another. Asking questions and getting answers instead of casting a line and hoping for a nibble, reeling it back in empty time after time.

Annis was asleep. Ada slid her finger into her little mouth to break the suction the way Matilda had taught her, then took her inside and put her down for the night.

When Matilda came in, she glanced at the open bedroom door. If she had asked about it, Ada would have told her what she had done and how it had made her feel. Stronger and more hopeful. But Matilda simply entered the bedroom and lowered the window against the coming rain.

Matilda missed supper the next evening, doing whatever she was doing out in the shed. It worried Ada, but it annoyed her, too. She did not fill a plate and leave it on the stove, but just put the food away. Then she readied Annis for bed and tucked her into her bushel basket next to Ada's own bed. Sitting by the window in the late light, she took up one of her mother's ruined magazines and paged through it for something she could read without a struggle. Reading had been put aside along with everything else she had lost when she stopped going to school. Finally, Matilda came in, nudging the screen door open with her foot and wrestling something big and heavy through the doorway. She set down her burden in the center of the room.

Ada stood up. "Where on earth…"

A cradle. Freshly painted a clean, crisp white and sturdy on four carved legs.

"Who brung this?" Ada knelt beside it and caressed the wood, smooth as glass. "It must have cost dear."

"Cost old Virgil his toolbox. And a nest of mice that old armchair rotting away out in the shed," Matilda said.

Ada could hardly believe it—that Matilda could have made such a thing, and that she *would* have.

"Unscrewed the hinges on the toolbox and took off the lid. Sanded it down past all the grease and splinters. The sanding was the worst of it. Sawed the legs off that old chair."

For the first time since she met her, Ada thought Matilda seemed as young as she really was, standing there proud of herself and looking to be told she had done a good job.

"It's beautiful. I never thought I'd ever have something like this."

"Every baby ought to have something decent to sleep in," Matilda said. "Not a bushel basket or a cardboard suitcase."

Ada woke Annis taking her out of the basket. She handed her over to Matilda, who took the baby in her arms and did not seem to mind having her there. Ada's heart sang. Annis fussed as Ada removed the square of wool cloth she had cut off the bottom of her own blanket, the worn-soft dish towels serving as tiny sheets, and the cotton-stuffed sack she had sewn up as padding. She transferred everything to the cradle. Matilda laid Annis gently inside, and the baby nestled herself in and instantly went back to sleep.

The girls looked at each other the way Ada imagined that real friends would. She felt as if she had finally reached the end of a long and treacherous bridge she had so hoped to cross.

34.
MATILDA

The shed was stuffy, the air faintly putrid, but privacy was worth some discomfort. Matilda latched the door. This was the most space she had ever had to herself. Once she had cleared it of Virgil's hideous paraphernalia, she found that being here in the place where he met his end at her own hand brought her an admittedly morbid sense of peace, something beyond, something higher than revenge. And Ada hated the shed. She had vowed never to step foot in it as long as she lived, which was an added advantage, especially when Matilda's grief overcame her and she came here to cry.

Morning light streamed onto the worktable from one of the high windows. She had stripped the burlap from the openings and covered them instead with wire screening. There was light enough that even with the door closed, she did not need the lantern. From a hiding place behind the deer sled—something else Ada was not likely to go near—Matilda took a pencil and one of the tablets Pastor Brown had sent to her. The pastor had trusted his eldest son, Byron, to meet her in the woods on the back trail several times during her first weeks in

the stilt house, to bring her things she and Ada needed and to take
away whatever Matilda sent back with him as donations to the swap
pile behind the church, Matilda's tithes and Virgil's involuntary offerings, as Matilda saw it. It was Byron who had traded the mule and
the wagon for her in the middle of a dark night, while she hid in the
pastor's barn.

"A time to every purpose under heaven" was what Pastor Brown
had told Byron with regard to misleading the community about
Matilda's supposed death. And Byron, training to be a preacher himself, had fallen back on the same reasoning when he found a buyer
for Virgil's liquor and his beaver pelts without telling his father. He'd
brought the proceeds back to Matilda, and she and Ada had hidden
the money in a cracker tin behind the stove along with the money
pouch they had taken from Virgil's pocket.

Now Matilda slid the tablet into the block of sunlight on the
worktable. She held her pencil over the blank page and felt the weight
of all that was impossible to put down in a letter. What could she write
to Rainy about her life since Teensy's death? What could she convey in
words that she could bear to form on the paper in front of her, words
that would be safe to send to the post office in town?

She wrote that she had moved. That unexpected things had happened and she had gone to live with a friend. She did not ask if she
could still join them in Cleveland, if there might still be a job for her
there. She did not write of the fire. Instead, she wrote about how hot
the past summer had been and that October wasn't looking to be much
cooler, that the tomato plants were still yielding in the garden and that
the water was high in the river. She wrote about the chicks that had

grown into hens. She filled an entire page with nothing. She did not mention the name of a single person. She put down no identifiable details regarding people or places. She wrote until she was fed up with writing around everything that was dangerous, of choosing safe words and arranging them in safe sentences, and then she put down the pencil.

She got up and paced the packed dirt floor, back and forth across the spot where Virgil's dead body had lain. Again, she asked herself what she was doing there. What crazed thinking had led her to the swamp? She was sick of hiding, sick of being careful, sick of pretending to be dead and sometimes wishing she were. Sick of keeping secrets for evil men.

She went back to the tablet and turned to a fresh page. In tiny print, she began again. She wrote about a man and his wife standing in front of a telegraph office, heads together reading their news, a cheery plaid handkerchief peeking from the man's shirt pocket. She described them as they had appeared that day, down to the color of the woman's only pair of shoes and the frayed brim of the man's hat. She wrote of the quiet determination in the husband's face as he stood on the sidewalk shielding his wife while trying to appease an arrogant, red-faced man twice his size. How the heels of his shoes hung off the sidewalk as he made more than enough way for a whole troop of such arrogant men to pass by. She bore witness to the sneers and snickers from the men gathered in front of the post office and to the fear in the young wife's eyes, the good news of her telegram forgotten.

The pencil in Matilda's hand was weightless now, words flying across the page. And then she was no longer writing to Rainy, she was just writing. About how time had seemed to slow as the big man's elbow slammed into the husband's jaw and how activity on the street seemed to freeze in place as he fell backward into the muddy road. That his mouth had filled with blood and his jaw had hung too low, unhinged, the angle wrong. Of the pain he must have felt as he wiped bloody drool from his chin with the handkerchief, and perhaps the greater pain, while hobbling down the road holding and being held by his wife, of not being able to defend his wife's dignity or his own. Of walking away uncertain of whether or not they would reach their home alive and what new horrors might still come of that simple trip to the telegraph office.

She stopped short of relating the rest of Buddy Jones's story. But setting loose even this small part of it had freed something inside her, had cleansed her somehow, like the cupping of bad blood. She did not care if Rainy thought she had lost her mind. For the first time since the shack fire, she thought she might actually be regaining it.

From one of Virgil's shelves, she took a box of peppermint candies that Byron had brought to her one day. She had kept them to herself because of the sweet look on his face as he gave them to her, hinting at something more than charity. She tore the page from the tablet and folded it in half, then in half again, over and over until it was the size of one of the peppermint squares. Then she unwrapped one of the candies and replaced it with the folded paper, retwisting the ends of the wrapper so that it looked exactly like the others before planting it among them. Turning back to her first letter, the one that had said so little, she signed it "Mary Potts," the secret name she and Rainy had used when leaving private notes for each other when they were young. Rainy would remember. She would understand and not write Matilda's name on a reply.

Under the name, she wrote that a return letter should be addressed in care of Miss Ada Morgan, to be held at the Bristol post office. With a brown paper sack hurriedly emptied of a handful of nails, she wrapped up the letter and the candy box, tied the package with a length of string, and addressed it to Rainy at her old address in Cleveland, hoping she still lived there after so much time had gone by. It would have to be taken to the post office, but for the time being, Matilda hid it behind the sled with the tablets and pencils. Byron would mail it for her, she knew, if she sent word to him through Gertie, but she would not ask him to do that. He had taken chances enough on her behalf. She would find another way.

35.

ADA

"She's awful little for such a long ride," Ada said, Annis asleep against her chest in the baby sling Gertie had brought. All that could be seen of Annis was a scruffy tuft of honey-gold hair peeking out of the sling. Matilda had wound it around Ada, tied it at one hip, and all but dragged her out to the wagon that was already hitched and waiting, the sun scarcely up.

"It ain't that far to Bristol. Just seems like it because it's so wild out here. Once you get off the Trace, you're almost there."

"But she's just two months, yesterday."

"I've seen babies half that old drug down a row of cotton on a pick sack. She ain't gonna break. And we're out of flour and meal. And lard."

Ada sighed. She picked nervously at a fingernail. "But I never drove the wagon anywhere but up and down the back trail with you. I don't know if I can do it."

"We been through that. You got that wrap, so you can nurse her while you ride. And her basket's in the back." Matilda patted Annis's bottom, a rare show of affection that Ada noted right off. She almost wanted to make the trip just to encourage that.

"What if something happens with the wagon? I won't know what to do."

"Ain't nothing going to happen. People ride to town all the time. I checked everything over yesterday—the wheels, the traces. Just stay out of holes and give the mule a drink when you get there. Like I told you."

"I wish I could leave her here with you, but she's got to nurse." Ada reached down into her blouse beneath the sling and adjusted the rags bound over her nipples to absorb any leakage, amazed, still, at how heavy and full her breasts had become. "And Lord knows I couldn't go long without some relief, anyway."

Matilda settled a basket of eggs into a nest of straw in the wagon, then handed Ada Virgil's old money pouch with eight silver quarters inside. "With what you get for the eggs, that ought to be enough for what we need. You got the list."

"What if nobody wants the eggs?" Or what if she couldn't bring herself to ask at the store or the feed-and-seed if anyone could see fit to buy her eggs.

"They're always wanting eggs in town. Won't be any trouble. Just walk in with the basket, and don't let them short you."

"You'd be better, taking them in. And driving the wagon."

"We been through that, too."

But they hadn't, really. Some time back, Ada had realized that rather than the two of them "laying low," Matilda was hiding out. From what, or whom, she wasn't sure. One day, out of the blue, Matilda had revised their practiced story. Now, if anyone ever came around asking questions,

Matilda would hide in the woods and Ada would make no mention of her at all. But no one had ever shown up. Virgil had been dead since spring, and here it was halfway through fall. Since the day she'd heard Matilda and Gertie whispering about nobody but the pastor knowing whatever secret was between them, Ada had believed that Matilda had reasons other than Virgil's death for being here on the swamp.

With Annis wrapped up against her like a second skin, wearing the diaper cover Ada had made from her mother's old oilcloth, she reluctantly climbed into the wagon. Unseating the brake brought on a rush of anxiety, but she could not deny that there was excitement, too, and some of the same resolve she had felt when scrubbing down the bedroom walls.

"Oh, and I got this I need you to mail." Matilda held up a small package wrapped in brown paper and tied with string. "Best if you go to the post office first. Won't cost much to send it."

Ada took the package and glanced at it. *Miss Lorraine Day, 13 Pency Street, Cleveland, Ohio.* She could not imagine knowing someone in Cleveland, Ohio.

"What is it?"

"It's some peppermint candy."

Ada wondered where on earth Matilda had gotten peppermints, but she asked a more important question.

"Who's it going to?"

"Just somebody that moved away from the Trace a long time ago. Somebody that loves peppermints. Somebody Gertie knows."

Three answers that told Ada nothing. She took up the reins and squeaked out a hopeful "Giddup!" To her surprise, the mule obeyed.

Ada fished one of Virgil's quarters from the pouch and set it on the counter next to Matilda's package. She shook her head when the clerk asked if she wanted him to check for mail. No one had ever sent her a letter, and until today she had never posted any mail. But she had driven herself into town with no trouble, proof that anything was possible.

Back on the sidewalk, she asked a woman walking past where she might sell her eggs. When the woman offered to buy them herself, Ada gratefully handed them over and took what she offered with no discussion. In front of the dry goods store, Annis started fussing, demanding a feeding though Ada had nursed her twice on the ride in. Ada struggled with her as she squirmed and twisted, drawing sympathetic glances from a young woman holding on to a rowdy little boy, and some that were not so sympathetic from a clutch of older women who had watched Ada ride into town. She saw herself through their eyes, young to be strapped to a baby, arriving alone in an ancient farm wagon hitched to a slump-backed mule, her husbandless situation on display. And now Annis was crying, and Ada felt more eyes on them. She'd been headed for the grocer's, but she pushed open the door to the dry goods store and escaped inside.

A friendly middle-aged woman with artificially orange hair and a bright and booming voice introduced herself. "Flora Rankin," she shouted over Annis's howls.

Ada apologized and Annis squirmed and Flora walked around the counter and lifted Annis right out of the sling.

"You are nothing but gorgeous, little lady." She tickled Annis's chin, and a perfect little smile blossomed on the baby's tearstained face. "There's a room in the back where you can feed her, if you're needing some privacy."

"I'd be obliged," Ada said, and a moment later she was sitting in a small room hung with cheerful pictures made of fabric scraps, scenes of galloping horses and children playing and houses with fluffy cotton smoke twirling from the chimneys. Ada thought she could live the rest of her life in that one little room and be happy.

"Those pictures in there," she said when she was done. "They're real nice."

"My idea of sewing. But ask me to make a dress that might come close to fitting somebody, and I'm hopeless."

"My mother sewed," Ada said shyly. "She could copy anything out of a catalog. She started teaching me soon as I could hold a needle. We sewed everything we wore. That was before she died."

The woman looked at her so kindly that Ada thought she might cry, so she kept talking. "She died way back. When I was a little girl. Not too little. Nine."

"I see. I'm sorry about that."

Ada bit her cheek to keep the tears back. She had no defenses against anyone's being soft with her. When she trusted herself to speak again, she said, "But I couldn't never have made anything like them pictures back there." She rocked Annis in her arms and went to stand in front of a sleek black sewing machine on a wooden table.

"Just got that in last week," Flora said.

"I never saw one like this. My mother had a sewing machine once.

It was real old. Rusty and all. But it worked. She let me run paper through it to learn how to stitch a straight line. I couldn't reach the treadle, so she'd pump it for me. Later on, when I really could sew, she tied a box to the treadle so I could reach it and work it myself."

"You don't have it anymore? That machine? People still buy the old ones, even if they don't work."

"No. I just sew by hand now."

Flora smiled. "Do you live in town?"

Ada shook her head.

"Close by?"

"Not too far," Ada said. "But out on the Trace."

After an intent look that seemed to tell her everything she needed to know, Flora asked, "Is there something I can help you find here?"

Ada looked around for something small and inexpensive, embarrassed to walk out without buying anything.

"Just a minute," Flora said, "I have the perfect thing for that little beauty of yours." She made her way between two long rows of fabric bolts to the remnants table, then returned with a folded-up square of soft, spring green cloth. "Now wouldn't this look pretty on her?" She held it next to Annis.

"I couldn't... I don't know that I have enough money for—"

"Oh, this is just a scrap. Not enough that anybody'd buy it. Just right for a little dress for this one. You take it, and I'll expect to see what you make from it the next time you come in."

Ada bit the inside of her cheek so hard she tasted blood, and then she said, "That's very kind."

"If you saw all the scraps I've got in the back..." Flora wrapped up the remnant in white paper, and Ada saw her tuck in a spool of green thread and a packet of buttons. "Dressing up babies is such fun. You know, my own little boy came along when I was about the same age you are. You should see him now. Six feet tall and got one of his own on the way. Wasn't easy, raising him by myself. I never married."

"Oh?" Ada couldn't look her in the eye. She smoothed down Annis's unruly hair and watched it spring back up.

"No. But it worked out. Who would have ever thought I'd run my own store someday? I guess I had to show everybody what I was made of."

"This is your store? Yours, by yourself?"

"It's a long story, how that happened. But yes, it's mine."

Before leaving, Ada made another trip to the back room to change Annis's diaper. Then Flora helped her get Annis back into the wrap.

"You come back soon and show me that new outfit."

"I will. And thank you again."

Ada left the dry goods store with her head higher. She made her purchases at the grocer's and climbed back into the wagon. On the ride home, she held the reins with more confidence, maneuvered around holes in the road with increasing ease, smiled at the autumn leaves raining down from the trees and dancing across the road in the wind. She would have liked to dance with them.

Ada turned Annis's new dress inside out and admired the rows of tiny, straight stitches, the blind hem, the button loops, her work as neat as her mother's had always been. She took the iron off the stove and ran the tip of it up the side seams, pressed them flat. It was a beautiful dress with a sweet little smocked bodice. She had separated the twisted strands of a length of Virgil's twine and used them to embroider a ring of daises around the neckline. Making something meant to be beautiful rather than simply useful took her back to the days when she and her mother had made clothes for Ada's doll, detaching bits of lace and ribbons, buttons, and hooks from old clothes in the rag bag and turning scraps of cloth into miniature versions of fashions in the magazines that Virgil brought home when he wanted to feel like the sole source of any happiness in her mother's life. As young as she was, Ada had soaked up her mother's lessons, mastering knife pleats and buttonholes and delicate embroidery. They sewed while Virgil was away so he would not see how much happiness they took from it.

One day he came in earlier than expected and caught Sylvie pinning up a hem on a dress she'd made for Ada from an old petticoat. "That's a awful fancy getup for a swamp rat," he said. "Wasting time on foolishness."

"I'm teaching her sewing. I can use extra hands, the way you go through shirts," Sylvie said, making it all about Virgil, which set well with him. So well that the next time he took a trip to Canton, he brought home a sewing machine, an ancient thing, dented and dirty, the cast-iron legs rusting, but it was a wonder to Sylvie. Ada saw her mother clap her hands and actually throw her arms around Virgil's neck, neither of which she had seen before.

"I figure that ourt to speed up the shirt-making some, leave more time for chores," Virgil said, and Sylvie promised to make him the best shirts he ever saw, as soon as she had some material. Material appeared after the next trip to town. Virgil made sure he let Sylvie know that he had scrimped on liquor to buy it, and Sylvie nodded acknowledgment of the sacrifice. She sent Ada out to the barn with a sack full of black walnuts and a hammer. "You work on shelling these here," she told her, shooing her out the door, "and don't come back inside till you see the back door open." Her father already had his shirt off in the middle of the day, and Ada knew her mother was about to pay for the sewing machine and material in some way that she did not want to spend any time wondering about.

That sewing machine was a joy, as long as it lasted. Ada and her mother spent hours together over it, turning out beautiful things from flour sacks and feed bags. Ada made her first dress when she was only seven, running up the seams in no time on that old machine. She loved the rhythmic movement as she worked the treadle with her feet on top of the box, the feel of the thread sliding through her fingers. The machine sat on its own little wooden table, and Sylvie polished the wood and oiled and sanded the rusted iron legs so that they gleamed like new. It was a sight to behold, sitting under the window for light while they worked. When she wasn't using it, Sylvie kept it covered with a soft, white tent she made special for it from a worn-out sheet.

Sylvie made a silly hat for Ada, all decked out in bows and tassels, and they took turns wearing it while they did their chores, making each other laugh, tying it onto the mule's head while they mucked out the barn, hanging it on the outhouse door to show that it was occupied. Virgil came in one afternoon while Ada was tossing balls of darned socks into the hat from across the room, her mother egging her on. Sylvie looked up from the sewing machine, her face full of delight over whatever she was sewing, which, as Ada would later remember, was not a shirt for her father.

"I see there ain't no supper on the stove," Virgil said, and Ada snatched up the hat and stuffed it into the rag bag.

"I ain't started it just yet. I'll get to it now. I got so caught up in sewing I lost track of time," Sylvie said. Not checking herself, Ada thought, as if her mother didn't know what he was like and wasn't taking the proper precautions about the things that were important to her.

The next morning, Ada woke to her father's raised voice from behind the bedroom door. He was shouting something about her mother coddling Ada too much, sewing her fancy clothes and putting foolish notions in her head. "You ain't doing that gal any favors dressing her up and frittering away time."

Ada slid out of bed and opened the chest she kept her clothes in. She found her oldest, most battered dress and quickly slipped it on. Her father's voice grew louder.

"Ain't nobody but me ever tried to teach her how to make herself useful around here. Carry her weight."

"She's only eight years old." Her mother softly speaking up for her broke Ada's heart.

"And good for nothing but dressing up the damn mule."

There was the sound of something slamming against the wall, then her mother's quavering voice. "Virgil, calm down."

Virgil thundered a response. "You been doing nothing but wasting time and money dressing you and her both up like dolls, and you telling me to calm down? I never should have brought that thing to the house."

And right then, Ada knew what he was going to do.

He stormed out of the bedroom and straight for the sewing machine, Sylvie following him.

"Virgil, please don't take it," Sylvie whispered like she was saying a prayer. With every movement he made—snatching off the cover, pulling out the drawers and dumping the contents, manhandling the machine until he had his arm locked around it tight enough to drag it across the floor, table and all—Sylvie begged, "Please." She got between him and the screen door and said she'd do anything if he would just put it down, but he stuck out his leg and shoved her out of the way, pushed open the door.

There was a mournful silence in the house the rest of that day. When Virgil wasn't in the shed, he sat on the porch keeping vigil over the liquor bottles at his feet, and Ada and Sylvie found work inside.

After an uneasy night, Ada rose before full light. She looked out the back door and saw that the wagon was gone, so she felt safe going to the bedroom to look for her mother. Sylvie was not there. She wasn't in the house. She wasn't in the yard. Ada braved her fear of the shed to check there for the sewing machine, thinking that maybe her father had hidden it so he could bring it back out again later when her mother had learned a lesson about wasting time and money and telling him to calm down. But it wasn't there. Nor was her mother.

Ada found her, still in her nightgown, sitting on the edge of the ditch that ran along one end of the canebrake. Ada walked over to her, stood behind her, and peered down into the ditch, knowing what she would see. It was wrecked, busted apart with some tool of her father's—the splendid machine hacked up, the wood table split in two, the little inside parts scattered in the ditch like jewels. Sylvie looked over her shoulder and saw Ada there. Silently, she stood up and took Ada's hand, and the two of them walked back to the house.

That image of her mother sitting in the dirt in her nightgown as if by the newly dug grave of a loved one was one of only a few that Ada could bring up clear and sharp. Most of her memories of Sylvie were blurred and faded, like chalk drawings on a slate carried too long under a child's arm. But she did remember, exactly, the joy in her mother's face when she sewed on that old machine, and sewing this new dress for Annis, with its fine embroidery and neat seams, brought Sylvie back to her. When the time came, she would teach Annis to sew, and she would tell her about her beautiful grandmother and pass on the things Sylvie had taught her. And she would teach Annis other things, things that Ada had yet to learn, things her own mother never had an opportunity to know.

Two weeks later, Matilda started pressing Ada to ride into town again. In case Gertie's friend had written a thank-you for the peppermints, she said. This time Ada did not mind making the trip. She was eager to show Flora the dress she'd made and to thank her again. She folded it up in Flora's white paper, took the coins Matilda gave her for the few things they needed most from town, and set out again.

"Beautiful work. Just beautiful." Flora Rankin turned over the hem of Annis's new dress, then ran a finger over the embroidered daisies. She praised the fine stitching, the clever design. "It's as pretty as any I've seen. And you did it all by hand."

"Same as you do with your pictures," Ada said. "It's no better'n that."

Flora held out her arms for Annis, almost asleep on Ada's shoulder, and Ada handed her over. "I have a proposition for you," Flora said, and Ada nodded as if she knew what *proposition* meant.

36.
MATILDA

"Flora Rankin says she'll take everything I can make out of all this, fifty cents apiece." Matilda watched Ada dump out a bag of fabric remnants— silk, satin, crepe, organdy, and everyday broadcloth—and leftover lengths of lace and braid and ribbon, tiny bows, and spools of thread onto the table. "She's planning on putting them in the store and selling them."

"Rankin's Dry Goods?"

"Yes. I can't hardly believe it."

Matilda had trouble believing it herself. She thought about how much cotton she'd have to chop to earn fifty cents.

"I don't know what to start with. They're all so beautiful, aren't they? And that's not all," Ada said, looking coy.

Like she wants me to play a blame guessing game.

"Come see," Ada said. They left Annis playing on a quilt on the floor and went out to where the mule was still hitched to the wagon, wet with sweat.

"It's not mine," Ada said. "Flora's just lending it to me. And it's pretty old. But just look!"

Matilda looked. Sitting in the back of the wagon, tied to the rails with rope, was a sewing machine. A big old-fashioned sewing machine with a cast-iron treadle.

They got it out of the wagon and up the steps the same way they had maneuvered Virgil's body, with a board ramp and the deer sled and some rope. The process was more laborious this time. They had to drag the machine up all the steps to the porch, Ada pulling as Matilda pushed. It called to mind their night at the tomb, and Matilda took care not to catch Ada's eye and let the memory drift between them. After an hour, the sewing machine sat in front of the window in the bedroom. It would require the filing away of a good deal of rust, and a liberal oiling, but it worked.

Matilda put up with Ada's fawning over it as if it were a living, breathing thing, listened to her go on about all the baby clothes she was going to sew and how she might be able to make enough money to see them through the winter easier, and only when Ada finally stopped for a good breath did Matilda ask, "Any mail come?"

"Oh, I forgot." Ada produced two envelopes from inside the sling on the table and handed them to Matilda. "From Cleveland, so I didn't open them. Not that anybody'd be mailing me anything from anywhere."

Matilda opened the envelope with the older postmark first, out in the shed with the door latched. It was two pages long. The Days were still at the same address, Rainy wrote, though instead of having the

top floor of the house to themselves—four rooms—the six of them
were now squeezed into two downstairs bedrooms with a view of the
moldy brick wall across the alley. Rainy still had her laundry business,
but she'd had to start offering home delivery to keep it going, rather
than her previous drop-off and pickup arrangement. Jobs were scarce.
Nearly all the factory work that had opened up for colored folks during
the Great War had gone back to white workers now. Everyone Rainy
knew who took in laundry was delivering now, and cutting prices, neither of which was sitting well with the white laundry owners. But they
were all doing well enough, the Days. All still glad to be there. Rainy
was working day and night. She was sorry she'd had too little time to
write, but would try to keep up now. She asked after Matilda's father
and the baby, without naming names. Asked if they were still at the
"old place." Matilda could read the concern in her friend's questions.
There was no mention of the message Matilda had hidden inside the
box of peppermints.

Next, she opened the second envelope and unfolded a single sheet
of paper. *The candy!* it began, and Matilda's heart skipped a beat. In
guarded language, Rainy wrote that she had "shared" a piece of candy
with her mother's uncle. *He loved it!* He loved it so much, she wrote,
that he wanted more. He would be sending Matilda a gift to thank her.
She should watch for it to arrive soon.

Rainy's mother's uncle. The uncle who ran the newspaper. He
had read her account of what happened to Buddy and Cassie Jones
in town, and he had "loved" it. Matilda felt as if she had been invisible all this time on the swamp and someone had finally seen her,
acknowledged that she was still here in the world, still living, not just

being. She hid the letters in a new secret spot and hurried back to the house, already working on how she could get Ada back to Bristol as soon as possible.

37.

ADA

Ada learned to use the sewing machine as if she were born to it. Sewing brought her the same joy she had seen on her mother's face, but more than that, it gave her hope. It was a skill. A way to contribute to their upkeep now, and maybe a way out of the swamp someday. She held in her mind an image of Flora Rankin running her own store and sewed toward some possibility that had not yet taken firm shape. All the while, Matilda pressed her to work faster, to get the batch of clothes to Flora as quickly as she could manage.

"You need to show her what you can do," Matilda said, and Ada's fingers flew, as much to prove herself to Matilda as to Flora.

Matilda finally seemed to be warming to Annis, and Annis to her. If Ada had not been longing for just that since Annis's birth, she supposed she might have been jealous as Matilda repeatedly took the baby from her so she could sew. But as it was, she was more content than she had ever been. Things were changing among them all, Ada thought, smiling to herself as she pulled a basting thread in a little puff sleeve.

At the end of six days, Ada had finished four showy dresses, a nightgown with a drawstring bottom, and two bonnets. A fifth little dress was in her lap as she blindstitched the hem, and another was still in pieces, pinned to a newspaper pattern.

"I never saw such," Gertie told her when she came by that afternoon, Job having fetched her to check on Irene down the road. "Not even in that there," she said, pointing to what was left of the old Sears catalog. She dropped a bundle of worn diapers onto a chair and picked up one of the little dresses. "Mighty good work."

"I didn't really know what I was doing, but it turned out okay, I think."

"Better'n okay. You got a gift, girl."

Ada basked in the praise. If Matilda was beginning to feel like a sister, Gertie was the grandmother in Ada's imaginary scenario.

Ada finished the last dress on the ninth day, a sweet little blue cotton smock trimmed with eyelet lace threaded with ribbon. Like something out of one of her mother's fairy stories, she thought. She would make one like it for Annis someday.

The next morning, after an early breakfast, Matilda hitched up the mule.

Ada was reluctant about riding to town. "I told Flora it'd be two weeks, at least. She might think I'm being greedy, looking to get paid sooner than we planned on."

"People in town'll be fighting over these clothes. They'll be standing in line to pay Flora Rankin way more than she's paying you. She'll be glad to get them."

Matilda seemed so excited that Ada let her wind the sling up tight, settle Annis into it, and hustle her out the door.

"Once she's eating real food, I can leave her home with you," Ada said. "She's getting heavy."

"A few weeks on and we can give her Gertie's formula, if we can get hold of some goat milk. Regular milk might do, watered down. A little cod liver oil. You can leave her here then."

Again Ada wondered how she ever would have managed without Matilda. She climbed into the wagon.

Matilda doled out her usual warnings about not talking to anyone on the Trace or anyone in town that she didn't have to, and Ada said, "I know. I won't."

"And you'll remember to check at the post office?" Matilda handed up the bag packed with the new baby clothes.

"I'll remember." Ada wanted to know more about who Matilda was writing to in Ohio. An old friend of Gertie's who moved up North, Matilda had said. Ada had seen that she was lying, or at least scrimping on the truth. It had bothered her. But she wasn't as concerned about it now that she was about to ride into town with baby clothes that Flora Rankin thought were worth paying for.

38.

MATILDA

"Looks like it had a rough trip," Ada said, handing Matilda a battered, grimy package about as big as a brick. Then she laid down the money Flora Rankin had paid her and rattled on about how Flora had sent her home with several yards of fabric—no remnants this time—with an order for more baby clothes, a few things for older children, and two dresses in Ada's size for which she had provided patterns.

Matilda knew that Ada was looking to be patted on the back and told that she could do it. But Matilda was having trouble getting past that four dollars and fifty cents lying on the table for work Ada had done while sitting in a chair. And the sewing machine that had dropped out of heaven into Ada's lap irked her some, too. Most everyone Matilda knew could sweat in the fields for weeks, months, and still have no hope of ever owning a sewing machine. She felt small denying Ada a word or two of encouragement, but when had that become her job, anyway? She took the package out to the shed.

She set it unopened on the worktable and took a closer look. It *was* a sad package, wrapped in mud-streaked paper and tied with so much string that Matilda had to cut through six or seven knots before she could get to what was inside. Candy. Homemade caramel patties, each one wrapped up in brown paper, greasy and unappealing. Her heart raced. She dug through the box looking for a message, uncovering patty after patty until she found it, wrapped around a small flat rock—a letter written in a bold and unfamiliar script. It opened with a quote:

For it is not light that is needed, but fire; it is not the gentle shower, but thunder. We need the storm, the whirlwind, and the earthquake. —*Frederick Douglass*

Rainy's mother's uncle wrote that he had read what Matilda had written and found her work remarkable. *Her work*, he'd called it. *Like it was real writing.* Then came a question. Would Matilda be willing to allow him, Henry Moser, to print in his newspaper her account of the assault she had witnessed? Anonymously, of course, and with the location, even the state, and other details obfuscated so no one could connect the story with Matilda or the victims or anyone else involved. "Our newspaper is not read in Mississippi. The citizens of your area know nothing of it."

Furthermore, Mr. Moser wanted to invite her to consider sending future pieces of that nature. His newspaper was documenting everyday life experiences of those "most severely oppressed among us who have been forced into silence." "Yours," he wrote, "could be a voice from within the lion's den of injustice. You write with fire and thunder and storm. Your outrage, your passion, your tender cries to be heard will move hearts. You would be doing meaningful work." There was risk, he wrote. "I would not want you to imagine that there would not be risk." But risk that others were taking, many of them no older than she. Should she be inclined to help, she should continue to mail packages of food to Rainy's mother. "Nothing pretty, now. Nothing anybody here nor there would be tempted to swipe. Humble wrappings and good tight string. Take some time to think about it." And if Matilda ever came to Cleveland, which Rainy had told him she had considered in the past, he would instantly offer her work on the newspaper. He might not be able to pay her much. Perhaps not anything, at times. She would likely have to clean houses or take in laundry to get by. But he would see that she had a safe place to stay, should she need one now or in the future.

Matilda read the letter four times. Then she looked up from it, knowing she had already stepped into that new world she had been wishing for. But to move forward, she would have to go backward, open herself up to facts and feelings and details and remembrances she had worked hard to shut out. Bringing it all back would not be easy. But there was something that would help her get started. She knew what she needed to do.

She didn't dare pass by Gertie's cabin. Go Away had taken up with Stella Mae after the shack burned, and he would not let a body past the cabin at night without waking up Gertie and Stella Mae and every sleeping creature within earshot. So Matilda cut through the woods to bypass the cabin, though she did not like stepping blind in the brush. Past Gertie's she met the road again just beyond the fork, followed it a ways, then slipped in among the tall trees at the rim of the gully. After sidestepping down a short distance, she stood on the firm foundation of the rock in the bank.

Perhaps she had been overeager. It was only about ten o'clock. She knew it would have been wiser to wait for the midnight hour before setting out. But Henry Moser's letter had filled her with purpose so righteous it felt like armor. Or maybe it was the feeling that she was part of a noble conspiracy, she and the newspaperman and the others taking risks, that gave her a heady sense of stealth and undetectability, a safety net of camaraderie. Whatever it was, she felt changed, and waiting for nightfall had been all she could manage.

She felt no kinship with her old rocky haven anymore, and she stationed herself there only to further the task at hand. Behind the buttonbush, she felt for the mossy plug, then pulled it out and slid her hand into the hole in the bank, retrieving what she had buried there the night her whole world had gone up in flames. Holding the coarse paper-sack notebook in her hands, Matilda felt affection for the girl who had buried it in those last moments of her baby sister's life, not knowing that she would leave the gully that day an orphan. It had been the final purposeful act of her former self, and digging the notebook out again felt like her first act with the new identity that Henry Moser's letter had given her. She shoved the pages down the front of her dress and climbed up to the edge of the road above.

Still in the protection of the trees, Matilda heard Go Away up the road yowling and barking until, after a final painful yelp, there was silence. She stepped back. Moments later, she heard familiar laughter. Camille Porter, the Porters' older daughter. Seventeen now, Matilda thought. A year younger than herself. Matilda had met her when she did the Porters' canning. And as Camille came closer, Matilda could hear her slurred speech.

"I shouldn't never have let you bring me down here. If my mama and daddy find out I'm not at Lucy's, I'm in big trouble." The footsteps stopped.

"They won't find out."

Frank Bowers. Matilda squatted among the trunks of the trees, making herself as small as possible in the darkness.

"How do *you* know? I'm taking a terrible chance for you, is what I'm doing," Camille said flirtatiously, then laughed that squealy laugh of hers, even more shrill than usual in her condition. There were a few silent seconds, then Camille's voice, husky and raw: "Why'd you leave the car up the road? We gonna walk all the way down to your house?"

"I'm taking you somewhere else. Somewhere special."

"I don't know as I can walk much farther after what all you gave me to drink."

"You're going to like this spot. Hid away from everything but the moon. Just behind those trees up there. You can walk that far."

The footsteps started up again just as Matilda realized where the two of them were headed.

It didn't take long.

In less than half an hour, Frank had desecrated not only Camille, but the rock and the whole gully forevermore. Crouched in the darkness a few yards below them, as far as she had been able to make it before it was too late, Matilda had soundlessly waited it out, the notebook pressed against her chest like a promise of retribution.

She waited where she was until Frank led Camille, who had ceased her laughing by then, back up the road toward wherever Frank had left his car. Then Matilda slipped up the road behind them as far as Gertie's to look for what she was afraid she would find. He was there, lying in the dirt road as if asleep, his head bloody, a fist-size rock lying beside him. Go Away. Matilda left him there and hid in the baby cemetery until she heard the car's motor start up in the distance. When the sound of the engine faded off in the opposite direction, she went back to him. She stroked his blond coat, wiped away her tears, and picked him up, carried him deep into the woods so that Stella Mae would not find him. Even so, she knew the girl's grief over the loss would be as wrenching as her own as she had to leave her old friend in the woods buried only in branches. And that grief was nearly overwhelming.

By the time the sun went down on the following day, Matilda had reread every detail she had entrusted to that old notebook, and Mr. Moser's box of candy had been rewrapped, addressed to Rainy, and hidden away in the shed. Inside the box, folded around the flat rock amid the greasy slabs of caramel, was a message from the lion's den that completed Matilda's previous story, recounting the murder of the man with a whimsical yellow-and-green handkerchief and a pocket watch with a fob shaped like a sailing ship.

39.

ADA

"Just like Sheba," Matilda said as Ada, bare to the waist, expressed milk and caught it in a tin cup. Sheba was the cow Matilda had begun milking every morning for someone at the other end of the swamp in exchange for a small amount of milk. This had come about after Gertie told them that Ada should be drinking milk while she was still breastfeeding Annis. The owner of the cow was Matilda's one exception to her rule about not talking to anyone on the swamp, and she had insisted that the exception applied only to herself. But most of the milk went to Ada, and Matilda made sure she drank it. "I ain't big on milk," Matilda said, but she went out at dawn each day, no matter the weather, and came back with a few inches of milk in the bottom of a bucket. "You drink that blame milk," she would say if Ada was slow to get to it. Sometimes Ada was slow just so she could hear Matilda say that. It made her feel cared for.

Since the day Flora sent her home with yards of fabric, money in her pocket, and a new fragile confidence, Ada had been harboring hope, frail as a cypress seed, that she might someday be able to sew herself and Annis out of the swamp. She set right in on the undertaking, sketching designs and cutting out patterns from Virgil's old newspapers, then pinning them onto the fine material with shiny new pins from the dry goods store.

Though she would never say it, hardly dared to think it, Ada felt like an artist as she sewed. It was like painting a beautiful scene or carving a block of wood, making something beautiful that had not existed before. Like Jesse filling their little apartment in Baton Rouge with some new melody that came out of his heart and went down through his fingers to the strings on his fiddle. Ada's instrument was the old sewing machine, those yards of cloth her canvas. She made up designs just as Jesse had made up his songs, and when she sewed to the rhythm of the treadle beneath her bare feet, she was dancing. Flora had given her a book on dressmaking techniques, and Ada turned to a new page each time she nursed Annis, dreaming of getting off of the swamp and sewing in a little airy room in town, maybe even owning her own dress shop someday in Bristol or in some other town she hadn't even heard of.

Matilda seemed different, too. She had folded Annis into her daily routine more and more, helping with feedings and diaper changes and rocking and through-the-night tending to free Ada up for sewing. She, too, seemed to have a new sense of purpose, Ada thought. A brighter outlook. Maybe that had something to do with the mail she was sending and receiving. Or maybe she was just becoming more comfortable in their life together. Without question, things were easier between the two of them. There were evenings when they sat together in the front room after supper, Annis already bedded down, Ada with some handwork and Matilda with one of Sylvie's old books, the lantern between them. On occasion, Matilda would read a passage or two aloud, Ada would quietly comment, and they would glance at each other companionably. It was, Ada thought, much like what she had imagined all those years before when she cut out a paper doll family for herself.

Ada was at the sewing machine in the bedroom one afternoon, stitching down pleats in a crisp cotton blouse, when a sudden shower began tapping the tin roof. Through the window she watched rain fall from a sunny sky, glittering as it pelted the green swamp water.

"Raining while the sun shines," she called gaily to Matilda. "The devil's beating his wife."

Instead of making fun of her, Matilda called back from the other room, "There'll likely be a rainbow."

When the rain stopped, Ada went outside and found a double rainbow arched over the swamp, all its colors showing. A sign, if there ever was one. She counted her blessings. The cupboard was filled with jars of fruits and vegetables from the garden, canned ahead of the cooler months. The chickens were thriving. Over winter they could cook the more sluggish of the layers and still have an abundance of eggs in spring, when the days were longer. Annis was strong and healthy.

And when the time came that Ada rode back to Bristol with the newly sewn garments for Flora and carefully opened the package Matilda had asked her to mail at the post office, all she found inside it was some sticky caramel candy. Nothing that threatened the life they were building together. She resealed the package, retied the strings, and rode on.

40.
ADA

"She don't look much like me, I don't think," Ada said early one evening in mid-December as she nursed Annis from a breast so full of milk that the overage spilled out of Annis's mouth and dribbled down her chin.

"Gertie used to say my baby sister looked more like her than any of us when she was new born," Matilda said, peeling sweet potatoes in the kitchen. "Wrinkled and squinty, like somebody's granny."

Matilda did not laugh often, but she did then. Ada was encouraged.

"I didn't know you had a sister," Ada said. Even though they had lived together through three seasons and into a fourth now, Matilda still kept such subjects closed. Ada decided to broach this one, this one time. "Where is she now, your sister?"

Matilda's smile fell away. She stabbed a potato and split it in half. "Who *do* you think she looks like?" she asked coolly, meaning Annis. She might as well have stabbed Ada with her paring knife.

"My mother, I think. Mostly like my mother," Ada said, her voice wavering.

A conversation from a few days back reared up between them. That day, Ada had confided to Matilda that Annis's eyes had begun to take on the same slate-gray color as Virgil's. Gertie had already told her to expect Annis's eyes to change color a time or two before they settled on the one that would stick, but Ada had confessed to Matilda her fear that Annis might grow to favor Virgil. And though Ada did, indeed, believe that Annis looked like Sylvie, with her pretty, pouty lips and hair the color of yellow pine, those eyes, for now, were Virgil Morgan's.

"Like your mother, huh? You think so?" Matilda asked, reaching idly for another potato. "I wouldn't know, not ever seeing your mother."

Ada was never fully sure of Matilda's motives, but she decided to believe that there was nothing hurtful behind her words. Because things had been so good between them lately, and because Ada desperately needed something to be sure of.

~

After that, Matilda's old moodiness returned. On some days she seemed to dote on Annis, and on others to push her away. She seemed to be waging a one-person tug-of-war with her feelings for both Ada and Annis.

I shouldn't never have asked about her sister. Ada had reason to know better. Once, alone with Gertie, she had asked about Matilda, about her family and why she was so tight-lipped with information about herself. Gertie had said, "Best to leave things be." She should have held to that.

Soon it occurred to Ada that Matilda never called Annis by her name.

"Why is it you always call her 'Little One' or 'Girlie' or something else when she's got such a pretty name?" she asked Matilda. *A name you picked out.*

"Why is it you ask 'Why is it?' so much? Can't you just let things be?"

The same advice Gertie had given her.

Matilda began pulling away from them. She spent more and more time outside, favoring mucking out the barn and chopping wood to conversation or companionship. Evenings spent sharing lamplight over books and needlework dwindled. When Matilda did take time with Annis, when she held her on her lap and played with her while Ada sewed, everything seemed as it should be. But those times came more and more infrequently. Matilda went back to her old all-business self, and Ada went back to worrying. She urged Annis on Matilda like a wife with a reluctant husband, hoping to strengthen the bond that held them all together. At day's end, Ada administered the much-dreaded rag bath, then handed over to Matilda the sweet job of tucking Annis into her cradle. She changed every diaper herself, took loads of them to the river to rinse them out before boiling them instead of handing over a bundle when Matilda set out to go fishing, as had been their practice before. And still Matilda was increasingly distant.

Christmas passed without fanfare. Then one morning, Matilda rose early and fed the stove. Ada woke to her stirring in the kitchen and reached for Annis, lifted her onto the bed. As Ada nursed Annis,

Matilda made pancakes—Ada's favorite—for breakfast. Ada watched her take out a jar of the muscadine jelly they had canned early in the fall and warm a tin of cane syrup on the stove. Annis especially loved to suckle a syrupy finger. Wonderful smells filled the house. While Matilda laid the table, Ada dressed, then hurried out the back door to do her business in the outhouse and draw a bucket of fresh water.

When Ada returned, lugging the heavy bucket, the pancakes were still warm. Annis was back in her beautiful cradle. And Matilda was gone.

41.

ADA

Ada sat on the porch steps with Annis in her lap, Matilda's last gift of pancakes untouched in the kitchen. She gave the sugar-teat, dry and unsweetened, to Annis to play with. The morning was quiet, the air clear of the smell of the starlings who had mysteriously abandoned their roost a month before. Today, Ada missed the familiar routine of the despised birds coming and going at dusk and dawn, as things should be. But nothing was as it should be. Matilda should be out by the shed feeding the chickens. Ada should be with Jesse in their room over the barber shop on Harlow Street in Baton Rouge. Her mother should still be alive. She lost herself in the stillness of the swamp until her gaze moved from some distant point over the water to Annis, asleep now in her lap, and she realized that some unaccounted-for period of time had passed.

She's not coming back. The old dress Matilda had been wearing the night of the shed fire was gone from its hook in the hall, as were the cotton shifts she'd brought back from the woods and the overalls she'd had Ada buy for her at the feed-and-seed with money from the selling of Virgil's liquor. Left behind were the nightgown and socks Ada had brought home for her from the dry goods store and the winter dress and shawl she had sewn for her, Matilda's way of closing the door firmly behind her.

She had left behind, too, the wagon and the mule, the chickens, and nearly all of the money hidden behind the stove. Gone were her dogwood-twig toothbrush, her comb, the old boots she'd arrived in, her scarf, the man's jacket Gertie had brought for her, and her quilts. She must have packed those things up and taken them out during the night or in the predawn hours of morning, hidden them in the woods, or passed them on to someone on the back trail while Ada slept.

The absence of those few things was enough to clear the air of Matilda. Now there was more of Virgil in the house than of her, and Ada felt that she was back where she had started before Matilda, her angel, had been sent to her. As if she had been picked up by Time and set back down on the day she first returned to the swamp with her pillowcase over her shoulder, except that now she had a baby looking to her for everything, for life itself.

Three days went by. Then, that fourth morning, Ada opened the front door and found a pint jar of milk on the porch, no one in sight, evoking memories of the pinecone on the table that long-ago night. Eagerly, she stepped out onto the porch, but there was no other sign of anyone's having been there. *Matilda.* It had to be her. *She's still milking Sheba and bringing me milk, because I'm nursing Annis.*

The next morning, she ran to the door again, but there was no milk, no friendly face, no angel. Again, the following day, there was nothing. When four days had passed since the milk appeared, Ada, hoping for a pattern, woke herself well before dawn and rushed straightaway to the door. There was a new jar of milk on the porch and a shadowy figure walking along the edge of the swamp toward a waiting wagon on the path. But it was not Matilda. It was Gertie. And likely the trusted preacher was in the wagon.

"Miss Tuttle!"

Gertie stopped for a second, acknowledging that she had heard Ada's call, then she started up again and moved more quickly toward the wagon. Then she was being helped up onto the seat.

"Miss Tuttle, wait!" Ada dashed down the steps and ran across the stubbly yard, slowed by her bare feet. But the wagon was already moving off.

Bereft, Ada stopped and listened to it rattle down the swamp road.

Ada grieved for days. She had no interest in filling the stove with wood for cooking. Instead, she took a canning jar at random from the cupboard when she was hungry, eating whatever was inside it—stewed tomatoes or green beans or sugar beets. Keeping the chickens and the mule fed were all she could manage outside of the basic necessities of existence: feeding Annis, changing her, drawing the necessary water, making the mandatory trips to the outhouse. She napped along with Annis and fell into bed each evening, still in her clothes, as soon as Annis was asleep.

There were no more milk deliveries. Ada had been sure that Gertie, at least, cared for her. For her and Annis both. But why hadn't she turned around that day? Why hadn't she knocked on the door when she brought the milk? Ada did not understand anything anymore. She mourned the loss of Matilda more than that of Jesse. She had never expected life with Jesse to last, but she had let herself hope that she and Annis and Matilda were forever bonded by all they had been through together.

Then one morning she got up and fed the stove. Heated water and filled the washtub. She bathed and washed her hair, pinned it back with the barrette Jesse bought for her in New Orleans. Put on one of several ladies' dresses she had finished sewing for Flora before Matilda left, before Ada set aside the sewing along with most everything else. From the little table in the bedroom, she picked up the cloudy hand mirror that had belonged to her mother, held it in front of her, and heard Jesse tell her she was beautiful. Then she watched herself cry.

Before the hour was out, she hitched the mule. She padded the washtub with a blanket and set Annis inside it in the wagon, gave her a freshly soaked sugar-teat and the rattle Flora had given her in town one day. Then, for the first time, she rode down the forbidden path that curved around the edge of the swamp.

The mule plodded past three widely spaced stilt houses, past a woman hanging laundry who looked up with surprise and another chasing a mud-crusted toddler. Past a small group of children tossing rocks into the swamp water. Ada waved at the children, and they stood with their rocks in their hands and stared. She longed for someone to stop her, to flag her down and offer a name, ask for hers. But no one did. From among the children, she picked out a little girl who surely belonged to Job and Irene, feeding scraps to a short-legged dog wet from a swim in the swamp.

When the road came out at the Trace, she followed it south for a distance. She did not know where Gertie lived, only that her house was across the Trace and that Matilda had been able to get there on foot the night Annis was born. She remembered that Matilda had said she took a route that night through woods along a creek bed, so when a dirt road appeared beside a piney wood with a creek running through it, Ada signaled the mule. They bounced over ruts and veered around holes until she came to a short row of old, dilapidated cabins. At first she thought they were all long forsaken—the roof of one of them had caved in, and another was missing a front door. But then a boy, seven or so Ada guessed, wearing only a man's long-tailed white shirt, stark against his dark skin, came out of a cabin that was still intact, trailed by a chicken. Ada stopped the mule. The boy ran up to the wagon as if he had been expecting her.

"Look," he said, holding up a finger with a strip of rag tied around it. "I cut it on the saw."

"Bet that hurt," Ada said.

"Naw, I'm strong."

"Do you know a lady named Gertie?"

"A white lady?"

"No. No, she's a colored lady. She's a midwife. A nurse."

"I don't need no nurse," the boy said, hiding his bandaged finger behind his back.

"Oh, I know you don't. No, Gertie is my friend. But I don't know where she lives."

"Mama might know her, but she ain't here."

"Is anybody else in there?"

"Just my granny. But she's taking a nap."

Ada glanced around at the landscape, so different from the swamp on the other side of the Trace. Wide fields and dry dirt. There was no one else to be seen.

"Do you know Matilda?" she asked, keeping her head down and her eyes lowered.

"You mean Mattie?"

"Yes, Mattie." Ada struggled to keep her voice even.

"Heard of her. I think my mama knowed her."

"Do you know where she lives?"

The boy shook his head. "I just heard of her because of what all happened over yonder, where she used to stay." He looked out over a field of corn stubble.

"What happened there?" Ada leaned eagerly over the side of the wagon.

"I don't think I can talk anymore," the boy said.

"Can you get your granny for me?"

"She's sleeping. She don't like to talk, noway. I gotta go," he said, scooting back across the yard. Then he ran up the porch steps and into the house and shut the door.

On the porch of another tumbledown box of a house a little farther along the dirt road, there was a woman whose pregnant belly was so enormous that Ada had to stop herself from gaping in amazement.

After Ada explained to the woman that Gertie had delivered her own daughter—reaching back to lift Annis out of the washtub for a moment—the woman directed her to the midwife's house.

"Just go on up the road a piece," she said, pointing. "Go round a turn and start looking for a big oak tree on the right hand. First place you come to after that'll be Gertie's. Ain't much," she said, "Gertie's place." The woman was sitting on a porch with her bare feet straddling an empty space where one of the floorboards had fallen through. The screen door behind her was hanging crooked across the doorway, the bottom hinge missing. Ada wondered what "ain't much" might look like. Then she noticed the boots standing by the door, the laces dyed a bright red. Virgil's boots.

"Thank you," she said, starting up the mule.

"My best to Gert. Tell her Sam'll be over to fetch her any day. I can't get much bigger," the woman said, laughing.

"Whoa, now." Ada pulled back the reins in front of Gertie's house. It was the smallest house she had ever seen. One narrow window. Two large flattop river rocks serving as steps to the porch. The yard was all dirt except for the lush, green oasis that was the vegetable patch. Gaps between the warped wallboards had been patched with stray boards nailed to the outside wall, or chinked with clay and mud. There was a bottle tree out front, a scrawny bare-branched Judas tree with the limbs cut back and glass bottles, blue and green, stuck over the stumps to catch the sun and, if one were of a mind to believe it, any evil spirits that might be on their way into the house. Ada's mother had pointed one out to her once on a rare trip to town with Virgil. A sign nailed to the house noted Gertie's name and her trade, "Birthing and General Nursing." Seeing Gertie's name boosted Ada's resolve.

"I'll be right back, sweet girl," she told Annis, kissing her forehead and pressing the rattle into her hand before climbing down from the wagon.

As Ada turned toward the house, Gertie appeared on the porch. The old woman stood there with her hands clasped over her apron and a look on her face that was as sorrowful as it was firm. Seeing her there, Ada almost fell to her knees with relief, but she caught herself on the side of the wagon.

"Miss Tuttle," she said, and the familiar name sounded like what it was—a plea, a supplication. Ada stepped up onto the first rock, but went no farther, halted by the lack of invitation on Gertie's face. "Where is she? Please tell me. Please."

Gertie reached up and scuffed her nose with the side of her hand as if ridding herself of an irksome itch. It wasn't so much a nervous gesture as the postponement of an answer. Then she spoke. "You ain't got half a notion what that girl be carrying around with her. What she been carrying around before she ever laid eyes on you. She saved your life. Saved your baby, too. Ain't that enough?"

The words struck Ada with the force of a bullet. She tried to think of what she might say, but crowding out everything else was the certainty that she was now, without any doubt, completely on her own in the world. And then the truth came like a blade of daylight pushing through a crack in a dark place. Gertie knew what had happened to Virgil. Matilda had told her. And now that Matilda had left the swamp, Gertie was no longer on Ada's side of things.

Then Gertie leaned down and put her weathered hand on Ada's arm, the same hand, Ada thought, that had brought Annis into the world. She wished she had the right to step up onto the porch and into Gertie's embrace, but she did not, and Gertie's arms were not open. Even as she had mounted that river-rock step, despite everything, she had believed that Gertie cared for her, and maybe she did, but she cared for Matilda more. It came down to that. She was protecting Matilda, and Ada wished that there was someone like Gertie willing to protect her, too. She had thought, had hoped, that Matilda would be such a person in her life. And now Gertie was protecting Matilda from her.

"Life is hard," Gertie said, her hand still on Ada's arm. "You got a hard row to hoe, I ain't denying. You find a way, is what you do. It's what we all got to do. They's things you can't understand, even if I tried to tell you. Things about Mattie and me both. We got different things at stake, you and us. It's the way it is." Then she turned around and went back into the house, closing the door without looking back and so softly that Ada only heard it in her heart, where the sound was deafening.

She couldn't go back yet. She could not go back to the stilt house, to pressing forward and being pushed back, to the laundry and the relentless cleaning and cooking and washing dishes and putting on clothes and taking them off and going to sleep and waking up to do it all over again. Not with her heart so heavy.

She nudged the mule forward, on past Gertie's house rather than back the way she had come. At a fork in the road, she turned left and followed the edge of a dense wood until it fell away into a ravine, then she rode on down a hill past cornfields and a hayfield and a few cows pastured behind barbed-wire fences. When the road leveled out and curved in front of a sprawling two-story redbrick farmhouse, she knew she was looking at Peggy Creedle's house. It was just as Peggy had described it in another lifetime, before Jesse.

Ada recalled the night she had gone to the carnival with Peggy, the last contact she'd had with her. Peggy scared her a little—she was so wild—but Ada would not mind having one friend in the world, now that Matilda was lost. Even someone as flighty as Peggy.

With Annis asleep in the washtub, sure to wake up hungry soon, Ada went quickly up the cobblestone walk and stepped up onto the porch. She knocked on the door and instantly heard footsteps. Then the door swung open on a man, tall and handsome with a thin blond mustache.

"Well, must be my lucky day," he said. "I'm Frank Bowers." He opened the screen door between them. "And who are you?"

Before she could answer, Ada let herself be ushered into the entryway, but she stood just inside, where she could see the wagon through the screen door. She could also see into the front parlor, and she tried not to stare at the costly furniture, the swirled plaster ceiling, the patterned rug on the floor. She was glad she was wearing the new dress instead of the one she woke up in that morning. She told Frank Bowers she had lost her bearings, which, considering everything, was not altogether false. Then, when he asked, she was forced to tell him where she lived.

"You mean there are houses up in that swamp? You don't live out there by yourself, surely," he said, sounding hopeful that maybe she did.

Ada hedged. She did not know this man, but more than her concern for safety or propriety, she was embarrassed to admit the truth about where she lived, especially while standing in that nice house. She called up the story she and Matilda had first concocted and borrowed from it. "Somebody lived there with me—another girl," she stammered. "My father hired her when he went on a trip. To help me with…" And now she had a baby to explain. She couldn't. She stopped talking midsentence.

Frank Bowers looked amused.

Ada tried again. "She just left recently. The girl. And my father isn't coming back. I mean, he don't look to be coming back. It's just a few months shy of a year he's been gone." She took a breath and tried to calm her nerves, hid her hands behind her back and dug a fingernail into her palm.

"So you're alone? On a swamp?"

"Not alone." Ada shot a quick glance toward the wagon. Annis was still out of sight in the tub. She took another breath and said, "My baby's with me."

"A baby." In that revelation Frank Bowers evidently found justification for a slow, bold assessment of Ada's physical attributes, causing her cheeks to burn, which seemed to further amuse him.

"I was looking for Peggy," she managed to say.

"Peggy? My cousin," Frank said, and having established that link, he stepped closer. "She got out of here a long time ago. Went back to Baltimore, to her mother. My aunt Rose. I spent a summer here with

Peggy a while back. Longest summer of my life. I never planned on coming back to this place, but life doesn't always run according to plan, does it?" He smiled in a way that brought out a dimple in his cheek and drew a shy smile from Ada.

"No. That's true," she said. "But I'd better get back now." Ada looked again at the wagon, expecting Annis to wake up at any moment and find herself deserted. "I didn't know Peggy was gone."

"Her mother is the reason I'm here. She asked me to look after the farm until I could sell it for her. I didn't expect to be here long, but then I decided to keep some of Uncle Curtis's business arrangements going for a while after he died."

"Peggy's father?"

"Yes."

"I'm sorry for her."

"I'll tell her. But you haven't told me your name."

"Ada."

"Well, Ada, it's just me here in the house now. Gets lonely, I can tell you." He looked at Ada as if she had a remedy for loneliness, and her face burned red again.

"I hate I missed Peggy," she said, pushing open the door.

Frank caught the top of the door and held it open for her. "You must be lonely, too, living on that swamp. It's no place for somebody as young and pretty as you. It's not safe out there."

"It's okay," Ada said. "I don't plan on being there too long. I've got a job sewing. For Rankin's Dry Goods. I'm thinking on moving to town, after I save up some. But I better get back to the wagon before she wakes up."

"You've got the baby out there?" Frank looked out at the old wagon and the sagging mule. "You know," he said, "I'm looking for some short-term help around here. A housekeeper. Just until I put the place up for sale in a few weeks. Uncle Curtis's housekeeper left when he died, and I need somebody I can trust to keep things up in the house while I do a little work on the place. That business of my uncle's is winding down, and I'm more than ready to get out of here. I'm thinking that if you could use some extra work while you're saving up, just a few weeks' worth, it might be perfect for you. It'd be an easy enough job. Just the usual upkeep and maybe some meals for me every now and then. Some laundry."

Ada didn't know what to make of Peggy's cousin or his offer, but she was leery of both. She shook her head and moved across the porch. "I was just looking for Peggy, is all."

Frank followed her down the wide brick steps that fanned out from the porch. "Uncle Curtis's housekeeper had a private room behind the kitchen. Comes with the job," he added. "Plenty big enough for you and your baby. And meals, of course—room and board—are included. You'd have total privacy. A stall and feed for your mule there. And Peggy can vouch for me."

"I couldn't. Really."

"Well," Frank said. "You keep it in mind."

"I will. But I hope you find somebody else, because I really can't."

Ada rode off with a picture in her head of what the housekeeper's room might look like—clean and bright and sunny, a varnished wood floor and a colorful rug. A year ago, maybe she would have seen a job like that as a way out of her troubles, but something about Frank

Bowers had made her feel dirty. She rode home grateful for the old stilt house. She would get back to her sewing. She would turn things around. It had hurt, being turned away by Gertie. And yes, she had no one now. But Annis, at least, had Ada.

Back at the house, she took stock of their supplies. It was into January now, the winter garden long done. She assessed the remaining jars of put-up vegetables and fruit, the staples in the larder, the last of the tart green apples wrapped in newspaper in the root cellar that Matilda had made usable again, the sacks of pecans they had stashed away. Her milk was still flowing for Annis. They would not starve. She gathered kindling and checked the woodpile. Matilda had left a good store of split wood, doing the hard work again. There was enough of the money she had made sewing, along with the remains of what Virgil's liquor and beaver skins had brought in, to buy food to get them by until spring, but the less of it she used, the sooner she would have enough to rent a room in town. She would ask Flora how much she would need for that. She had been thinking that if she lived in town she could continue to sew clothes for Flora's store and maybe even offer herself as a general seamstress, making clothes to order and doing alterations and mending and such. Any kind of sewing work she could do from their room while she took care of Annis. It was the beginning of a plan.

In the days that followed, Ada cleaned out the chicken coop and shoveled the barn, did all the chores she had been neglecting. Then she sat down again at the sewing machine. Using every spare minute she could steal from Annis, she worked on turning out new things from Flora's latest assortment of fabrics. She sewed, on the machine and by hand, until her fingers were sore, then she sewed more, often into the night by candlelight, because kerosene for the lamp was so dear. When she laid out the last dress on the table, she knew she had done her best work. She would be late getting them to town. Flora was probably worried about her by now. But looking at those beautiful clothes, she began to believe again that it was possible to take care of herself and Annis by her own effort rather than depending on someone who might leave, like Matilda, or who might send her away, like Jesse. She would sew them out of the swamp yet.

You find a way, is what you do.

42.

ADA

A storm set in that night. Instead of blowing off, it settled over the swamp for days, an evil counterpart to whatever good the double rainbow had once foretold. Thunder and lightning came and went and came again, booming and crackling and rattling the two windows, waking Annis and frightening her before the storm would dwindle, for a while, to a light patter of rain that lulled her back to sleep.

Daytime was as dark as dusk. The swamp flooded its low boundaries, and water flowed under the house, lapping against the stilts. Muddy water carved a cavern under a section of the chicken-wire fence, and all but a few of the chickens disappeared, gone to predators or escaped in panic. Only the tips of the cypress knees that stood guard around their trees in the swamp could be seen, and a tall tree in the woods fell with a booming crash, split and charred by a lightning strike. Ada fought to not see that, too, as a sign.

Finally, the storm died out, the rains moved on, and the sun returned. It was warmer than usual for January, which was a blessing. Slowly, the water receded. The mud firmed up. As soon as the trail was passable, Ada hitched the mule, who seemed as eager as she to head out of the swamp. Ada settled Annis again on her blanket in the washtub with some favorite playthings. There was room enough in the tub for Annis to roll over, something she had become adept at doing, and she was content to entertain herself there with her toys and her sugar-teat and her endlessly interesting toes. The clothes Ada had made—for women, children, and babies—were ironed and neatly folded, the dress she had worn to Gertie's washed and as good as new.

"May I help you?" A man behind the counter at Rankin's Dry Goods glanced at Ada, Annis in her arms with a lock of Ada's long hair clutched in her hand. He eyed with distaste the new baby dress folded over Ada's arm, as if he expected a returned purchase. Ada had left the other garments in the wagon, expecting to pass Annis off to a delighted Flora and go back for them. She had brought in the prettiest of the baby dresses as an apology for having taken so long to finish the work.

Ada glanced around the store for Flora. She shifted Annis in her arms and explained why she had come, after which the man informed her that Flora, his wife's sister, had fallen ill. "She is not," he said, smoothing his bushy gray mustache, "expected to return to running the store." As he spoke, he picked at the lace dress with what looked to be disdain, but might be worry over Flora, Ada thought, as her own worry engulfed her.

"What's happened to her?"

"Apoplexy." Ada did not detect any concern in the way the word was spoken. The man took in Ada's blank look and said, "Left arm paralyzed. Face drooped down on that side. Can't talk right. Stroke, some call it."

"I'm sorry. Flora's been so—"

"Yes, well." The man cut her off to ask about her financial arrangement with Flora. When Ada told him what Flora paid her, he replied that under the circumstances he would agree to take what she had already made at half that price and that no more garments would be needed in the future. "Flora always was too soft to run a business."

This man was no friend to Flora; Ada could well see that. She did not ask to use the back room to nurse Annis and change her diaper, although both needed doing. She went out to the wagon and returned with only two boys' shirts and an apron. The rest—the five ladies' dresses that had turned out so well and the beautiful things for babies and children—she did not mention, hoping to strike a better deal for them somewhere else, some other time. She left the store with the few coins the man shoved across the counter and no remorse.

She and Annis rode slowly back to the swamp on roads made treacherous by the storm. After they turned off the Trace and onto the back trail, Ada was so intent on avoiding mudholes that might catch a hoof or seize a wheel that she did not see it until she had pulled to a stop. Even then, she could not register what her eyes were taking in. She sat in the wagon, Annis softly babbling now in the tub, the mule calmly standing in his usual spot between the swamp and the stilt house as if the house were not tilted precariously to one side, like a child's first building-block tower about to tip over. As if the top plank in the long column of cypress plank steps had not detached from the porch and smashed through the front window to disappear inside the living room. Ada sat suspended in the moment, a familiar feeling from the past, and though the motion was dreamlike, unreal, she flicked the reins and the mule moved forward in response. She urged him onward, down the still-foreign swamp path, straight to Job Farley's house.

~~~

"She'll go down," Job said. He stood back a ways from the house with his hat in a fist clamped to his hip. "Ain't no stopping it now."

It was the storm, he told her. The flooding had dislodged the stilt frame, though it had probably been loosening its hold for a while. The old house had stood as long as it was going to. He said she was lucky they had not been inside when it slid.

"It ain't safe to go up there," he said.

"But all our things are inside." Their linens, their food, the tin of money behind the stove, her mother's hand mirror, Flora's sewing machine. Everything they owned except the laundry Ada had hung on the clothesline that morning, the bag of Annis's necessaries she had taken with her into town, and the stack of newly sewn outfits still in the wagon.

"It's just things. They ain't worth dying over. It won't stand for long. Once it comes down, you can pick through what's there, save what you can. I'll keep an eye on it, if you want. Collect anything I can for you when it goes. Till you can get back for it."

Ada thought of how long she had hated that old house and how much she needed it now. While they stood there, a cracked stilt broke off under the house and fell into the mud.

"You got somewhere to go?"

The same question Jesse had asked her in Baton Rouge. This time, she shook her head.

The oldest daughter set a place for Ada at the table in Job and Irene's house. Over a shared supper—milk and corn bread mush, put-up string beans and new potatoes, and a jar of bread-and-butter pickles—Ada asked Irene if she knew Matilda. She and Job passed a wary glance, but did not answer.

"I know she came from across the Trace," Ada said, aware of the desperation in her voice. "She lived over there somewhere before she came to live with me. I think she had a sister."

Job cleared his throat. "Can't help none, there. Sorry."

Ada and Annis slept that night on the floor in the small front room along with four of the Farley children who hugged the walls to clear as much space for them as possible.

The next night, they slept in the housekeeper's room in the big house on the Creedle farm.

43.

MATILDA

Matilda woke up mad every morning. Not because of Leeta's incessant chatter, or because of Leeta's no-account boyfriend who resented Leeta's sharing her room with a friend when he had been accustomed to slipping in through the open window whenever he had a mind to, or even because of the mindless hatred that met her every day, one way or another, in Jackson. All of that was only kindling for her anger at herself for having lived in that stilt house, having taken up with the daughter of that devil and allowed her outrage to bend into acceptance. She hadn't expected to leave so suddenly, but then, she'd had no obligation not to. She had never wanted Ada to depend on her. She had been at Gertie's cabin the day Ada came there, saw her pull up in the wagon and watched from inside while Gertie sent her away. She had felt bad about that. But when Virgil Morgan's house began to feel like home to her, when she realized she had developed a fondness for his daughter and his granddaughter that turned what began as justice into something that felt like betrayal, she'd had to leave.

On this morning, she lay on her cot in Leeta's room, the sun not yet up, and knew there would be no getting back to sleep. The other cot was empty. Leeta spent more nights at her boyfriend's place than in the tiny room the two girls shared in the shoddy boardinghouse next to the colored funeral parlor. Matilda did not miss her when she was absent. Leeta had taken her in, and she was grateful for that, but Leeta had two settings—asleep or complaining—and that wore on Matilda. And Leeta came in late and loud, when she did come in, which did not win her any friends among the other boarders who got up early and went off to their various jobs, worked hard and did their best to sleep at night behind their paper-thin walls.

Matilda had a new job at the fancy movie palace on Capitol Street, cleaning up after the afternoon matinees and the evening shows, picking up trash and mopping the floors and scraping the occasional pieces of chewing gum off the bottoms of the plush velvet seats that Negroes were not allowed to sit on. After work, she walked back to the boardinghouse, most often in the dark, entered quietly, closed her bedroom door softly, then undressed and lay on her cot. Sometimes she was still awake when faint light filtered through the curtain at the window and Alice and Verbie and Shirley and Vera and the Johnson twins, Serena and Tranquilla—wishful thinking, those names—were stirring awake in the other rooms in the house.

She could hear the other girls now, making their way to the kitchen, their voices drowsy and soft, heard the wooden scrape of the bread box sliding open, plates being set down on the table. She stayed in bed until she heard them all leave, each one on her way to a different house to work as a maid. All except Verbie, who worked in the kitchen at the insane asylum on the edge of town. The asylum paid more than what any of the rest of them earned, but no one envied Verbie her job. They had all heard the stories she brought home with her. The asylum put even the worst aspects of Matilda's work at the theater into perspective. The asylum put a lot of things into perspective.

Matilda made enough at the theater that she had been able to put a little back, and she hoped to find a second job soon. When she had enough money for three train tickets and a couple of months' living expenses, she would somehow convince Gertie to go with her to Cleveland, if only for Stella Mae's sake. With that in mind, she had been spending her mornings walking up and down manicured streets and knocking on the doors of prim houses, inquiring about maid work. Almost always, the door was opened by a maid. She decided to stay in this morning, to allow herself some rare solitude. The city crowded a person; there was no escaping it. She missed the woods and the gully and, truth be told, the strange beauty of the swamp. She went into the empty kitchen and poured herself a glass of water. She was sitting at the kitchen table eating a cheese sandwich when the back door opened behind her.

"Mattie, you here by yourself?" Leeta spoke in an urgent whisper, and Matilda knew something was wrong.

"It's just me. What's the matter?"

"Oh, God, Mattie. Come help me."

Leeta darted back out of the doorway, and Matilda followed her over to the funeral parlor. Leeta knocked on the back door, and it opened a few inches, then wide enough for Matilda and Leeta to slip inside. The room was dim, heavy drapes drawn, and to Matilda's horror, there was a body laid out on the cooling board. As Matilda stood gaping, wondering why they were there, Leeta threw herself over the body and an arm came up and clutched her neck. The body on the board was Alvert, Leeta's boyfriend, and he was alive, or something akin to alive. Mr. Lewis, the undertaker, locked the door behind them and turned on a second lamp. Alvert's clothes were thick with mud, as were his hands and his bare feet and most of his face. His eyes were sunken and red, and he was muttering feverish pleas to his mother, who was not there. Leeta was wailing. Mr. Lewis was attempting to dribble water into Alvert's mouth with a ladle, but Alvert had the shakes and not much liquid made it into his mouth.

"Bad dehydrated. We don't get some water down this boy, there's no way he'll make it," Mr. Lewis said.

Leeta climbed up onto the cooling board and lay close to Alvert, holding him still by the force of her will, cooing and caressing him until he was calm enough to let Mr. Lewis drip some water down his throat.

Matilda stood useless in the center of the embalming room, her hands at her sides feeling like wooden weights, the sounds coming from Alvert all too familiar to her after Verbie's descriptions of the asylum. She knew it was not the right time, but she had to ask. "What happened to him?"

"Sonofabitches buried him," Leeta hissed. "Out by Bent Creek over in Mozeville. Jumped him and beat him up, hog-tied him and buried him up to his nose. Left him there two days and nights. Me back at his place mad as hell, thinking he was sniffing around Mavis Odell, and all the time he..." Leeta started wailing again and Alvert starting crying for his mama and Matilda laid her hand against Leeta's cheek and told her she was strong enough to get through this.

"Strong enough to kill them sonofabitches, soon's I know who done this," Leeta said, and Matilda nodded as if she believed that Leeta would do that very thing. She understood firsthand how comforting dreams of revenge could be, as long as they never came true.

In the elegant lavatory at the movie palace that night, Matilda filled a bucket with soapy water and hooked a trash sack over her shoulder in the same way she used to wear a pick sack in the cotton fields on the Trace. She drowned a mophead in the bucket, then rolled the bucket on its little metal wheels into the ornate auditorium, a wet cleaning rag tucked into her waistband soaking through her skirt. Mr. Massey, the white night guard, eighty years old and nearly deaf, was dead asleep in the projector room, as usual. His only job, as far as Matilda could tell, was to watch her and the other night workers actually doing work.

Matilda had not wanted to leave Leeta, but they both needed her to hold on to this job, so she had come, carrying with her the memory of Alvert on the embalming table with Leeta draped over him.

She tried to keep her mind on her work as she wrung out the mop and swabbed the floor between the front row of seats and the foot of the stage where the movie screen was hidden behind gold-tasseled burgundy curtains, but every stroke made her angrier. When she could not bear it anymore, she plunged the mop into the bucket with a force that matched her feelings, sending the bucket scudding across the floor and splashing the satin curtain with grimy gray water.

She turned away from the mess and stormed over to the orchestra's piano, which Mr. Massey had warned her to never touch. She pressed the forbidden keys with her forbidden fingers. Then she marched down the front row of blue velvet seats, flinging herself into one after another, as Mr. Massey snored away upstairs. She did not let up until she reached the last seat. Then she spat on the beautiful upholstery and kicked the fancy cast-metal leg until her big toe was bleeding inside her shoe.

And then, because she had to, she got down on her knees in front of the burgundy curtain and began scrubbing out the stain. She tried to hold back the hot tears that came. Tears that came because she was angry, she insisted to herself. *Not afraid. Not broken. Angry.*

~

Alone in her room the next morning, while Leeta was back at the funeral parlor, Matilda wrote a new article for Mr. Moser's newspaper. She recounted everything that Leeta and Mr. Lewis had learned during periods in which Alvert was lucid and able to tell them more about what had happened to him, as they sat with him in shifts all day and all night. That three young men, white men, around twenty years old, had cornered him and taken his week's pay because Alvert had been hired by the railroad while one of them had been turned away. That they had pushed him into the back of a car and driven him to a wooded creek across the county line, beaten him until he could not move, hog-tied him and buried him in a hole he had watched them dig. He'd thought they intended to bury him alive until they packed mud around his neck and up past his mouth, stopping just short of his nose. Two days later, just yesterday, a man intending to fish in the creek had come upon him at dawn, rescued him, and taken him to the funeral parlor, knowing that Mr. Lewis provided help and a safe haven for people in Alvert's particular sort of need.

Matilda wrote, too, that there had been moments on the cooling board when Alvert believed he was still buried in the hole, and others when he thought he was a little boy at home with his mother. And that Mr. Lewis had been afraid to take him to the hospital, bringing in a trusted doctor for help instead, out of fear that Alvert would be sent straight away to the asylum and never leave it again.

When Matilda finished writing, she folded the paper and slipped it into a pocket she had sewn onto the inside of her dress, inspired by Job Farley's secret pocket back on the Trace. Tomorrow she would mail a box of Vera's molasses cookies to Cleveland, in a homely box sealed tight and tied with lots of string.

At the funeral parlor that afternoon, Mr. Lewis discussed Alvert's options with Leeta and Matilda while Alvert slept in an upstairs room.

"He could try to bring charges. He works for the railroad, and they've got clout. Could be they'd get behind him," Mr. Lewis said doubtfully, passing a hand over his cap of graying hair. "There would be people here in the city who would stand with him. White folks, too. But it'd mostly come down to them in Moze County, since it happened across the county line. And Moze County..." He shook his head. "Well, it wasn't any accident they took him there. It's up to you," he said to Leeta. "He's too foggy-headed to think it through."

It was the real possibility of Alvert's ending up in the asylum that made up Leeta's mind. Alvert's family lived down near the Gulf Coast. He had been headed up North, had gotten as far as Jackson when he ran out of money and took a job with the railroad. Met Leeta.

"I'll take him home to his family," Leeta said. "Soon as he can ride the train. Let them decide from there."

44.
ADA

Ada spent most of their first week in Peggy's father's farmhouse alone with Annis. Other than Frank, the only people left on the farm belonged to one sharecropper family, and they would be leaving soon. Frank was away much of that week, in Canton contesting what he believed to be surveyor's mistakes in the deed to the farm, and then in Jackson scouting for office space for the law practice he had decided to open there when the farm sold, rather than returning to Baltimore.

He had been surprised when Ada showed up again at the house.

"Every house this size has a live-in housekeeper," he'd assured her, quick to dispel her discomfort. "It's a perfectly normal situation."

And maybe that was true. Ada's only references regarding living situations were the swamp and her one-year reprieve in Baton Rouge, neither of which could be counted as normal.

When he was on the farm, Frank stayed busy with what he said was shipping off the last of his uncle Curtis's peaches and corn, which seemed odd this time of year, but Ada understood little more about farming peaches and corn than she did about the propriety of her new job. She enjoyed the work, cleaning the rooms of the big old house, polishing the hearts-of-pine floors, and beating the dust out of the nice thick rugs she draped over the railing of the wide wraparound porch. Arranging things in ways she imagined would be most pleasing to potential buyers. It was more like playing house than work. She did laundry in a hand-crank washing machine on the porch instead of in a tub in the yard, and she helped Annis learn to belly crawl on soft rugs in bright, spacious rooms with no mouse droppings in the corners. Still, it was hard not to lose hope.

She held to her dream of a room in town and a job sewing. And though she avoided Frank as much as possible, she did mention to him her desire to retrieve the sewing machine and Annis's cradle from the stilt house. She could never get them out by herself if the house was still standing, or even into the wagon if the house had tumbled down. She did not mention the money in the cracker tin behind the stove, but that was on her mind, too. Frank had promised to find someone to help her, but as of yet, he had not.

With Frank so occupied with other matters, Ada's last name did not come up between them until he paid her wages at the end of the first week, recording the sum in a leather ledger.

"Morgan," he said, squinting as he mulled that over. "There was somebody who did some farmwork for Uncle Curtis that summer I was here. You aren't related to Virgil Morgan..."

Ada almost dropped the glass vase she was filling with daffodils. She did not have to reply; her stricken look was answer enough.

"Your father?"

"Yes."

"He's the one that ran off and left you alone on a swamp? Can't say I'm surprised, from what I saw of him."

"I wasn't alone. There was a girl, like I told you. She came to help out before Annis was born. Stayed close on to a year." Ada tugged at the flowers nervously. She, at least, was still sticking to their original story about Virgil's disappearance, even though Matilda had left her.

"How did ugly old Virgil ever come up with anything that looks as good as you do?" Frank asked then, taking her in with a look that broke his weeklong streak of gentlemanly behavior.

Once Virgil's name had been spoken between them, Frank began treating Ada more casually. He offered her Peggy's old room with its lace-canopied brass bed and flowered wallpaper. Ada insisted that the housekeeper's room suited her and Annis fine. Peggy's bedroom was upstairs, just down the hall from Frank's, while the housekeeper's room was on the bottom floor at the opposite end of the house and near the back door, should she need it.

At the end of the second week, as Frank handed Ada a considerably larger payment than the one from the week before, he asked her to eat supper at the table with him instead of taking a plate to her room as she had been doing. Ada did not trust herself to judge his intentions. She had not known enough men in her life to determine where Frank's place was between men like Jesse and men like her father. *Probably, he's just being kind*, she thought. So she obliged, sitting at the table with Annis in her lap. After that meal, and for the next several nights, there was an offer of a glass of peach brandy, which Ada politely declined. Twice, Frank knocked on her door after sundown to ask a question that could well have waited until morning. Each time, Ada made sure to have Annis in her arms when she opened the door.

Occasionally, she felt Frank's eyes on her when he was in the house. But he never suggested anything unseemly. Never took any liberties. Still, Ada began sleeping in her clothes rather than in her lone night-gown, snatched from the clothesline before she left the swamp. She sensed that Frank was toying with her in some way that she did not understand. One day soon, she decided, she would tell him that she was going to drive the wagon into Bristol to visit a friend. Surely she was entitled to a day off. Then she would go to the dry goods store and hope her prayers had been answered and Flora was back, recovered. If not, she could walk from one business to another, asking for work. But carrying Annis with her? And who would watch Annis if she did find work? She thought of Gertie, so near that Ada could easily walk to her house, yet so far removed. She wondered again where Matilda was.

Early on Thursday morning, Frank went into town to officially put the farm up for sale and to meet with a man who, according to Frank, had had his eye on the farm for years. "Uncle Curtis bought it out from under him, and now I'm going to dangle it under his nose."

Late that afternoon, Ada was scrubbing out the kitchen sink and Annis was sitting in a laundry basket happily waving a wooden spoon when Frank's car came down the farm road. Ada heard his steps in the hall, then heard him open the cabinet where he kept a bottle of brandy in the parlor. He sauntered into the kitchen, full glass in hand.

"It's sold—the land, the house, and all the furnishings, right down to the pictures on the walls and the spoons in the drawer. I threw out the highest number I could get away with, and the old codger didn't even dicker over it. The guy's oozing money. Paid me cash on the spot, and I signed the deed over and wired Aunt Rose her share before he could change his mind. Then he paid me extra to be out of here by next week."

Next week. How could she possibly have enough money to rent a room that soon? Ada did not even know what a room would cost. She didn't know anything about living in town.

As if he'd read her mind, Frank said, "There's a bonus in it for you, too. Enough to cover a couple month's rent in Bristol for you and Annis. Aunt Rose cut me a big slice of what I got for the place. Or what I told her I got for the place," he said, winking. "I can afford to be generous."

He lifted his glass and said, "Say hello to a room in civilization, Ada Morgan. And goodbye to this damnable Trace. I'm driving to Jackson first thing in the morning to sign the lease on my new office. I've already put money down on it. Why don't you come along and we'll stop at Bristol first. I'll help you find a room, make sure the rent's fair. That sharecropper woman can look after the baby."

Ada was so relieved that she did not offer any objections. How could she? She imagined herself in a cheery little room in Bristol, free of the swamp and her father and Frank. Free to make a life for Annis and herself, by herself.

Frank went upstairs—he had already eaten in town—and Ada took Annis to their bedroom. It was all going to be okay. She laid out one of the dresses she had sewn for Flora, to wear the next day. Then she danced around the room with Annis in her arms, telling her about the new life they would have. An idea had come to her a while back.

She had seen a shoe repair shop in town, and she thought that maybe she could make up a little sign with prices for various sewing services and persuade the shop owner that she might bring in extra business, offering sewing for his customers. And maybe she could put signs in other places, too. She would need the sewing machine from the swamp, and then she could set it up and work right from their rented room. And who knew? Maybe Flora would come back after all.

"We're almost there," she told Annis, spinning her once more, then setting her down on the floor. Spellbound, Ada watched her beautiful baby girl sitting upright without any help, until she leaned to try to catch a last golden beam of sunlight coming through the window, toppled over, and giggled.

45.

MATILDA

Mr. Moser sent Matilda the latest edition of his newspaper in a box of ripe cheese. He had hidden it between layers of cardboard in the bottom of the box, glued around the edges so that Matilda had to tear the box apart to discover it. In one of the margins, he had scrawled a note instructing her to burn the paper immediately after reading it, no matter how tempted she was to hold on to it. "A safeguard for you." He had given her a pseudonym, L. D. Daniel, and under cover of that byline, Matilda Patterson had told readers in Cleveland, and who knew where else, the truth about Buddy and Cassie Jones, about the red-faced man in town, and about Frank Bowers, all with aliases of their own.

Verbie was home sick that day, so after Matilda had read every word of the newspaper in her room, she slipped over to the funeral parlor and knocked on the door. Mr. Lewis let her use the sink in the embalming room to burn the paper. He did not ask her what it was or why she wanted to burn it; he just told her to be right careful, then climbed the stairs to his living quarters and left her to it. Matilda struck a match and lit the paper on fire. It curled into a charred black scroll, then disintegrated into ashes, and Matilda washed all evidence of L. D. Daniel down the drain.

She had sent three stories now, including the one about Alvert that she had mailed only two days earlier, after Leeta left to take Alvert home. Mr. Moser had written that Matilda's first piece had garnered attention in Cleveland and beyond, and that while no one knew where L. D. Daniel lived, her words had an even greater effect because readers knew they were arriving from the Deep South. Matilda saw this as more reason to remain in Mississippi until she was able to take Gertie and Stella Mae with her when she left.

Matilda soon learned that the funeral parlor was a meeting place for the kind of risk-takers that Mr. Moser had mentioned in his first letter and that Mr. Lewis tended to more than the dead. He lived as frugally as Matilda did, and she came to understand that he was aided in his efforts by donations from many people who were grateful to him for one thing or another. Those donations had enabled him to buy the shiny new truck he had turned into a hearse, boarding up the sides and topping it off himself with rough scrap lumber, then painting on the name of the funeral parlor in crude letters because there were people who would not have stood for his owning a brand-new truck like that one if he had not made it look as homely as Mr. Moser's packages of candy and cheese.

When the time came that Matilda decided it would be good for one person in Jackson to know what she was doing, in case she was ever caught by someone who took exception to it, she sat down with Mr. Lewis. She told him she was writing stories for a newspaper up

North, said enough that he was able to form an understanding of the nature of the stories.

"I don't need names or details," he said. "It's usually best that way." But he took her hand and looked at her in a way that made her feel proud.

After that, Mr. Lewis was like family to her. He looked out for her, lent her books from the floor-to-ceiling bookcase in his living room, and taught her to play chess. There was a camaraderie between the two of them borne of their separate efforts to make a difference in the world.

Even so, Matilda was tired. Mississippi was wearing her down. She was eager to leave. Leeta had put in a word for her with Eunice Wickerson, a woman Leeta had worked for as a maid, and Mrs. Wickerson had agreed to an interview. Matilda was to knock on her door, her back door, the following Saturday. If she could get that job, as well as working at the movie palace, it wouldn't take long to have what she needed. And then perhaps she would enlist the help of Pastor Brown in persuading Gertie to leave the Trace. Gertie was stubborn, but she was not one to argue with the pastor.

46.

ADA

"It's perfect," Ada said.

The room was so perfect that she wished she had never seen it, as it was almost certainly beyond her reach. It was just one street over from Front Street in Bristol, a ten-minute walk from the dry goods store and the shoe repair shop and no more than fifteen or so to most every other place she would need to go in town. It was small, built onto the back of the banker's house for his wife's mother just months before she passed away. But it was sunny and new, and there was a separate door to the outside, so whoever lived there needn't enter the main house to come and go. And there were electric lights and an electric fan! A small section of the larger yard was fenced in behind the room, with a clothesline and, on a small covered patio, a hand-crank washer like the one at the Creedle house. It came with the room, as the banker's wife had an electric washing machine. They would not mind, they told her, if she wanted to take in laundry as well as sewing, as long as anyone coming to see her used the street behind the house and came through her little gate.

With all eyes on Ada, she tried to think of how she might manage it. In her handbag was all of her last three weeks' pay, but surely not enough for a place like this. There was Frank's promise of a bonus from the sale of the farm, but that was still just a promise. She hoped she might still recover the money from the stilt house. Perhaps Job Farley had found the tin and saved it for her. She would need time to find out.

"Could you wait until—"

"No need. We'll square it later." Frank took out his wallet and handed the banker three months' rent on the room.

Frank's making that decision for her made Ada uneasy, as had his introducing her to the banker and his wife as his recently widowed cousin. "On my father's side," he'd said smoothly, while Ada had concentrated on keeping her mouth from falling open.

"Easier than explaining the situation," he said when they were back in his car. Meaning Ada's being a young, unmarried mother. "They're old fogies. Had to give them a reason not to hike up the rent so either you'd go away or it'd be worth their while to overlook a little disgrace."

It was like being doused with a bucket of water.

Frank noticed. "It got you the room," he said.

Being so close to a whole new life, and not wanting to appear ungrateful, Ada said, "I'm beholden."

"Good," Frank said, laughing.

Frank drove fast, and Ada, who until that day had never been in an automobile, was still trying to acclimate herself to the noise of the engine. She was nervous, particularly as Frank was never the one to give

way when they encountered another vehicle—car, wagon, or buggy—
on the rough, narrow roads. She had been nervous, too, about leaving
Annis behind, although Doreen Braswell was a friendly woman with
two little girls of her own and had seemed happy to look after Annis.
The Braswells had already begun packing up their belongings, readying themselves to leave the farm.

Ada was amazed at how quickly they covered the distance between
her new room in Bristol and Frank's new office in Jackson. When they
arrived, Frank reached behind his seat for the sign he'd had made up—
"Franklin T. Bowers, Attorney at Law"—and Ada remained in the
car while he went inside to sign the lease. She was eager to get back
to Annis, to start packing up her own meager belongings. She would
load them into the wagon and drive first to the swamp, ask Job Farley
to help her rescue the sewing machine, pay him what she could, then
she and Annis would be on their way. And whether or not Frank's
promised bonus ever came her way, in time, she would pay back every
cent of what he had given to the banker to hold her room.

When Frank returned to the car, he opened her door instead of
his.

"It's a done deal. My sign's going up today. And now," he said, "it's
time to celebrate."

"Celebrate?"

"The sale of the farm. Your new room. My new law practice." He
offered his hand, and Ada stepped onto the sidewalk. "Have you ever
been to a theater?"

Ada shook her head.

"Then I'm going to treat you to a movie."

"What? We can't. I need to be getting back to Annis."

"It's early still. We'll be back before dark, or soon after. The drive's shorter without going through Bristol. So there's nothing to worry about." He smiled, bringing out that disarming dimple, then said, "So stop worrying. You deserve a day out without a baby under your feet."

⁓

The film that day was *Robin Hood*. Ada passed through the elegant pillared lobby and into the grand auditorium as if stepping into one of her mother's best stories. She sat on a velvet seat under an arched ceiling painted with flowers and vines in diamond-shaped panes and let herself be pried loose from all her worries, her awareness of Frank sitting next to her all but gone. When the lights went down and the red and gold curtains swooshed open, Ada was transported to a world of kings and castles, clashing swords, knights and fair maidens. And there was music like she had never heard, could never have imagined, from the theater orchestra. Ada Morgan from the swamp on the Natchez Trace did not exist until the final frame faded and she floated out of the building and back to reality.

"Frank Bowers!" A portly man in a black suit, smoking a cigar, clapped Frank on the back.

"Mr. Bonner." Frank thrust out his hand.

"I've been hearing rumors about you, young man. I understand you're putting up a shingle here in Jackson."

"Yes, sir," Frank said.

"So you won't be signing on with a firm here?"

"No, going to go it alone."

Ada hoped this man would not require her to speak, which he did not. Frank turned his back, standing in front of her as if making her disappear, and Ada wished she truly could. She stood by silently as they talked about real estate and the law and a seemingly endless number of related topics while the moviegoers all cleared out of the theater and dispersed in their various directions. After a while, the two men moved to a bench under a lamppost in front of the jewelry store next door, and Mr. Bonner pulled a second cigar from his pocket and passed it to Frank. Frank bit off one end, accepted a light, and they were off again, discussing cigars and the curse of Prohibition, all without so much as a glance in Ada's direction. She saw that as an opportune cue and wandered down the sidewalk, peering into shop windows and imagining herself with a storefront of her own someday. Finally, the men stood and said their goodbyes, and Frank joined her on the sidewalk.

"Chet Bonner. Land commissioner," he said. "Come next election I'll be running against him, but he doesn't know it yet."

Frank slid an arm around Ada's waist, and she quickly stepped out of it.

"Jackson's not far from Bristol, you know," Frank said. "I'll be close enough that I can look in on you from time to time. Make sure no one's taking advantage of you. Make sure you're not having trouble keeping up with the rent." He took hold of her elbow, leaned in close to her ear and whispered, "I expect you'll be willing to show your gratitude then."

Ada's heart froze. She wanted to walk away from him, but that would only leave her stranded. She wanted to go immediately to

Annis, but she had no way to get to her except in Frank's car. So she
bit the inside of her cheek and drew up inside herself, just as she had
with her father when she'd felt trapped. She wished she had stayed on
the swamp until the stilt house fell down around her. Or gotten on a
train and gone to Red Dog, Texas, looked for Jesse and told him he had
a daughter. Anything but driving that old mule to Peggy's house after
Gertie sent her away.

Frank moved his hand to the small of her back, then turned to
flick his cigar into a gutter along the street behind them. Suddenly he
pulled away and spun around, staring at the entrance to the theater.

"What is it?" Ada asked, alarmed. There was a look on Frank's face
that scared her, the look of an animal in the woods alert to some kind
of danger and deciding whether to hide or attack. Ada peered around
him, but there was no one else in sight except a colored cleaning lady,
her back to Ada, slipping into the empty theater.

"I thought she was dead," Frank murmured.

"Who?"

Frank turned back to her. "The actress," he said. "From the movie.
Up there on the marquee. Let's go."

47.

ADA

Frank was different now, as if a gear had turned as he stood in front
of the theater and all his dangerous interest in Ada had fallen away.
He touched her only to clutch her hand and pull her across the
street.

"I've changed my mind," he said. "We're going to stay here tonight.
There's something I have to do."

"No. No, we can't. I have to get back to Annis." Ada took a deep
breath, tried to calm herself.

"I said I have something I have to do." Frank spoke coldly now.
"The croppers have Annis. We're going to go over to the hotel now,
get checked in."

The hotel. What was happening? Could it be possible that she had
led him to believe she would go to a hotel with him? She had no experience with men other than Jesse, and Frank was nothing like Jesse.
She stuffed her trembling hands into the folds of her skirt and made
herself look Frank in the eye the way she imagined Matilda would in
her place. She tried to muster some of Matilda's bravado and insisted

that he take her back to the farm. Frank did not answer. Ada was not sure he had even heard her.

Then he said, "I have no choice," and Ada understood that she was the one who had no choice.

"I wouldn't never have come if I'd known it was going to cost you so dear," she said. "A fancy picture show and two rooms at a hotel…"

"Don't be a child."

The room was on the second floor. Frank was preoccupied, agitated, though the cause seemed to have little to do with Ada. He sat staring out the window, nervously kneading the back of his neck with one hand.

Some other time, under other circumstances, Ada would have been delighted by the room—the floral wallpaper and lace curtains, the brocade chairs and the plush spread on the bed—but now it turned her stomach, too sweet a background for what was playing out on this night.

Frank stood abruptly and said, "There's somewhere I have to go. I'll be gone a good while. Don't leave this room."

A moment later, he was gone. Ada's head hurt so that she could not bear the light from the window. Her vision blurred, and even the whispery sound of her thoughts was painful. She thought she might faint. She pushed the two brocade chairs together as far away from the bed as possible and curled herself onto them. With her shoes still on her feet, she gave herself up to the blissful oblivion of sleep.

Ada woke the instant the door opened. She did not move on the chairs. There was still a little light outside, and she opened her eyes just enough to watch through her lashes as Frank paced back and forth on the rug, then sat on the edge of the bed. He cursed under his breath, punched a pillow with his fist. Ada hardly dared breathe. Then in a low and bitter voice befitting a curse or a challenge he was privately accepting, Frank said, "Matilda Patterson."

Ada gasped, and a whisper escaped her—"Matilda."

Instantly, Frank was on his feet. Their eyes met, and Ada knew he had heard the recognition in her voice, could see it now in her eyes. She sat up. Frank crossed the room slowly, then leaned over her to turn on a lamp behind the two chairs. He caught his bottom lip between his teeth and nodded slightly, as if he had part of something figured out and Ada had what he needed to finish the process. Then he lifted his chin and raised his eyebrows, and Ada saw things fall into place for Frank.

"It was her. By god, it was her, wasn't it? The girl living with you on the swamp. It was her."

Ada said nothing.

"I saw her on the street tonight. But what I don't get is how old Virgil figures into this." Frank sat down on the chair pressed close to the one on which Ada sat. He draped his arm across the back of her chair.

Ada wanted to tell him he was wrong, but she could only close her eyes, try to shut him out.

"She's a bootlegger—did you know that? I found out about it, and she attacked me. Drew blood," he said, leaning over and showing Ada a scar, a thin white line on the back of his hand. "Did she tell you what happened to her family?"

Ada could not stop herself from looking up at him then, waiting for the answer to her long-held question.

"Their house burned up. A sharecropper cabin on the farm. It was just after Uncle Curtis died. At first they thought it was the woodstove that caused it, but the deputy told me later that someone started that fire deliberately. They never found out who. There was a baby inside. Her own sister, they told me. And here we all thought your Matilda died in that fire. Just like she wanted us to."

"What do you mean?"

"I mean she started that fire. Why else would she run off and let people think she was dead?"

Matilda hiding out on the swamp. "Turns out I'm needing a place to stay." Her driving off with Virgil's liquor. Her anger at a question about her sister. Ada's thoughts scattered like leaves in a wind; she could not catch hold of any one of them before it skittered away. She couldn't reason, she could only feel, and the feelings did not seem to belong to her, but her to them. The strongest, though, was disbelief, and she shook her head fiercely.

"I don't believe she done that."

"Ask around. Ask the Braswell woman. She was there. Your little friend let them all believe she was dead. And all the time, you were hiding her. That's against the law, you know." Frank slid off the chair, slippery as a snake, and stood in front of Ada.

"I think she murdered them. Her own family. And what I'm wondering is, first off, why you'd be hiding a murderer when a person can go to prison for that." He leaned in closer. "And second, I'm wondering what really happened to old Virgil. She hated him."

Ada's pulse roared in her ears. A herd of horses galloped in her chest, and her temples throbbed. Frank terrified her. She heard more words through the pounding in her head, things that Frank said should happen to Matilda, *would* happen to her, now that he knew she was alive. Knew where she lived, he claimed. She heard him accuse Matilda, and Ada herself, of killing Virgil. Then she heard her own voice break through it all.

"No! You're wrong. This is the truth. The real truth." She was screaming now, and Frank did not stop her, didn't try to quiet her. "She saved my life. My daddy lit the shed on fire with me in it, and he was latching the latch—just like he done to my mama. And Matilda saved me. She hit him with a hammer and pulled me out. I would have burnt up. Annis wouldn't never have been born. She saved us."

And there on Frank's face was a look that Ada knew. A Christmas morning look.

"What did you do with him? After she killed him. Murdered him."

"We—" Ada stopped herself, swallowed hard, and started again. "He wasn't hurt bad, my daddy. He went off to sell some pelts and never come back. Like I told you back at the house."

Frank grabbed Ada's wrist and wrenched it behind her back. The lamp fell over as he drew her to her feet. When the glass shade shattered, Ada was back in the stilt house and the broken glass was her father's empty bottle smashed on the kitchen floor; then it was shards from the kerosene lamp her mother took to the outhouse the night she died; then Virgil was kicking over the glass lantern in the shed.

Frank held her wrist in one hand and her face in the other and spoke calmly and slowly. "Your old friend killed Virgil, and you're up to your neck in it. Don't think you aren't." He let go of her, and she slumped to the floor as if his grip had been the only thing holding her up.

He kept talking. "Maybe she had a reason that you thought made it all right, or maybe you hated the miserable bastard enough to want to see him dead. I don't care. But she's had it in for me for a long time, and she's not going to cause trouble for me now that things are going my way for once. I'm going to take care of this, and you're going to do everything I tell you to do. Do you understand that?"

Ada had heard stories. Even on the Trace where she had known so few people, almost no one after she stopped going to school, she had heard about the kinds of things that had happened over a lot less than a dead white man and a colored girl with a hammer. Her face was still as a stone.

"Let me be clear. You are going to tell me what you two did with Virgil. And if you don't, I will see that both of you are arrested and that Annis becomes a ward of the county. That means you never see her again. I can make that happen, or I can keep you out of trouble. You have less than a minute to decide before I decide for you. Now I'm going to ask one time. What did you do with him?"

She couldn't lose Annis. She could not let Annis lose her mother the way Ada had lost Sylvie. Leave her in Frank's hands. *I'm all she has.* Maybe she could find Matilda. Warn her. Maybe Gertie…

"All right, then," Frank said. "Time's up." He turned, took a step away from her.

"The woods. We buried him in the woods."

Frank slept on the floor in front of the hotel room door, wrapped in the spread from the bed and barring any exit. Before he lay down, he took Ada's shoes and her handbag. Ada sat in a chair across the room, clearing her mind, looking for strength. *You find a way, is what you do.*

48.

MATILDA

"A white man," Mr. Lewis said. "Trailing behind you a ways off when you came in. Could be he had some kind of business down here, but I don't know as that's likely. Just keep an eye out."

Mr. Lewis and Matilda were standing behind the boardinghouse an hour after Matilda had returned from the theater, having cleaned up after the midday matinee. Mr. Lewis had knocked on the back window, and Matilda had rushed out to meet him.

"What'd he look like?" she asked him.

"Couldn't tell much. He stuck to the other side of the road. About as tall as me. Medium build. Hat pulled low. Walked on down the road after he watched you go in."

"Could be somebody carrying a grudge against Leeta, looking for her." Leeta had always had a way with making enemies for herself.

"Could be that."

"You think somebody might know about my packages?"

"I don't think so, but he did look to be following you. I had a thought it might be somebody looking into what all I do at the parlor, but he just walked on by. Stayed back while you went into the house. That tells me he didn't want to be seen."

Matilda had not told Mr. Lewis about Virgil Morgan lying in a tomb on the Trace, or about Frank Bowers sitting in the springhouse with Buddy Jones's watch in his hand. The man was already carrying more secrets than she was, and she knew how heavy each one could be. And how could she have explained killing a man and hiding his body in a borrowed tomb? Or letting people think she'd died in a fire she might have stopped if she hadn't taken a walk when she should have stayed home?

"Could be somebody just liked the way you look. Or could be nothing to do with you at all. But you might want to hold off on trips to the post office. For a while. And it wouldn't hurt if you started looking like you had you a boyfriend walking you home at night. I've got somebody in mind."

It was late, well past midnight, when Matilda was finally able to sleep. At nine o'clock in the morning, she set out to meet with Mrs. Wickerson about Leeta's old job. The Wickersons lived in a pretty two-story house on Congress Street just a short walk from the movie palace. It was a beautiful, sunny day, not quite spring by the calendar, but full-on spring in the air. Matilda was early, so she stopped here and there to do a little window-shopping on her way up Capitol Street. The sun felt good on her skin. Flowers were blooming in pots on the sidewalk, scenting the air in a way she did not notice when she walked home hurriedly at night. And tonight, she remembered, she would be walking home with Mr. Lewis's friend.

"His name is Robert," Mr. Lewis had told her before she left the boardinghouse that morning. "And don't go slapping his face when he holds your hand. I told him to make it look good. You hear anybody behind you, you cozy up to Robert like anything getting to you is going to have to get past him."

Matilda had to admit that holding a male hand on the way home did not seem all that awful. She wondered what this Robert was like as she cut a path to North Congress Street. She wasn't far from the Wickersons' house when she passed a storefront office with a new sign outside that stopped her cold: *Franklin T. Bowers, Attorney at Law.*

Frank is here. In Jackson. He could be behind her on the sidewalk right now. Or inside that office. She turned around quickly and walked all the way back to the boardinghouse without breaking her stride, then over to the funeral parlor. She knocked on the back door, and when it opened, she collapsed into Mr. Lewis's arms.

Before dawn the next morning, laid out in a body basket in the back of Mr. Lewis's homemade hearse, Matilda cracked open the lid with her toe to let in some air. The prickly horsehair cushion underneath her smelled of antiseptic. The wooden ceiling over the enclosed truck bed was too low to allow her to sit up without bumping her head, so she lay on her back taking shallow breaths and estimating the passing miles between herself and Frank Bowers in Jackson. Mr. Lewis was driving the hearse in the wrong direction—away from Jackson—for there to be a body in the back. A body would be headed to the funeral home for embalming and the other professional ministrations and dignities Mr.

Lewis provided for the departed. And they were now well outside the limits of his general funerary jurisdiction. Folks this far out just dug their own holes for their loved ones. But should anyone stop them, he had explanations prepared.

Matilda had told him everything. About the shack fire and the hammer coming down on Virgil Morgan's head and the tomb on the Trace. That she was the only person, other than Frank himself, who knew that Frank Bowers was a murderer, though she could not prove it. That she had let most everyone believe she had died in the fire. She told him that Frank was in Jackson now, that she had seen his sign downtown. That he must have been the man who had followed her home. And that she would not leave Mississippi without Gertie and Stella Mae. Within an hour, Mr. Lewis had her hidden inside the hearse.

Finally, the truck slowed and shuddered, then stopped. The wooden door at the back swung open on its barn hinges, and Mr. Lewis's face appeared. They were on the Trace, had made it there unseen. He had gone on a mile beyond the road that led to Gertie's and to the farm, as Matilda had requested. He lent his hand as she climbed out of the basket and crawled from the truck bed. She stretched her stiff limbs in the clear light of the beautiful morning, and Mr. Lewis lifted out the bag she had filled with her scant possessions, set it on the ground, and refastened the door. He had agreed only reluctantly to letting her out there, and he argued again now for driving her down to Gertie's cabin.

"I'd like to pass you off to somebody I could say a word to," he said. "See you safe inside."

Matilda insisted he take her no farther, but turn around and head back to the relative safety of the funeral parlor. "I'll backtrack through the woods. I can walk it easy," she told him. "You took a big enough chance driving me this far."

"What if your friend's not home?"

"The preacher's not far. He knows about me. Knows I wasn't in the fire. I could go there."

"Pastor Brown," Mr. Lewis said, nodding.

"You know him?"

"We have crossed paths," he said, and Matilda understood that to mean that Pastor Brown was not unacquainted with risk-taking and meaningful work himself.

Mr. Lewis asked once more to drive her the rest of the way, but they both knew that it was not wise to draw any more attention to the hearse than they had to. Which meant not standing alongside it there on the Trace much longer.

"Can't fight stubborn," Mr. Lewis said, handing Matilda her bag. He took a minute to watch her shoulder it, readying herself for what lay ahead. "I forget, sometimes, how young you are," he said.

"Sometimes I do, too."

"It's important that the young hold hope for this world. Otherwise, we're every one of us lost." He held open his arms, and Matilda walked into his fatherly embrace, his gray beard and his shirt smelling of tobacco and soap. She breathed in his scent, then broke away.

"You need to get on," she told him.

He slipped an envelope out of his pocket. "Take this," he said, "and get yourself and your friends on that train to Ohio bright and early tomorrow. From Canton, like we talked about. Less chance of seeing anybody you know there than in Bristol."

"The pastor's son'll take us."

"Send word as soon as you get to Cleveland. I won't rest easy till I hear."

"I don't like taking this," Matilda said of the envelope. "You've already done so much." She swiped a hand across her eyes. "You know I'm good for it. I'll pay it back. Look for a package of smelly cheese," she said, smiling and crying at the same time. Mr. Lewis jerked a handkerchief out of his pocket, blotted his own eyes, then swung open the driver's door of the truck. He stepped up and slid onto the seat, and Matilda ducked off the road into a familiar thicket of thorny trees.

49.

ADA

When Frank woke on the floor of the hotel room in Jackson, he balled up the spread and tossed it back onto the bed. He walked past Ada without a word, then went into the little lavatory. Ada sat in a chair by the window where she could see the people on the street below and feel connected to the world outside that room. When Frank returned, he pulled the lace curtains closed.

"This is what we're going to do," he said, his voice stone cold. "First, I'm going to go downstairs for some coffee. Then I'm going to start the car and drive you back to that swamp, and you're going to show me exactly where you buried old Virgil. Then Sonny Platt, the deputy sheriff, is going to see to it that your old friend and mine doesn't get in my way going forward. And before we pay him that call, you need to know that I've got more on old Sonny than your Matilda thinks she's got on me. Enough that I can keep you out of this or I can put you right in the middle of it. So do we understand each other?"

Ada did not believe any of Frank's accusations. She had stacked everything she knew about Matilda against everything she had seen of

Frank, and put all her faith in Matilda. If Matilda had left that scar on Frank's hand—and she doubted that was true—Ada knew she'd had a good reason. She had to warn Matilda. And she had to get to Annis, get her off the farm. She felt herself shutting down as she had so often as a child, drifting out of time into a secret, safe place where she was untouchable. But now she worked to bring herself right back, because she could not fight for Annis from that place. And she had to fight.

She looked at Frank and nodded.

"All right," he said. "I'm going now. You pull yourself together and be standing out front of the lobby in twenty minutes."

In the lavatory, Ada poured a pitcher of water over her head, then twisted her wet hair into a bun. The dress she had been so proud to sew for Flora was wrinkled and twisted and forever marked by her time in this place with Frank. She never wanted to wear it again. She put her shoes back on her feet and looked for her bag, but didn't find it. She supposed Frank had taken it.

She sat for a moment, thinking wildly about what to do, trying to focus. Surely Matilda knew something dangerous about Frank. Was it Frank that she had been hiding from on the swamp? Ada was sick with fear. What would become of Annis if she couldn't reach her? And Matilda. Matilda had been more than a friend to her, more than a sister, and Ada had handed her over to Frank. And though she was certain, in that moment, that she was too evil for anything good to hear her, she dropped to her knees and prayed for help. *Light a path for me.*

Twenty minutes after Frank had left the hotel room, Ada was standing on the sidewalk, hoping for a miracle.

Frank pushed the Ford to its limits. His knuckles were white as he gripped the wheel. The stutter and whine of the engine was so loud that Ada was spared any more of his vile words. As the streets of Jackson, then the rural houses on the outskirts, then wooded countryside rolled past the car window, Ada was torn between relief that she was that much closer to Annis and panic at the events she had set in motion when she whispered Matilda's name. Better that Frank had had his way with her in that hotel room than that she had betrayed Matilda. She knew that now her only value to Frank was in her recounting to the deputy that Matilda had killed Virgil. She had to protect Annis, and protecting Annis, as Frank had ordered things, required condemning Matilda. Everything was tied up together and revolving around Ada, spinning and moving forward toward some horrible end.

When they finally reached the Trace and slowed enough that Ada could shout over the noise of the engine, she tried again to undo some of the damage of the night before.

"You're wrong about Matilda."

"Not now," Frank shouted back, holding up a hand between them to stop her. "It's too late for that."

Ada wanted to yank the door handle, fall out of the car, and run to the shelter of her childhood woods. And she might have, if not for Annis. And Matilda. At the road that led to the farm, Frank turned hard and Ada slammed into the car door. When she realized he was taking her to the farm instead of to the swamp to look for Virgil, she thought that maybe her prayers had been heard after all. When he turned left at the fork, toward the farmhouse, instead of right, toward the Braswell's house, she spoke up again. "I've got to get Annis. Doreen's expecting—"

"Doreen can wait."

They were at the house only long enough for Frank to change out of his dress pants and white shirt and into old work clothes. He threw a shovel into the car, and they were off again, driving away from Annis. He stopped where the farm road met the Trace and turned to look at Ada. His eyes, she thought, were as dead as Virgil's just before he dropped into the tomb.

"Which woods?" he asked her. "Which way do I turn?"

She had not told Frank just where they had buried Virgil or that they had buried him in a tomb. She had let him bring a shovel without telling him it was the wrong tool. As if that one omission might stop him. She hesitated before answering.

"Let me spell this out for you again," he said. "You're going to take me to where you put him, and I'm going to make sure he's there. And he'd better be. And then we're going to go see the deputy in Bristol, and you're going to tell him that Matilda killed your father. That you tried to stop her, but she was crazed and too strong for you. And unless you want to go down with her, you'll tell him that she said she would kill you, too, if you didn't help her bury him. And then, if you do all that, I'll clear you with him, and we'll go get Annis. But if you don't, if you miss doing any one of those things, I'll take you into town with another version of the story. You don't look so good in that one. In that case, I'll be leaving you with the good deputy, and I'll go for Annis myself. You might not want that."

"He won't believe me." Ada's voice shook, as did her whole body. Her teeth clicked together as she spoke. "I don't lie good."

"That won't be a problem. There's one thing you need to understand. That deputy and me, we've been in business together since I came back to the farm. Exporting, you might say. It's quite lucrative. And he's got a lot of important friends he's done favors for. So either way, your friend's going to hang. You're the only one I'm not sure about yet." He put his hands back on the wheel. "Now which way do we turn?"

Ada had only seconds to make a decision. For once in her life, she thought, she would do something herself rather than waiting to see what might be done to her.

She directed Frank onto Virgil's weedy back trail, told him to stop halfway down it, long out of sight of the stilt house. They got out of the car, Frank with the shovel, and Ada led him into the woods. Her knees were unsteady. She reminded herself to breathe, told herself that so very much depended on her right now.

"I'm trying to remember," she told Frank. "It was pitch-black that night. It's back through here. I just have to get my mind clear."

Frank stayed on her heels, pressing her forward, warning her against wasting his time. He was angry one minute, then dead calm the next. She steered them east for a while, away from the swamp, then bore north into denser woods crowded with young pines that had sprung up amid the old hardwoods. Here there were no discernible paths, and moving through the undergrowth was difficult. Ada knew that a half mile or so on, if she missed the red maple she was looking for, they would come out at the Pearl River. If they got that far, she would have to tell Frank she was lost, and then backtrack. She did not know what he might do to her if that happened. But then, there was the maple, showing her the first of its frilly red blooms.

"This way," she said, turning east again, then cutting a wide half-circle through tall trees that spread their crowns overhead and blocked the sun, casting shadows that Ada hoped would keep Frank from gaining his bearings in her woods.

"How much farther?" Frank was breathing hard. "It's almost like night in here. I'll bet this place is crawling with snakes."

From tree to tree, Ada navigated a careful way forward until she could make out what she was aiming for: Virgil's old deer stand, the boarded-in platform high in a massive sweet gum tree with woody poison-ivy vines as thick as her wrist climbing the trunk like hairy serpents guarding the place where Virgil had hidden his stolen pelts.

"It's just on from here," she said, and Frank moved more quickly in response.

Ada paused. She crossed her arms over her chest and tucked her hands into her armpits to ease their shaking. She tried not to think about what she was doing.

"We're real close," she said. "Just let me try to remember right." Her voice broke, and she jumped when Frank took her arm, not harshly this time, and turned her around. When he spoke, she could hear the forced patience in his voice.

"Look," he said. "I'm not a monster. You do this right, and we can both have a good future. The truth is, your friend knows some things that could hurt me. I sowed some oats the summer I spent on the farm. But her father was a bootlegger. He was a sharecropper for Uncle Curtis and sold liquor out of his cabin. Matilda was all up in that. I was on to them, and she had it in for me. Started making up lies and threatening me. And that's the thing with politics. It doesn't have to be true, what people say when you're running for office. Rumors and lies will take a person down just as quick as truth. Lucky for me, she did old Virgil in. She's a murderer. Problem solved. You just need to grow up and learn how life works. If you don't strike first, you get struck. I'm going up in this world. You show me I can trust you, and you'll go up, too. Do you understand?"

"I understand." Ada held her voice steady.

"Now. You know exactly where Virgil is, don't you?"

Ada nodded. She hung her head in the old show of defeat that had usually disgusted her father enough to disarm him. "Around back of that big tree," she said, "there's a board ladder nailed to the trunk. He's up there. In a deer stand." She raised her head and pointed, sure that in the dim light Frank would not notice the other way, the safe way, up—an old stump, and above it, four footholds carved discreetly into the opposite side of the trunk of the sweet gum tree. Afraid he might try to push her ahead of him, she sank to the ground and sobbed.

"Why didn't you tell me I wouldn't need this?" Frank threw the shovel to the ground. "Putting him in a deer stand isn't burying him."

Ada kept sobbing, real tears rolling down her face as Frank moved off. *Merciful God, let it be the same as it was. Let it do what it was made to do. For Annis. For Matilda.*

Frank stomped through the brush. Ada heard the rustling of the dry leaves around the base of the tree.

"I don't see how two girls got somebody his size up—"

His scream was bloodcurdling. It raised the hairs on Ada's neck, though she had expected to hear it, had hoped to hear it. There was the faint barking of a dog, probably one of Ansel's. Then there was nothing. She thought there should be some sound, but there was nothing that did not belong to the woods. She was afraid to look, afraid of being tricked by Frank. Several silent minutes passed before she found the courage to step forward. She moved past the tree inches at a time, imagining Frank standing behind it, waiting for her. Two steps more, and she saw him. Lying at the foot of the tree, the large, cruel teeth of Virgil's enormous bear trap embedded in his calf. His shredded pant leg and the ground underneath him were soaked in blood, and still, blood spurted from his leg, coursing with his pulse. His face was ghostly white. He was deathly still.

Ada turned away from him and ran back through the woods. There was only one place to go.

50.

ADA AND MATILDA

The latch had been drawn at the door, the window behind the porch closed and braced, the curtains pulled together. Ada's chest was heaving after the trip across the Trace. Her legs were weak and wobbly. She had run nearly the whole way, slowing to walk only when the stitch in her side doubled her over.

She banged on the front door.

"Miss Tuttle! Please. I'm in terrible trouble. Please, please open the door." She invoked Annis's name, hoping that might sway the old midwife. She cried out that it was a matter of life and death, appealing to Gertie's holy call to nursing. When there was no answer, she ran around to the back door and found the latch drawn there, as well.

Inside the cabin, Matilda watched Ada through a crack in Gertie's wall. Ada was in the backyard, now, looking into the lean-to. Now she was walking among the stones in the baby cemetery. Soon she would come upon the stone that Matilda had discovered when she arrived at the cabin that morning, after saying goodbye to Mr. Lewis on the Trace. *She'll see it, and she'll leave.* But when Ada did see it—a large rock marking a fresh grave and painted with *Gertrude Tuttle, Born 18?, Died 1924*—she did not leave. Matilda saw her look up at the sky as though Gertie were there among the clouds, then return to the back porch. She heard Ada slump against the door, and Matilda hardened herself. She was in no position to trust anyone other than the pastor. She had been about to go to him when Ada arrived. She listened through the old dry wood of Gertie's back door, making no sound. She heard a soft whimper, then "Oh, Miss Tuttle. I killed Frank Bowers, and I don't know what to do."

Matilda drew back the latch and pulled open the door.

51.

ADA AND MATILDA

The sense of danger that had hung in the air of the stilt house in the days just after Virgil's death hung now in the air of Gertie's cabin. Ada had told Matilda everything, the events of the past several hours spilling out in words so caught up in sobs that Matilda had had to work hard to piece together the horrid details. Now she and Ada sat silently across from each other at Gertie's table, Ada as anxious and Matilda as wary as they had been on that first night together on the swamp, and in as much need of a plan as they had been then. So much had been demanded of each of them in the past hours that both were worn raw, and they allowed themselves some time to think separately before attempting to renew a mutual resolve.

When talk resumed, it circled back to Virgil. Ada spoke first.

"He used to say that anybody fool enough to try to steal his pelts wouldn't live to try again. He worked on that trap a long time. Making adjustments. I didn't know if it was true, what he said—that it would kill somebody right off. And I wasn't sure it would still spring. Mostly, I was afraid it would, I think."

"It had to have cut through an artery, for him to bleed out like that," Matilda said. "Gertie saw it once. A plow. He's done for now, for sure. Probably didn't take long."

They were quiet for another moment, thinking about that. Then they turned to the situation at hand.

Matilda had already made her own plan, had rescued herself from Frank, she and Mr. Lewis together. Frank's death had little bearing on that. She would be on a train bound for Cleveland in the morning. But without Gertie. The pastor would tell her where Stella Mae was, and if that little angel was in good hands, Matilda would go on without her, too. In the minds of everyone else on this side of the Trace, other than Pastor Brown and Byron, Matilda was still conveniently dead. She was not required, she told herself, to clean up this mess.

"I'm not looking to you to help me," Ada said. "I done this myself." She thought of Gertie's last words to her, on the porch of this very cabin: *She saved your life. Saved your baby, too. Ain't that enough?* And yes, it was enough. More than anyone had ever done for her. She would not ask Matilda to involve herself in another man's death. Not even for Annis's sake. "If I can just rest here a little while, I'll go and leave you be. I won't never let your name slip like that again. You don't need to worry about that."

If she had said anything else, Matilda thought, *I could have sent her on her way with nothing more than goodbye and good luck. Maybe.*

They made a new plan. They both understood that it was far too dangerous to risk Matilda being seen at the place where Frank died. To

THE GIRLS IN THE STILT HOUSE

be seen alive anywhere, under the circumstances. So Ada crossed the Trace again, alone.

She went first to the stilt house. It had not completely collapsed, but was severely tilted. The tin of money from behind the stove had rolled out, and Ada saw it half buried in mud under a pile of broken stilts. But there was no time for that now.

In the shed, she found Virgil's deer rifle just where Matilda had told her to look for it, and she loaded it with the bullets Matilda had saved for emergencies. With a gun under her arm for the first time in her life, she trekked back through the woods, in a straight line this time, to the deer stand.

She allowed no emotion to slow her down. Each step she took was one step closer to Annis, and she would have her baby in her arms by nightfall even if every demon in hell tried to get in her way.

Frank was still there. Of course he was still there, one more victim of Virgil's traps. Blood no longer spurted from his leg. All color had drained from his face. His eyes stared, unseeing but still as cold and menacing as they had been at the hotel that morning. Frank Bowers had joined Virgil in the just hereafter.

With none of her old fear, with only purpose, Ada laid her father's rifle beside Frank's open hand and slipped the last of the bullets into the pocket of his pants. Then she picked up the shovel and headed back with it to the shed.

"If anyone finds him," Matilda had told her before she set out, "they'll see a hunting accident, plain and simple. A man in the woods with a rifle, about to climb up a deer stand. Stepped into an old bear trap some hunter left out there. Ain't nothing odd about a hunting accident on the Trace."

Back at the stilt house, she left the shovel in the shed and latched the door. She did not rescue the tin from the mud and rubble under the house. Her hope was that, eventually, when it was clear that no one was coming back for it, Job Farley would take it and use the money for his family. She doubted he would, though.

She turned a last look on the swamp, the tall trees throwing long shadows over the surface of the water, a blue heron gliding overhead, making its own escape. She bid a silent farewell to everything good and beautiful about this place and let go of everything else. Then she headed for the Trace, and Annis.

Ada made it back to Gertie's cabin, and then to the farm, in time to retrieve Annis from Doreen Braswell just as the sky was hinting at dusk. She made her apologies and offered excuses for having been an extra day getting back, for worrying them. She added lying to Doreen, telling her that they'd had trouble with the Ford in Jackson, to the long list of things she was hoping to be forgiven for.

"We're all packed up. Leaving first thing in the morning," Doreen told her, passing Annis into Ada's arms at last. "New Orleans. Got family there. No more cropping for us. Charles's brother got him on at the docks. Can't say I'll miss this place," she said, her face full of pure relief.

"One thing," she said then. "That name. Annis. I was wondering where you got that from. I knew somebody once, named their baby girl that."

"It's pretty, isn't it? Somebody else picked it out. A friend," Ada said, and Doreen seemed to ponder that as she held open the screen door for Ada.

In the housekeeper's room at the Creedle house, Ada stood at the window watching the farm road in the last light. Matilda was on the floor, Annis crawling over her feet.

"You did good today," Matilda said. "It might not seem like it—taking a life. But you can think of it as saving your own. He wouldn't have left you in peace any other way. Wouldn't have let you go off safe, knowing you could tell the truth about him anytime. He was right about me knowing something about him. And I can tell you, you saved your life."

Ada did not need to know more. She already felt pardoned.

Later, they talked through the rest of their plan, the part that Matilda had arranged while Ada was back at the swamp. Byron would meet them—Matilda, Ada, and Annis—in the barn at four o'clock in the morning. They would hitch the mule to Ada's wagon, then Ada would drive all four of them off the Trace before sunrise, Matilda's face hidden as much as possible under a field hat. Byron and Matilda would ride in the back of the wagon as if catching a ride to Canton, a detail that embarrassed Ada, but was the course least likely to raise any eyebrows. After the trip to the train station, Byron would drive the wagon back to the Trace, the mule and the wagon his then.

While they waited for the appointed hour, Ada quickly packed her things. Matilda rocked Annis—at least one of them would sleep that night—and Ada went upstairs to look for her handbag. She found it bunched up with the clothes Frank had worn to Jackson. Then she worked on a plan of her own.

She went into Peggy's room and took a stuffed bear off the bed, ripped out a section of the back seam, and pulled out the stuffing. Then she went through the house visiting each of the spots where she had discovered, while cleaning and exploring when Frank was away, stores of hidden cash. Frank's "exporting" money, she supposed. Probably some of his uncle's, as well. Perhaps, too, the under-the-table money Frank had kept from the sale of the farm. There was so much money that after she had restuffed the bear with some of it, she went back to the house-keeper's room for Annis's drawstring nightgown and tied up the rest inside it. She offered it all to Matilda, figuring Frank owed her that much and more. And what Ada's father owed Matilda could never be repaid.

"Frank was making bootleg, shipping it up North," Matilda said. She divided the money equally between the bear and the nightgown, after setting aside a portion for Byron and Stella Mae, then passed the bear back to Ada. "Looks like we won't have any trouble buying train tickets to any place we want to go. We might could buy the whole blame train if we wanted to."

In Canton, they bought tickets to Memphis, thinking only as far as get-ting across the state line as quickly as possible. They traveled north in separate cars on the same train, Matilda in one of the colored coaches at the front of the train, subject to smoke from the locomotive, and Ada farther back. Ada held Annis in her lap, petting her sweet head, playing patty cake and peekaboo, offering a finger for her to chew on with her tiny new teeth. Ada could not get enough of her, now that she had her back.

In Memphis, they bought tickets to Louisville, Kentucky, heading northeast. Ada had no plan; Matilda seemed to have something in mind that she wasn't talking about. Each had more than enough money for a fresh start somewhere, together or separately. Ada was hoping for together. But it wasn't hope soaked in her old desperation. When she looked back at everything she had been able to overcome and the events of the last two days, she felt sure that she would be able to handle whatever the future might hold. She gave her thoughts free rein to venture there. And when doubts crept in on that train ride, usually in Virgil's voice, she drowned them out with Flora's encouragement and Matilda's confidence and Gertie's gentle wisdom.

Three stops after Memphis, there was a two-hour delay in Amona, Tennessee. It was a pretty town, smaller than Memphis but larger than Canton, with tree-lined streets and dogwoods in bloom along the trimmed edges of wooded areas so different from the wild, tangled woods of the Trace. Hazy blue mountains rose in the distance, along the horizon.

Ada bought sandwiches and Coca-Colas at a diner, then joined Matilda on a bench in an empty park across the street from the train station. They ate while Annis lay on a blanket in the soft grass at their feet, playing with Peggy's teddy bear stuffed with money. With an hour left before their train was scheduled to depart, they strolled up the main street, past a bank and a hotel, past painted lampposts and colorful awnings over store windows filled with nice things. In one of the windows, a dress shop, there was a sign: *Seamstress Needed*.

Ada looked at Matilda, and Matilda nodded toward the door. Ada paused for a moment, unsure, then brushed stray crumbs from the bodice of the dress she was wearing, a dress she had sewn from Flora's finest material. She straightened Annis's pretty little smock and took her inside.

Matilda went back to the park, where some children had arrived. She watched them, colored children playing on one end and white children on the other. A decrepit set of swings and slides for one group, shiny new models for the other. Two little girls stood facing each other at the border of their separate worlds, chatting across the invisible divide. Matilda felt overwhelmingly tired.

When she saw Ada come out of the shop bouncing Annis on her hip, Matilda knew that those two would not be on the train when it pulled out. Things would be easier that way. Still, she felt a pang of something she did not try to attach a word to.

"There's a room I can rent over the shop," Ada said, looking down at Annis as she spoke. "And the lady who runs it loves children. She asked if I thought a half-and-half split would be fair pay for dresses I make, after taking out for fabric and such. And a bigger share for taking in and letting out the ready-mades. I told her I'd come back about that." Ada looked up then.

"Sounds fair," Matilda said, and Ada nodded.

At the train station, Ada cried. Annis put her hand on her mother's wet cheek, her little chin beginning to quiver. Matilda took her from

Ada and held her close as long as she dared, then passed her back. She reached into her pocket and pulled out a folded slip of paper.

"An address where you can get word to me," she said.

Ada unfolded the paper. *13 Pency Street, Cleveland, Ohio.* She smiled.

"Don't write about anything that could cause any trouble," Matilda said. "No names or places from back home."

"No," Ada said, tucking the paper into her handbag.

"But send me an address, soon as you have one."

"I will."

"And maybe write here and there about how things are going, with the job and all. With Annis."

Annis. She called her by her name, Ada thought. She took that as a sign that something between them had healed.

Annis. A baby named by the wind, Matilda thought. Her mother's beautiful baby, gone to a better world.

Matilda stepped onto the train platform alone. There was much that she would miss about the Trace, its harsh beauty so intertwined with every good thing she had known. Dark memories would haunt her, and new evils would meet her ahead, but she would confront them with fire and thunder and storm. In Cleveland, when she lay down at night in the apartment she would share with Rainy, it would be mostly the strange noises of the big city that kept her from sleeping. And in time, she wouldn't notice them at all.

AUTHOR'S NOTE

The word trace *comes from the Old French* tracier: *a path;
a course; to walk over; to pass through; to traverse.*

The setting of this book was the setting of my childhood. I grew up—
though not in a stilt house on a swamp and certainly not in the 1920s—
in Natchez, Mississippi, the starting point of the Natchez Trace.

And here I should note that "the Trace" is an ambiguous refer-
ence to locals. It can mean the Old Trace, the wilderness path that
once linked the Choctaw, Chickasaw, and Natchez Native American
territories, originally forged by bison and deer roaming between riv-
ers. It can mean the more recent Natchez Trace Parkway, the historic
highway that roughly follows the same course between Natchez and
Nashville, Tennessee, and is dotted with historical sites and milepost
stops. The term also refers to the remote communities, farms, woods,
and swampland that flank the roadway, well known to authors William
Faulkner, Richard Wright, and Eudora Welty. If you are "from the
Trace," it means all of these things.

Mississippi leaves its mark on a person. Much of my childhood was spent filling coffee cans with dirt-crusted arrowheads and spear points dug up in orchards and fields, playing in sparkling clear creeks with pristine white sandbars, and later, taking my teenage angst to the loess bluffs overlooking the ever-surging Mississippi River for the wild comfort it never failed to offer. When I was quite young, my much older sister and I often trekked through overgrown cemeteries on the Trace, rubbing chalk over worn tombstones, looking for lost ancestors. It was one of those treks that lent me the image of the cracked and buckled tomb in which Ada and Matilda bury a body in the prologue of *The Girls in the Stilt House*.

It is my hope that readers of this novel will view the Trace as something of a character itself, as it was to me as a child and is, still, in my memory, though I left Mississippi as a teenager and have lived in many diverse and far-flung places since then.

In writing this book, I wanted to use the landscape, both physical and cultural, of 1920s Mississippi to convey something universal—the contrast between beauty and brutality inherent in our world, and sometimes in ourselves.

Because Mississippi has always been steeped in its past, a native writer does not have to dig very deep to find herself immersed in an earlier time. It's right there, just under the surface, like all those old arrowheads buried under a thin layer of soil.

READING GROUP GUIDE

1. How did you feel about Ada's return to the Natchez Trace? Why do you think she decided to come back? Do you think there were any other choices that she didn't consider?

2. Describe Matilda and Ada's relationship after their first fraught night together. Who is in charge? How are their actions shaped by Virgil's lingering presence?

3. Why do you think Matilda insists that Ada call Gertie "Miss Tuttle"? How would you characterize the relationship between Matilda and Gertie throughout the story?

4. What did you think of Peggy Creedle? Is there a difference between how she treats Matilda and how she treats Ada? How do her whims shape the story?

5. Think about Virgil Morgan and Frank Bowers. Are they

comparable villains? How does social class affect their actions and demands? What did you think of their ultimate ends?

6. Why do you think Matilda withholds so much information from Ada?

7. Teensy always looks for something beautiful in her day, even if she ends up being grateful for something very small. What do you think of that philosophy? How do Matilda's feelings toward the practice evolve throughout the book?

8. Matilda blames herself for losing Dalton and Annis to the fire. How does that guilt motivate her? Do you think she ever forgives herself fully?

9. Describe the events that lead to Ada accepting the housekeeping job from Frank. Can you imagine something similar happening today?

10. By the end of the book, how has the relationship between Ada and Matilda changed since their first meeting?

A CONVERSATION
WITH THE AUTHOR

What was your first inspiration for *The Girls in the Stilt House*? Did you start with a particular character or scene?

One image that was in my head before the story or the characters took shape was of the cracked and buckled tomb overtaken by woods that first appears in the prologue. I have long been fascinated with old cemeteries and tombstones, and the idea of hiding a body in the way that Matilda and Ada did was irresistible from the beginning. Beyond that, I knew there would be themes of loss and struggle, and some grappling with the meanings of family and belonging. And that trees would play an important role. Landscape is often my starting point with a new project.

The landscape surrounding Ada and Matilda takes on a personality of its own, and you grew up in the same part of the state. What was most difficult about setting a novel on the Natchez Trace, especially in a historical period?

The Trace *does* have a personality of its own. Many personalities, really, as it stretches about 440 miles from Natchez, Mississippi, to

Nashville, Tennessee, once connecting Choctaw and Chickasaw lands. Several of my ancestors lived and died on the Trace. That old wilderness pathway and the surrounding landscape were influential aspects of my own coming of age and my early awareness of the displaced and oppressed people to whom the Native American ceremonial mounds, the ornate antebellum mansions, the crumbling river shacks, and the old frontier outposts testify. History haunts the Trace, and it haunted me as a child. It haunts me still.

Although Ada's swamp is not meant to represent any of Mississippi's numerous swamps, it was loosely inspired by a bald cypress/water tupelo swamp at one of the Trace mileposts. A swamp setting seemed to be a perfect metaphor for the juxtaposition of beauty and brutality in 1920s Mississippi. With such an atmospheric backdrop, I did have to rein in my tendency to ignore the forest for love of the trees (literally and figuratively).

The historical period in which this novel is set came with its own difficulties. Research was intense. I did not want to make that period seem more genteel than it was by avoiding dark truths, yet I did not want to overstep in bringing Matilda's story forward. Navigating that line in a respectful and honest way was very important to me.

What kind of research went into Gertie's remedies, recommendations, and overall role in the community? Is there anyone in your life who inspired her?

So much research! The rural midwives of the early twentieth century were astonishing medical practitioners, despite their scant resources. Although Gertie, as the oldest character in the story, did hold some ideas that some people might view as superstitions, I wanted her nursing practices to have a genuine basis in science and herbal medicine. For instance, there is a scene in which Gertie has Teensy close a fist around a carrot, then tries to pull it out of her hand to test the strength of her grip. This came of my having researched a modern medical study about testing hand-grip strength to screen for preeclampsia, or pregnancy-related hypertension. So while some of Gertie's methods might seem unorthodox, the reasoning behind them was medically sound. There are many excellent resources about midwives in this period. And I went down many research rabbit holes learning about medicinal plants and natural remedies.

As for Gertie, she came entirely from my imagination. I wish there were a Gertie in my life!

When Ada sought Gertie's help in locating Matilda, the midwife turned her away, saying, "She saved your life. Saved your baby, too. Ain't that enough?" What was behind Gertie's response?

In the story, Gertie is a caring and tender soul. Turning away a young mother in need, especially as a midwife, would not have been easy for her. On the porch that day, Gertie was refusing to put Matilda, Stella Mae, and herself at risk to further aid Ada. But behind her words, as well, is an acknowledgment of the many generations of Black women forced into caretaking roles for White families at the expense of their own children and loved ones and their hopes for their own lives. Although it is not mentioned in the story, Gertie, an old woman in 1923, would almost certainly have been born enslaved in Mississippi. She would have been intimately acquainted with the horrors endured by enslaved mothers and with the domestic roles that were so often the only options for Black women in later years. Providing nursing care to Ada was Gertie's choice, and in that scene on the porch, it was also her choice not to lay responsibility for Ada's well-being on Matilda's shoulders. Ada, I think, comes to understand this by the end of the book.

Did you have a hard time deciding on the "right" endings for Matilda and Ada after everything they had been through, separately and together?

Yes. I wrote several endings before settling in with one that seemed to hit the right note. I wanted a tender, poignant ending rather than a traditionally happy one, an ending that was triumphal and uplifting without minimizing all that stood between Matilda and Ada, both in their relationship, so laced with trauma, and in their world.

What advice do you have for aspiring writers, especially writers trying to wade into historical or regional fiction?

Spend more time reading than writing. Read books by authors who write better than you do, and pay attention. I've attended workshops and writing conferences and done coursework, but the most meaningful and impactful lessons I've learned about writing, by far, have come from reading.

This is your debut novel. What has surprised you most about publishing a book? How does it differ from the other types of publication you've done in the past?

Writing is a solitary endeavor, and as an introvert, I generally enjoy that. But working with a team of book-loving professionals—my agent, my editor, and everyone at Sourcebooks involved in making this book shine—has been a wonderful experience. As for surprises, I'm guessing that most of those are yet to come.

What books are on your bedside table right now?

Some new, some old, some I set aside until after all work on this novel was finished because I knew they would be all-consuming experiences. Among them are Colson Whitehead's *The Nickel Boys*, Elizabeth Strout's *Olive, Again*, and Michael Farris Smith's *Blackwood*. Right now, I'm reading Natasha Trethewey's *Memorial Drive: A Daughter's Memoir*.

Any new projects in the works?

I'm working on a new novel, this one set in both Mississippi and western North Carolina. As usual, the landscape came first. And an image of a small child and a shadowy figure standing on a front porch on a rainy night in the 1930s.

ACKNOWLEDGMENTS

The following quote found in Henry Moser's letter to Matilda in chapter 38 is from the speech titled "What to the Slave Is the Fourth of July?" delivered by Frederick Douglass on July 5, 1852, to members of the Rochester Ladies' Anti-Slavery Society in Rochester, New York: "For it is not light that is needed, but fire; it is not the gentle shower, but thunder. We need the storm, the whirlwind, and the earthquake."

Douglass went on to say, "The feeling of the nation must be quickened; the conscience of the nation must be roused; the propriety of the nation must be startled; the hypocrisy of the nation must be exposed; and its crimes against God and man must be proclaimed and denounced."

More people than I can name here offered support and guidance as this story became a book. I am grateful to each of them. My thanks, especially, to:

My agent, Peter Steinberg, for his belief in these characters and his unwavering determination to see this story through at every turn.

Shana Drehs, my editor, who championed the work wholeheartedly and navigated the journey with keen insight and a shared vision. Everyone at Sourcebooks Landmark who worked to give this book its best possible entrance into the world, among them Heather Hall, Heather VenHuizen, Molly Waxman, Cristina Arreola, Valerie Pierce, and Bridget McCarthy, as well as Diane Dannenfeldt.

Karen Dionne, writer and friend extraordinaire, for reading drafts and offering wisdom, for cheering me on and lifting me up, and for expectations that were always greater than mine. Jon Clinch, for clear-sighted advice, writerly generosity, and work that both inspires and sets the bar way too high. Elizabeth Letts, my reading twin, for every word. Writers Sandra Kring and Terez Rose, who were always there for any reason, literary or otherwise. Katrina Denza, writer and lover of books and authors, who almost certainly underestimates the impact her support and friendship have had on my work and in my life. Pat Riviere-Seel, whose poetry and camaraderie were, and are, essential.

The confidential society of extraordinary writers who enfolded me into their fellowship. What a roundtable! I am indebted to each of you.

The Weymouth Center for the Arts and Humanities, for a room with a view, dedicated writing time, and incomparable support for the creative writing community of North Carolina. Kathryn, Katrina, Ry, Alex, Dottie, Marianna, Brittany, and everyone faithfully upholding James and Katharine Boyd's tradition of hospitality

to writers, as well as my fellow writers-in-residence, who have so
enriched my work.

Paul, my best and most trusted reader, for invaluable feedback and
countless walks and talks about books, this one and others.

Grace and Andra, whose support meant the world, and Margeaux,
who is appreciated more than she knows.

David B., Sandra, Twyla, and Jo, for answering so many questions
and keeping faith for so long.

Michael, Shea, April, Megan, Matt, Paul, and David, for things far
beyond the writing of books.

And Cierra, Amari, and Linc. May this world grow more beautiful
along with you.

ABOUT THE AUTHOR

Photo © Rachelle Thompson

Kelly Mustian grew up in Natchez, Mississippi, the southern terminus of the historic Natchez Trace. Her work has appeared in numerous literary journals and commercial magazines, and her short fiction has won a Blumenthal Writers and Readers Series Award. She is a past recipient of a Regional Artist Project Grant from the North Carolina Arts and Science Council. Kelly currently lives with her family near the foothills of North Carolina. *The Girls in the Stilt House* is her debut novel.